STEAMED UP
A DREAMSPINNER PRESS ANTHOLOGY

Dreamspinner Press

Published by
Dreamspinner Press
5032 Capital Circle SW
Suite 2, PMB# 279
Tallahassee, FL 32305-7886
USA
http://www.dreamspinnerpress.com/

This is a work of fiction. Names, characters, places, and incidents either are the product of author imagination or are used fictitiously, and any resemblance to actual persons, living or dead, business establishments, events, or locales is entirely coincidental.

ISBN: 978-1-62798-330-3
Digital ISBN: 978-1-62798-331-0

Printed in the United States of America
First Edition
October 2013

TABLE OF CONTENTS

FIVE TO ONE

ANGELIA SPARROW

"DEE!" Jonathan bounded through the backyard to hammer at the door of the little shed, his tiredness from his day at the mill forgotten. "Dee, come see what I have. We're gonna be rich!" He hammered some more, but the door remained resolutely shut. "Declan Ferguson, open this door before I knock it down!" he bellowed.

"More fuel for an engine!" came the retort from inside. But the bar slid open and Declan peered out, oil in his bright-red hair and a smudge of soot across his freckled nose.

"No, no engines. Look, Dee." He shoved the rumpled paper at his roommate, who smoothed the handbill and read it aloud.

"Preliminary qualifying race for Transcontinental Manpower Road Race. Human-powered vehicles only. The item must manage a minimum speed of twenty miles per hour for at least half an hour or successfully complete the twenty-five-mile course in less than an hour and twenty minutes. All qualifying vehicles will be entered in the race and will be required to journey from historic Boston Harbor to San Francisco Bay. The prize for the race...." Declan looked up. "Jonny boy, what's that number? Does it really say one million dollars?"

"It does." Jonathan nodded at his oldest friend. He gave Declan a wide grin and imitated the bit of an accent Declan had never shaken, "Oh indeed it does, Dee, me boyo."

"Oh hush, I'm not that bad. Da and Mum worked to make sure we could speak proper English." Dee tended to be touchy about his second-generation accent, because even in Boston many shops still sported "No Irish Need Apply" signs.

"Aye, larnin' it from your father and mither and the priest and the constable on patrol," Jonathan teased him, the fake accent getting broader and more obnoxious.

"Half a minute and I'll knock you down," Declan threatened, as he always did. Jonathan noticed his accent was indeed getting thicker and his face was reddening around the freckles. Before he could do violence, Dee returned to reading the flier. "Each vehicle must have a two-man crew. The race begins on Independence Day."

"You can do it, right? And by the qualifier on Saturday?" Jonathan asked, ending his teasing. He knew how far he could push Dee and when to back off. "I'll help."

"You'll bloody drive, because I'll get lost," Declan said. "Of course I can build it. Gonna take all the time I can scrape. Might have to burn some lanterns." He gave a wicked grin. "Hope you're not afraid of heights, Jonny boy. This is going to have some powerful big wheels."

Jonathan smiled as Dee vanished back into the shed. Soon the familiar squeak of chalk on slate filled the backyard. Dee might reappear for supper. There was bread and cheese if he did. Jonathan went up the stairs and grabbed his apron from the back of the door.

He brought in an extra dollar a week by sweeping up for four different stores in the neighborhood. Sometimes the grocer let him have bread that was just starting to mold or wilted vegetables. Everything helped. Dee didn't work a steady job, preferring to pick up odd bits here and there to pay for his inventing.

It was an arrangement that suited them fine, but Jonathan wanted more for them both. Nobody would ever say Jonathan Crawford didn't take care of his own.

He wanted them to have a fine house and people to take care of it and them. No more sharing a fifth-floor room barely big enough for their narrow bed and the washstand, with no heat and half a window. No more shriveled apples. No more stews cooked on Dee's alcohol burner while he invented, cooked until everything was mushy to disguise the texture of limp carrots and potatoes. No more carefully paring off the smallest bits of bread he could and hoping he'd gotten all the mold. He wanted a cook to rival the one at the Parker House and a fine carriage and nice clothes. He wanted Dee to have all the tinkering equipment he wanted and a fine workshop and a personal courier to the patent office.

He didn't want Dee to darn his socks ever again. He didn't want to mend the threadbare elbows of his shirt one more time. They were going to get into this race and they were going to win it.

"I said, do you want this, boy?" Old Mr. Connor held out the last quarter of a meat pie. "It'll be no good tomorrow. Take it home to your layabout friend for a treat."

"Sorry, Mr. Connor. I was thinking."

"Spending money you don't have yet, or I don't know the look of it. What's he inventing today, Crawford? A mail pulley for the upper apartments?"

Dee's mail pulleys were one of his few successes. Most of the tenements in the neighborhood boasted several, raising the mail to the sixth and eighth floors, which saved the postman and the tenants a lot of stairs. He charged a dollar to install each pulley, and the landlords quickly found they made it up by charging fifty cents more a week for rent.

"A vehicle." He wasn't ready to talk about the race or the million-dollar purse.

"Oh lordy, an engine-driven nightmare to stink up the neighborhood and scare the horses." Mr. Connor looked over the vegetable bins. He pulled a couple of carrots well past their prime, three slightly sprouted potatoes, a shriveling turnip, and an onion just showing green sprouts. He held them out, along with the quarter for the previous week's work. "I can't sell these. Keep him fed, son. I hope this is the one that works for him."

"Thank you, Mr. Connor." Jonathan tied the produce in a corner of his apron and carried the pie home carefully. Millions on his mind couldn't compare to the real wealth in his current possession. He had a whole dollar in his pocket, a pie for dinner tonight, and vegetables for stew tomorrow. Maybe he could afford a bit of meat bone to go in the pot. With oatmeal or barley, they could eat for three days for nearly free.

The light was out in the shed and in their rooms. Dee seldom burned lamps or candles, calling them wasteful. He invented all day and would sit under a streetlight and design in the evening if the mood took him. Jonathan climbed the stairs to their room. Dee was already asleep.

He bent over his friend and brushed a kiss over Dee's temple.

"Wake up, you lazybones, and see what delicacies I brought home for you."

"Mmph," Dee grumbled, turning over in their narrow bed.

"Rich lamb stew, fine beer, good bread, and a bit of cake," Jonathan teased.

Declan opened one eye. "Really? Did you mug a swell, then?"

"No, but I have a meat pie, some vegetables, and I got paid. Eat up. The pie's about to go off and won't keep until morning."

Dee sat up. "Jonny, how are you at pedaling? This is going to be a powerful long trek across country. Even the twenty-five miles is a fair piece to ride. I'll do my best to make sure that you get the most out of each stroke, but it's gonna be hard on you, my bonny boy."

"I figured we could trade off if we had to."

"Not for the qualifier. Love, you want to travel as lightly as possible for that."

Jonathan knew Dee was worrying if he was into affection words. Or maybe he'd just woke up desirous. That happened too. Dee tended to pour his affections out on Jonathan verbally. Jonathan assumed it was for lack of female company.

"But for the actual cross-country?"

"There we'll trade the time spent powering and have to pack along some necessities. Clothes, shelter, bedrolls, food, and money. But to qualify, not even a sunshade."

"Oh yeah, I'll look fine cycling along under a tattered umbrella." He chewed thoughtfully on the last bit of pie crust. "But won't the gear and your weight cut the speed when we get rolling?"

"Not if you can qualify pedaling at a comfortable speed and then step it up for the actual race. I've got a line on some ordinary wheels. Fifty-six inchers. I figure we use a really tiny drive wheel and a standard pedal wheel. So one turn of the pedal wheel would turn the drive wheel three or four times, and that will send you.... Hmmm." He picked up a slate and moved into a patch of streetlight.

"You'll wreck your eyes, Dee."

"And I'll never get back to sleep without knowing. The wheels are fifty-six inches tall, so they're a hundred and seventy-six inches around.

That's about fourteen feet, eight inches or four and five-eighths yards. I'm rounding up here, Jonny—bear with me." He scratched some more with chalk. "Three rotations would send you about fourteen yards. Four would go eighteen yards."

Jonathan listened. Dee might not be able to write very well, but he was a wizard with numbers. Dee mumbled to himself a little more.

"There's one thousand, seven hundred sixty yards in a mile. It will take you ninety-eight full circle pedals to make a mile if I use a four, a hundred and twenty-six on the three. Hmmm. Now you have to go twenty miles an hour. That's about thirty-three circles a minute at the faster one or forty-two at the slower. Yeah, better use the smallest gear I can get my hands on. Wonder if I could make it go five to one?" He scribbled a little more and looked up. "We can do it at eighty rotations per mile and twenty-seven pedals per minute."

Jonathan winced at his memory of rides on borrowed boneshakers and ordinaries. "And my seat will be a deal sorer for it."

Dee grinned. "I have a plan, but it'll keep until morning." He took a long drink and settled back on the bed. "And your mill whistle blows a sight earlier than either of us will like."

Jonathan stripped out of his vest and shirt and shoes to join Dee. The summer night was warm and the bed was narrow. "Maybe I should take the floor," he suggested.

"Going nowhere, Jonny boy." Dee wrapped arms around his neck and pulled him in tight. "Need you right here."

Jonathan remembered the nights he had tried sleeping on the floor and always migrated back to the bed. He had slept beside Dee for five years now, since they were both just kids finding their way alone and had tumbled together as roommates. He couldn't sleep comfortably anymore without Dee's arm over his ribs and Dee's breath on his shoulder. The soft little kiss that pressed on the back of his neck let him know Dee felt the same way.

The next morning came around much too early, as Dee had said it would. Jonathan rose and dressed, washed his face and hands, and nudged Dee.

"Make stew for dinner. I've left you fifty cents. Get some meat and bread, a bit of barley or rice if you can afford it, before you start tinkering. For once you begin, you'll barely remember to eat, let alone buy food."

Dee sat upright. "You really did get food, then. I thought I woke fuller than usual." He glanced at the slate. "I calculated in my sleep, then?"

"I thought you were awake enough when I made passionate love to you." The joke was an old one and Jonathan gave him a saucy wink to go with it.

Dee laughed. "Oh indeed. And not even a kiss before you go? Be off with your sweet-talking ways, then. I've work to do." He pulled on his shirt and Jonathan saw him pick up the fifty-cent piece.

The mill work moved quickly, but it never varied. Jonathan carried bolts of cloth from the docks to the cutting tables. Then he carried the cut cloth up two flights to the sewing girls. The finished dresses came down to the sorting room, and he was back on the dock moments later to do it all again. The hot air hung thick with lint and thread, and by noon, he'd sweated through his shirt and his breath came in rasps.

Up and down. He tried to think of the stairs as training. There would be a lot of pedaling. It was a long way to San Francisco. Dee would know how far. Up and down for twelve hours. His legs felt as mushy as the potatoes would be when he got home to eat them.

He dragged home in the June twilight. There was still some hammering coming from the shed. Dee was hard at work. Jonathan hoped the ordinary wheels had come through. The smell of cooking filled the backyard.

"You put more onion in it," he said as he leaned against the shed's doorframe.

"Stew needs good flavor. The one you brought had no strength in it. Got 'em from Mrs. Farrell. She offered and I said please."

"How much hammering did you do?" Jonathan asked suspiciously. Mrs. Farrell, two floors down, was generous with her onions and bread but tended to take advantage of the sturdy young men and their tool use.

"I rehung her door. Only a few minutes of work."

"Worth it. It smells good." He gestured at the wheels in the back of the shed that loomed nearly as high as Dee's head. "They came."

"That they did. And I've ten minutes more of good light, so get out of it. Go sweep for the shopkeepers and I'll bring you dinner when we both finish."

Jonathan gave him a smile and set out on his appointed rounds. He came home to find Dee sitting on the back stoop with a bowl of stew in his hands and another beside him.

"How far is it to San Francisco, Dee?" Jonathan asked.

"About three thousand miles, give or take a hundred or so."

Jonathan blinked. "Three thousand. And I'm pedaling."

Dee got the usual manic grin he wore when he'd just made a grand invention. Jonathan hoped the news was better than the bed maker that had nearly strangled them both in the night. "It's all right, love. I got the five-to-one gears. So each time you pedal, it's an eightieth of a mile. Two hundred and fifty thousand pedals will bring us to San Francisco." He pulled a bit of chalk from behind his ear and figured it, drawing on the stoop and stairs. "One hundred and thirty-eight hours or six days of pedaling. Less if you pedal faster."

"My legs ache after twelve hours on the stairs. I'll never make it."

"I'll spell you. We can win this thing, Jonny boy."

"Will it be ready by Saturday?"

"It's the midnight oil for me. You wash up and go to bed. I'll be up after I've got the works framed up. Tomorrow, I decide how to put this together."

Jonathan went up and lay in the empty bed. Dee was the best friend a fellow ever had. Jonathan rolled over, trying to find a comfortable spot. The bed didn't feel right. Too big. He smiled as he realized he was missing Dee being curled around him. He sounded like some love-struck girl tossing and turning as she dreamed of her sweetheart.

The thought made him sit straight up. He was in love. And not with any girl—with his best friend. With Dee, who breathed on his shoulder in the night and was even now staying up late on his behalf. In love with Dee. The notion sounded less silly the more he thought of it. Dee took care of him, almost as a wife would. Cooked for him, made sure his shirt was clean for work, built what he needed, did bits of work to bring in extra money or food. And hadn't some of the soldiers taken male wives during the war, as he'd heard tell?

He wanted Dee up there now, right now. He wanted to pull Dee into his arms and whisper, "Declan Ferguson, I love you." He wasn't sure how Dee would take it. Would he just laugh or would he throw a punch? Would he wrap his arms around Jonathan's neck and say "I love you too, Jonny boy" and kiss him?

No, better not to say anything. Such deeds were illegal at best, so the feelings must be too. He couldn't risk losing his friend over this. A practical corner of his mind suggested that if he won the million dollars, no one would care if he loved Dee then.

Jonathan lay back down, straining his ears for noises from the backyard shed. He fell asleep listening. He woke to the usual rattle of pebbles from the Waker on the street below.

"I'm up," he yelled out the window and flipped the boy a penny. The urchin ran next door to send a gravel hail against another window.

Dee reached and mumbled in his sleep. Jonathan smiled to see he wasn't the only one who didn't sleep well alone. He bounced on the edge of the iron bed.

"Wake up, Dee. Daylight's burning. There's a lot of work to do."

"Yes sir, mister foreman," Dee grumbled and rolled away to clutch the pillow closer.

Jonathan laughed. "Right, then. For my handsome, brilliant inventor, there will be something nice for supper that he did not cook himself. We've made the rent and we can eat. So there should be a treat."

Seized by a sudden whim, he bent in and kissed Dee's lips. Dee opened his eyes.

"What's this, then?" he asked when Jonathan sat back up.

"Awakening my sleeping beauty. I'm off to work, my darlin' boy. Be good. Stay out of saloons and in your workshop."

Dee sat up, not awake enough to take issue with Jonathan imitating his accent. "What's gotten into you?"

"June madness. I'll tell you tonight if it lasts."

Jonathan walked out the door, hoping he actually heard Dee whisper, "I hope it does." The four words haunted him as he carried and climbed all day long. He had an idea. If Dee's vehicle didn't work, maybe there was an invention he could make for the factory.

The taste of Dee's lips stayed with him. Soft and warm under his, they'd been exactly what he was looking for in a kiss. He hoped to get more kisses tonight.

Instead of going right home after the whistle blew, Jonathan made his stops at the shops. It was Wednesday. They had two days to finish the vehicle and test it. He made it home just as the lamplighter was making his rounds.

Dee was on his back in the middle of the yard, under a contraption the likes of which Jonathan had never seen. He stood and stared. The great high wheels of the bicycle stood well above a narrow platform with what looked like a battered old easy chair with no legs, a wheel on a post, and a set of bicycle pedals attached to a little wheel in the floor.

"Is this it?'

Dee sat up and banged his head on the platform. "This is it. For the real thing, I'll add another seat, a shade, and a box for our goods."

"It's amazing. How fast?"

Dee's grin looked as though it wanted to wrap clear around his head. "Streetlights are on. Let's find out." He pushed it toward the gate that led to the backyard. "It's narrow enough to fit out the gate. I made sure."

They got the contraption onto the street. Jonathan planted one foot on the platform and hauled himself aboard. "Just pedal, right?"

"And steer with the wheel. Pedal very slowly until you get the feel for the steering. The brake is the lever beside you. Don't crash it, Jonny boy. I put my whole heart into her."

Dee's heart, in his hands, under his control. The thought made Jonathan bite his lips together, sealing his mouth shut lest he say something untoward, and resolve to be extremely cautious.

The streets had mostly cleared of their daytime traffic. He settled into the seat, more comfortable than any bicycle he'd ever been on, and gave an experimental push of the pedals.

The half turn sent the contraption whirring down the street. He held the steering wheel tightly, keeping it steady. When he coasted to a stop, he looked back and saw Dee half a block away waving his hat in the air.

"Take her around the block! Learn to steer her." Dee whooped again as Jonathan tapped the pedals just enough to get himself moving and rolled out of sight around the corner.

The contraption steered beautifully, and Jonathan managed to roll to a stop right in front of Dee. "What do we call it?"

"She's the *Ruagán.*"

"Rue again?"

"*Ruagán.* It's what Da called a fast, cold, biting wind off the ocean. We're going to sail by like a wind and bite them all!" Dee tossed his cap up, spun around, and caught it. "You're going to qualify, Jonny boy. You're going to qualify and we're going to win that race and we're going to be rich!"

Jonathan set the brake and lightly hopped off the *Ruagán.* He seized the moment fate had handed him and grabbed Dee, kissing him to within an inch of his life. A brief moment of fear that Dee would bite him or hit him crossed his mind. Instead, Dee's arms went right around his neck and his mouth opened softly under Jonathan's, his lips making little motions of desire.

Jonathan pulled back and Dee looked at him, merry green eyes and impish face stark and serious under the streetlight. They'd been kissing like a wanton and her evening's meal ticket, on the street in plain sight of anyone who cared to watch. Jonathan had a brief moment of shame.

Declan's sweet smile and next words dispelled it. "So that's how it is, then, Jonny, my love?"

"Don't say that unless you mean it, Declan. Because I do love you."

Dee reached up and planted a fast kiss on Jonathan's nose. "I knew that, stupe. You take care of me better than my own family ever did. Come on, let's put her away and head for bed. It's late."

"I forgot your supper," Jonathan said.

"Ellie's open around the corner."

They pushed the *Ruagán* back into the yard and into the shed. Jonathan dusted himself off, wiped a smudge of grease off Dee's cheek, and couldn't resist stealing another kiss.

"Easy or we'll not get that bite of supper."

Ellie, her gray hair tied up in a kerchief, stood over her sidewalk booth, singing about her new beer.

"Pint and two thins for each of us," Dee said, stepping up. "And make it the good beer you drink, not the stuff you brew in the washtub."

Ellie laughed. "Of course, my boy." She handed over four slices of bread and butter and drew two mugs of beer.

"You got anything else tonight?" Jonathan laid four cents on the counter.

"Aye, cold coffee for the evening ladies and their cads. Then more in the morning for working boys like you."

"Anything solid?" Dee asked around the end of his bread and butter.

"Couple of pigs' feet, if you got a nickel."

Jonathan wrinkled his nose. "No pickled oysters?" She shook her head. Jonathan drained his beer and handed back the mug. "Thanks, Ellie."

"It'll hold me until morning," Dee promised.

They headed back to their room. Dee moved with his usual quick step, hurrying up the narrow stairs and throwing open their door. He stood in the center of the moonlit patch on the floor, smiling with his arms open.

"Jonny, love, come here and let me show you how I feel. You show me every day. You work two jobs, feed me, and let me invent instead of tossing me out on my ear or demanding I go to the mill as well. You sleep in my arms every night. Do you think I don't feel it when you wake up with a bit of iron between your legs? Do you think I don't want to kiss you every morning, hold you every night, and feel your cock in my hand all night long?"

Jonathan blinked at the outpouring of words. He had no idea Dee felt so about him. He stepped into the waiting arms and Dee yanked him down for a kiss.

This one wasn't playful or overjoyed. It took its time learning his mouth, tasting him, exploring him, and making him hard in his trousers. Jonathan breathed hard when Dee let him up.

Dee shrugged out of his shirt and suspenders and dropped his trousers and underwear. He sat down on the edge of the bed, naked as the day he was born, and kept smiling.

Jonathan hurried out of his clothing. He couldn't stop looking at Dee, half in shadow, half in the moonlight. Shadows played over his light skin, made deathly pale in the wan light, but the smile gleamed in the darkness. He wanted to touch all that skin, kiss Dee, and tell him over and over how much he loved him.

Jonathan walked to the bed. A plunge that knocked Dee flat would be undignified. He sat beside Dee and took the much-loved face in his hands. He brushed light kisses over the freckled nose and cheeks before settling on Dee's lips. He liked the way Dee felt pressed against him, the softness of his mouth, the little moans Dee made as he kissed. He slipped his tongue into Dee's mouth, tasting him as Dee had tasted him earlier. There had been a few girls here and there. But sweethearts were expensive and wives more so. He grinned into the kiss. Dee had been serving him as a wife for a couple of years now and never a complaint about it.

Dee rested his hands for an instant on Jonathan's chest and stomach, the touch seeming to sizzle on his skin. He ran teasing fingers over Jonathan's arms and stroked his legs. When one hand landed on his crotch, he nearly jumped. Dee closed his lightly callused fingers around Jonathan's cock—which was standing as proud and straight as any soldier—gripping him as though he were one of the many tools in the work shed.

"You're good with tools, Declan. See what you do with mine."

Dee laughed at that and stroked him, a slow, steady motion that mimicked the piston strokes of one of Dee's beloved engines. Jonathan wondered for a strange moment whether Dee had ever handled himself so, in time to one of his machines.

"Like this?"

"Perfect." Jonathan kissed him again.

"And I promise you, my lad, if you don't quit calling me by name, I'll give you no release."

"Evil. You are wicked and evil, boyo."

"Watch it, Jonny boy."

He kissed Dee again, pleased to finally be in his lover's arms. Getting up his courage, he reached for Dee's cock. It felt much the same as his, heavy and warm, a firm thing, not hard like a bony knee or sharp finger, but solid. He wondered how it would taste.

"About time," Dee said, nipping his earlobe and neck. "Any idea what should be done about this distressing predicament in which we find ourselves?"

"Mmm, a little." Jonathan shoved Dee back to lie on the bed. "I think our hands will serve for tonight. I know there are other things that can be done, but we'll leave them for a night less rushed."

"You've never—"

Jonathan cut him off with a kiss. Dee didn't need to know he was still a virgin. He had kissed a few girls and felt one's breasts, but none of them had interested him enough to try for more. Now he knew why. He'd been waiting for just the right person, a bright Irish boy with a knack for inventing and a taste for adventure.

"It's all right, my love. I know how to make it sweet." Dee rolled them onto their sides to face each other. "Let me lead. You just ride along. You'll be driving soon enough."

Jonathan chuckled. "All right."

Dee kissed him over and over. Quick pecks, long invasions, and everything in between. His hand never stopped moving. Jonathan thrust into the fist that held him at a perfect tightness, urgency building in his belly and in his balls. He needed to spend forth, shoot out everything in him, painting Dee with the same white streaks that had fascinated him when he was younger.

"Just like that, precious boy. All of it. Give it all out." Dee's soft words rang in his ears and Jonathan did. Everything in him shot out the end of his cock, all his fears about Saturday, all his tension, all his exhaustion. He lay limp and panting in his Dee's arms. Dee just smiled and kissed him.

"Sleep now. You've much work tomorrow."

"But you—"

"Shush. I'll keep." Dee kissed him until the onrushing wave of sleep took him.

Jonathan woke to Dee sitting up and dressing. He grabbed his lover and pulled Dee down for a kiss.

"Good morning."

"A fine morning to you too, my heart. Now, I'm off to find a bit of work for some parts." Gravel hit the window. Dee looked over. "And you need to be off to the mill. We'll go for speed tonight, see how fast you can go with the *Ruagán*."

"Fast, are we, Dee? How fast are you?" Jonathan pulled him close. "You know an awful lot about the ways of men. Care to show me more?"

"I think it's my turn. You came off like a steam whistle, but I got nothing."

"You told me to go to sleep."

"That I did. Now, let me teach you something fun."

Dee lay back down and fished his cock out of his fly. Jonathan looked at it in the daylight. It was as fair as the rest of his lover, with a sprinkling of freckles and auburn hair at the base. He took hold of it at once.

"Can you kiss it?" Dee asked. "Lick and kiss and let me feel your mouth all over it?" He ran one thumb along Jonathan's lower lip. "You've a beautiful mouth. And I love kissing it. But I want to fuck it now."

Jonathan flinched at the crudeness. They had both been careful of their language, neither wishing to scandalize the other. But he looked at the cock that lay in his hand and nodded. He wanted to do this. He wanted to taste Dee and make his best friend and lover feel the way he had last night, as if his entire being was unraveling like a bolt of cheap cloth, as though he was exploding like a Chinese firework.

"Ever had this done?" he asked and licked the head. He wasn't sure how to pleasure Dee this way, so he stroked with his hand and ran his tongue over the head, flickering under the foreskin, across the tight spot on the bottom where it hooked on, and around the ridge.

"Oh, Jonny." Dee gasped. "You're a quick study."

Jonathan experimented, tasting and licking more. He ran his tongue down the shaft and back up. He took the head in his mouth and blinked when Dee arched up into his mouth before he remembered the rude words.

He wondered how much of the cock would fit in his mouth, so he worked his way down, getting most of it before the head pressed something in his throat and made him gag. He spat Dee out and tried to compose himself.

"It's all right," Dee said, stroking his hair. "Happens to everyone the first time or two. Some never do manage it. You did just fine."

"I'll be late for work."

"Three more strokes. Just, please, don't leave me here."

Jonathan looked up at Dee's face and wanted him more than ever. He wanted to tell the mill and shops to go take a flying leap off the harbor wall. He wanted to make love to Dee all day.

Instead, he gave Dee a wicked smile, shoved him flat on his back, and loomed over him. He grasped Dee's cock and descended for a harsh, demanding kiss. Dee moaned under his touch, not quite whimpering at the sensations.

"Rough, is it?" Dee whispered.

"Mine," was all Jonathan could say. He wanted to imprint his claim all over Dee's body now that he knew Dee's heart was securely his.

He took a slow and steady motion with his hand, wanting Dee to explode as he had. When Dee started thrusting, he gave a hard squeeze in warning and took his hand away. He propped up and looked down seriously at his boy.

"My turn. I'll give you pleasure when it suits me and how it suits me."

"You bastard," Dee said with no heat behind it as he attempted to flip them over so he could take control.

"My mother was a married lady, thank you kindly." Jonathan took hold again and jerked Dee's cock hard twice before he let go. Dee gasped at the suddenness.

"Really, now. And here I thought you hatched from an egg that washed up in the harbor."

Dee always made him laugh. But Jonathan wanted to make Dee lose all his words with desire and need. He ducked back down, found a good position, and sucked Dee to the root. A gasp from above told him he had succeeded in silencing Dee's thoughts and tongue.

Jonathan sucked hard, wrapping his tongue around Dee's cock, imagining this would feel good. He moved, sliding off and on, as if Dee was actually getting to fuck his mouth. Dee grasped the bedding and lay still, panting. Jonathan sucked more, wanting Dee's climax. There would be other days to see Dee explode, his eyes rolling back, his mouth going slack. But for now, Jonathan wanted it to be his mouth that did the work.

It didn't take long. Dee gasped again and spent, thick salt filling Jonathan's mouth. He stayed until the cock stopped pulsing against his lips, until Dee relaxed. He thought his options through while he waited for Dee to finish. A conclusion reached, he swallowed, taking Dee's very life into his own body.

Dee had barely rolled over when Jonathan dressed and headed for the mill, pausing only to kiss him and say, "Speed trials tonight, my sweet."

When he came home, Dee was waiting on the street with the *Ruagán*. He'd added a sunshade, a second seat that looked like a scavenged wingback chair, and a wooden box. Lanterns hung from the corners.

"I thought I didn't get a shade," Jonathan said.

"It's got most of the gear for the race in it. We're doing a fully loaded speed trial. No sense qualifying if we can't win." Dee hopped up and made himself comfortable in the second seat. "Get aboard. The daylight's wasting. We need to get out of town so I can clock you without traffic."

Jonathan climbed up and seated himself. He pedaled slowly, the high contraption more stable and smoother than he had expected. The extra weight seemed to make it ride better. Dee sat behind him, whistling through his teeth.

"Not bad. We're managing about fifteen miles an hour even with traffic." Dee clicked his watch shut.

Jonathan steered, following Dee's directions until he parked them out in an abandoned field where the weeds grew half as high as the wheels of the *Ruagán*. He let Dee down to pace off a course for him.

"All right, love, that's a quarter mile from here to that big rock. To qualify, you need to do a mile in three minutes. So you have to pedal from here to there in forty-five seconds or less." Dee climbed back aboard and took out his watch. The great silvery turnip was his one vanity, the one gift his parents had given him when he left.

"On your mark," Dee said.

Jonathan adjusted in the seat, gripped the wheel, and made sure his feet were on the pedals.

"Get set."

Jonathan fixed his eyes on the big rock Dee had indicated. He could do this. He would do this. Forty-five seconds, fully loaded, over terrain that was undoubtedly much more rugged than the course. He took a deep breath.

"Go!" Dee barked.

Jonathan shoved the pedal down with all his might. The wheels whirred. The weeds tapped against the wooden platform with a sound like pebbles on his window. He was awake, alive, and the speed thrilled him as he whooshed past the rock.

Behind him, Dee whooped. Jonathan let the *Ruagán* roll to a stop, well past the rock. "We did it! Forty seconds, Jonny!" Jonathan heard the ever-present chalk scratching against wood. "Forty seconds for a quarter mile is a minute twenty seconds for a half mile, and that's two minutes forty seconds for a mile." More scratching and mumbling. "Twenty-two and a half miles an hour over an ugly course and fully loaded. We're in. We're in!" Dee leaned forward and kissed his neck. "Do it again to prove it wasn't a fluke."

Jonathan obliged, pedaling even harder to get back to the starting point. The wind whistled around him and he laughed, half-exultant, half-terrified by the speed.

Dee gasped. "Half a minute. That's thirty miles an hour. As fast as a train!"

Jonathan laughed again, stopped the *Ruagán*, and turned around to kiss Dee. "Amazing. We are going to win this."

"Let me drive us home. I need to do this too. You'll be the primary racer, but if I can pedal too, it will get us there faster."

They switched seats. Dee edged along the plank on the right sides of the chairs and Jonathan took the left. Dee's chair was very comfortable after a full day on his feet. Dee pedaled them home, keeping to a slow and safe speed.

He stopped a few blocks from the room and bought two bowls of jellied eels for their supper. Jonathan didn't protest although eels were not his favorite. He ate without descending, handing the bowl back to Dee when he finished.

They made the stairs to the room, the whole week settling like a great weight on Jonathan's shoulders. Dee washed his hands and then brought Jonathan a cool cloth.

"We're going to do brilliantly. And I haven't been letting you sleep nearly enough, have I, love? Rest now. Work tomorrow and then the race."

Jonathan woke to the pebbles on his window, growling. Dee was snoring into his shoulder, as always. He wanted to stay right where he was and sleep longer. But work had to be done. They had to eat and lay up what money they could between now and July fourth. The qualifier was only one step. Then there was the whole weeklong race to San Francisco. He left without waking Dee.

Dee had a bit of supper going over the alcohol burner when he came home and was happily squeaking the eternal chalk over a slate. He looked up from the map he was poring over.

"Do you know, Jonny, my love, that if we leave here on July fourth, pedal at thirty miles an hour for twelve hours, we'll be into Pennsylvania by bedtime?"

Jonathan shook his head. "I've never even been out of Boston."

"It's here that worries me." Dee tapped the map. "Between Denver and California is all desert. Hope we can carry enough water."

Jonathan kissed Dee's neck. "To bed, sweetheart. We'll worry about that when we qualify."

Dee smiled and blew out the alcohol lamp. "And am I, then? Your sweetheart?"

"For always, whether we qualify or no, whether we win or not." Jonathan draped one arm around Dee's shoulders and steered him upstairs.

"Oh good, then you'll take me riding and for ice-cream sundaes and all the other frills a sweetheart gets," Dee teased.

"If we win this, you can have ice-cream sundaes for breakfast every morning if you like. Delivered as you lie abed until nine or ten."

Dee laughed and kicked the door shut as he kissed Jonathan. "You kissed me sweetly yesterday morning." He yanked Jonathan's pants open and went to his knees. Jonathan liked the look of this but wasn't sure he could stay on his feet through the torturous pleasure Dee would be giving him.

A warm, wet tongue slid along the bottom of his cock and then circled the head. Jonathan sat down hard on the edge of the bed. Dee stayed on the floor and slipped his tongue into the slit of Jonathan's underwear to lick his balls. Jonathan held still and didn't groan as he wanted to.

Dee knew what he was doing, and Jonathan wondered if there had been others before him. Probably. It didn't matter as long as he was the last one. He wanted his boy with him forever, inventing delightful nuisances and making bad jokes.

When Dee swallowed his cock, Jonathan shut his eyes and let his lover control the moment. There would be nights for thrusting and nights for gentle licks. Tonight was for whatever Dee wanted to do.

What Dee wanted was long and wet and delightful. His wicked tongue teased and tormented until Jonathan nearly wept with need. Then he concentrated with a firm suction and plenty of tongue. Jonathan listened and heard Dee making soft little moans around his cock, the sounds of pleasure and desire. He was pleased that Dee was enjoying this as well.

A deep swallow and tongue press sent him over the edge. Dee's tongue whispered over him until he finished spending. In a moment, Dee brushed a kiss over the head and came up to sit beside him.

Jonathan turned them around so that they were lying down. Dee kissed his ear.

"Tomorrow morning, my heart. Tomorrow. We'll sail by them all and win the qualifier and then we'll pedal our way to San Francisco." He hesitated. "Jonathan."

Jonathan knew it was serious if Dee was using his name. "Yes?"

"Let's not come back. After the race, I mean. Might as well stay in San Francisco. Both our folks are dead. Nothing holding us to Boston. We won't have jobs if we come back."

Jonathan kissed the top of his head. "I had been thinking much the same as I carried cloth today. Pack everything and we'll go. I'll bring all the money I have and we'll light out as Mark Twain says."

"Anywhere with you, my love. Is it to be Jonathan Ferguson or Declan Crawford when we finish?"

"Anything we want."

They woke to the Saturday pebbles, but Jonathan did not go to work. He hurried down and paid his awakener a nickel to take a sick note into the mill. After a fast breakfast of bread and the end of the jam, he and Dee got the *Ruagán* from the shed.

Dee was unusually quiet as they drove out to the raceway. The *Ruagán* jostled over the cobbled roads and handled the ruts of the dirt roads with aplomb. Jonathan found himself loving the machine as well as the man who had made it.

They pulled up to the registration table. Jonathan climbed down, put his goggles up, and pulled down his scarf. They had stopped a couple of times to make themselves more comfortable from the rushing air and the flying grit.

He looked at the crowd. Dozens of young men in all manner of vehicles waited, some in line, some already wearing a numbered cloth. He got in line and got his number.

"Lucky thirteen," Dee teased when he came back scowling at the cloth.

He let Dee tie it around him and they went to the starting area. There was nothing to say. He wanted to tell Dee he loved him, tell him they would win, but the time for those words was all past now. He gripped the wheel as a man with a megaphone requested the first ten racers to the line.

"The first ten will begin the course now. The second ten will go in ten minutes. And so on, until all have left the starting area. Follow the marked course, watch for stations along the way. You must collect a ticket at each station as well as bring the vehicle in on time to qualify. Good luck, gentlemen."

Dee's breath on the back of his neck was followed by, "Less than an hour to make the run. Can you do it, Jonny boy?"

Jonathan reached up and pulled Dee's hat down over his eyes. "If I can't, your father's a London night soil driver."

Dee nipped his ear and settled back into his seat. The first group was off and Jonathan joined the other racers at the starting line. It looked as if many of them had had the same idea of using large wheels, but none of the devices looked like his and Dee's.

"*Ruagán,*" he whispered as he snapped the goggles down over his eyes. The biting wind that left all shivering in its wake. He was the wind. The starter waved his flag and Jonathan pumped the pedals with all his might.

The course whizzed by, impossibly fast, each station barely within view of the next. He would slow at each station and Dee would lean down for the ticket. They could do this. Most of the other devices were a station or two behind. They passed one of the first group who had lost a wheel.

They crossed the finish line barely behind the last member of the first group, and well ahead of the rest of theirs. The timekeeper blinked at his watch.

"*Ruagán,* by Jonathan and Dee Crawford, qualifies!"

Dee whooped as he brought the vehicle to a stop. They sprang off and into each other's arms, shouting and pounding each other on the back.

"I told you we could do it, Jonny!" Dee bounced out of his arms and thrust a fist at the sky with a leap. He calmed a bit and cocked his head. "And when did I become Dee Crawford?"

"When I was afraid they would see Ferguson and say 'no Irish' like half the places in town." He pulled Dee back into a hug, wishing he could kiss his boy right there.

Instead, Jonathan just held his lover, feeling the barely contained energy and excitement. In a week, they would be on their way to California.

ANGELIA SPARROW is a five-time loser of the Darrel Award (the Memphis SF and Fantasy Award), a double loser of the Gaylactic Spectrum Award, and a frequent convention guest around the Southeast and Midwest. She has been writing professionally since 2004, and writing steampunk since 2008. When not traveling with The Literary Underworld author consortium, she is a part-time inventory clerk and full-time trucker's wife. She has two children still at home. She can usually be found at conventions wearing goggles and a battered leather hat and wielding knitting needles or a crochet hook with reckless abandon.

Website: http://www.brooksandsparrow.com

Blog: http://angelsparrow.blogspot.net

Twitter: @asparrow16

Facebook: Author Angelia Sparrow

Livejournal: valarltd

E-mail: angeliasparrow@gmail.com

THE CLOCKWORK NIGHTINGALE'S SONG

AMY RAE DURRESON

NIGHTINGALE No. 48 had stopped singing.

Its brass head should have been raised, not hanging low, and its jeweled wings were meant to whir. Instead, it stood atop its marble pillar (not real marble, of course, any more than the paste jewels were real, but wood painted well enough to fool the eye by gaslight) in the most secluded glade of the Vauxhall Flying Gardens. None of the thousands of visitors who flocked to the pleasure gardens every night had yet stumbled across it. Give it an hour, Shem thought dourly, once the ladies of the *ton* went home and the strumpets came out to play, and this would be a far more popular spot.

Better do something before then. This was the third time this month Shem had needed to repair this nightingale. Time for it to be taken apart for a proper look at its clockwork innards.

"What should we do, Mr. Holloway?" the boy asked.

"Put a cage over the top until morning," Shem said. "Stop the guests from interfering with it. Young gentlemen don't have much respect for property."

"The *gentlemen,* Mr. Holloway?" the boy protested, his eyes going wide. "But they're brought up proper."

"Proper*ly*," Shem corrected sharply. No apprentice under his charge was going to wander around the Gardens with a gutter accent. "Higher they're born, further they fall with a drink in them. You steer clear of gentlemen, boy."

"Yes, Mr. Holloway," the boy said, but he still looked puzzled.

Shem sighed. He liked to take new apprentices with him on the late shift until he was convinced they'd learned some common sense (at which point it was safe to assume they were staying, and he would deign to learn their names). This one had him worried. He was hardworking, no doubt, and the masters at the training orphanage had been right when they said he was bright. Unfortunately, he was too eager to please, and pretty besides, all coltish limbs, pink lips, and slim hips.

It wasn't just the mechanical devices the young gentlemen liked to interfere with. Some of them had a taste for mechanics. Shem kept a fatherly eye on his apprentices, for all they were only ten years younger than him. It was going to be a job to keep this one safe from wandering hands.

Shem unlocked the gate that connected the concealed path to the grove. It took an army of mechanics, gardeners, and servants to keep the Gardens running efficiently, and keeping everyone hidden maintained the illusion of magic.

"Always lock these gates behind you," Shem instructed the boy, who nodded earnestly. It was bad enough the whores of London plied their trade in the quiet groves and dark walks. Give them access to the secret paths, and the place would be a brothel within a week and shut down within two, putting all the staff out of work. Shem had grown up poor; he had no desire to be jobless.

The cage clicked into place over the silent nightingale, and Shem showed the boy how to lock it shut. He'd come back for it once the Gardens closed, but for now the nightingale was safe.

He and the boy continued on their rounds as the Gardens grew rowdier around them. Dining was over, and the supper boxes in the central grove were overspilling, lewd and drunken chatter drowning out the wheezy music of the steam orchestra. Some young blood, likely straight down from one of the better universities, had managed to get a foothold on Atlas's brass globe, and was being hoisted toward the smoggy heavens as his friends cheered. Neptune's water fountain had gotten clogged and was spewing bubbles sideways, an urgent repair that made Shem glad to have an apprentice to send wading into the foam to clear the pump.

He paused at the end of the Grand Walk as the horns mounted in the trees suddenly blew in perfect synchrony. Nudging the boy round, Shem watched his amazed face as the fireworks began. Vauxhall was unique, and he loved knowing the whole of London looked up at them every night, watching the lights blazing in the garden in the sky.

Only once did they encounter trouble, when a ruddy-cheeked gentleman came stumbling toward them, winking at the boy. Luckily, all Shem needed to do was tap his wrench meaningfully against his thigh, and the hopeful lecher hurriedly found business elsewhere. Even when he'd been a piston boy, running coal through the tunnels below the Gardens to feed the great burners that kept them afloat, Shem had never been waifish. These days his shoulders were too wide for the tunnels, and he carried the muscle to match them. Being a senior mechanic was no light duty. Only a brave man would risk his ire.

When the trumpets sounded for closing, long after midnight, he sent the yawning boy back through the hidden paths to wait in the staff canteen until the Gardens returned to earth. Shem himself retraced his steps toward Nightingale No. 48, the Gardens going quiet around him. He could now hear the distant clang of the last airship undocking from the quay, the wind sighing softly through the treetops, and the night birds, ones that weren't formed of gears and metal.

The ground surged beneath his feet as the first heated air was released from the floats, and the Gardens began to slide steadily back toward the earth, guided into place by chains and pulleys. A waft of steam floated across the stars, scenting the night with ash and hot metal.

As he stepped into the grove, a real nightingale began to sing, its voice rising in loose, breathy notes. And inside its cage, for the first time that night, the brass nightingale lifted its head with a soft whir and began to sing in reply, its mechanical melody just as yearning.

THAT afternoon, Shem took apart the nightingale, unscrewing its chest panel to expose the mechanisms. He'd replaced its spring twice already, so he could discount that. He checked for worn, strained parts and joints in need of oiling. There was nothing obvious wrong.

The bird had sung, just not at the appointed hour. Perhaps there was a problem with its circuitry. Shem was a cog and piston man, not a circuit expert, but he knew how to replace a faulty chip. Ignoring the dull sheen of the nightingale's glass eyes, he opened up its head. He checked that the circuits were secure, and no wires burned out, and then looked more closely.

He'd had No. 24 open last week, to replace a scratchy music roll, and this one didn't look the same. It had the usual miniature pianola rolls to dictate its melody, but this one seemed to have an extra circuitry chip: one to control movements, one that switched between tunes, and a third, unfamiliar chip, connected to all the rest with thin filaments.

Time to consult the manual.

The nightingales were not very complex mechanisms, and their book was little used. Shem had to blow off cobwebs (he'd have to talk to the matron about whichever of the orphanage girls was supposed to be cleaning in here, because a well-ordered workshop should be clean even in the corners). To his surprise, each of the fifty nightingales had a separate listing in the book. Nine of them, including No. 48, had a symbol inked across the top of the page: a simple figure of an angel standing on a wrench. Some later hand, in red ink, had added small horns and a forked tail to the figure.

Shem wasn't going to guess at what that meant. Instead, he tossed a dust cloth over the nightingale and took the manual to the man who might know.

NATHANIEL DAWKINS had been a senior mechanic back when the Flying Gardens were merely the Mechanical Gardens. These days, Dawkins was one of two Chief Mechanics. His office, unlike Shem's workshop, had a view of the swaying treetops of the daytime Gardens, currently resting against the ground while gardeners and day-shift mechanics rushed to prepare them to rise again once the sun set.

Dawkins took one look at the picture in the manual and groaned. "Oh, not today."

"What does it mean?"

"Only the angel bloody Gabriel coming down from heaven. Or, in his case, from Mayfair."

Shem must have looked baffled, because Dawkins sighed. "Oh, you've not the pleasure yet, have you, Holloway? This is the inventor's mark. Your broken nightingale is one of Lord Marchmont's specials."

That made more sense. Even Shem, who had no interest in aristocratic nonsense, had heard of Gabriel Marchmont, the Earl of Godalming. He was the darling of the Royal Society, the genius inventor whose rank protected him from accusations of madness, and the man who had, whilst punting up the Cam one May Week, casually devised a way to make a garden (and, more to his government's interest, an ironclad) hover above the ground for twelve hours at a stretch. Shem, who worked with his inventions every day, had always rather wanted to meet the man.

"So?" he asked, thinking about the extra circuit.

"So, he'll want to repair it himself," Dawkins said glumly and then raised his voice to roar, "Ruth! Telegraph Lord Marchmont. We broke one of his toys."

There was chorus of groans from the outer office.

"God help us all," Dawkins muttered.

AFTER all that, Shem was alive with curiosity and half expecting an old curmudgeon, although he knew Lord Marchmont had started inventing as a Cambridge undergraduate twelve years ago.

The Marchmont steam carriage drew to a halt outside the Mechanics' Hall, behind an unusually sleek engine. Steps unfolded from the carriage with a neat click, each one locking smoothly into place. Only then did Lord Marchmont emerge.

He was beautiful. His hair was golden, pulled into a queue at his nape. His face was narrow and high-boned, almost ascetic until you saw the fullness of his mouth. He was tall, looking down on Shem and Dawkins with ease, and slim as a snake. He was dressed for dinner, in somber colors, save the bright white fall of his cravat.

"Dawkins," he drawled, "what have your oafs broken this time?"

"A problem with one of the nightingales, my lord," Dawkins said politely, as Shem blinked and began to seethe. Typical gentleman, then, despite his genius.

"Break the key off as they were winding, did they?"

"No, my lord."

"What, then?"

Dawkins waved Shem forward. "One of my senior engineers, my lord. Mr. Holloway is in charge of repairs."

"I wish you wouldn't palm me off on your lackeys, Dawkins. I don't have time to run a remedial school for your rude mechanicals."

"Mr. Holloway will take you to his workroom, my lord," Dawkins said. "He'll explain the problem to you, sir." Then he abandoned Shem to face the earl's disdain.

Shem never quite knew what to do in these situations. He didn't have gentry manners; he'd never had them ingrained into him as a child, and he fumbled whenever he was faced with a social situation. He didn't know how to address the man, or whether he should bow (though he knew he didn't want to). Gruffly, he said, "This way, your earlship."

"Dear Christ," the earl remarked, but as he seemed to be addressing the air, or possibly the heavens, Shem ignored him. He strode back toward the workshops, assuming the earl would follow.

Strolling along beside Shem with his nose wrinkled, Lord Marchmont remarked, "This place feels more like a factory every time I visit."

"We like to be efficient, sir," Shem said, bristling. If Marchmont was going to sneer at his attempts to be polite, a simple "sir" was all he'd be getting.

"Napoleon was not wrong to call England a nation of factory workers."

"I'm sure, sir."

"They don't waste any time teaching you people the art of conversation, do they?"

"No, sir." Then, prompted by some inner devil, he couldn't help adding, "They taught us that old Boney lost, though, so forgive me if I don't care much for his opinion of working men. Sir."

That was met with silence. Shem wondered if he had pushed his luck too far. Then Lord Marchmont laughed. It was a surprisingly nice laugh, full and merry, and Shem was startled to see genuine amusement crinkling the corners of the man's eyes.

"A hit, a very palpable hit," the earl said and doffed his top hat mockingly. Then he grimaced and tucked it under his arm. "These things are absurdly uncomfortable. What fool invented them?"

"Someone who never had to crawl into a beam engine," Shem said and was relieved when the earl laughed again. He could tolerate arrogance better in a man with a sense of humor.

Once they arrived in the workshop, however, things took a turn for the worse again. The earl took one look at the nightingale dismembered on the bench and drew in his breath with a distinct disapproving hiss.

"I'm supposed to be called in before maintenance is done on any of the special automatons," he said, pursing his lips.

"First place it mentions that is in the manual, my lord."

"And you touch my mechanisms *without* consulting the manual?" the earl demanded incredulously.

Shem couldn't hold back a snort of derision. "Wouldn't be much of a mechanic if I needed the manual every time I replaced a spring."

The earl stared at him for a moment before he turned back to the table. "True. Perhaps I should have marked their casing instead, to prevent well-meaning meddling."

Shem didn't particularly appreciate that description of his job, but he bit his annoyance back. "So far, I've checked—"

"I have no interest in your opinion," the earl interrupted. As Shem glowered at him, he added, "I prefer a fresh perspective."

"Shall I leave you to your work?" Shem asked hopefully. He had other repairs to make and an apprentice whose work needed assessing.

"No, stay and tell me your observations, without conjecture. When did it first go quiet?" Even as he spoke, his hands were moving with swift competence, performing all the checks Shem had already done, at twice Shem's speed. Shem found himself fascinated, watching those long fingers move with such dexterity. He'd always assumed aristocrats had plump, soft hands, but Lord Marchmont's were long and narrow, with callused fingertips. Ink and oil were smudged across the base of his thumb, and Shem indulged himself for a moment. He had a weakness for men's hands that he rarely acted upon. There was no danger he'd be tempted to flirt with Lord Marchmont, so it was safe enough to look, as long as the earl didn't notice.

"Is that all, Holloway?"

"Yes," Shem said, realizing he had gone quiet. "That's when I brought it in for a better look."

"Quite right. Nothing obvious is wrong, so it must be the special circuit. A shame. It was an interesting experiment. I was hoping it would work." He snapped his fingers. "Clippers, please. I'll remove the empathy circuit, and we'll see if that fixes your problems."

Shem passed him the tool, asking, "The empathy circuit?"

"Oh, it was an idea I had." Marchmont paused, his hand hovering over the nightingale's innards, and looked slightly indignant. "Some people found the early prototypes unnerving—unnatural, they said!"

"Some people are idiots," Shem said and was startled when Marchmont smiled at him. It was broad and bright and chased any hint of arrogance out of his face. Again, the realization of just how beautiful this man was hit Shem, stealing his breath and making his cheeks heat.

"Quite," Marchmont said. "So, the empathy circuit should cause the bird to simulate simple emotional reactions: fear, surprise, joy. If it's interfering with its primary function, however, I'll pull it out." He reached forward with the clippers.

Without thinking, Shem grabbed his wrist to stop him. Marchmont swung to stare at him, his face affronted, and Shem remembered that working men did not lay their hands on lords of the realm. What Marchmont had just said changed the way Shem thought about the automaton, though. He wouldn't let drunks abuse his apprentices, and he wasn't going to let Marchmont cripple the nightingale without a little more explanation.

"You gave it a heart," he said, not releasing Marchmont. He could feel the pulse in the man's wrist beating beneath his thumb, steady as a clock.

"Strictly speaking," Marchmont said slowly, "the mainspring is its heart. That's what powers it, you see."

"That wasn't what I meant," Shem said. Marchmont didn't have blue eyes. Shem had thought he would, with all that cold blond hauteur, but his eyes were brown, as rich and warm as licorice.

"I see you're speaking metaphorically. It doesn't have real feelings, you must understand. They are simply produced by the circuitry."

"And what produces our emotions?" Shem asked. He'd never been taught to be good with words, and he was struggling to find the ones to express the little clutch of panic and wonder in his throat. "The bird doesn't know they're not real, does it? You gave it a heart. Don't you want to know why it's breaking?"

Marchmont just stared at him, his brows furrowed a little. Then he cleared his throat and said, "Oh." Shem wasn't sure what that meant, not until that bright smile dawned across Marchmont's face again, and he breathed, "Oh, let's find out!"

THAT night, Shem found it hard to concentrate on his rounds. He was distracted by the thought of a brass nightingale that refused to sing and, more and more as the evening underwent its daily transformation from charming to wild, of its creator, his unguarded smile, the arrogance Shem wanted to slap off that pretty face, and his fine hands.

"Should we check the fountain, Mr. Holloway?" the boy asked, breaking him out of his daydream.

Shem glanced at Neptune's fountain, currently occupied by three very drunk young men: one sitting in the water up to his waist and the others, shirtless, copying the pose of the great statue for the benefit of a squealing crowd of women who were clearly no better than they ought to be.

"Have some sense, boy."

The boy's eyes were wistful, and he wet his lips a little before venturing, "But they might need our help, Mr. Holloway."

Like that, was it? Shem could see they were pretty, for drunken louts, the water slicking across their bare, muscled chests, and the colored lights which hung in the surrounding trees washing them with a gold-and-purple glow. Still, anyone who stripped off in a fountain on a June night in England deserved to get pneumonia, and he wasn't going to let his apprentice lust after buffoons. "The constables will be along in a moment to help them all the way to the dock."

"But, Mr. Holloway…."

"Come along, boy." Shem firmly steered the boy away.

He wasn't expecting a firm clap on his shoulder and an all-too-familiar posh voice to say, "There you are, Holloway. Must say the entertainment's changed in tone a little since I was last here."

"I can assure you that the management does not…." Shem started and protested as Marchmont plucked the key from his hand and unlocked the gate in the hedge. "My lord, the paths are for employees—"

"I'm on a retainer," Marchmont said cheerily, pushing them through the gate. He was still in evening dress, but there was a lot more ink smudged across his cuffs.

A loud splash and a roar of jeering laughter sounded behind them, and both Marchmont and the boy craned in that direction, as if they could see through three inches of dense laurel hedge. Irritated, Shem said, "We weren't expecting you quite yet, my lord."

"Oh, I couldn't stop thinking on it. I've revisited all my notes, and the standard reference texts, and now I must see the bird *in situ*. You've restored it to its post?"

"Some hours ago, sir."

The boy was quivering with curiosity, so Shem said to him, "Nightingale No. 48. Show me that you can find the way."

The boy darted ahead a little, and Marchmont commented, "It's a veritable maze behind the scenes. You could make a fortune opening this up to the public. Mazes are all the thing, you know. I designed revolving hedgerows for the one at Blenheim."

"We do try to keep undesirables out of the staff areas, sir," Shem remarked. Marchmont seemed to have relaxed considerably since the afternoon, and Shem eyed him suspiciously. Was he drunk?

"Luckily, I am considered quite the catch," Marchmont said as a money capsule went rattling through the pneumatic tube attached to the side rail of the path. "I say, what do you do about rust?"

"The exteriors are specially treated," Shem said, relaxing a little. Mechanics he could talk about comfortably. "We also replace sections during the quiet season."

The boy came rushing back. "There's guests there, Mr. Holloway."

"We'll wait for them to be done," Shem said.

"The devil we will," Marchmont snapped and marched straight out into the glade. Shem just had time to glimpse a corpulent gentleman with his hands busy on the bare bubbies of the girl on his lap, before Marchmont swept by with a comment of, "Evening, Shackleton. How's your wife?"

Within moments, they had the grove to themselves.

"Was that necessary?" Shem asked. They did need to keep the customers happy, after all.

"Absolutely," Marchmont said. "Can't stand the man. Tried to court one of my sisters, but Rosalind has far too much sense to be taken in by that type."

The boy piped up to ask, "Do you have many sisters, my lord?"

Shem clipped him on the ear. "Don't ask personal questions, boy. It's impertinent."

"But—"

"And I've told you not to talk to gentlemen."

The boy looked rebellious, and Marchmont was smirking at them over the nightingale, so Shem pointed to the gate in the hedge and said, "Mr. Ferrars needs another pair of hands at the dock. Off you go."

The boy trailed off, and Shem turned back to Marchmont, who said, with a note of amusement, "Five, for the record."

"Sir?"

"Five sisters, all my elders, from Rosalind down to Miranda."

"That's nice, sir," Shem said, ignoring the little twist of bitterness. He had no family.

"You're supposed to make a remark about my family's evident fondness for Shakespeare," Marchmont informed him, sprawling comfortably on the bench. "No? Ah, no small talk from the working man? I hope you're not going to be dull, Holloway."

"I shall endeavor to entertain you, my lord," Shem said drily.

He was rewarded with laughter, and Marchmont delved into his pocket to produce a slim notebook. "To work, then. What time did you wind the bird?"

After a while, Marchmont patted the seat beside him with an irritated look. "Sit, will you? You're giving me a crick in my neck."

It felt strange, sitting down in the middle of the garden with a handsome man. He'd never come here as a guest, and it felt oddly sinful to just sit and talk, even if they were exchanging technical details. Marchmont was jittery, obviously desperate to take the nightingale apart again, and so he talked freely, ideas and explanations bubbling out of him. He wasn't drunk at all, Shem realized gradually, just so caught up in the problem the nightingale posed that he couldn't be calm. He seemed to want Shem's reactions now, leaning forward to gesture at him as he described literal castles in the air. It was fascinating, principles Shem worked with every day sliding up against each other in unthinkable ways to make the impossible possible, and it made him a little breathless at times. As Marchmont's face lit up in response to his careful questions, he wondered if the man had anyone at home who understood his ideas.

A few guests stumbled into the grove, but the sight of the two of them sitting comfortably sent them away again, several sniggering into their gloves.

"What's wrong with them?" Marchmont demanded.

"They're probably assuming the worst," Shem said, shrugging uncomfortably. Dawkins knew Marchmont was here and why, so his reputation was safe at work, but he didn't like the idea that strangers were judging his morals. "There's some gentlemen have a taste for engineers."

"For engineers?" Marchmont echoed, as if he had never heard such an absurdity. "Really?"

"It's to do with the tool belt, sir, or so I'm told."

"*Oh*," Marchmont said and then added thoughtfully, "Hence Viola breaking Lord Rochester's nose in the workshop all those years ago. I always wondered why she hit him so hard."

Shem really didn't want to know any more than that, but had to ask, "How old were you?"

"Fourteen," Marchmont said absently. "I should really make her something to say thank you. Do you think her children would like a mechanical pug?"

"I think children like anything mechanical," Shem ventured, keeping his voice steady.

"I could adapt a design," Marchmont started and then was off into flights of fancy again, even as Shem swallowed back fury. If it had been one of his apprentices....

He reminded himself that Marchmont was not a defenseless boy and had clearly had his own protectors.

By the time the sky began to lighten and the crowds thin, Marchmont was yawning. His gaze remained fixed on the nightingale, but he was beginning to slump sideways, tilting closer toward Shem's shoulder with every yawn. Shem did his best to prop him back up with a discreet nudge, but Marchmont merely smiled vaguely and slid back down.

"When," he asked as the closing trumpets sounded, "do we call it a night?"

"Not yet," Shem said, watching the small brass shape atop the pillar. It looked very sad, with its head slumped and its wings still, and he wondered how much of his sympathy for it was simply because he knew it had feelings.

As the garden began to sink to earth, and Marchmont made a little notation of the time in his book, the bird stirred. Its head lifted, and its wings whirred, and a strange music burst out of it: a string of notes from one of its melodies jarring into another in a patchwork, inelegant song.

Marchmont froze, his fingers tightening on his pencil.

A shadow flitted out of the trees on the edge of the grove, landing softly on top of the abandoned cage. As the brass nightingale fell quiet, the real nightingale sang in reply, its song arching up into the dim dawn, throbbing with yearning.

And the brass nightingale began to sing again, clumsily matching its song to the little brown bird's until the two threads of music merged into a hopeless, lonely whole.

MARCHMONT was still spluttering incomplete and incoherent sentences when the Gardens finally landed, so Shem marched him back through the hedge paths to the staff canteen. They were greeted by the scent of bacon frying. The tea urns were hot, so Shem deposited the earl at a table, got them each a sturdy mug of the strong milky stuff, and went to join the queue of yawning night-shift men waiting for their breakfast.

Dolly, behind the counter, winked at him when he asked for two plates and replied in a hoarse whisper, "Who's your fancy man, Shem?"

"That's Lord Marchmont, come to examine his inventions," Shem said, and there was a rumble of interest around him.

"Never knew a lordship to eat his breakfast with us before," Dolly said. "I hear he's not married, girls."

"Think he'd fancy you, d'ya, Doll?" someone shouted from farther back, and there was a wide roar of laughter.

Shem, embarrassed, said, "Enough. I doubt he fancies more than a fry-up right now."

Dolly nodded vigorously. "Looks like he needs a good feed. Reckon them lords and ladies don't know how to eat proper."

"Pay a fortune for Vauxhall fare every night, don't they?"

"Maybe they think that *is* good food."

"Can we just feed the man, Dolly?" Shem asked quietly as the conversation rolled on.

She slipped an extra bit of bacon onto the plate and winked at him. "That's for him, and don't you growl and scare him off, Shem, my boy."

No one else had heard, but Shem narrowed his eyes at her anyway, even as she turned to the next in line. She'd known him too long, had Dolly, ever since they sat in the orphanage schoolroom together.

Back at the table, Marchmont had started sipping his tea. He put it down as Shem approached and said, his voice bewildered, "It's in love."

"Looks that way," Shem said and passed him a plate. "Eat your breakfast."

"That wasn't in my design."

He looked so genuinely taken aback that Shem had to hide a smile behind his mug. "That's what happens when you play god, sir. I'm fairly certain God was surprised when we started building steam engines."

"Not a believer in providence?" Marchmont asked.

"Not a believer in arguing religion over breakfast," Shem said quellingly, and had taken a good mouthful of bread and bacon before he remembered that Marchmont wasn't one of his apprentices.

"I won't take out the empathy chip," Marchmont said fiercely.

"I didn't think you would," Shem said. "Your bacon's getting cold."

"Oh," Marchmont said and began to dip the edge of his bread into his egg in a distracted way, until he said suddenly, "I'll replace it! I'll take it home with me, and it can sing in my garden, and I'll give Vauxhall a new one, free of charge."

It was a generous offer, because a mechanism like the nightingale didn't come cheap, but something still troubled Shem. It was the end of a long shift, so he took his time to tease it out as he ate. It wasn't until his plate was clean that he said, "What about the other nightingale?"

"The real one?"

"Are you going to take it to your garden too? Put it in a cage there?"

Marchmont blinked at him. "Oh." He frowned, putting his knife down.

"Don't waste food," Shem said automatically.

Marchmont started eating again, the frown still knotting his brow. At last he said, "One of them has to be in a cage, either way. The brass nightingale—its wings don't work."

"Why not?" Shem asked.

"It wasn't necessary for its original function, and so the weight.... Unless I apply.... I could extend its wings.... Membranes and some gliding function.... It's not.... I need a pencil. Paper!"

"In your pocket," Shem reminded him, and Marchmont blinked at him. Amused, Shem said, "No, not now. Go home and sleep on it."

"But the nightingale!"

"Will still be here when you wake up."

"I need it in my workshop."

"I'll bring it by," Shem said. He'd had a few apprentices like this, boys who got so entranced by mechanical problems they couldn't bear to eat or sleep, and knew quite well that Marchmont would just keep going until exhaustion overwhelmed him if he took the nightingale now. The poor bird deserved better.

"When?"

"When I've slept," Shem said. It was his half day, but the nightingale had caught his heart, and he didn't mind giving up a few hours of his afternoon to help save it. "That will have to do." And, belatedly again, he remembered to add, "My lord."

BY THE time he made it across the river, Shem was already beginning to regret his offer. He had lived out his entire life in the confines of Vauxhall, moving from the orphanage to the boardinghouse across the road. He rarely ventured far from the comfortable green shade of the

Gardens. This side of the Thames felt like a foreign country, for all it was shrouded in the same heavy pall of smog. He tensed at every steam carriage that came looming and huffling out of the fog, chimneys chugging dark smoke into the mist. How did the rest of London stand it, when they didn't have the freedom to soar above the murky streets every night?

When the great bell in the new Westminster tower boomed out two o'clock, he jumped. He hadn't realized he had walked so far, so he pulled his muffler up, braced himself against the wind, and turned away from the river. The Gardens' advertising claimed only at Vauxhall could Londoners experience a true English summer, and Shem wondered what these streets had been like before the invention of the steam engine. Had Westminster ever been green?

On his arrival in Albemarle Street, his heart sank. The Marchmont town house was huge, with tiers of windows. The black door was framed by pillars, with gleaming brass numbers. It wasn't the sort of door Shem could ever imagine approaching. Looking at it, he was ready to turn tail and scurry back to Vauxhall. He could send a courier with the nightingale.

He was no coward, though, so he pushed open the gate to the basement stairs and walked down to the tradesman's entrance. He knocked, but there was no reply.

Then he noticed a small sign tacked to the side of the door frame. A neatly drawn arrow pointed to an ornate brass daffodil, and the sign read, in scrawling handwriting, *This is a BELL!!*

Dubiously, Shem poked it.

Like a fan, the door folded up into the corners of its frame, revealing a sheet of metal studded with dials, sliding panels, and cogwheels. Another shutter rose to reveal a round-keyed typewriter. At just above his eye level, there was a clack of rotating flaps which revealed the command *PLEASE ENTER YOUR DE—*Another whir and it now read *LIVERY NUMBER OR THE—*It whirred again.—*PURPOSE OF YOUR VISIT.*

Shem reached for the typewriter warily and tapped in *shem holloway bringing the nightin—*

The panel slid down before he was done, almost catching his fingers, and Shem stepped back indignantly as a bell began to ring and the flaps whirled again to reveal red letters reading *ERROR!*

"Obviously," Shem told it.

He shifted uneasily from foot to foot as the bell kept shrilling. He really hadn't anticipated such a palaver. He was ready to shove the nightingale at the first servant he saw and leave.

Then the entire door—panels, typewriter and all—slid silently sideward into the wall to reveal Lord Marchmont.

"Why are you at this door?" he demanded. "I told the footman to expect you."

Shem decided not to try explaining. There wasn't much point arguing about class with folks who were rich enough to disregard it at a whim. Instead, he proffered his package. "The nightingale, my lord."

"Well, of course," Marchmont said, backing away into the basement. He didn't look as immaculately tidy as he had the day before: his hair was standing on end in places, and he had clearly been chewing his quill, because his lips were stained blue. He hadn't shaved, and although he had abandoned his dinner jacket, he still wore last night's shirt, its sleeves now grease-streaked. He grinned at Shem as if it were Christmas morning. "Come on, now. My workshop is this way, and I've been experimenting with wing components, but all the aerodynamic principles in the world are no use without experimental data, and...." He stopped and stared at Shem, who was still standing on the doorstep, feeling too bulky and grubby to set foot in a place that was too pricey for him to spit at.

The thing was that it never lasted. Shem had kissed a few gentlemen in the shadows of the Gardens, before he learned better, and none of them had looked for him again. One or two had even walked past without a glimmer of recognition. A gentleman could indulge himself by befriending a working man, for an hour or a day, but it was his whim that governed when and how the friendship ended. God help the ordinary man who misjudged that friendship or overstepped his mark. Shem was used to the ground moving under his feet, but everything else in his life needed to be steady to compensate. He didn't want to be charmed by Marchmont or risk responding to his excitement, only to be frozen out when the technical challenge was solved.

"Afraid to enter my lair?" Marchmont asked sharply, his smile dimming. "I assure you that, contrary to rumors, I am not building an army of mad automatons to conquer London, nor am I attempting any unholy rites or sacrificing virgins."

"Of course not, sir," Shem said, giving up. He didn't like the note of defensiveness in the earl's voice. "Blood would make a terrible mess of the gears."

Perhaps the most worrying thing was that Marchmont found that funny. It was hard to maintain proper detachment from someone who laughed at your darkest jokes. Biting back a sigh, Shem stepped into the inventor's basement.

The first thing that struck him was the heat and racket: the air rang with the wheeze and clang of pistons. It wasn't until his second cautious step that he realized he wasn't in an engine room.

This was a kitchen. The hobs on the polished black stove were glowing, and spits of steam escaped the chimneys that sprouted from its side. Pots and pans were suspended from a pulley that swung them from the hob, lowering them under taps and onto conveyor belts to be filled with chopped ingredients. At the table, the cook, a sturdy woman in a wide black dress, was chopping carrots with a relentless efficiency Shem only understood when he took a second look and realized that she was made of metal, her arms ending in an array of swiveling tools: carving knives, mixing spoons, whisks, even a gleaming potato masher.

Marchmont paused for a moment, sucking his breath in. "Damnation, not again. I swear, no matter how I adjust the programming, Cook always makes enough to feed a family. You'll have supper, I hope."

"That's very kind, sir," Shem said, eyeing the cook with interest.

"Excellent. Now, downstairs. These are the old cellars. Medieval in parts, I've been told. My sisters insisted I put my workshop here to save the house from any accidents. Demmed inconvenient, when I haven't started any serious fires in years, but not worth the family row, so here we are."

He swung open the door and waved Shem in. There was a note of nervousness in his voice, and Shem wondered again if the inventor's friends ever visited his workshop. Surely there were other inventors in the great city of London who shared Marchmont's passion for his work. Or was it just that Marchmont didn't trust them in his lair? To Shem, accustomed to collaboration when there was a problem to solve, it seemed a sad way to work.

Unbending enough to smile at Marchmont with some warmth, he stepped inside.

The ceiling was vaulted, crisscrossed with beams and lines of wire threaded with cogs and gears, nuts, latches, clips, bolts, and clasps, the brass gleaming dimly in the gaslight. Racks were bolted onto the ancient walls, but most lay empty, their tools scattered across the cluttered workbenches: wrenches balanced precariously on tins of tacks; pliers and pencils jumbled together in mugs with broken handles; a drill marking the place in a battered book; saws half-hidden below sheaves of blueprints that drifted onto the floor as Marchmont rushed past. There were half-built devices everywhere, many clicking and ticking. A small tin drummer marched along the edge of one bench as the key turned in its back, and a whole tray of fist-sized glass eyeballs rolled around to stare at Shem.

A slight sucking sound made him jump, and he looked up to see a brass turtle crawling across the ceiling, lifting one sucker-tipped foot at a time. A small spider dangled off the edge of its shell, spinning busily. The whole ceiling was lightly coated in cobwebs, and Shem wondered if Marchmont would notice before the turtle lost its grip and fell on his head.

Every tool he had ever wished for was scrambled into this mess somewhere, but he would fire any apprentice who left one of his workrooms in this state.

Then he recalled Marchmont's anxious look and bit back his criticism to say, "Magnificent."

"Naturally," Marchmont replied, the arrogance back in his voice. He pushed aside books and papers to make a space in the midst of one of the benches and put the nightingale down carefully. "Let's get her wings off." He looked up, blinking. "If I can find the right screwdriver."

Shem looked over the chaos and spotted one the right size in amongst a tottering heap of camshafts. He extracted it carefully and offered it to Marchmont without comment, although he suspected his expression said too much.

Marchmont took it eagerly, his fingers brushing against Shem's. The touch made Shem jump, as if he'd been caught by static, a warm shudder arching up his arm to make him catch his breath. He wanted to touch Marchmont again, for longer, to see what it led to, but that was a bad idea, a very bad idea.

"Holloway?" Marchmont was staring at him, his eyes narrowed so he looked both quizzical and intent. He was breathing fast, and Shem realized they were both still holding the screwdriver, their fingers separated by a mere length of polished steel. A step would bring them up against each other, and he'd be able to find out if Marchmont kissed with haughty arrogance or wild enthusiasm.

Summoning his willpower, Shem stepped back. "Shall I be getting out of your way now, sir?"

"No!" Marchmont seemed have surprised himself, as he blushed a little and added, "Stay, do. You understand the designs, and some of the work will go faster with some help. I shall probably talk, of course, but you're not obliged to listen. I shall just be thinking aloud."

Shem knew he should not allow himself to become any more fascinated with Marchmont, but it was so hard to resist, especially when he wanted to know what the man had planned for their nightingale. It couldn't hurt to stay a little longer, and he would almost certainly learn a great deal, skills to help him in his own trade. "May I make suggestions?"

Marchmont looked a little puzzled. "If you like. People don't usually…. If you're interested, of course."

"I'm interested," Shem said, and it came out with slightly the wrong emphasis, making Marchmont's eyes go dark and intent again. Hastily, Shem sidestepped and picked up the nearest drill bit. "I'll just tidy this up, then."

"Tidy?" Marchmont echoed, as if it was a foreign word. "Whatever for?" As Shem eyed the nearest bench meaningfully, he added, "I suppose it is a little messy. There's just so much to do."

"And think how much more you'd get done if you weren't constantly searching for your tools," Shem said tartly and then picked up a fretsaw that caught his eye. "Or replacing them because you haven't cleaned off—what *is* this? It's corroded the blade."

"I honestly don't know," Marchmont said, taking it off him with interest. "Shame. I need a good corrosive sometimes." He put the fretsaw down on the nearest stool and returned to the nightingale. "Do what you like. I'm going to start by replacing some of the heavy parts with lighter prototypes. Wingspan and body weight ratios are the key, I think…."

Shem moved around as he listened, slowly imposing some order. It was easy to fall into the usual back-and-forth of problem solving, and he soon found himself matching his comments to Marchmont's rambling. Shem couldn't spin ideas as fast, but he could pull Marchmont's wilder flights of fancy back, and he was starting to learn how to ask questions that would make Marchmont's eyes narrow with interest. It was a shock when he realized the clocks scattered around the room were striking seven.

"My shift starts in an hour," he said, stepping back from where they were both leaning over the nightingale. "I should go."

"Fine, fine," Marchmont said without looking up, which disappointed Shem (which, in turn, made him want to slap himself in the face for pure stupidity). "Come back tomorrow."

"I start work at four tomorrow," Shem told him, not even surprised that Marchmont intended to commandeer his free time without apology.

"Must you?"

"Must I work for a living?" Shem asked pointedly. "Yes, my lord."

"Fine," Marchmont said with a note of irritation. "Be here by two, and come in the front door." He pressed a lever above the desk, and a bell tinkled somewhere in the house above. "The footman will show you the way."

The footman was another automaton, balanced on a pair of ratcheted gears that allowed it to climb the stair rails. Upstairs, it took a photograph of Shem and slotted the resulting slide into a rack behind the front door, and then Shem escaped from the dull and featureless hallway with relief.

All evening, making his rounds and teaching his apprentice, he turned over what he had learned until it fit into place against what he already knew. The engineering knowledge was easy, but the man was a puzzle. Marchmont was rude to strangers, oblivious to anything outside his own social realm, arrogant and demanding; he was sharply defensive of his work, overflowing with words once he realized Shem was willing to listen, living in a house full of automatons, and flustered by a small touch.

Perhaps, Shem thought, it was as simple as loneliness.

It was a quiet night, the fog lapping as high as the edges of the Gardens. The steady mechanical progression of symphonies was underlaid by the distant boom and cry of foghorns on the river. The dirigibles came nosing slowly out of the mist to nudge alongside the wharf, their sides lined with red-and-green lights and their horns sounding steadily. Despite that, there was a quiet to the Gardens tonight, especially in the less frequented corners, where the trees bent deeply over the alcoves and gazebos, their leaves slick and heavy with the damp. He wasn't surprised when he found Marchmont sitting in their nightingale's grove after closing, his fingers laced beneath his chin as he contemplated the bird, which had been restored to its perch. It looked different, its wings wider and less adorned.

"Were you successful, my lord?" Shem asked.

Marchmont startled, as if he hadn't noticed they were there. Sighing, he said, "Not yet."

He'd shaved since Shem had left him and found a clean shirt, but there were shadows under his eyes. He clearly hadn't slept, and Shem's heart went out to him. Didn't rich people have faithful old servants to look after them? What about those sisters he had mentioned with such affection? Why wasn't someone looking after him?

"Go on, boy," he said to the apprentice. "Shift's over."

Left alone with Marchmont, he went to sit beside him on the damp bench, grimacing at the cool press of the stone. He didn't say anything, but after a few moments, Marchmont said abruptly, "I thought there was little point if I didn't bring it back in time for dawn."

"I understand," Shem said.

The dim sky lightened so slowly it was barely noticeable. The birds were quieter than usual, but the little brown nightingale sang brightly. It didn't seem to care that the brass nightingale had new wings, but Shem had to catch a breath when he saw them unfold into the gleaming span of brass rods and thin leather, more like a bat's than a bird's.

It wasn't until the brown nightingale flitted away that he realized Marchmont had fallen asleep on his shoulder.

"My lord? Marchmont?" All that got him was a small snore, and shaking Marchmont just made him grumble and slump closer, his hand catching on Shem's collar.

"Gabriel," Shem said softly, swallowing the shiver of nerves and the fear of going too far, of falling over the edge of his secure, orderly life. "Wake up."

Marchmont opened his eyes, hunching up his shoulders in protest. Shem offered him a hand up and again felt Marchmont's touch shiver right through him. As Marchmont paced, yawning, Shem packaged up the nightingale and walked back through the Gardens with Marchmont plodding slowly beside him. They were sinking through the sky now, the slow hiss and ease of the floats sounding through the ground beneath their feet, and the fog was closing over their heads again, hiding all but the dim shadows of the hedges from their sight.

If they were to step aside now, into one of the hidden alcoves, no one would see them. Shem would be able to slide his hands up into Marchmont's hair and tip his tired face down to meet his own lips, and there would be no one to witness it or condemn them.

Reckless men couldn't keep secrets, though, and society would not forgive Marchmont such a sin, let alone Shem. What was silently tolerated in drunks and foolish boys would be roundly condemned by daylight. He would not take not that risk, not even here in the illusory safety of the Gardens.

They had to wait for the gates to be unlocked. Marchmont leaned more precariously to the left the longer they stood, and Shem decided that was a good enough excuse to slide his shoulder under the earl's hand and prop him up. It had nothing to do with wanting to test how long he would keep reacting to Marchmont's touch, not at all.

The shivers were almost wearing off when Marchmont moved his hand slightly, his bare fingertips brushing Shem's throat, and Shem's whole body tightened in response. When he managed to catch his breath and look round, Marchmont was staring at him. His eyes were still heavy and sleepy, but there was a heat in them that hadn't been there before. Holding Shem's gaze, he shifted his fingers again, an almost imperceptible stroke.

Shem barely bit back a gasp.

The gates rattled up, signaling the Gardens were safely lodged into their daytime spot, and Marchmont leaned forward to say, straight into his ear, "See me home."

Shem wanted to, so much he couldn't speak for a moment.

But he knew better, so he took a slow breath and stepped back. "I'll see you this afternoon, my lord. You should sleep."

He carried the memory of Marchmont's puzzled disappointment away with him as he trudged through the breakfast hall and then on to his narrow and lonely bed.

HE WAS expecting it to be awkward when he arrived back at Marchmont's workshop, but Marchmont merely greeted him with, "Weatherproofing?"

"Could we add caulking and a protective coating without changing the weight distribution?" Shem asked, coming over to the bench. The workshop already looked messier than it had when he left the day before.

They fell back into yesterday's rhythm easily enough, though there were a few moments when Shem looked up to find Marchmont staring at him with a faint frown, as if trying to work out a puzzle. Neither of them mentioned the previous evening, and Shem knew he should have been relieved that Marchmont dropped it easily. He just felt sad, though, and a little more conscious of how easy it was to be alone in this world. It didn't help when their hands bumped over their work and sent another pang through him.

An hour didn't seem like very long, and Marchmont was clearly irritated when he left. It was no surprise when Marchmont appeared in the Gardens again, bringing the nightingale home to sing out its heart. He wasn't as tired tonight, or maybe just more guarded, but Shem walked him back to the gate anyway, neither of them saying much.

There was no easy solution to the challenge posed by the nightingale: it had never been designed to fly. Marchmont continued to work on it with an intensity Shem didn't quite understand. He knew there were other projects waiting for the inventor's attention, but this one seemed to have become an obsession.

By the end of the week, they had a routine, and something that, if it wasn't for the class divide, Shem might have termed a friendship. He learned his way around Marchmont's workshop and ventured the odd comment about his own life in response to Marchmont's babble. He managed to make Marchmont fall quiet and think a few times too, by challenging the little sneering comments Marchmont made about people less brilliant or educated than him. Shem was fairly certain there was no real unkindness in the man; he had simply never bothered to think about society in the same way he did about his designs. It must be nice to have that freedom.

The summer turned sweltering. At least the air above the permanent veil of smog was cooler, and Shem was always awed by the nights when lightning crackled across the skies and caught at the tips of the firework towers, even though it was bad for profits. His work settled back into its usual pattern, and he gradually entrusted the boy with more independent work.

Marchmont appeared in the nightingale's grove before every dawn. Sometimes he stalked straight off home again, but often he stayed for breakfast, addressing most of his conversation at Shem, but learning the names and skills of some of the other mechanics too. They all regarded him with a wary interest that slowly changed to a careful tolerance. The rich were odd, everyone knew, and geniuses even more so, and if his lordship wanted to eat with them, that was just another eccentricity.

Shem was beginning to feel comfortable, when it suddenly became obvious he had been neglecting at least one of his duties. He hadn't been watching the boy well enough.

His mood was black when he reached the grove that dawn, and Marchmont immediately asked, "What's wrong?"

Shem choked on it, his fury and disappointment tangling with what could and could not be said aloud. Closing his eyes didn't help, because all he could see was the boy's face, head thrown back and mouth hanging open with delight as he was fucked over the side of a fountain by a man old enough and, by the few items of clothing he was still wearing, rich enough to know better.

Some semblance of what he'd seen must have stumbled out of his mouth, because Marchmont went still and calm. "Was he willing?"

"He's a child," Shem said. "It doesn't matter if he was enjoying it."

"He's well past the age of consent," Marchmont said, giving Shem that puzzled frown again. "You keep teaching me not to judge on first appearances. Shouldn't you ask—"

"He's been told," Shem said flatly. "Time and time over. Stay away from gentlemen."

"He resents that," Marchmont remarked. "Everyone's stupid at that age. There's little harm in it."

"That shows how little you know," Shem snapped and stomped across the grove to scowl at the nightingale, yet again restored to its pillar, rebuilt but still essentially whole. He'd waited until the boy and his fancy man were done and then sent the boy running back through the hedge paths with tears on his cheeks. It hadn't made him feel any better.

Marchmont's hands landed softly on his shoulders, not clutching but simply there. "Shem."

He'd never used anything other than Shem's surname before, and it meant something, but Shem was too tense and furious to care what. He lifted his shoulders, ready to shrug the man off, but Marchmont's thumb brushed the back of his neck lightly, and some of the tightness eased out of his spine.

"You can't expect me to solve a problem if I don't have all the information," Marchmont said. "What aren't you saying?"

"It's not your job to fix things," Shem reminded him. "You make things. Beautiful things. *I* keep them running."

"Too simple," Marchmont complained. He was close to Shem, not quite pressed against him, but his presence was tangible just behind Shem's back. His thumb kept circling on Shem's neck, soothing and steady. "Occam's razor is a terrible obstacle to creative thought, you know."

"I have no idea what you're talking about," Shem said, but his mood was beginning to lighten, and he took a slow breath, closing his eyes.

Marchmont was quiet for a long while, and Shem could almost hear him thinking. He imagined gears clicking rapidly together in Marchmont's mind and smiled.

"Did you never indulge?" Marchmont murmured. "Did you never get tempted?"

"A few times," Shem admitted, lulled by the way Marchmont's other hand was rubbing around the curve of his shoulder, warm and kind. "A few kisses." Marchmont wouldn't understand without more than that, though, and Shem didn't want to make him ask. "I had a friend...." Marchmont's fingers tightened, digging into Shem's shoulders, so he amended that quickly. "No, an actual friend. This isn't a story about me. I never...."

"Never what?" Marchmont prompted. His fingers had moved into the ends of Shem's hair now, distracting him. It had been so long since poor Giles was attacked, and the details had lost their immediacy. He could barely remember the clean lines of Giles's young face and the freshness of his laughter.

"Never had a weakness for rogues," he said. When he had indulged, it had been with shy, earnest boys, whose kisses were as sweet and clumsy as his own.

"But your friend did?"

"One of them came back for seconds," Shem said, his throat closing around the words. "And brought his friends, to which Giles said no. They forced him, and then they beat him, for presumption, they said. By the time we found him...."

"How bad?"

"He lived," Shem said, but that didn't say it all. "He works in the tunnels now. Doesn't leave them much. His face is...." He swallowed. "They put worse scars on his heart. He doesn't speak much, and never to anyone who knew him before. The boys who work for him tell me he screams sometimes while he lies sleeping."

"I'm sorry," Marchmont said. He was close enough now that his breath stirred the hairs on the back of Shem's neck.

"And then there are the girls," Shem continued. "A lot of the girls I grew up with, they found respectable work or they married, but not all of them. Some of them got tempted into something foolish and ended up on the street. Others... there's men out there who think if a girl is poor she's theirs for the taking, whether she wants it or not. A lot of those girls, the ones who lost the fight to be respectable, are dead, whether it was violence or the pox. Most of the rest are sick or gone to drink. So don't you tell me it's just harmless fun."

"I won't, not again." Marchmont slid his arms around Shem's waist, holding him lightly. "I never did anything like that. I swear."

He should have been concerned with how inappropriate it was and castigating himself for hypocrisy. Instead the warm clasp of Marchmont's arms, hugging him close, threatened to tear him apart. Half of him wanted to take the offered comfort, but it made him twitchy, aware of every point where their skin brushed, desperate for something different, either to be held tighter or to fight free. He couldn't remember anyone ever holding him like this.

Marchmont hummed a little in his ear, one of his thinking noises, and Shem relaxed a little at the familiar sound.

"So," Marchmont said at last. "You don't take risks, and you don't indulge. Would you marry?"

Shem considered it. There were times when his little room in the boardinghouse felt very lonely, especially as his contemporaries married and moved out. Much as he respected the women around him, though, he could never imagine touching one of them, not in the way he dreamed of men, dreamed of Marchmont.

His life was already organized, everything regimented. He wasn't happy, as such, but he was safe and content in his work. There was no place for a wife, let alone….

"No Mrs. Holloway on the horizon, then?" Marchmont asked, sounding amused.

"No."

"No Mr. Holloway, either?" Marchmont kept his voice quiet, right into Shem's ear.

He had half been expecting the question. He hadn't been vigilant with Marchmont as he would have been with anyone else, and the man could not have missed the way Shem was slowly melting under his hands. Keeping his voice quiet, he said, "That brings other dangers."

"If it was someone you could trust?" Marchmont asked. His lips caught the edge of Shem's ear, and Shem shuddered against him. He wanted to take what Marchmont was offering: wanted to turn in his arms and meet his mouth, wanted it so much.

But the world wasn't made for happy endings, so he simply said, "If."

Marchmont groaned heavily behind him, dropping his face against the back of Shem's neck. "Why is it never easy with you?"

"I couldn't say, my lord."

"Gabriel," Marchmont corrected him, a little crossly, and then froze. "Look!"

They had been too busy to notice that the nightingales were singing, their voices twining together.

"Persistence," Marchmont remarked vaguely. "It's rather…. Hmm."

He'd vanished into thought again, so Shem indulged himself for a moment, leaning back against his shoulder to watch the nightingales' devoted, hopeless courtship.

He was a little surprised when Marchmont released him without further demur. They walked back through the Gardens together, not quite touching, with Marchmont mumbling to himself. Shem recognized the look by now: inspiration had struck. He wondered what they would be trying with the poor nightingale tomorrow.

But the work continued as it had done. What changed was Marchmont's behavior. He didn't press his case in words, but little things changed. He touched Shem more, a squeeze of his shoulder to get his attention or a bump of hips as they leaned over the bird together. Midway through their hour, the footman came rumbling down the stairs with a plate of chocolate éclairs, which of course spurted cream across Shem's cheek as he bit into one, giving Marchmont an excuse to wipe it off and then suck his fingers clean.

It wasn't the least bit subtle, and Shem was torn between laughter and constant arousal. By the way Marchmont grinned at him, as if it was some shared joke, he was in exactly the same state, which didn't help at all.

When Shem left that afternoon, he got a warm, chaste kiss pressed to his cheek, and a murmur of "I'll see you at dawn. Good-bye, Shem."

"My lord."

"No," Marchmont chided, pressing his finger to Shem's lips. "You're supposed to say 'Good-bye, Gabriel' now."

"Good-bye, Gabriel," Shem said drily, amused and secretly liking having the name to use.

He got another kiss for that, and a chuckle.

In the Gardens that night, though, Gabriel's behavior was beyond reproach, and the same pattern continued all month. Gabriel flirted shamelessly in private and showed perfect respect in public. He came to breakfast with Shem, and every afternoon he fed him cake and kissed him good-bye.

Over orange sorbet, a delight in the heat of August, Gabriel remarked, "You shall have to be careful when you meet my sister Rosalind. They're her favorite, and she's vicious with a cake fork."

"When?" Shem repeated skeptically.

"When."

"I know what you're doing," Shem informed him. "You can't seduce a man with domesticity."

"Can't I?" Gabriel sucked on his spoon, clearly pondering it. "Besides, it's a courtship, not a seduction."

There was nothing Shem could say to that, so he muttered a little, aware he was blushing.

Kissing him good-bye later, Gabriel murmured, "Come home with me tonight. You can sleep in the spare room if you like. No one will know. My servants don't have voices. I want more of you."

"Gabriel."

"Stay," Gabriel sighed, pressing second and third kisses against his jaw.

"I have to work." But Shem regretted every step out of there.

To his surprise, the tension didn't stop Gabriel from working on the nightingale. If anything, the flirtation seemed to make him think faster and work more smoothly. He flitted from tool to tool, fitting pieces together with growing confidence, his explanations compressed into cryptic comments and incomplete sentences. Shem gave up trying to follow his train of thought and just leaned on the bench to watch him. Once you stripped away the arrogance, he was lovely. It would be good to have all that intelligence focused on him, Shem thought vaguely. It would be good to strip away Gabriel's clothes as well.

He wasn't thinking about the nightingale when Gabriel stepped back decisively, dropping his screwdriver on the floor.

"Respect your tools," Shem chided him lightly. "That has a place."

Gabriel scooped it up with a grin and stalked toward him. Shem realized, too late, that it hung on the wall behind him. He couldn't move, but just watched Gabriel approach. He pushed off the side of the bench a little as Gabriel stepped close and reached over him to hook the screwdriver up. They pressed together from thigh to chest, and Shem went from pleasantly aroused to hard as iron, his cock pressed against Gabriel's lean thigh.

"Does *that* have a place?" Gabriel inquired, his breath coming a little fast. "Because I certainly respect it."

Shem looked up at the sly curl of his lip and the bright laughter in his eyes and gave up. Pressing up a little farther made Gabriel actually gasp, and Shem wasn't the only one who was desperately hard here. Wrapping his arm around Gabriel's neck, he tugged him down into a kiss.

For a moment, Gabriel's mouth was soft and shocked beneath his. Then he breathed out in a great fierce sigh of relief and kissed Shem back fervently. It was so easy, in the end, and Shem lost himself in it, happiness sparking through him as his worries faded.

When the music began to play overhead, he thought it was an illusion. It wasn't until Gabriel slowly pulled back to catch his breath that either of them looked up.

The brass nightingale was perched on the beam above them, singing joyfully.

"How did it get up there?" Shem asked.

Gabriel just grinned at him, beyond words. As they watched, it spread its gleaming wings and took off again, swooping along the length of the workroom, music tumbling from its polished beak.

"You did it," Shem breathed, and then kissed Gabriel again, just to celebrate. Within moments, they were both distracted, their hands wandering across each other to the sound of the nightingale's song.

They didn't break apart until it went quiet. It took them a moment to spot it. When Shem saw it perched completely still on one of the benches in the back corner, he pulled his hand out of Gabriel's shirt to point. "What's wrong with it?"

"I don't…," Gabriel started, and then chagrin swept across his face. He spat out a couple of words Shem didn't think gentlemen knew and went striding across the room. "It needs rewinding, and it will keep needing it, and so we're not done at all!"

"It can be solved," Shem said, because there was no need to despair, not when his skin was still warm from Gabriel's hands. "Can you harness the bird's own movement with a winding rotor?"

"I could," Gabriel murmured, but he still looked distressed. "But then what? It's a machine, not a living creature. There are so many parts that could fail or break. How can I be sure it will last?"

"How long does a real nightingale live?" Shem asked.

Gabriel turned to frown at him.

Of course he wouldn't understand. He was too much a perfectionist, too good at creating and with no instinct for when something could no longer be repaired. Trying to find the right words, Shem said, "You can't make it immortal. You shouldn't. Give it the chance to live as long as its mate, and then let it be free. It's the opportunity that matters. Just let it have the *chance* to live and love."

Gabriel stared at him with his fiercest problem-solving glare, his hands curling into fists. At last, he said, his voice a little plaintive, "You believe that? That happiness is the freedom to take a chance on love?"

It wasn't quite what Shem had been trying to say, but it was close, so he nodded. "What the bird does with the chance is out of your power."

"I'm not talking about the bird!" Gabriel snapped, taking a step closer. "Why won't *you* take that chance? Why can't you forget about making everything in your life safe and perfect and orderly? Why won't you just take the risk and *love me*?"

The last words rang out like a slap, and Shem felt like he'd been hit, all the breath rushing out of his lungs.

Love Lord Marchmont, the hoity-toity Earl of Godalming?

Love the inventor who was determined to save one brass nightingale from a broken heart?

Love Gabriel?

As he caught his breath, he began to feel like the nightingale, free to fly for the very first time. His hand was shaking as he raised it to cup Gabriel's cheek. Swallowing, he said, "I will." It came out choked and quiet, so he tried again, watching Gabriel's eyes widen with hope. "I'll try that. It's not something I've got much skill at, taking risks, but I will try. Loving you, I mean, not doing foolish things for the sake of—"

Gabriel cut him off, not kissing him this time, but grabbing him tight. This time Shem didn't want to twitch his way out of his lover's hold. Instead, he wrapped his own arms around Gabriel and let him murmur wild, disorderly words into the crook of Shem's neck, until Shem just had to kiss him quiet again.

A FEW weeks later, they stood in the misty dawn. The first hints of autumn were touching the leaves here in the Gardens, and Shem was glad of the warmth of Gabriel's hand in his. They watched as, yet again, the little brown nightingale came flitting out of the trees to sing to its metal lover. And this time, when it flew away, the brass nightingale followed it, vanishing into the dawn on shining wings.

AMY RAE DURRESON teaches in an eccentric boarding school deep in the English countryside. When not teaching, marking or trying to fathom the mysterious logic of the typical teenage brain, she likes to go wandering across the local hills with a camera, hunting for settings for her stories. She has a degree in early English literature, which she blames for her somewhat medieval approach to spelling, and at various times has been fluent in Latin, Old English, Ancient Greek, and Old Icelandic, though these days she mostly uses this knowledge to bore her students when they foolishly ask why English spelling is so confusing. Amy started her first novel nineteen years ago (it featured a warrior princess, magic swords, elves, and an evil maths teacher) and has been scribbling away ever since. Despite these long years of experience, she has yet to master the arcane art of the semicolon.

She can be found online as amy_raenbow on LiveJournal and Dreamwidth. Amy is also now on Twitter (amy_raenbow) and has a blog going at http://amyraenbow.wordpress.com.

ACE OF HEARTS

MARY PLETSCH

AEROPLANE Mechanic First Class William Pettigrew of No. 2 Heavier-than-Air Squadron, Royal Albian Flying Corps, slammed the hatch of the Sopwith Pegasus's rotary engine closed with a loud bang. "That's it: one more fixed."

And, he noted ruefully as he looked around the hangar, *only four more to go*.

He wished, once again, that the Sopwith Aviation Works had been given more time to work out the design flaws with the Pegasus single-seater fighting biplanes. Unfortunately, the war against the Boche had already been raging for more than a year when the first Pegasus prototypes had been rushed into production. Most of the improvements to the Pegasus had been invented on the fly by enterprising mechanics, including the sonic emitters mounted to the main wing spars—William's personal contribution.

Wartime meant privation. William understood that. Still, every time a dirigible passed overhead, William was reminded what he had to lose. The Albion High Command had been using dirigibles in combat for decades; heavier-than-air aircraft were something new. They had to prove themselves in battle, or they would be scrapped as obsolete.

And William had more than just *his* job on the line, if they did. His mother, after all, was one of the Sopwith firm's chief inventors.

William's superior officer, Flight Sergeant Prospere Doucette—a native Burgundian attached to the Albian squadron—walked over, rubbing his whiskered chin as he considered the aeroplane thoughtfully.

"I'm not entirely convinced there aren't still a few gremlins in there. Perhaps you ought to take it up for a test flight, just to be sure."

For a moment, William wondered if Prospere really didn't have faith in his skills. Then he caught the twinkle in the flight sergeant's eyes.

"Yes, sir," William managed to say, though he couldn't keep the grin off his face and was certain that his good eye was lit up like a beacon.

Prospere folded his arms and feigned a stern tone. "Just a few circuits of the aerodrome, mind. Petrol's hard to come by, and I wouldn't want you bumbling into the path of any Boche zeppelins."

Just that swiftly, William felt his high spirits come slamming back down to earth. If it weren't for the patch where his left eye had been, William would certainly be a *chasseur* right now—a heavier-than-air fighter pilot whose job was to protect the skies of Burgundy, Albion's ally nation, from the predations of the Boche.

William felt as though he spent every day of his life cursing the stupid decision he'd made when he was only seven years old. He'd been making a model glider with real metal ribs, and rather than glue it together, he'd decided it would be more durable if he welded it. He'd snuck into his mother's workshop and messed around with her tools. Hot sparks flew, and the next thing he knew was a kind of pain he'd never felt before... or since. His left eye had been beyond saving.

Since then, his life had been all about settling for the next best thing. He couldn't get a job as a dirigible pilot, or even a crewer, thanks to his eye, but his mama had taught him to fly heavier-than-air gliders and, later, the petrol-powered aeroplanes. When the war broke out, he'd joined the Royal Albion Flying Corps as an aeroplane mechanic and came overseas to Burgundy—with the war fliers but not one of them. Someday, he thought, he'd like to meet someone special and have a home of his own, perhaps even a family... but for now, he contented himself with admiring the handsome pilots while hiding behind the wings of the aeroplanes and taking whatever opportunity he could to slip into a cockpit and take off into the clouds, leaving his inadequacies on the ground below. William loved to point his plane's nose toward the heavens and watch the world shrink into insignificance below him. Up in the skies, he could do anything, be anyone.

Here on the ground, he was always a little bit less than good enough.

Eager to escape for just a few minutes, William clambered up into the Pegasus's cockpit. "I promise," he said as he flipped the magneto switches on. "Give me a swing."

William wrapped his hand around the control column and leaned his toes forward, pressing down on the Pegasus's brakes. When Prospere swung the prop, the crankshaft would start turning and the fuel inside the engine would be sparked by the magnetos. William wanted to be sure he had the brakes held down long enough for Prospere to get out of the way of the wings when the Pegasus started to move.

Unfortunately, just as Prospere was getting into position, a towheaded figure in the uniform of a batman—a soldier-servant who acted as assistant to a flying officer—darted out in front of the Pegasus. William muttered a curse under his breath and turned the mag switches off again. The last thing he needed was to hit another Albian with his aeroplane.

Even an Albian like Alex McKinnon.

"New pilots," Alex cried, his eyes lit up with excitement. "New pilots arriving in new aircraft at two o'clock this afternoon. I overheard it walking past the major's office."

William stretched his arms over his head and leaned back as though he'd been intending nothing more exciting than a nap. "So?" he drawled, trying his best to appear nonchalant—to hide the flutter of anticipation in his stomach.

"So," Prospere said with a scowl, "our bold batman here loves to keep abreast of squadron gossip. And I suspect he's hoping one or two of them will be interested in his *very special services*."

William felt his excitement transform into a slow sinking feeling. That was the difference between him and Alex: Alex had the courage to act on his feelings. Alex had more notches on his bedpost than most of the pilots had kill markings on their aeroplanes. William, for his entire life, had done nothing more than look and wish. He hid his feelings so well that not even Prospere knew Alex wasn't the only non-commissioned officer in No. 2 Heavier-than-Air Squadron with an inclination for men.

Was it jealousy that riled him so whenever Alex came around the hangars?

Alex crossed his arms in an exaggerated pout. "You know that in this war, the average lifespan of a heavier-than-air pilot is less than a month," he retorted. "I'm just making sure their final days are happy ones."

"That's a disgusting thing to say." The words were out of William's mouth before he could take them back, driven by the tide of bile rising up his throat. Alex stared at him, shocked, but no more so than William himself.

No, it wasn't jealousy. It was Alex's unutterable selfishness.

"The mouse finds its tongue," Alex said tauntingly. "My advice to you, Pettigrew, is don't knock it till you've tried it."

William just sat there, searching for the words to explain that his objection was to Alex's cavalier attitude and failing to find anything at all. Alex winked, smirked, then turned on his heel and began a slow saunter back toward the officers' barracks.

It was Prospere who finally broke the silence. "For all the rolls in the hay that young man takes," he said, "I don't think Alex has the slightest clue what love really means."

William nodded his assent, and Prospere, mercifully, returned his attention to the Pegasus's propeller. When William didn't see any other aircrew in range of the aircraft, he turned the magneto switches back on and yelled "Clear!" as a signal to Prospere. The flight sergeant swung the propeller, and with a throaty growl, the rotary engine came to life.

William pushed the throttle forward, feeding more fuel to the engine. The Pegasus trundled forward, slowly at first, then faster over the rutted ground. William used a bit of left brake to turn her nose into the wind; then he gave her full throttle and her engine roared its glory song. The Pegasus skipped once, twice, and then the air was under her wings and she was flying, carrying William into the clouds.

The Pegasus flew like a dream. Hand raised to block the sun, William searched the blue vault above. A dirigible formation was limping home above the eastern horizon; William could see the hindmost of four skyboats trailing a plume of smoke from its left maneuvering fan. His gaze probed the brilliant blue sky, and he blinked hard against the dazzling glare. Was that—yes, a formation of three single-winged aircraft, coming in high from the north. The pilots were arriving in the new Sopwith Gryphons—the first monoplane aircraft to ever serve in combat.

William pulled his ocugoggles over his head and rapidly flicked through the lenses until the distant aircraft popped into sharp relief. He admired the distinctive silhouettes of the monoplanes and the brilliant purple streamers attached to the head aircraft, marking it as the formation leader. Fresh from the factory, the Gryphons were painted in standard Royal Albion Flying Corps colors: khaki green on top, pale blue underneath. That would change. William looked at the colorful yellow-and-black checkered wings of his Pegasus and grinned. On closer examination, it seemed as though the flight leader was already aware of the tradition of customizing aeroplanes: he had already added a violet stripe painted around each wing and down the length of the Gryphon's fuselage.

Violet stripe. The thought tugged at some half-forgotten memory in William's mind.

The aircraft overhead cut power to their engines and glided on the breeze like hunting hawks. William felt a stab of scorn for those stuffed-shirted officers back in Albion who called heavier-than-air flying machines "toys for the idle rich." What gasbag, tossed about at the mercy of the winds, could ever chart so swift and straight a course? What skyboat could swoop down out of nowhere to strike a threat below and vanish just as suddenly into the clouds?

William rocked his wings to signal a greeting to the Gryphons. The squadron leader dipped his wing in return. Grinning, William sent the Pegasus into a climb topped off with a half roll. Soon he'd caught up with the Gryphons. Still, he kept flicking the settings on the ocugoggles to sneak close-up looks at the three new pilots.

The man in the rearmost Gryphon was a young fellow, even younger than William. He looked as though he was barely out of school: grammar school and flight school both. His hands were obviously full keeping the Gryphon in place in the formation. The middle pilot had an aristocratic bearing and might have been handsome were it not for the sneer on his face. All William could see of the lead pilot was the back of his leather-helmeted head.

On a whim, he slipped his Pegasus into the formation, taking up the rear position. The young pilot waved, clearly grateful that William hadn't tried to shove him out of his spot.

If only they knew.... William pushed the defeatist thought out of his head. All too soon, these new pilots would learn he wasn't a flight officer. In the meantime, the ocugoggles hid the patch over his left eye. In the meantime, he could dream....

The formation of three Gryphons and William's Pegasus circled the airfield. William watched the tiny figures of the squadron's personnel come running out of the barracks, mess hall, and hangars, standing in rows along the sides of the airfield, waving at the new pilots. Swept up in his fantasy, William held his place in the formation as they landed, pretending the crowd was waving to him.

Then the Gryphon in front of him wobbled and his dream disappeared in a blink. The young pilot couldn't control his aircraft. It was bouncing over the rutted airfield, blown by the wind right into William's path.

William considered turning, but he was very close to the ground now. If his wingtip touched the ground, the Pegasus could flip over. Even if the crash wasn't fatal, No. 2 Squadron had more than just an aircraft to lose.

No. 2 Squadron had experienced more than its share of losses in the past month. Two pilots shot down in flames. A third whose engine failed behind enemy lines; whether the man had been captured or killed, William could not say. A fourth killed just like this, when a wheel strut snapped during landing and flipped the plane over. A hangar filled with Pegasi waiting to be repaired.

Prospere had been cracking down hard on the mechanics ever since, ranting and roaring about the number of pilots lost to equipment failure. William couldn't blame him. If the heavier-than-air squadrons didn't prove they were worth the cost, the heavier-than-air flying program would be scrapped permanently.

And Prospere might be held responsible for allowing a one-eyed man to fly.

William's right arm pushed the throttle open. His left arm pulled back on the control column. His actions were instinctive; when his brain caught up, his own audacity chilled him, but by then it was far too late to attempt a turn.

Instead, his Pegasus caught air under its wings again and flew over the top of the bumbling Gryphon.

William braced himself, expecting at any moment to hear a hideous snap as his undercarriage tangled in the Gryphon's tail, but instead the airfield dropped away below him.

He'd done it.

Heart in his throat, he circled the airfield, giving the Gryphon pilots time to get out of their aircraft and the mechanics an opportunity to push the planes clear of the landing area. By the time he came around again, the field was clear. William glided the Pegasus down into a smooth landing.

William taxied up to the hangars and cut the engine. The young flyer stood with his back against the wall of the barracks, receiving a stern dressing-down from the squadron commander, Major Lacey. The aristocrat wiped the mud off his high boots, curling his lip in distaste. And the flight leader....

The flight leader stood next to his Gryphon, watching William.

And the flight leader was the spitting image of Dirigible Captain James Hinson, two-time winner of the Distinguished Flying Bar.

William felt his jaw drop. The man looked exactly like Hinson's newspaper daguerreotypes—strong chin, chiseled features, a tousled lock of hair tumbling over his forehead—except that his hair was sandy brown. Funny how William had imagined him as a ginger, like William himself. William had spent a lot of time in the past year fantasizing about the famous ace Captain Hinson, but he'd never dared dream he'd get to meet the man himself.

William blinked, revised his personal image of Captain Hinson, and then dared to look again. He had to be mistaken. But when he opened his eyes, the newcomer was still the spitting image of the famous dirigible pilot, and he was standing in front of his purple-striped aircraft. The buried memory dislodged itself and swam up to the surface of William's thoughts. Hinson's dirigibles' baskets had always been marked by distinctive purple stripes, just like the lead Gryphon.

What business would a hero like Captain Hinson have in a heavier-than-air squadron?

"Don't just sit there like a lump," said a voice at his side, making William jump. Prospere stood right next to the cockpit. William hadn't even heard him approach. "Come on," the older man chided. "Help me get this Pegasus back into the hangar."

William shoved his goggles onto his forehead and climbed out of the Pegasus. His mind was whirling and his knees were still shaky from the near miss. "Am I seeing things?" he whispered to Prospere as the two men placed their hands on the forward struts of the Pegasus and began to push it backward into the hangar.

"No," Prospere said with a chuckle. "That's really Captain James Hinson."

William shook his head in disbelief. He snuck a peek as they pushed the Pegasus past the group of pilots. Major Lacey, his lecture finished, was speaking to Hinson, but Hinson's gaze was elsewhere. For an instant, his eyes locked with William's eye.

William ducked his head and pushed harder. "What's a dirigible pilot doing here?"

Prospere mumbled something under his breath.

"Sorry, Sergeant, I didn't hear you," William said.

Prospere didn't answer until the Pegasus was safely settled in the hangar. Then he circled the aircraft and muttered in William's ear. "I said I don't like this. I heard rumors the government wanted Hinson to quit war flying. Said it would bring down morale if he got shot down and killed. I thought he would go on a publicity tour or maybe teach at a lighter-than-air flight training unit. Instead he's here, and I'm... I'm afraid he's here to evaluate us."

"You mean, to tell the government to shut us down."

Prospere nodded.

William scowled. *Let this be a lesson*, he thought. *A handsome face does not make a friend.*

The barracks door opened, and three batmen—including Alex—appeared. These non-commissioned officers acted as servants and assistants to the pilots, who all held officer's rank. William watched as the first batman walked up to the nervous young pilot, introduced himself, picked up the man's luggage, and headed toward the barracks to show him to his new quarters. Alex was the second batman in line, and though he cast a speculative glance over the aristocratic-looking pilot, he turned his attention to Captain Hinson and then stumbled, as though on a rock. He gestured for the batman behind him to pass him and take the aristocrat's baggage.

William clenched his hands into fists, seething. Alex had done that on purpose so he could be Captain Hinson's personal servant.

"Problems?"

William jumped. He'd forgotten all about Prospere. Muttering an oath, he gestured toward the scene in front of him.

"Mmm." Prospere nodded as he took it all in. "Alex being Alex." He paused, studying William. "Why does it bother you so much?"

William scowled, because he had no idea why. "You aren't too fond of him either, as I recall," he said defensively.

Prospere watched as the captain shrugged off Alex's hand on his forearm and strode into the barracks, leaving the young batman struggling with his heavy trunk. "I knew a girl like that once," he said quietly. "I cared about her very much. But all she cared about was how many men's heads she could turn." William expected to hear Prospere's words grow twisted with bitterness, but instead the older man's expression turned distant and wistful. "I tried my hardest, hoping that if I gave her all my love, someday it might be enough."

"What happened?" William dared to ask. His head was spinning. He'd been at No. 2 Squadron for over a year, and all that time he'd figured Prospere's problem was with Alex's attraction to men.

Prospere shrugged. "I got posted to another air base, and we lost touch. It was just as well, son. I'd already guessed by that point that she'd never change. Sometimes the best you can do is know when to let go." He looked at William and his gaze sharpened. "And sometimes the best you can do is know when to hang on."

William fidgeted, suddenly uncomfortable. He didn't like the knowledge in Prospere's gaze, or the revelation that he'd figured the old sergeant all wrong. "I... uh... how am I to tell the difference?" he stammered.

Prospere laughed. "I'll let you in on a secret, William—if you were anyone else, I'd tell them they don't get to know until they've lived as many years as I have. But truth be told, I think I'm still figuring it out myself."

William felt a question on the tip of his tongue and had already begun swallowing it down before he realized this was precisely the sort of thing Prospere had been cautioning him against. Just once, he'd dare to take the chance. "So, ah, your issue with Alex isn't that he prefers the company of men?"

Prospere shrugged. "I don't understand the appeal myself, but I've only ever been in love the once and never had it returned. If you're luckier than I, William, I'm in no position to judge you."

William shivered. He thought he'd hidden his longing looks from everyone at No. 2 Squadron. On the other hand, Prospere was an unusually perceptive man, both in his role as a mechanic and as a human being. William's secret might be safe after all.

A sudden surge of recklessness tore through him, like a mighty updraft buffeting the wings of an aeroplane. Where was his secret getting him? No further than Prospere's unrequited love had taken the older man.

One of these days, William vowed, one of these days, when he found the right man, he'd take the risk. He wouldn't let love slip away from him because he hadn't the courage to try.

But, he thought as he watched Alex follow Captain Hinson into the barracks, *one of these days isn't today.*

PROSPERE chuckled as he walked into the hangar the next morning. "William," he called, "I've got a juicy bit of squadron gossip for you."

William looked away from the Gryphon he'd been inspecting. They were beautiful machines; the Sopwith works had really outdone themselves. He told himself that his feeling of admiration was wholly due to his mother's involvement in their design. It was purely, *completely* coincidental that he'd been looking at the Gryphon with the distinctive purple streaks on its wings. "What's that?" he murmured, his mind still half on the Gryphon—and its pilot.

"It's something you won't be hearing from our friend Alex McKinnon, that's for certain."

Prospere had William's attention now. "What?"

"A little birdie told me that Mr. McKinnon spent last night all alone in his quarters like a good little boy."

William swallowed. "Hinson?"

"Turned him down flat."

"How did he take it?"

"Not particularly well. He thought he'd misheard. Hinson's door slamming in his face convinced him otherwise."

William found his emotions curiously mixed. On one hand, he was glad Alex's slick and smarmy act didn't work on all the men. On the other hand....

William circled the Gryphon, running his hand along the purple streak, and saw a name painted just in front of the cockpit.

Violet.

William felt his stomach sink. Captain Hinson had a lady friend. Of course he did. How could he not? He was a famous flying ace, after all. Hinson must have chosen one out of the bevy of beauties that surrounded him in his publicity photos. No wonder Alex's advances held no appeal. Hinson's heart belonged to the woman he'd named his plane for.

I hardly know him, William told himself, *and wouldn't stand a chance if I did. I've got no bloody reason to be so disappointed.* He resigned himself to a gray and dreary day working on the endless line of damaged Pegasi; Prospere was already hard at work on the other side of the hangar. With a deep sigh, William stuck his head into a huge gaping hole in the first Pegasus's fuselage, checking to see if the aeroplane could be fixed with a simple patch or if there was structural damage inside that would need repairs first.

Then, like an aeroplane in a stormy sky, a sudden updraft struck him out of nowhere and sent his emotions tumbling once more. The unexpected wind came in the form of a low, deep voice sounding just behind him.

"Hello? Mechanic?"

William jerked his head out of the fuselage and straightened up. Behind him was a broad chest, strong arms, and two of the brightest blue eyes he'd ever seen. He could smell Hinson's scent over the smell of grease, petrol, and the thick "dope" used to protect and seal the fabric that covered the Pegasus's wings. Hinson smelled like fresh air, like a spring breeze blowing through a pine forest.

"Captain Hinson," William blurted, pulling his arm up into a salute. He was acutely aware of the oil stains on his hands, the little hole in the front left breast of his mechanic's coveralls, and his hair sticking up in every direction from the protective goggles shoved up on his forehead. What would Hinson see when he looked at him? A perfectly average young man with an average build, average ginger hair, average looks. Run-of-the-mill in every way save for the patch over his missing eye. Almost, but not quite, good enough.

Hinson was wearing the same clothing as the other squadron pilots. A leather flying jacket lined with fleece stretched across his broad chest. Heavy pants outlined his muscular thighs. A flying cap with goggles perched on his head, and a single sandy lock escaped from beneath it, curling down over his forehead. Hinson's scarf was snowy white, his calf-high boots were obviously fresh out of a supply crate, and his gloves were neatly tucked in the left pocket of his coat. A few trips over the other side of the front lines would change all that. Heavier-than-air planes were dirtier than dirigibles, and soon Hinson's clothes would be covered in petrol and castor-oil stains, just like all the other pilots'. Somehow, William knew it would just make Hinson look battle worn and dangerous rather than dirty or disreputable.

"I'm looking for someone," Hinson said quietly.

William waited.

"The pilot who met my flight in the Pegasus. Who is he?"

William felt his stomach sink. "That was… that was me, sir."

Hinson raised an eyebrow. "Your rank badges say you're an aeroplane mechanic, first class."

"I often test fly the aircraft, sir. Particularly if a new mechanic's been working on them or if the repairs were particularly difficult."

"That seems like a dangerous thing to do, isn't it?"

"The *chasseurs* take those aircraft over enemy territory, where the Boche do their best to shoot them down. They don't need to worry about being let down by their own equipment. No, if the *chasseurs* are going to take these aeroplanes into battle, the least I can do is be certain they're safe to fly."

Hinson threw back his head and laughed. "I suppose you've got me there. You take one kind of risk, so we don't have to."

"Ah… *we*, sir?"

"Pilots."

"You have someone test fly your dirigibles, sir?"

Hinson paused for a moment, then spoke carefully. "I don't fly dirigibles anymore. I'm here to be a *chasseur* with your squadron." Suddenly, his eyes sparkled with mischief. "I'm surprised, Mechanic, that the vaunted squadron gossip grapevine has failed you."

William didn't know where he found the courage to say what he said next. Perhaps Hinson's playful spirit was contagious; perhaps it was the comfort Prospere's news had provided. "The squadron gossip grapevine is your batman, sir, and he's none too pleased with me right now."

Hinson took a step backward. "Oh?"

"He and I had a disagreement on the value of quantity versus quality," William said.

The captain laughed again. William enjoyed the rich, hearty sound of his voice. It was the tone of a man who loved and savored living.

"I'm a proponent of quality myself," Hinson confided. "How about you?"

It sounded like flirting. William shook his head. Hinson was just being nice. After all, the newspapers said he was a natural charmer.

"If I preferred quantity," he said, "all these aeroplanes would be out on the flight line, and I'd be relaxing right now."

"With my life riding on the condition of my aeroplane," Hinson said, "I think I'm glad you prefer quality."

William offered him a grin and then dared to say, "May I ask why you're flying aeroplanes now?"

Hinson took a deep breath. "Because I believe in heavier-than-air craft and what they can do." He pushed his hands down into his pockets. "The European air services have all been flying dirigibles for decades. The Boche have their zeppelins; the Flemish have their blimps; the Basques have their balloons. We make huge dirigibles to haul cargo, armored dirigibles to act as frigates, light dirigibles covered in directional propellers to do the work of gunboats. Our strategists take the methods that have served our navies for hundreds of years, slung the ships underneath gasbags and thought no more of it." His eyes swept the hangar and a note of iron crept into his voice. "The aeroplane is not a dirigible. It's faster, more maneuverable, and more flexible. It can chase down dirigibles and pop their gasbags. It can go into areas where there are no dirigible docking towers, no helium pumps, no crewers by the hundreds. I am certain it would take only a little modification to create an aeroplane that could land on water or on snow. And if we were to marry dirigibles and aeroplanes, we could create a mother ship that carried her own scouts and defenders everywhere she went."

William's lips curved in a grin. His mother had a sketch of such a mother ship pinned to the wall of her workshop.

"But," Hinson continued, "none of it will happen if the generals don't open their eyes and see what potential the heavier-than-air flying machine holds. Hidebound fools!" he cursed.

William struggled to stop his jaw from dropping open. None of the newspapers had ever reported on Captain James Hinson being anything but 100 percent behind the decisions of High Command. "So," he said carefully, "you've transferred to the Heavier-than-Air Corps to prove the value of aeroplanes to High Command?"

Hinson nodded. "I'm a dirigible ace. The eyes of the Albian public are following me, even here in Burgundy. If I can show those eyes that aeroplanes can make a vital contribution to the war effort, High Command will have to listen." He paused. "And I want the help of the man who designed the wing mount for the sonic emitters all our Gryphons now carry."

William froze.

Hinson continued enthusiastically, "Our country needs that kind of innovation. Tell me, where can I find the Sopwith designer Vera Dunsany's son? I heard he was assigned to this squadron."

William swallowed, his mouth dry. "I, ah, I use my father's name. Sir. Aeroplane Mechanic First Class William Pettigrew, at your service."

Captain Hinson regarded him for a moment and then his mouth curved into a slow and lazy smile. "You're a man of surprises, Mr. Pettigrew, I must say. Not only could you see a problem in your pilots' aeroplanes and invent a means to fix it, but you also handle those planes so very well." He reached out and ran his thumb over William's cheek, just under his eye patch. "And yet I suppose that when the system looked at you, they did not see what you could do, and judged you only by how well you fit their mold."

William struggled not to flush. Captain Hinson was regarding him so intently, and he was leaning forward, his face mere inches away from

William's own. William held his breath, refusing to flinch, wondering what might happen if Hinson closed that distance and….

"Captain Hinson?" Major Lacey's voice echoed through the hangar. Hinson pulled away from William, but not before William saw what he thought—or hoped—might be disappointment in his eyes.

"Sir?" Hinson said, turning toward the commanding officer.

"I want to speak to you about the reporters, Hinson. Reporters! Camped out on our doorstep, right outside my office."

Eyes on him everywhere, William thought. Meanwhile, William himself had faded back into invisibility. He sighed and put his head back into the Pegasus's fuselage. Both the war and the validation due the Heavier-than-Air Corps weren't going to win themselves. He might as well do his bit.

LIFE at No. 2 Squadron settled into a new routine now that Captain Hinson had arrived. William still spent most of his days repairing aeroplanes, but now those days were brightened by Hinson's regular visits to the hangar. Hinson liked to tell William about his experiences on his sorties over enemy lines and suggest possible devices to make the aeroplanes more effective in air combat. William stayed up late into the nights, tinkering, mounting the new devices on the Gryphon called *Violet* for Hinson to test in flight.

Despite William's secret hopes, the incident in the hangar that first day had never repeated itself. Some nights, William hoped that maybe, just maybe, the chance would come again, and this time he might actually kiss—or rather, be kissed by—the handsome ace. Other nights he chastised himself for what had to be a preposterous misinterpretation of a comradely gesture. Just keeping company with Captain Hinson was both good and not quite good enough.

William, however, was used to settling for what he could get, and for a month, he settled. Then one morning as he shuffled into the mess hall, he was met by a smirking Alex McKinnon.

McKinnon had gotten over his disappointment with Hinson in the arms of the sour-tempered aristocratic pilot. William thought Alex was ready to let bygones be bygones. The malicious smirk playing on the batman's lips warned him otherwise.

Alex informed him, with a self-satisfied gloat, that Captain Hinson had gone out on dawn patrol with Lieutenant Stewart—Alex's new lover—just before sunrise. Stewart had returned with some bad news.

Captain Hinson had been shot down by a Boche zeppelin over the town of Rassicot, five miles on the other side of the front lines.

USUALLY William was fascinated by the beauty of brightly painted fabric-covered wings and the delicate cat's cradle of wires that ran between them, the streamlined fuselages, and the powerful rotary engines that inspired heavy materials to take flight. Today, William could think of nothing but Captain Hinson. He saw the ghost of Hinson's reflection in the aeroplanes' propellers, caught breaths of his scent in the breeze blowing over the Gryphons' wings.

Disconsolate, William paced at the mouth of the hangar, a wrench in his hand as an excuse to justify his presence. Nobody paid him the slightest attention—and why would they? The pilots and aircrew walking by had no idea that William was giving serious consideration to stealing an aeroplane and flying out in search of Captain Hinson.

It was a stupid thing to do. Never mind that he had a pilot's license, or that he had more flying hours than most of the pilots in the squadron. He wouldn't have the slightest idea what to do if enemy zeppelins attacked him, and theft of an aeroplane was a court-martial offense. William had to trust that Major Lacey would come up with a plan to rescue Captain Hinson, if indeed he'd survived the crash.

William didn't trust himself to work on any aeroplanes today. His mind was with Captain Hinson. The smart thing to do would be to plead sick and spend the rest of the day in his bunk, but William wasn't sure he could stand the hell of lying there with nothing to do but wonder whether Captain Hinson was being tortured by the Boche at that very moment. He wandered aimlessly, delaying the inevitable, and had only just turned his feet toward his barracks when he heard voices drifting out of Major Lacey's open office window.

"It's a black eye on the honor of the squadron, is what it is." William knew that voice: his flight sergeant, Prospere Doucette. Prospere was just an enlisted man, but his age and experience had won the respect of Major Lacey and all the other officers. William tilted his head and slowed his step, wondering what his supervisor and his commanding officer were talking about.

"Men get lost in wartime every day," Major Lacey replied dismissively. "He's no more immune than any of the other pilots."

Prospere's temper was riled up as he retorted, "If it were Hebblethwaite or Shaw down behind enemy lines, you'd have the whole squadron airborne, looking for him."

"That's precisely what the Boche would expect of us. They're sure to have zeppelins with skynets, flying gunboats, and God only knows what else waiting for us."

"And you wouldn't give a damn! I know Hinson's only been here a few weeks, but surely he's earned as much respect as any of our other boys."

"Hinson," Lacey growled, his voice low and tense, "is here to shut us down." There was a long silence, as though Prospere was flabbergasted. William gritted his teeth, knowing Lacey had jumped to a mistaken conclusion about the dirigible ace. The commanding officer continued. "This is supposed to be classified, Doucette, but I know that you hear things, from the pilots, the other squadrons, I don't know where. I'm sure you're already aware that the Royal Albion Flying Corps is top-heavy with pro-dirigible sorts who consider the Heavier-than-Air Corps to be some sort of bastard offspring to be shoved aside and forgotten. Now think. Hinson is a hero to High Command, and he's here to provide the confirmation they need to eliminate us completely."

William couldn't see either of them and didn't dare peek into the window, but he could imagine Prospere's face as he asked cautiously, "Do you have any proof of that?"

"Good God, man, you've seen the articles in the papers. What more proof do you need?" William could hear Lacey making a tutting noise under his breath. "I know it's a terrible thing to say. Captain Hinson seems a pleasant enough chap and I would hate to wish him ill. Still, it might be the best for us if Hinson never gets his chance to submit his evaluation to High Command."

William turned away and clenched his fists until his knuckles turned white. He suddenly felt sickened, both with the major and with himself. Alex, promiscuous though he was, wasn't afraid to be honest about his interests and intentions. Prospere had the courage to disagree with an officer who far outranked him. Hinson had traded his fame as a dirigible ace to fly with the Heavier-than-Air Corps because he believed in their aeroplanes. And William… all William had the courage to do was watch from afar and listen at windows.

Well, not anymore.

This wasn't about his reputation or his rank or even about his mother's career. This was about the life of a decent man. William Pettigrew no longer had the luxury of hiding in the shadows.

This time he was going to do the right thing.

As he walked toward the hangar, he took only a moment to consider that the right thing involved deceiving his fellow mechanics, stealing an advanced machine of war, and taking on the might of the Boche *Luftstreitkrafte* all on his own. Then—before such notions could invoke any misgivings—he blotted them out with the memory of James Hinson's touch.

He briefly considered taking a Gryphon but instead selected the yellow-and-black checkered Pegasus. He knew the machine and was familiar with it. Nobody questioned him when he climbed into the cockpit and asked another mechanic to swing his prop; they were all so used to his test flights by now that he would be out of sight of the airfield long before he was missed.

Moments later, William looked down at the ground below from the Pegasus's cockpit, hoping to experience the familiar sensation of watching his problems shrink into insignificance along with his view of No. 2 Squadron's airfield. He had climbed up to six thousand feet, and the airfield had vanished behind him, before he realized his old comfort had eluded him. This time, he'd brought his problems with him. This time, he'd done something that would change his life forever—just as he had when he was seven years old, tinkering with his mama's tools.

William gritted his teeth and pushed those thoughts from his head. No, it wasn't like that at all. This time he hadn't needed to take to the skies before he could pretend to be the man he'd always dreamed he could be. This time he'd been that man on the ground, when he'd climbed into this cockpit with purpose. And this time his life had already been changed forever by Captain Hinson's caress.

No, William would not sit and wait and let life pass him by again, because this time it was not only his life at stake. William leveled out the Pegasus and turned its nose toward the enemy lines.

ANTI-AIRCRAFT fire never hits anyone. Anti-aircraft fire never hits anyone.

William repeated the phrase like a mantra as puffs of black smoke erupted all around him. He was climbing at the Pegasus's ceiling—as high as the aeroplane could possibly go—yet somehow it didn't feel quite high enough.

William had learned a lot from listening to the flying officers trade stories. He knew it was very difficult for gunners on the ground to hit a moving target in the air, particularly one as high up as he was. He knew most of the fatalities from anti-aircraft fire came when inexperienced pilots got spooked and did something stupid. He knew the wisest course of action was precisely what he was doing now, and in a few moments he would be out of the guns' range.

Still, for the first time in his life, he was facing enemies who were doing their level best to kill him, and the notion was terrifying.

He thought, again, of Captain Hinson's hand on his cheek, of the scent of the captain's jacket, of that small smile curving his lips. He surrendered his senses to the memory and felt his fear wash away.

William could fantasize forever, but when the anti-aircraft fire died down, he forced his attention back to reality. He was on the Boche side of the lines now, and perversely, the anti-aircraft fire had protected him from enemy zeppelins, because the Boche wouldn't risk being shot down by their own gunners just to pursue him. Without it, his single lonely Pegasus was an easy target for zeppelin gunboats. His gaze scanned the sky, but he saw nothing other than a few scattered clouds off to the west.

Looking down, William saw the front lines below: the trenches where two great armies faced off against one another. From this height they looked like crude scrawls of black crayon, inscribed by a preschool child over what had once been the rich farms of Burgundy. Here and there he saw a dilapidated barn or a burned-out house. He expected to see, at any moment, one group of soldiers go over the top and the other group to rise to the challenge, but the lines were quiet and still. William supposed the two armies could not sustain constant combat, and most of a soldier's time must be spent squatting in the dirt and the muck, waiting. He shivered. Far better to belong to the skies, where death, when it came, was quicker and cleaner.

He checked the surrounding airspace again—still clear—and began searching. Alex had said that Captain Hinson's Gryphon had crashed near the village of Rassicot. William couldn't see a village, but he could see a river meandering its way through the countryside, now rutted with the scars of war. He also knew Rassicot lay east of No. 2 Squadron's aerodrome. Gently banking his wings, William guided his aeroplane eastward, following the river.

Someday, he vowed, Burgundy would be green and rich once more. The torn mud below would once again nurture grain and flowers. Burgundy, Albion, and their allies had heroes who would make it happen. If William's mission was successful, they'd have one more hero on their side.

The shape of a small village coalesced on the horizon. Sunlight glittered off the bronze-colored roof of Rassicot's church steeple as the Pegasus approached. William caught his breath: there, in a field not far away from the church, lay the carbonized skeleton of a burned-out aeroplane.

William pulled back on the throttle and let the Pegasus descend a few hundred feet. This was a dangerous time. If enemy zeppelins pounced on him from above, he would need height to get him home safely; an aeroplane trapped between a gunboat and the ground had little room to maneuver. In a pinch, he could lower his nose and trade height for speed. Yet if he stayed at the Pegasus's ceiling, he would not be able to properly identify the wreckage. William took one last look around, confirming the sky was clear, and then dove toward the ruined aeroplane.

The second he'd flown over it, William pulled the Pegasus into a climb. His mechanic's eye had discerned the unique shape of the Gryphon's tail section—about the only part of the aeroplane that hadn't been burned to a cinder. Even though the telltale violet stripes had been burned away, William was certain he'd found Hinson's aeroplane. Since the Gryphons were so new, Hinson's was the only one that had been reported lost in battle.

The fact that it was burned gave him a perverse sense of hope. Yes, it was possible Hinson had perished in a fiery crash, but it was also possible Hinson's aircraft had been merely damaged. He might have landed it safely and, once it was down, set fire to it to prevent it from falling into enemy hands. The shape of the charred fuselage suggested it had landed wheels-down, further supporting this theory.

Which then begged the question: if Hinson had survived and torched his own aeroplane, where was he now?

The Boche would have seen the aeroplane going down and raced to the site. To avoid capture, Hinson would have had to put some distance between himself and the wreck.

William groaned. Hinson could be hiding just about anywhere. However would William find him from up here? And yet, to land and search for him on the ground would be the height of stupidity. He knew there were a multitude of Boche eyes down there keeping close watch on the Pegasus. He would have only a matter of moments to touch down, pick up Hinson, and take off again before the Boche arrived.

This trip was hopeless.

Hinson turned his gaze toward the church steeple, praying to God for a miracle.

And then, a miracle he saw.

A long purple streamer fluttered from the church's belfry.

William remembered the bold purple streamers fluttering from the lead Gryphon on the day he'd slipped his Pegasus into the formation of new pilots. The lavender stripes on the Gryphon's wings. The aeroplane's name written under the cockpit: *Violet*.

Holding his breath, William dared buzz the steeple. He flipped the lenses on his ocugoggles, zooming in on the belfry. The streamer was none other than a minister's silk stole, one end tied in a knot around one of the pillars lining the belfry, the other snapping in the breeze like a flag.

William turned the Pegasus around and came back for another pass, rocking his wings in a gesture of greeting. Yes! A figure emerged from between two of the pillars. Captain Hinson waved from the belfry, then pointed down at the churchyard.

William rocked his wings again to indicate he understood. He cut power to the Pegasus's engine and sideslipped to lose altitude. With his propeller turning slowly, William circled the church, carefully studying the ground below.

He didn't dare land in the churchyard itself. The scattered tombstones of the old church cemetery could damage his wings or take his undercarriage clean off. Fortunately, there was a recently cut hayfield next to the churchyard. William checked the trees to see which way the wind was blowing, and then he turned the Pegasus's nose in the same direction as the wind, coming down for a gentle landing in between the rows of cut hay.

William looked up and saw Captain Hinson struggling to climb the fence between the churchyard and the field. His left arm was pressed close against his body, indicating he'd not escaped the crash unscathed. William let the Pegasus taxi as close to the fence as he could, and Hinson made a dash for the aircraft.

William caught his breath when Hinson skidded to a stop next to the Pegasus. He wondered how the dirigible ace would feel when he realized his rescuer was nothing more than a mechanic. Disappointed? Angry?

Hinson's crystal-blue eyes met William's gaze. The ace's mouth crinkled into a smile.

William couldn't help it. Here, on the ground in the middle of enemy territory, William smiled back.

The moment was all too short-lived. Hinson leaned forward, shouting into William's ear over the noise of the Pegasus's engine: "Cavalry."

William frowned. Cavalry, as a rule, were hopelessly outdated in modern warfare. Machine-gun nests could cut down a cavalry charge; sonic emitters caused equines to panic, rearing and bucking wildly, casting down their riders. Still, a troop of Boche cavalry were more than a match for a grounded Pegasus. The sooner they got airborne, the better.

Hinson clambered up on the Pegasus's lower right wing root and looked up questioningly at William. The Pegasus, unfortunately, was a single-seater aircraft, and Hinson was far too large to fit on William's lap in the cramped little cockpit. The noise of the propeller made it difficult for the two men to talk, so William gestured to Hinson to wrap his strong right hand around the closest strut between the Pegasus's upper and lower wings, and to sling his left arm around the rim of the cockpit. William bit his lip when he saw the bloody scarf wrapped around Hinson's wrist.

"Hang on," William shouted, and just then, a loud *sprang* caused the Pegasus's airframe to shudder.

William whipped his head around and felt his heart constrict.

There were Boche cavalry in the vicinity, all right, but not the old-fashioned kind.

In the early days of the war, both the Allies and the Boche had taken their horses onto the field of battle, only to incur frightful losses. The Allies' response had been to abandon horses in favor of large, armored, slow-moving battle tanks. William had heard rumors that the Boche were taking a different approach.

Those rumors had just been confirmed.

A troop of Boche cavalry charged through the churchyard, and the horses they rode were not flesh and blood, but clockwork machinations. Their iron hooves threw off sparks against stones and their brass trim flashed pain-bright in the sun. Great wing-shaped projections rose from their chests to provide armor for their riders. Long plumes of exhaust streamed out behind them like tails. They were tireless, pitiless, immune to sonics, undaunted by bullets. And they had the Pegasus in their sights.

William pushed the Pegasus's throttle full forward. The plane began to lumber forward, far too slowly. Another bullet whistled overhead and William felt a sudden sting on his cheek. One of the wires strung between the Pegasus's wings had been severed, and the sudden release of tension had caused the wire to snap like a whip and cut him.

The Pegasus's guns and sonic emitters fired in one direction only: straight ahead. William could not halt his takeoff roll to bring his guns to bear on the horses. His only hope was to take off before the cavalry caught them. As he glanced backward again, he realized the mechanical horses were too fast for them to escape.

Hinson tugged on William's sleeve. William had never dreamed to see such a look of desperation on the ace's face.

Then Hinson let go of the cockpit and fumbled in his pocket for… what? A metal object with a bell-shaped muzzle quivered in Hinson's crippled hand. Unable to grip it properly, he leaned bodily against the fuselage, sending the object tumbling into William's lap.

William reached down for what he thought at first was a revolver, but the distinctive bell-shaped barrel told him it was a signal-flare gun. Of course—Hinson would have fired a flare into his Gryphon to start it on fire. He grabbed the weapon and turned around, pointing it in the direction of the cavalry.

The lead Boche cavalryman pressed his heels into the launch buttons located on his horse's sides. The mechanical creature leaped into the air, soaring over the fence and landing neatly in the hayfield. His comrades followed suit, brandishing pistols and sonic emitter staffs.

William pulled the trigger. He turned his face forward quickly, but even so, he saw the flash of the exploding flare cartridge reflected in the metal and glass surfaces of his control panel.

He wasn't certain if he'd hit anything. The Pegasus hit a rut, popped into the air, and drifted to the left. William was forced to put both hands on the control stick to keep the aircraft traveling straight as it touched back down on the other side of the row of cut hay. The drying hay twisted up in the undercarriage could be disastrous at these speeds.

Hinson poked his shoulder and flashed him a thumbs-up with his left hand.

William risked a quick look back. The Boche cavalry was in disarray.

The flare gun hadn't done anything to the clockwork horses: the flare was nowhere near hot enough to damage them, and their sensors were immune to the blast of light. The same could not be said for their riders. The Boche cavalrymen had been utterly unprepared for the brilliant flare. They were now charging forward blindly, firing wildly along the row to the right, where the Pegasus had been only an instant before. A single blast from a sonic emitter staff caused one of the Pegasus's wing struts to disintegrate, but that was all.

The Pegasus leaped again; this time it was going fast enough for the air moving under its wings to lift it up. William carefully rotated the control column backward. Much as he wanted to climb for the sky and get out of the cavalry's range, he knew a too-steep climb could send Hinson tumbling off the wing. There was no help for it. He was going to have to do what the pilots called "hedgerow hopping"—nerve-racking flying close to the ground. He would be forced to constantly dodge tall obstacles while risking the fire of every Boche with a weapon. All the while, if he maneuvered too sharply, he risked throwing Hinson off. At least he hadn't run into the airborne defenders Major Lacey had told Prospere about in his office.

Suddenly a terrible notion occurred to him. William hadn't seen Boche zeppelins on his trip over the lines, but that didn't mean there hadn't been any, lurking in the clouds, waiting. Waiting for the whole formation of Allied aeroplanes anyone would have expected Major Lacey to send to Hinson's rescue. Soon those cavalry officers would be on the horn, calling every *Luftstreitkrafte* unit they could find, telling them the Gryphon pilot was escaping in a lone Pegasus.

William bit his lip as another strike vibrated through the Pegasus's airframe. He didn't dare look back; he was too busy weaving the aeroplane around chimneypots and gables. Hinson gave him another thumbs-up, which William guessed meant they'd finally escaped the cavalry's range. Keeping the throttle on full power and climbing just enough to clear the rooftops of Rassicot, William raced for the front lines.

Every once in a while he glanced over at Hinson, just to be sure the man's grip on the strut remained tight. Even at this low altitude, a fall would likely kill him. Hinson kept smiling, but over time, William noticed his smile was becoming strained and his knuckles were growing white. His left hand hooked into the cockpit began to tremble. Impulsively, William took his hand off the throttle and folded it over Hinson's.

He didn't dare look at the captain's eyes to see his response to the gesture.

There! The lines were in sight! William thought he recognized the large bridge ahead from the stories told by the *chasseurs*. No. 2 Squadron had been attempting to bomb it to prevent the Boche from using it to bring war materiel to the Front; the area around the bridge was pockmarked with craters, but the bridge itself was still standing. The bridge was a good mile west of the aerodrome, suggesting William had allowed the Pegasus to drift with the winds.

Right then, though, William didn't care. All he had to do was get the Pegasus back on the Allied side of the front lines. From there, he and Hinson could fly, hitchhike, or hell, even walk back to the aerodrome. William braced himself, realizing he was going to have to run a horrific gauntlet of anti-aircraft fire in order to reach safety.

Hinson's hand twisted under his. Surprised, William looked over reflexively. Captain Hinson jerked his chin upward and to the right. William followed Hinson's line of sight and automatically tightened his hand on Hinson's.

High above and to the left, the expected Boche defenders had arrived to deal with the Pegasus that had dared invade their territory and snatch their prize. But William did not see zeppelin frigates with long, trailing skynets—frigates the Pegasus could outrun. Nor did he see zeppelin gunboats, whose shots he could probably outmaneuver. Instead, William saw a sight he'd only heard about in furtive whispers, some from the pilots spinning tales around the fire, once in a rumor confided by his mother. She had told him that the Sopwith Works owner believed a Boche spy had stolen some of their experimental blueprints.

William now knew this rumor was absolute truth. He had seen sketches on his mother's workbench before he went to war; sketches of a three-winged fighting aeroplane. Those sketches had now come to sudden, horrifying life in the skies overhead.

The Allies were no longer the only ones with heavier-than-air flying machines. William, who'd never even taken the Pegasus up against a zeppelin, was now about to face a squadron of seven Boche triplanes.

Well, William was not about to beetle along like a duck in a shooting gallery. He gave Hinson's hand one last squeeze: then with one hand on the control column and the other on the throttle, William jinked and weaved the Pegasus from left to right as the triplanes descended from on high, swooping down on him from behind, their six wing-mounted sonic emitters sending out pulses of energy that could shatter wing spars and cripple engines.

William's erratic maneuvers, made even wilder by his lack of skill at war flying, allowed him to survive the first Boche attack, though not unscathed. There was a series of holes seared through the Pegasus's left-side wings, causing strips of torn fabric to flutter behind in a grotesque parody of Captain Hinson's purple streamers. Hinson clutched desperately to the Pegasus, kicking his left leg when the aircraft's maneuvering caused him to lose his footing on the wing. Worst of all, the time William had spent zigzagging had slowed his progress toward the safety of the lines. William watched the Boche triplanes whirl about, preparing for another pass.

Hinson tugged at his sleeve. William turned to his passenger, and though Hinson once again jerked his head skyward, this time he was smiling. When William saw what Hinson had noticed, a similar grin spread across his own face.

A full squadron of Sopwith Pegasi, accompanied by the squadron's two remaining Gryphons, were headed their way from the east. William did not know, and in that moment did not care, whether Major Lacey had experienced a change of heart, or whether Flight Sergeant Prospere

Doucette had leveraged every favor he'd ever been owed to talk the squadron's pilots into his mad scheme. Regardless, every airworthy aeroplane that No. 2 Squadron possessed was on its way to the rescue.

The high-pitched pulse of sonic emitters warned William that the rescue might yet come too late.

No. 2 Squadron descended like avenging angels, taking full advantage of their height to pounce on the triplanes and riddle them with bullets. Four or five of the Boche planes broke off their attack on William's Pegasus and rose to greet them. That still left far too many enemies against William and Hinson.

William's mind raced. His skill was with his innovative abilities, not with his guns. He wished he could tinker up some kind of gizmo that would allow him to stall the Boche, even just for a moment, until the rescuers arrived. He was flying at less than a thousand feet; there was nowhere he could hide....

Or was there?

William looked up at the Boche and a little grin spread across his face. As the triplanes dropped from the sky, William skidded his aeroplane to the right until he was flying over the river. Then he dropped lower... lower....

Just as bullets began hitting his fuselage in a storm of deadly rain, William sideslipped as low as he dared....

And flew the Pegasus underneath the river bridge.

William held his breath. Concrete pillars flashed by on either side of his wingtips. If he'd judged wrong, he and Captain Hinson would die together in a fiery cartwheel.

Sunlight flooded his wings. They'd survived.

William pulled back on the control column for a little more altitude as he emerged from beneath the bridge. All the triplanes were behind him now, having reached the low point of their dive right when he was underneath the bridge. The structure had protected the Pegasus from the worst of the triplanes' attack.

The enemy aircraft were turning again, but William and Hinson were no longer alone. The two Gryphons passed by William's left wingtip, with the other Pegasi close behind. The sky became a deadly dance of whirling, spinning aeroplanes. Lieutenant Stewart flashed by so closely that William could see the lethal grin on his face as he pursued a tiger-striped triplane.

William felt somewhat badly for running for home while his squadron mates were in danger. Logically, though, he knew he could not take part in a dogfight while Hinson still clung to his wing.

Unfortunately, one of the triplanes didn't want to let him go. Sonic pulses tore into the Pegasus's frame. The Pegasus's propeller coughed, sputtered, and ground to a halt. He looked back....

Only to see the triplane roll over onto its back and plummet to the earth. A small figure stood up in the cockpit of its Gryphon and waved. It was the young pilot who'd had such trouble controlling his plane on the day the Gryphons arrived. Apparently the fellow had learned a few things.

He wasn't the only one.

Right now, though, William's attention was taken up with keeping the Pegasus in an even glide. A few puffs of anti-aircraft fire gave him a scare, but for the most part, the Boche anti-aircraft gunners had been forced to hold their fire for fear of hitting their own triplanes. Then the guns were behind them, and they were back on the Allied side of the front lines; William barely noticed a platoon of Burgundian infantry waving to him from their trench. The Pegasus was going down, and all he could do was pick the best available landing spot.

Just a little to his right there was a churned-up field, and to his left, a ramshackle outpost that might have been a division headquarters. A dirt road ran between them. William tightened his grip on the control stick. The road was rutted and bumpy, but it was the best he had.

"Hold on!" he shouted to Hinson.

William let the Pegasus descend until it was only a few feet off the ground. He pulled back on the stick just a little, knowing too much would cause the plane's wings to stall and it would flop to earth like a pancake, possibly breaking its airframe—and its passengers. Carefully, he set the Pegasus down....

To discover he hadn't pulled back too much. No, he hadn't pulled back *enough*, and the Pegasus was still traveling forward at an alarming speed. William stood on the brakes until the Pegasus's tire caught in a rut and the aeroplane whipped around to the right, slamming William into the far side of the cockpit.

"Hinson!" he called, and then, with one last shudder, the Pegasus was still.

William attempted to release his white-knuckled grip on the control stick and found himself trembling instead. It was as though his mad airborne dash across no-man's-land had enabled him to outpace his own fear. Now that the Pegasus was no longer moving, that terror had caught up to him, causing his heart to hammer and his throat to constrict.

We're safe…?

William had a sudden terrible image of Captain Hinson losing his grip on the Pegasus's wing strut during the rough landing. William turned his head to look, only to see the captain looking back at him with a sheepish grin, leaning against the fuselage where the force of the landing had thrown him, his own hands clenched just as tightly to the lip of the Pegasus's cockpit as William's were around the control column.

Only then did William's airway open enough to allow him a deep breath.

"Welcome home," he said to Captain Hinson with a nervous grin.

"You almost died." Hinson's tone was strangely admonishing.

"So did you."

"If you'd gotten yourself killed," the captain said sternly, "who would have championed the heavier-than-air cause?"

"Nobody. I'm kind of relying on a certain hotshot ace to do that job," William retorted. "Seems he got himself stuck behind enemy lines, so I had to go get him back."

Hinson grinned. "I heard my former batman refer to you as a little mouse. I think Mr. Alex McKinnon was just unable to recognize a lion in disguise."

Dwelling on the compliment would certainly tangle his tongue, so instead William said, "Former batman?"

"I switched with Lieutenant Stewart. Seems that he and Mr. McKinnon are having a good deal more fun together, though I wish they'd be more considerate—the walls of the barracks are awfully thin."

William sighed. "I suppose you'll want to tell Violet that you're all right."

Hinson tilted his head. "Violet?"

Was Hinson going to make him say it? "The girl you named your Gryphon for?"

And then Hinson laughed. Outright guffawed. William sat thunderstruck.

"William, my plane is named for an old nickname. Shrinking Violet. That's what the bullies in my grammar school called me."

William held his breath. "You?"

Hinson nodded, his eyes sparkling again. "When I joined the Royal Dirigible Corps, I decided I would finally show them just what a coward I could be."

"So there's no girl?" He paused, then dared to speak the captain's first name. "James?"

"There's no girl, William." His mouth curved in an inviting smile.

Once again, William wasn't quite sure what to do. He awkwardly climbed out of the Pegasus's cockpit, covering his nervousness with inane chatter. "We're well back from the front lines, but it's going to be a long walk back to the squadron's airfield," he said as he slid to the ground. "If we're lucky, we can catch a ride with a...."

His feet hit the earth and an instant later, his knees buckled. William realized too late that he was still a nervous wreck; his legs had outright refused to support his weight.

Then James was there behind him, his right arm braced across William's chest, his front supporting William's back. William flushed, for it was not at all unpleasant to be held that way by a strong man.

Perhaps it was the adrenaline still charging through his system that gave him the nerve to turn around. Perhaps it was the realization that he had been given a chance and he'd let it slip away. He was not about to squander another.

So this time, Aeroplane Mechanic First Class William Pettigrew did not stand there and hope that Captain James Hinson might kiss him.

This time, William rose up on the toes of his work boots and proved he was more than good enough to deserve his happiness.

MARY PLETSCH is a glider pilot, toy collector, and graduate of the Royal Military College of Canada. Administrator by day, writer by night, she stays up late to indulge the voices in her head, powered by the lunar tides and too much caffeine. She lives in Ottawa with Dylan Blacquiere and their four cats. She can be found online at http://www.fictorians.com.

CARESS

ELI EASTON

I.

London, 1857

THE child's mother was asleep in the chair when I climbed in through the window. I was small and light and well versed in the science of being invisible. *Two, three, four* steps to the bed. I placed the mechanical lark on the table, moving aside bloodstained tissues and a bottle of laudanum that had likely cost this family a month's wages. When I looked up, the child's eyes were open. They were huge in her pale face and blue as the Crimean sky. I placed a finger to my lips and winked.

"Who are you?" she whispered, joining in the conspiracy at once.

"An angel," I whispered back, unable to resist the irony.

"Is this from heaven, then?" Her bony fingers reached for the lark.

I nodded solemnly.

She picked up the automaton as if it were so fragile a breath could break it. But despite the delicate look of its enameled wings, it was strong.

"I love it so," she whispered fervently. She started to turn the key. I touched her hand and put up a finger. *Wait.* She stopped.

I attempted a smile in lieu of a good-bye. But I could already see Death's hand on her in the purple tinge of her lips and the gray around her eyes. My smile felt like the white flag of a traitor.

I slipped out the window. As I climbed down the building—it was so close to its neighbor that even my short legs could meet both walls—I heard the key wind. *Snick, snick.* I dropped to the ground and scooted out to the street, the lark's song playing sweetly behind me. I'd given it a real lark's voice but the tune was *his.* I could almost see the throat and breast pulsing, see the tiny wires that made the eyes blink. *Nictitating membrane, upper eyelid, iris contracting, repeat.*

HER name was Grace, and two days later I watched them carry her from the building in a box. I wondered if the lark was in her cold, still hands, or if her parents had decided to sell it. The lark would pay their rent for a year, so it was only logical. But I knew the heart was an irregular clockwork, untidy. There were enough larks of mine buried in the pauper's cemetery to found a feathered choir. It had been a hard year for cholera and consumption.

Grace's mother, Molly, was a pretty barmaid at the Dunswood pub. I went there when the silence of my lonely rooms became too full of remembered screams. She was back at work a few days later, her eyes swollen and red.

"Aye, the Angel of Seven Dials brought my poor Grace her treasure," I overheard her tell some fellow customers. "I caught nary a glimpse of him, mind. But I'll tell 'ee this: that man has a heart of gold."

I nearly spewed out my drink of ale. I wanted to laugh until I cried.

They had no idea the sins I atoned for.

MY HEART was not gold, in fact. But it wasn't human either.

I stood next to the mirror, taking deep breaths to calm myself, and watched my bare chest rise and fall. *Pulse 120, 110, 95.* At twenty-five, I still had a boy's frame. Early privations had stunted me. Or perhaps my father was small; I never knew his name.

I had the gauze and bandages ready along with the three new valves, perfectly calibrated. *Inverted piston design, powered off the electrical impulses of the heart, warm from the sterile bath.* Albertus had instructed me on the method to replace the valves. It was done once a year, just before my birthday. But since the war I'd not been able to stomach the sight of blood, not even my own.

I used the tiny key to open the chest plate. Inside, the mechanical heart beat steady and sure. I could see the purple of my lung as it inflated in and out, the pink of my esophagus. Living arteries attached to gold couplings, but the heart itself was made with the thinnest plates of steel—*a pump, a work of art, the clockwork engine of a monster.*

I used a small pick to turn off the blood to one valve and remove it. Bright red spurted from the coupling, making me feel faint. My gloved fingers grew slick as I set in the new valve and hooked up the pins. I forced myself to replace the other two, despite my shaking hands.

I closed the chest plate and sterilized it. Done. The entire thing had taken less than five minutes, but darkness threatened the edges of my vision and my skin was clammy. I lay down on the bed. Since the war I'd had the urge, as my birthday neared, to ignore the procedure. How long would it take for the valves to wear out? Knowing Augustus's craftsmanship, it might take years. They might slow down before stopping entirely, or miss beats, causing me to lose consciousness. They might fail one by one. I deserved such a death, but I hadn't yet found it in me to ruin Albertus's masterpiece. Not when there was any lingering chance that *he* might come.

Albertus had made the mechanical heart for me when I was fourteen to replace the faulty one I was born with. If he'd known the horrors I would commit, the thousands of people I would murder, he might have thought twice.

I am sorry.

London, 1844

I WAS twelve when my mother and I stood in the queue, in the cold rain, for two whole days and a night to see him. I counted the cracks in the sidewalk and the bricks on the wall. *Two hundred forty-two to the bottom of the second-story windows.* My clothes grew wet and my teeth chattered like castanets. Hunger was always with me, a snake in my belly that coiled and bit. But by the second day, it was enraged and tormented me.

I was smaller than the next smallest boy in the line, *three inches shorter, two stone lighter*. Twelve was the minimum age, though there were boys who looked as old as sixteen. My body had always been little, but it ran hot as a furnace, and the broth and scraps of bread my mother could afford to feed me were never enough. I dreamed heady dreams of boards groaning with meats and heaping bowls of potatoes. All I understood or cared of my mother's determination to get me in to see Albertus was that it might lead to food. *A piece of cheese or an apple. Tangy apple, thirty grams.* Beyond that, I cared not.

Of course, everyone knew Albertus was the greatest machinist in London. But I thought nothing of my chances. I was no one, a lad frequently weak and ill, with pockets too mean to even afford lint. But the hope that they would feed me inside, and the fierce determination in my mother's eyes, gave me the strength to endure.

When I was finally seated at a table in Albertus's workshop, and the wondrous tools and puzzles were placed in front of me, I forgot my hunger. I forgot about being wet. My brain was caught like a gear engaging, and I reached out my fingers to touch. I'd never imagined such marvels.

I moved tiny copper fragments around under a magnifying glass with the aid of pin-thin tweezers—*red ones to the left, black ones to the right*. There was a game with turning pipes and dials and getting a flow of water from point A to point B, and a lovely sorting game involving parts that looked nearly identical but weren't.

I was so enamored with the sorting game that I jumbled the pieces up and replayed it three times. By the time I came to myself, Albertus, all gangly limbs and gray hair, was discussing the terms of my apprenticeship with my mother. He required nine years, a long term for an apprentice, but the post was a coveted one and there was a lot to learn. My mother gave him her hand, and my fate was sealed.

"This is the greatest opportunity of your life, Tinker," my mother said through her tears as she hugged me good-bye. "Be good. Be brave. I'm so proud of you, my brilliant boy. This will change your destiny."

I clung to her, sobbing out protests that were ignored. She forced me from her arms and hurried away. It was the first time my heart broke, but it wouldn't be the last.

II.

Crimean Peninsula, 1854

HE HAD green eyes.

Irises the color of Kolmården green marble with flecks of gray and gold and a black outer band.

Major Barker had been summoned to the hospital, and I went along. He'd been called from our work in the machinist's hangar, and that could only mean one thing: a potential for flesh and metal to mate in a bloody marriage.

Tingles of excitement wanted to tug up the corners of my mouth, but I was adept at keeping my face blank. Even after a year in the army, surgery was still a savory puzzle to me—*repair, stitch, restore.* Flesh was simply a gorier form of clockworks at such times. But that was only if I managed not to think about the weapons testing room.

Don't think about that.

Our outpost of Her Majesty's Service had taken over a small village south of Simferopol. The machinist's hangar was a giant collapsible tin box assembled on the outskirts of the village and heavily guarded round the clock. The hospital was in the old church. A nurse ushered us to the patient. He was lying on an exam table and the colored light of an Orthodox stained-glass window fell across him, dissecting him with yellow, blue, and purple.

His skin was white with shock but he was awake. When I saw the horror of his injuries, I wished to God he hadn't been.

"Dynamite blast, poor chap," said the doctor, Major Winslow. "The arms are the worst of it."

I stood two steps behind Major Barker, as was my lot, but I assessed the damage as if I were in charge, also my lot. *Forearms ended below the elbows, stumps coated in gore, edges raged and torn and partially cauterized.* Part of a radius bone jutted an inch from the torn muscle on his right. Tourniquets above the elbows stanched the bleeding, but they could have done nothing for the pain. His khaki uniform was stiff with blood.

And his eyes. I looked up into the most beautiful eyes I'd ever seen. The soldier's face was handsome, even with the damage from the blast—a gash in his cheek that would leave a scar and a mosaic of soot and blood. Pain dug deep into his features, but what struck me the most was the defeated resignation in his eyes. It was an expression you might expect to see on a man's face seconds from death, as a lorry slides toward him on a slick road.

Major Barker looked over the stumps with a petulant moue. "Far too damaged," he pronounced, annoyed at having been disrupted from his work. "There's nothing to connect to. It can't be done."

Brigadier Warwick, the man in charge of the outpost, happened to be walking by. He stopped and approached us.

"Most unfortunate," he grumbled. He gave the soldier a smile that was both falsely sympathetic and told him to buck up. Warwick was a man of the times, not a terrible commander, but at that moment I disliked him intensely. "Well, put him under, for God's sake, and clean up those stumps."

"Wait," I said, stepping forward.

Three pairs of eyes gazing at me, four, five. Sweat skittered down my spine. I don't know what made me do it. Well, that's not true. His beauty stirred me, even in his bloodied state. But more than that, I could read his future clearly in his eyes. He would be sent home to England with two stumps and no way to fend for himself or make a living. Like so many before him, he would take his own life. It was already there in his eyes.

"Well? Speak up, Tinker," Major Barker said impatiently.

"I can salvage the connections," I said. "Permission to try, sir."

Major Barker glared at me angrily. I had contradicted him in front of the brigadier. That was unforgivable. But I knew my master well. I put an adoring regard on my face.

"Your marvelous golem, sir," I purred. "He'll need hands, and I have so little experience of them. Perhaps I could practice by making hands for this man."

"Capitol idea!" Brigadier Warwick said. "What do you think, Major Barker? Won't hurt to give it a go, hey?"

Barker smiled tightly, but I knew he was still angry and that I would pay for it sooner or later. "I doubt my apprentice will be able to pull it off. The forearms are too damaged. But he does need the surgical practice. If"—Baker picked up the chart—"Captain Davies does not object to being operated on with so little chance of success."

Captain Davies. The tattered rags of his uniform came sharply into focus. *Officer. Cavalry.* He was still clinging to consciousness, his jaw shaking with the pain. He looked at Barker, then at me. I tried to reassure him with my eyes. *I can do it.*

He nodded once.

Barker turned to me. "I can't have you skimping on your regular work, Lieutenant. It's far too critical."

"I'll operate tonight. I'll be back on the job in the morning," I promised.

Barker's eyes narrowed, telling me he'd better not regret it. Then the brigadier started asking questions about the progress on the golem and the two of them strolled away.

The doctor prepared a hypodermic and sighed. "I can't assist you in surgery, Tinker. I have a dozen other patients. If this were a simple amputation, it would take me ten minutes, but this…. I've no time for this."

"I'll make do," I said. I stepped closer to Captain Davies. His gaze never left mine as I gripped his upper arm, offering comfort, I suppose, and a distraction from the hypodermic. *Right biceps muscle, diameter of the plunger one centimeter, needle point-three-oh centimeters. Unconscious in ten, nine, eight….*

"If you can't—" Davies whispered. He didn't get to finish before the drug took him. Nevertheless, I knew what he wanted—a reprieve I would never have it in me to give.

Don't let me awaken.

"I hope you know what you're doing," the doctor muttered as those green eyes slid closed.

III.

ALBERTUS made me a new heart, and he gave me an even more precious gift—knowledge. He taught me everything he knew. Hunger of the mind replaced hunger of the belly. There was always enough food in the genius's rambling London workshop. And enough food for my mind as well.

He taught me how to work with fibers as delicate as the hair on a lady's arm. He showed me the magic of tiny gears that ran in perpetual motion, feeding each other energy like an ouroboros. He built mechanisms as large as an elephant for the queen. Albertus's creations were unique. He gave them little flaws—a dandy's shoe with a cracked heel, a horse with a bump on its nose, a shepherdess's stocking that was falling down. Because reality was never perfect, he said, and it was the imperfections that made his creations feel real.

But I, I preferred tiny things, miniatures so complex not one more filament could be crammed into their perfection. I made frogs and spiders and glittering eggs that opened a dozen times to reveal smaller and smaller works of art. They sold to the highest bidder. Victoria herself carried one of my mechanical butterflies in her purse. And we made limbs too, when St. Bart's sent for us. Men often lost parts of themselves in the maw of the Industrial Revolution. *Snip snap.*

One day in the operating theater, Albertus suddenly stepped away from the patient with the halting gait of one of his automatons. His scalpel dropped to the floor. He fell and I reached for him, barely catching him before he hit the boards. He looked into my eyes for a second and then he was gone.

Unlike mine, his heart had given us no warning. He saved me and then died in my arms.

I was twenty and only a year away from my freedom. *Three hundred sixty-three days, twelve hours, ten minutes.* But Albertus, the greatest mind of the century, had forgotten to mention me in his will. My contract went to his widow, a woman neither Albertus nor I could abide. She sold me, for a great deal of money, to Major Barker. Barker had been after Albertus to work for the British Army for years. Albertus had refused; I could not.

Albertus placed his deepest secrets in me, and Major Barker bought them as if they were nothing more than a cheap whore.

IV.

I OPERATED on Captain Davies from seventeen hundred hours till four in the morning. *Eleven hours, twelve minutes.* Major Winslow sent in a nurse to assist me for a short while, but when she had to leave, I didn't get another. This was a war zone, and the battle that had brought in Captain Davies had brought in other wounded. The hospital staff had no time for the delicate work required.

As I worked into the night alone, I was gripped with doubt. Why had I said I could do this? What if I failed? The arms were terribly ravaged. I had to saw off and smooth the edges of the bones and shave the ragged flesh before I could begin to coax the delicate nerve fibers and tendons to the surface. I would need them to connect to the prosthetics. I had to control the bleeding and recirculate the blood. The IV sedation had to be monitored and clean, sterile water applied regularly to keep the tissue pliable.

By midnight, I knew I would succeed. By four I was finished and dead on my feet.

I wrapped the prepared stumps and gave Davies more morphine. I wanted to stay with him, be there when he awoke. But Major Barker would expect me in the hangar in an hour to begin a day's work.

I bent over his bed. In my exhausted state, and after so long focusing on minutia, his face was blurred and soft in the glow of the lamps. He was a large man, at least six two and fifteen stone. His shoulders were broad and muscled. But in my altered state he looked angelic lying there. His hair was dark blond and clipped short. He wore a slim mustache. He looked young. His lips were full and soft, his jaw square and rough.

"Don't die," I told him. "I'll make you hands, marvelous hands. You'll see."

V.

FOR three days, Major Barker had me working on the golem around the clock. He refused every request I made to go the hospital to check on Captain Davies. Barker said the stumps should not be disturbed for a week so there was no point in checking them. The truth was, he resented any moment I was not slaving on *his* project. Barker had made big promises to the brigadier, and he knew no one else had the skill to accomplish the thing.

I often contemplated how to turn his need of me to my advantage. But Barker was hard and ruthless. And while I could see wires and rods in my head as clear as day, people remained a mystery to me. When I tried to insist on seeing my patient, Barker threatened to ban me from the hospital for good. I relented.

I'd never liked Barker, but in those few days, I learned to hate him. I felt a craving to check on Captain Davies, an obsession of the sort I developed around important projects. Having it thwarted was painful.

On the fourth day, Major Barker was summoned to the hospital by Brigadier Warwick himself, and he nodded at me tersely to go along. We found the brigadier standing at Captain Davies's bed. The patient's color had returned, a rosy glow, and he was sleeping peacefully. He looked much improved.

Deliberately, I stepped around Major Barker to check the captain's forehead for fever. There was none.

"Well?" the brigadier asked. "What's the prognosis? Can we use Captain Davies to prototype the golem's hands or not?"

Major Barker went a little red, having ignored the issue for days. "Unwrap his hands, Tinker," he ordered. "Show the brigadier how he's got on."

"Yes, sir." I unwrapped the bandages, anxious to see the stumps for myself.

As I reached the final layer, I took care, checking his face frequently for pain. But he didn't awaken. The nurse must have given him something strong. I exposed both stumps. The flesh around the connectors was red but healing nicely. The stitched seams were tight and pale. I touched the connectors one by one with a steel rod I'd brought for the purpose. Each time, the small tube on the end of the rod lit up. The connectors were live.

Major Barker's expression cleared and he smiled like the satisfied fox he was. "As you can see, it's going splendidly. The nerves and tendons are attached to those connectors. The mechanical hands will slot right onto them. And then they'll be screwed into these divots here and secured to the bones."

He went on to point out all my hard work as if it were his own marvelous doing. I was used to it. He always took credit for my skill. I only felt relief that Davies was living, that he was healing, and that the arms were excellent candidates for my prosthetics. I would be able to give him a future in which he was not helpless.

"But the golem won't have nerves, will it?" Brigadier Warwick asked.

"No, the golem will have wires and gears," Barker said. "And it will be powered by a small engine in the torso. The prosthetic hands will be run by the electrical pulse of Captain Davies's heart. It's a technology I myself invented."

Albertus had invented it, and I'd refined it, but I wasn't going to argue.

Barker continued. "But the basic function of the hands will be the same. They'll be exceptional weapons."

"Crushing, as I recall," the brigadier said. The golem was an important project and he knew the design well.

"Yes. The hands will be far stronger than human hands. They'll be able to crush a throat in seconds. And of course, the grip for climbing will be superb, and the force of a fist blow will shatter bone on contact."

I knew all this about the golem. It was, after all, laid out in my own blueprints. But now the words sank into me as if I'd never heard them before. I looked at Captain Davies asleep on the bed and felt a sharp pain of regret and guilt. Suddenly the hands did not seem so much a gift as a curse.

"I say!" The brigadier was impressed. "But the golem will be controlled with code words. Will we be able to control Davies the same way? Or will he have his own mind? I suppose he must. He's a man, after all."

Major Barker looked at me. He didn't know the answer, but he was warning me to say what he wanted to hear.

I swallowed. "He'll have his own mind, sir. Of course. But the hands could be engineered to override that on a code word. However, it might be best—"

"Marvelous!" Brigadier Warwick said. "Naturally, one would hardly expect to need such a thing, but do put it in, put it in. I'll want a list of the code words. I suppose they'll be a different word for each possible action, hey? 'Crush,' for example. Not that we'd call it that! It wouldn't do to have him killing someone accidently, would it? For example, if you said 'It's a crush in here.' No, that wouldn't do at all."

"The code words will be things unlikely ever to be spoken aloud," Major Barker assured him.

The brigadier seemed so cheerful at the prospect. And after all, that was what the HRH Machinist Corps was for, wasn't it? To invent new weapons, to take life. From the first time a caveman raised a bone and struck a rival over the head, it's been a race to create the biggest stick. We were the British Empire. It was our right to create deterrents. Our duty, even. That was what they'd told me.

I'D BEEN so naïve when I first came under Major Barker's wings. He'd been nice to me then—fatherly, even—and I'd been grieving for Albertus. I bought into every platitude he'd uttered. "For queen and country." "To end the war and bring our boys home." I preened under his praise of my skills like a wallflower soaking up compliments from a handsome gentleman. I'd been putty in his hands. *Foolish Tinker. Foolish, queer Tinker.*

I knew Albertus had rejected Barker time and again, but I'd always assumed he was too busy making pretty marvels for royalty and couldn't be bothered. For a short time, I considered myself *better* than Albertus for using my skills in service of our fighting forces, of England, of *peace*. I took up the mental challenge to make killing things as if it were a delightful puzzle to be solved.

It wasn't until I saw my weapons tested on prisoners of war that I realized the obvious—why Albertus had rejected such work. *Blood, brain matter, bones, screams, pleas....* But it was too late. They put my designs into production. There were thousands of them out there. *My* devices.

I would never be forgiven—not by God, if there was such, not by the spirit of Albertus, not by my victims, and not by myself.

"WHEN can a prototype be ready?" the brigadier asked. He and Major Barker strolled away together, chatting enthusiastically.

Dismissed, I stepped closer to Captain Davies's bed and looked down at him. He opened his eyes. There was a dull horror in those deep green pools and a grievous crease between his brows. He'd been awake, then, the entire time. He'd heard.

"I'm sorry," I whispered to him. I began to rewrap his stumps. *Over, under, gentle on the connectors, don't touch the inside of the sterile gauze.*

"What's your name?" he asked me quietly.

He didn't sound like he hated me. I looked at his face. We were only a few feet apart, stooped as I was to bandage him. It felt troublingly intimate but I didn't look away.

"Lieutenant Gray," I said.

"Gray. Like your eyes." There was nothing in his voice but weariness, but the mere fact that he'd noticed the color of my eyes made me feel a wave of something—simple gratitude, perhaps—at being seen for once. More than that—pleasure.

Gray like my heart, I thought, meaning the steel of it and also the fact that it was no longer pure. But black would have been a truer color. I said nothing.

"You're the one who'll be making the hands?"

I nodded. "Yes. I'm a machinist." I went back to bandaging his stumps. I wanted to say I was sorry again, but that was stupidity.

"*Gray…*," he murmured, and he fell asleep.

VI.

NOW that the brigadier was excited about the hands, Major Barker allowed me to spend as much time on them as I liked. Two days later, I brought the skeleton of them to Captain Davies to test the couplings. I found him awake and sitting up.

"The fittings will be painful," I told him regretfully, "but once the hands are finished, you won't have to remove them. I can give you some morphine now."

"No. No more morphine. Just do what you must."

I wanted to argue with him. But his face was determined, his resolve as solid as a barred door.

"All right, Captain. But I'll stop the moment you say."

I fitted the hands. *Gold connectors, pins to pin fittings, snap, secure.*

Even though the connectors themselves had no sensation, just shifting them caused waves of pain to shoot up the living fibers. But Davies never said a word. By the time I was done, he was pale and sweating, his jaw clenched so tight it would surely ache for hours.

"I'm sorry about the pain," I said. I seemed to do nothing but apologize to him, like a toy drummer that could only beat one note. I wet a cloth in a nearby basin and wiped his brow, waiting for the pain to fade. The mechanical hands lay on the bed like dead things attached below his elbows.

"What these hands will do…. I deserve to feel every bit of the pain of attaching them," he managed when he could finally speak. He sounded bitter.

I didn't know why he felt he owed me an explanation for his behavior, or why he would be so honest. I was no one. I didn't know how to respond. But I couldn't seem to stop wiping his brow and face. The nurses shaved the men when they could stand it, but it had been at least a day for him. The stubble on his jaw tugged at the cloth. I found it fascinating.

"Where are you from?" I asked, to change the subject.

"North Hampshire. My father was a small landholder. Fifty acres. We raised sheep and we had horses."

I smiled tentatively, but I was surprised. He had a sort of noble bearing I would not have expected from a sheep farmer, though at fifty acres, his family were not paupers.

"We used to slaughter the sheep, you see. So I was a perfect candidate for the army." He attempted to make a joke of it, but there was no humor in his voice. I rewet the cloth and began to wipe down his upper arms.

"I always hated it," he said.

"Farming?" I met his eyes.

"Killing," he answered. I didn't know if he was talking about the sheep anymore.

"You made captain. You must be a good cavalryman."

"Effective at least," he said flatly.

I should have moved on with my work then, but he was still pale, though his trembling had lessened. I told myself I should give it a few more minutes for the pain to fade before I made him move the hands. I rewet the cloth.

I continued to wipe down his left arm, holding it gently at the elbow—and I became mesmerized at the sight and feel of his muscle and skin. I lost myself for a moment, then realized I'd become aroused. I was aroused by touching him, a patient, and I was touching him all wrong. The slow drag of the cloth against his skin could not be mistaken for clinical duty.

Shame and fear flooded me. I felt my face burn. I turned, put the cloth back in the basin, and breathed deeply, schooling myself. *Pulse 130, 120, 110.* When I had myself under control I turned, my face deliberately blank. He was watching me, but he looked thoughtful, not angry. I stuffed my hands into the pocket of my lab coat. Thankfully, it covered up my sins.

"Where are you from, Gray?" he asked.

"No one calls me Gray."

"What, then?"

"Tinker."

"Is that your Christian name?"

I smiled. "Yes. It's a family name. My mother's ancestors made clocks." I had never told anyone that. No one had ever asked.

"Tinker," he said as if testing the word. "And you must call me Colin."

I started to protest, but it would just sound like another apology. I shut my mouth. I could not seem to look away from him.

The way he studied my face, so openly, stole my breath. I'd never had anyone look at me like that. Albertus was usually distracted by his work, and when he did look at me it was either with a paternal fondness or annoyance, depending on what I'd done. Major Barker treated me like a tool he could manipulate as he liked. I was small and mostly I was ignored. No one saw me the way Captain Davies—*Colin*—was seeing me now, like a person, an interesting one, one worth studying and puzzling over. It made me shiver with alternating twinges of hot and cold. It made me want to excuse myself and escape, and at the same time it made me ache for more, for my allotment of human contact.

I told myself it was just his way. There was nothing in Colin's face that indicated more than curiosity, nothing to suggest his interest in me was carnal. But my body reacted to the weight of his gaze as if it was a physical touch. And oh, I craved that touch.

"You don't like being a solider," I said, forcing my eyes to look away from his.

"It's my job. It's what I signed up for," he said with no emotion.

"If you weren't a soldier, what would you be?" My eyes shifted back to him of their own accord.

He looked surprised at the question. "I… write music. In my head." He started to gesture toward his head and his right hand obeyed, fingers flowing. He stared at them for a moment, swallowed audibly, then carefully let the hand rest back on the bed.

"You're a composer?" I asked.

He shook his head. "Nothing so grand. Never been published. Never even heard my music played other than in my head. I've written reams of it, though. Foolish. Helps me cope, I suppose."

"Not foolish," I said. "Do you write it down?"

"Yes."

"I'd like to see it."

"Why?"

Green eyes. Very frank green eyes. Should I not have said that? *Be quiet, Tinker. Know your place. Hands, mechanics, work. Do your job.*

"Is the pain bearable now?" I asked hastily. "I need to test the hands."

"It's bearable."

I held out my palm, waist high. "Place your hand on mine, very gently."

His left hand moved and slowly raised to mine. It rested there.

"Excellent. Can you turn it over so that your palm faces the ceiling?"

He did.

"Now wiggle your fingers."

The tapered steel fingers moved up and down.

"Make a loose fist. Good."

We repeated the test with his right hand. I had him grasp a pencil.

"I'll be able to eat by myself? To write?" he asked.

"Of course."

He looked relieved. I wondered if he was thinking about writing his compositions. Or perhaps he had a girl back home whom he wrote to. Of course he must.

I tested each finger in turn. Though the hands worked, the pinkie was slow to move on the left and the thumb almost immobile on the right. I would have to make adjustments.

"There will be at least one more fitting," I told him as I removed the hands. "And then... we'll have to test the full range of features for the brigadier."

He looked down at his chest, his brow furrowing. He knew exactly what I meant.

"I'm sorry," I said again. It was such a weak thing to say. I had to stop saying it. But I could hear his voice in my head.

I always hated it. The killing.

He raised his eyes to meet mine. "Thank you, Tinker," he said, absolving me in a way I didn't deserve. He turned his back to me and pretended to go to sleep.

VII.

WHEN Albertus gave me a new heart, he gave me other things as well.

A love of walking, which I had never been able to do as a child without getting winded. I roamed all over London when I had the chance. I particularly adored Highgate Wood and Queens Wood. My mind would slide over problems during such walks, as if the faster-pumping blood and fresher air were feeding my brain. I would return to the workshop eager to test new ideas.

The heart also gave me a less useful thing—crushing sexual desire. Perhaps I was not unlike any other fifteen-year-old boy, but it didn't seem that way. Once I was healthy, I was always randy. Even when my mind was deeply engaged in my work, there was a tingling little itch in my groin that begged for attention. And when I was not working, it became a need that was impossible to ignore.

At the slightest provocation, I would harden. My baggy trousers and long waistcoats were my greatest allies. It didn't take me long to discern that, while the barmaid's breasts did little for me, my prick would stiffen at the merest glimpse of broad shoulders in a fitted jacket, the muscled thighs of a man on horseback, or glossy black hair curved near a masculine jaw. I never spoke of these things to anyone, but I listened to others talk. I came to understand the condition I had and its relative rarity. It was a crime under English law.

I'd never been what you might call normal, so my irregularity in this regard did not distress me. I felt no shame. But it did convince me that my life would be one of work and invention, not love and family. I was unlikely to find many willing partners, nor I was prepared to take on the wife society would expect of me. I would be alone.

We often had great lords and ladies visit the London workshop. Lord Winthrope was fascinated with mechanisms and he came often. Sometimes his son, Rupert, would accompany him. While Lord Winthrope and Albertus discussed projects out in the shop front, Rupert would wander back to my workbench, a place well tucked away from patrons' eyes.

Rupert was a pompous ass, so I would work on, ignoring him as best I could. But he loved to tease me just to see the blush that stained my cheeks. One day he leaned over my back, placing his chin on my shoulder as I worked. I should have shaken him off, but the warmth of his chest pressed against me, his breath in my ear…. It felt good. I must have groaned or sighed, for he guessed my predicament. His hand stole over my thigh to my groin. He purred in my ear at what he found there.

"Ooh… you have a big tool for such a little lad, Tinker."

His tongue flicked my ear. My hands stopped moving but I kept my tools clenched in my fingers, my breathing harsh. He rubbed me through my trousers. I felt his answering hardness thrust against my rump and lower back as I sat on the stool.

I knew we could be caught at any moment, but I couldn't make him stop. It felt so delicious to have someone else's hand on me, to feel a stiff prick against my back. I floated in delight for an endless few minutes.

Stroke, once per second, twice per second, applied pressure thirty psi. Harder, oh God, harder. Please.

With a small whimper, I spent in my trousers. I felt him tense up and spasm too.

He left without another word and never came back with his father again. I was only a mechanic's apprentice, after all. I did not miss him.

It was the only sexual experience I'd ever had with another person. I knew where the johnny boys worked, and I always had a few bits in my pocket. I daydreamed about sneaking out to see them, just to feel another's hand, mouth, on me. But the threat of disease, and the fear of getting caught and shaming Albertus, kept me from acting on the fantasy.

I made do with my own clever hands and the boundless plains of my imagination.

VIII.

MAJOR BARKER was most particular about the killing features of the hands. I programmed them and tested them in the lab while he watched, running them through an engine that would eventually empower the golem. Either hand could crush a brick to dust in seconds. They responded to spoken command. Barker was pleased.

On the next fitting, I had no choice but to explain the features to Colin.

"Only think what you want the hands to do, and they will do it," I told him. "But you'll have to strongly will it. Don't worry about doing something accidently."

I placed a towel over his lap and gave him a brick. "Squeeze it as hard as you can."

He looked down at the hand.

Thought impulse sent to receptors, receptors filter out minor impulses, strong impulse drives the hands. Three thousand psi. There.

The brick disintegrated. Colin huffed something that was part laugh, part sob.

"You'll be able to climb anything," I assured him.

"And to punch hard enough to shatter bone," he said flatly. He *had* been listening that day when he'd pretended sleep.

"Yes. Maybe the hands will save your life one day."

"But I won't always control the hands, will I? The brigadier said… they'll respond to spoken commands too. From someone else."

There was a catch in his voice, and I knew the idea truly frightened him. I focused on the hands, adjusting a screw that didn't need adjusting. "Yes. But hardly anyone will know those commands."

He sighed as if defeated. "It's all right, Tinker. The army doesn't build hands like these without asking for their pound of flesh. I know I should be grateful. Without them…."

He lay back on the pillow, and I cleared away the brick dust and towel. I cleaned the hand of tiny red particles. I liked holding the hand while he was wearing it. Just the simple act of attaching it to his connections, slotting it to the end of his arm, made it *alive* to me, made it *his hand* in a way that was completely illogical. By now, the skeleton was sheathed and there were enough feedback sensors in the fingers that I knew he could feel me as I stroked them clean. It gave me a strange thrill.

He didn't pull away. I could feel his gaze on my face as I worked. Maybe it was the intimacy, but he began to speak haltingly. "I was in the expeditionary force that landed at Eupatoria. I fought with the Light Brigade at Balaclava. Almost half our men were killed or wounded in that battle. But I wasn't. I mowed down everything in my path. Do you know why? Because I was terrified, you see. I killed so I wouldn't be killed, like a sick dog lashing out. And the Russians, by God, they were so young and inexperienced. It was like scything down tender grass. I still see their faces when I close my eyes. Since then, there've been too many battles and too many faces."

"I have killed too," I said before realizing I was going to say it.

He looked at me in surprise and I could see the question in his eyes. At twenty-two I was still small and ever would be. My hair had been cut short when I joined the army but as a machinist it was not tended to with much frequency. It lay against my nape and, unruly and thick, stuck up on the top of my head. My face was thin and pale, the face of a scholar. To put it bluntly, I probably looked as dangerous to him as a plate of peas.

"Weapons," I said with a tight smile. "I design weapons."

"Like what?" he asked, curious now.

"The dervish," I admitted. It was a device shaped like an orange. But when it was activated, slicing blades emerged and spun. They acted like wings, allowing the device to fly. A mercury core steered its course to the nearest warm body. Its navigational system was calibrated to move forward for a dozen yards, and from thence in a widening cone seeking a target. This would presumably ensure that the sender, and his fellow countrymen, would be safe. And yet I could not pretend the thing had not killed the innocent or even a horse or dog unlucky enough to get in its path. I had nightmares about it chasing me.

His eyes widened. "That was yours?"

I nodded. "And the stinger." The dart was a better design; it carried death a little less randomly. It had to be aimed at a specific target and engaged. Then it would fly to that target with the speed of an arrow. *Point-one millimeters of poison injected into the flesh, a killing dose.*

He was staring at me in shock. I felt a debilitating pain of the heart. He saw it now: I was a monster. I looked at the floor, blinking back the unfathomable threat of tears.

His left hand closed over mine and tugged me closer. If I'd been less embarrassed, I might have felt a creator's pride at the tenderness with which he could grasp my fingers.

"You're brilliant, then, Tinker," he said quietly. "A genius."

I gave a bitter laugh. "Only a trained mind, one in the service of the devil."

"*No,*" he said firmly. "We need all the help you can give us out there. But—I do understand."

I looked up and saw regret and sympathy on his face. I swallowed a lump and nodded.

"Liberty and ease for those at home—it has a high price," he parroted.

Did he still believe those words? That the scrabble for bits of the Ottoman Empire really affected the lives of people back in England? If he could believe it, I was glad for him.

I suddenly realized how close we were. I was pressed against the side of the bed. My left hand rested in his mechanical fingers and my right, somehow, had moved onto his chest, which was covered only by a thin hospital johnny. We were staring deeply into each other's eyes. It was rather a shock to realize how we were arranged, as if I'd woken from a dream with no idea how I'd gotten there. I almost pulled away, but I stopped.

If this was being offered to me, why shouldn't I take it?

It was a moment of vulnerability, a moment of understanding, of humanity, a moment of something else too—lust, not to put too fine a point on it. He was strong, rugged, and handsome, the stuff of my erotic dreams. And what I saw in his eyes was no less longing than my own. I didn't understand how it could be there, not for me, for small, unimportant Tinker, but I drank it in greedily. Heat rushed through my body.

In my mind, I drew back, knowing this was dangerous ground. But my body didn't obey. My hand remained heavy on his chest, my fingers barely stroking. I was painfully aroused where I pressed against the bed, but thankfully, my white coat covered my folly. If only I could as easily hide what must be written all over my face.

"Tinker," he said, questioning.

I nodded, not trusting my voice.

"Could I ask you something terribly personal?"

I nodded again.

He blushed. "I—" He tried again. "I know the hands must be set to kill. I know this. But...."

"Yes?"

"Can you make them do other things as well?" He looked down where his hand held mine, frowning at it as if he didn't trust its current gentleness.

"Anything."

"Can you make the hands... caress?" His blush deepened and he couldn't meet my eyes. "No one will want a mechanical man, you see, to be touched by things like these." He held the hands up to look at them. I missed the weight of his hand on mine immediately.

"That's not true. Many men have prosthetics. And you're a handsome man."

He looked at me sharply but without much hope. "You're used to mechanisms. But for most people.... They'll frighten away any lover."

I noted that he did not say the word *woman*. I swallowed.

"And if the hands don't keep them away, the blood on them will," he said roughly. "I'm already a killer. But with these.... If I ever see England again, I'll be soaked in blood."

I couldn't argue with him. I knew what duty he and his hands were bound for. But my fingers rubbed his chest to offer comfort, as if they had a will of their own.

He closed his eyes as he choked out the request. "Allow me to be tender to myself at least. No one else will ever want to touch me."

I felt my face heat, understanding his meaning perfectly. *Ten pounds psi, twenty, scrotum, shaft, glans.* The ideas it sent rushing through my head overwhelmed me, intellect and body both.

He mistook my silence and pulled away, rolling onto his side to put his back to me. "My apologies. I didn't intend to ask. I shouldn't have. Please forget I ever said it. Please, Tinker."

He was distraught. I felt the strongest urge to lean down and kiss his hair. I was losing my mind. I did lean down, but only to whisper in his ear.

"I will teach the hands to caress, Colin," I vowed with all my heart.

He froze, then nodded.

And before I could do anything else irredeemably foolish, I removed the hands and took them away to be finished.

IX.

SO I taught the hands. During the days, I taught the hands to grip and climb and maim. At night, I taught them to caress.

I was fortunate that, although I was a mere Machinist, Second Class, I had privacy. As Major Barker's apprentice, I slept near his quarters in a room that was little more than a closet. But I had a cot with an iron frame as sturdy as a granite mountain and a lock on the door.

By now, I was an expert at touching myself. It was my only relief from the sexual demands my body made upon me, demands more incessant than even hunger and thirst. But though I knew how to pleasure myself, usually it was done furtively, expediently, and, to pardon the pun, mechanically. I'd never made a study of the thing.

Now I was motivated to use my art to its highest effect. I wanted to give Colin some beauty to cling to in the midst of the darkest night, in the mud and filth of a foxhole. And my only means of doing so were through my own body. How could I teach the hands unless I first taught myself?

Every night when I went to my cell, I would take the hands with me. I'd lock the door and remove my clothing. My own hands played upon my body, learning, feeling, and then I'd adjust the delicate gears and wires. I imagined I was touching Colin, or that Colin was touching me.

I composed odes for fingertips and palm, teasing touches of adoration, strokes upon his length, circles in tender places, ancient rhythms of cresting need and completion. *You are beautiful,* the hands said as they caressed. *You deserve to be loved.*

Of course, the hands would be wired to his will. He could override their training, tell them what to do with a mere thought. But when his will softened, when he stopped consciously guiding and gave in to sensation, the hands would revert to the blueprint I'd given them and perform upon his body the notes of the composition I had written.

The thought turned me on unbearably. And as the mechanisms of the hands became ever more finely tuned, I tested them upon my own body, imagining that I was Colin, that the hands were giving him the sensations I was feeling, sensations *I* had created. They teased and tickled, handled the ball sac gently, rubbed the space behind, stroked with exquisite pressure, thumbs circling just under the glans. When I was certain they could wring no greater pleasure from my body, I considered them complete.

X.

MY TIME with Colin was shorter than I'd ever dreamed. The war was not going well, and there was a push from the top for the golem army Major Barker had promised. They wanted the prototype hands in the field as soon as possible. So it was only a matter of weeks before we stood in a bunker with the brigadier and demonstrated the hands. There was a wall, which Colin easily scaled. Stacks of bricks were broken; steel rods were bent. The brigadier was thorough. He enjoyed seeing Colin use the hands on his own, and then he'd read from his list of commands and watch the hands take over, his eyes gleaming with satisfaction.

Colin steeled himself not to give anything away, but I knew him. I could see the fear in his eyes every time the hands moved with a will of their own.

Then they brought in the prisoner of war. He was an older Russian, afraid but holding his chin up proudly. I wished I could stop it or at least turn away. But if Colin had to bear it, so did I. I was concerned he would refuse, but the brigadier was too interested in his own power to even test Colin's will. He himself ordered the hands to crush the man's throat and they did, thoroughly and quickly, without even a spurt of blood.

One thousand psi crushes the windpipe and the arteries. Death is inevitable within five seconds, complete in thirty.

When it was done, I turned away, unable to bear the look on Colin's face.

I WENT to say good-bye to him and to give the hands one final adjustment. The hands were his now; he'd been wearing them for nearly a week. He was sitting on an exam table, dressed in a new uniform. His packed kit was next to him. We were in a room where they gave exams, which had the advantage, at least, of being private. My heart was hammering in my chest, an engine run amok. This was the last time I'd ever see him.

It was disturbing how much my mind had become wrapped up in him, how deeply he'd burrowed under my skin. Even when I worked in the hangar on the golem, he was never far from my thoughts. If I opened my chest plate, would I see the stain of him against the silver of my artificial heart? If I drew my blood, would I find tiny traces of him in it, like the filaments we used in the automaton oils to keep them fluid? Would each filament be engraved with his name by a miniscule pen? Foolish thoughts—and ghoulish as well. But I knew I would remember him always, like some pathetic spinster who remembers the one man she'd danced with once in her youth, the one man who'd looked at her kindly, who made her feel beautiful.

"Tinker!" Colin said as I entered the room. He looked relieved. "I didn't know if I'd be able to say good-bye to you."

I gave him a tight smile, not trusting my voice. I hoped my singularly stupid adoration was not on display all over my face. I took a tool from my pocket and placed his left hand, palm up, on my sternum. I opened the plate on the forearm.

I looked up into his eyes, which were watching me, and then used a small pick to make an adjustment.

Flip switch to disabled. Smash the switch with a hard tap so it can never be reset.

I closed the plate and repeated with the other hand. This time, I left the hand on my chest when I was done.

I spoke aloud the command I'd given the brigadier, the command to crush.

Colin recognized it. For a moment, his eyes flared with panic. But the hands did not move. He stared at me, wide-eyed. Slowly, the steel fingers on my chest turned and closed around the lapel of my jacket. He blinked his eyes, which were suddenly bright.

"These are *your* hands," I said quietly. "They'll do everything we tested, but only when *you* ask." I moved my fingers of flesh and blood up to squeeze his metal ones.

He breathed out a shaky sigh. "Thank you, Tinker. God bless you." His voice wavered.

"Mechanisms fail," I said with a tight smile. "Most unfortunate."

His gratitude, and the admiration on his face, flooded me with joy. At least I would have that. At least I would know he didn't hate me in the end. But there was nothing else for me to do, no reason for me to linger. I took one last look at him and turned to go. But his fingers firmed in my lapel, not allowing it.

I turned back to him. We were close. I was standing between his knees. His gaze on my face was intense and I could feel the heat rolling off him. I suddenly found it difficult to breathe, as if the need for oxygen had been replaced by a need for something else, and my body was struggling to make the adjustment.

"The hands…. The way they touch me…. You did that." He was blushing, but he stubbornly held my gaze.

I knew at once what he meant. He had tried it—the caress. I looked down, feeling my face burn. I placed my hands on his steel forearms as if studying them.

"When you need comfort," I said, "pretend the hands belong to someone who loves you, someone who accepts you as you are, someone who… who aches to please you."

I bit my lips, my gut twisting with anxiety. I'd meant for him to understand, yes, to understand that it was me. But I imagined it would happen once he was far away, where I couldn't see how he would feel about that knowledge.

"Is that someone you, Tinker?" he asked, his voice rough.

I was too afraid to answer.

He pulled his hands free and clasped my shoulders. "Look at me. Is that someone you?"

I looked into his eyes. "Yes."

He sighed and leaned slowly toward me, his eyes reading mine, giving me plenty of time to pull away. I didn't. No, I fell into him like a collapsing bridge, meeting him more than halfway. His mouth on mine was needy and commanding. He parted my lips with his tongue. I'd never been kissed before, didn't think I ever would be. It was heaven. Our tongues met and slid and teased and I was swept away on a wave of lust and need and natural instinct.

He moved his hands down to grasp my waist, then slid them around my back and pulled me close, never breaking the kiss.

Oh, the marvel of those tender hands, controlled not by me this time, but by him. I'd never been held in passion, and not at all since my mother's last clasp as she left me with Albertus. My body craved it like it was water and every cell was dying of thirst. A storm of feeling overwhelmed me. I pressed closer, between his legs, wanting to never leave his arms. I felt his prick stiffen as it pressed against my own. *I am desired! Me, Tinker Gray.* My heart thundered like a million bells tolling. This was too wonderful to believe—and too dangerous to sustain, for both of us.

We were not alone in the hospital and we both knew it. We could be shot for this. He withdrew from me reluctantly and I from him. I took a step back. We stared at each other.

"Tinker," he choked out. "Will you... if I make it...."

I could hear footsteps approaching. *Dear God, not yet.*

"Find me in London," I said hurriedly. "I'll wait for you."

"No, don't wait. I probably won't make it. Only...."

"*Live*," I said fiercely. "I'll wait."

AFTER they took Colin away, a nurse gave me a parcel from him. I didn't open it until I got back to my quarters. Inside were five notebooks filled with handwritten music. I was no expert on musical compositions, but we'd made music boxes in Albertus's shop, so I knew how to program notes. I stole some bits from the hangar and made a simple music box. I programmed it to play one of Colin's pieces. It was a melancholy and haunting little tune.

A composer. He was truly a composer. Oh, the terrible irony of war. A composer and a maker of miniatures, made to dance to the song of death.

XI.

London, 1857

IN THE spring of '55, we got news that English citizens had protested the war by throwing snowballs in Trafalgar Square. That made me laugh so hysterically that Major Barker threatened to have me thrown in the stockade for madness. By February of '56, the war was over.

Barker tried to convince me to work for him, to keep my commission. But he didn't try very hard. The golem had been a failure.

Pins misaligned by point-oh-two millimeters, engine cross-wired, runs briefly, then fails. Pretend frustration, pretend chagrin.

Barker hated me by the time I took my leave of him; he gave me nothing. I didn't care.

In London I had a safe-deposit box. Albertus had allowed me to make creations for myself in my spare time. *To start your own shop someday, Tinker*, he'd said. My miniatures took so little material, after all. He was a good master.

I rented a few rooms at the edge of Seven Dials and went to see some of Albertus's most faithful clients. The marvels bought me a year's rent and the material to make many more.

I was in business. I was alone.

I sought news of Captain Colin Davies, but the war department could tell me very little except that he was not on the lists of the dead. I made larks and gave them to dying children. I made inventory for my store. I worked until my eyes could focus no more and forced me to sleep.

In my dreams my devices lived on. Perhaps a dervish would be discovered in a barn in Russia tomorrow. Perhaps it would be activated and kill a young sheep farmer's son. How many did the army make? One thousand? Two thousand? Ten? I would never know.

I had only one reason to live, to prosper—a hope lodged deep in my mechanical heart.

IT WAS a Wednesday and the skies were drenching London in rain when the door to my shop opened. I looked up from my tools. He was in a rain cape, hood up. My pulse started to race even though I couldn't see his face.

Adrenaline released 500ng/L. Heart pump accelerates in response. Pulse 90, 100, 120. Fingers drop tools, clutch counter.

He lowered the hood.

"Colin," I said.

He'd aged ten years. His hair was longer and there was heavy stubble on his face. He had dark circles under his eyes and he'd lost weight. He was the most beautiful thing I'd ever seen.

I was frozen in place but he came to me, his gaze searching mine.

"Is this all right? Do you still want to see me?" He looked anxious, as if I would tell him no, as if I hadn't been dragging through the months in agony for him to appear. The shop door wasn't locked, the blinds were not drawn, but I didn't care. I wrapped my arms around him and pulled him tight.

"I waited," I said.

His body was solid and hard and wet against me. He ran his hands up my back and into my hair. He kissed my forehead and then he was kissing my mouth, hot and hungry.

I wanted him so fiercely I thought I would die. I'd been denied for so long, a lifetime of want. I had to get him out of those wet clothes and into a warm bed, with me.

I pulled away from him long enough to cross the room and lock the door. I turned the sign in the window to *Closed*.

"I live in the back," I said, not hiding the need on my face. "There's a bed."

He shrugged out of his rain cape and held up his hands. "These first," he said, his voice strained. "Can you make them normal? Remove the killing strength? I want to touch you, but I...."

I understood. I swallowed down the ruthless passion raging through my veins and took up my tools. My hands trembled.

Grip strength down to seven hundred pounds. Blow force five hundred. Set the maximum duration to something human; blood and bone tire even if steel does not.

"It's done," I said, closing the panels.

"Can you be sure?"

I pointed to a mannequin, a ballerina with a long steel throat and an egg-shaped head. He looked at me, silently asking permission.

"Try it," I urged.

He walked up to the mannequin, raised his right hand to her throat, and frowned in concentration. His fingers closed around the silver tube. He squeezed, then smiled. He tried harder. He threw back his head and laughed. I grinned at the sound.

He took two long strides and caught me up, spinning me around.

"Oh, Tinker. What I owe you. What I owe you!" He trembled with emotion.

"Shhh. In the back." I began kissing his neck, and he carried me into the back room.

As soon as the curtain closed, my lips were on his. We kissed until we were drunk with it. His breathing turned harsh and his caresses needy. The fire in my blood roared back hotter than before. He was still lifting me, my feet off the ground, but he finally put me down so he could undo my clothing. We fumbled with each other's collars and shirts. The air was cold against my skin as he bared my chest. I worried about him catching his death, wet as he was.

"Let me get the fire," I said. "You climb into bed."

I pulled away to light the tinder in the stove. I heard him undressing behind me, and a thick surge of lust threatened to make a quick end of things right then. The fire caught at last, despite my fumbling. Dreary daylight spilled in through the curtains over a small window. I felt terribly self-conscious as I dropped my trousers and smalls. I crossed my arms over my chest, held my breath, and turned. He was already in the bed, but he had the covers back, waiting for me, and I could see his bare chest, his arms, his muscular thighs, the thick, hard shaft of him, its foreskin fully retracted.

Scarred body, too thin, strongly aroused, male, beautiful.

I couldn't believe this moment had come, that I had a lover, that we had both survived the war, that Colin was really here. I went to him, slipped between the covers, and pulled them up to hide myself. I was so hard I throbbed like a metronome.

"I'm sorry I'm not more to look at," I said, even as my fingers, caring nothing for my modesty, stroked the heavy muscles of his chest.

"Tinker"—he laughed sadly—"you are sweet as an orchard peach. I thought so from the first moment I saw you."

I looked at him skeptically.

"Lovely and brilliant and brave. What you gave me. What you risked for me…." He took a deep, shaky breath.

"Hold me," I said, desperate. I could feel his naked skin next to mine, still cold from the rain. I pressed against him, needing more.

He took my lips with a groan and rolled on top of me. *God.* The weight of him pressing me down was the remedy to everything my body had ever craved. I put my arms around his ribs to cling all the tighter.

There was no more talking then, only his tongue stoking my mouth, his hands, the hands I had taught to caress, teasing my sides, my arms. His prick lay heavy against my hip.

His is two-point-five centimeters longer than mine, hard and hot with blood (a quarter pint, circulating), pulsing every third beat, bollocks tightening in preparation for release, male, my Colin, mine.

I had no finesse in me. I'd taught the hands to tease but at that moment I wanted him so violently I was incapable of subtlety. I slid my hands down to cup his arse, and I began to thrust against him. I was making embarrassing sounds in my throat, but it was like distant thunder for all I could control it or cared. He broke the kiss to pant my name and I latched on to his throat, his collarbone.

"Please," I begged over and over as I rutted against him. The indescribable pleasure in my prick and in every centimeter of my skin where he touched me made my eyes roll back in my head. *"Colin."*

I don't know what I was begging for, only that it never stop, that he never leave me. He grunted on top of me, thrusting. I fell over the edge, convulsing as my release emptied out. I felt him jerk, his seed mingling with mine.

"Tinker," he said, burying his face in my neck. A pained sound, deep and terrible, escaped him.

He rolled off me and covered his face. I found a cloth and cleaned us both. I lay back down and held him as he trembled. "Shhh. It's over now."

He shook his head. "I killed so many. Soldiers all, but still…."

"Shhh." I rubbed his arm, wishing I could take away his pain. When his breathing slowed, I got up and pulled on my trousers. I went into the shop and picked up one of my favorite automatons. I took it into the back and sat on the bed.

Wait and see. Do not hope too much. He may still leave.

"Look," I said with false cheer.

He did, rubbing his eyes to see more clearly. On my palm was a piano four inches long. A tiny man in a top hat sat at the keyboard. I wound the key. A melody began to play as the tiny man moved his hands and pressed keys. The tune was bittersweet.

"Mine?" he asked, surprised.

I nodded. "Didn't you see the sign over the shop?"

He blushed. "Yes, but I didn't want to presume."

"*Gray and Davies, Musical Wonders.* I put your songs in my automatons. If you don't like it, I can remove them. But I thought… if you *liked* the business and wanted to stay…."

He took my hands in his and squeezed. "You were with me in the night, Tinker, when I was alone in the cold and the dark. You were a caress on my cheek. It was only thinking that you might be here waiting for me, that we might be together in the end…."

"Me too," I whispered.

"But I never expected all this. I'm not worthy of you. Of your talent. Of your faith. But I'll try hard to be. I swear on my life."

In answer, I kissed him.

Two hearts broken. Two souls lost. The figures move together, holding each other up. An artificial heart, artificial hands, a love outside the lines. It is the imperfections that make something real.

Dance.

ELI EASTON has been at various times and under different names a minister's daughter, a computer programmer, a game designer, the author of paranormal mysteries, a fanfiction writer, an organic farmer, and a profound sleeper. She is now happily embarking on yet another incarnation, this time as an m/m romance author.

As an avid reader of such, she is tickled pink when an author manages to combine literary merit, vast stores of humor, melting hotness, and eye-dabbing sweetness into one story. She promises to strive to achieve most of that most of the time. She currently lives on a farm in Pennsylvania with her husband, three bulldogs, three cows, and six chickens. All of them (except for the husband) are female, hence explaining the naked men that have taken up residence in her latest fiction writing.

Her website is http://www.elieaston.com.

You can e-mail her at eli@elieaston.com.

THE GALATEA'S CAPTAIN

ANKA GRACE

THE frigid air of Alba, capital city of Camlaan, sends a phantom ache through Kamil Ramses's bad leg. Despite the chill, a light sheen of sweat begins to mist across his brow when he steps out of the horse-drawn carriage the Duchess of Althea had reserved for them.

Seeing his pinched expression, she hooks his right arm in her left and says, "Oh, Mr. Ramses, please do not tax yourself! I just *knew* we should have brought along your chair!"

He winces. Ever since his arrival in Camlaan, he'd been sequestered away in the Altheas' sprawling estate, stuck convalescing in the wooden wheelchair its master had commissioned on his behalf. The cane he now holds, made from ironwood and embellished with gold, is also a gift from the wealthy old couple, but he prefers it immensely. It allows him *some* autonomy, at least.

"Don't worry, Your Grace, I've become quite accustomed to this by now," he replies after a moment, smile stilted. If he could, if it would serve to allay her doubts, he would pat her hand.

Instead, he gazes out at the harbor ahead of them. The sea breeze tickles his nose, whipping his long, dark swath of hair around his narrow face in spite of the cord around it. No boats are visible on the water, hidden by the colossal bodies of anchored airships, comprised of various woods and metals, fantastical figureheads carved into their bows. Their colorful sails billow in the wind, blotting out the gray sky above.

Although he misses Siro, his homeland, rather intensely, Kamil admits to himself that Camlaan has many virtues, many incredible, beautiful sights. Perhaps when he recovers, he can pay proper homage to them. *If* he ever does.

"Shall we continue?" The duchess's hesitant voice disrupts his reverie.

He flashes her another smile, disarming this time. "Yes, I'm ready now."

She beams up at him through the netted veil of her hat. Elaborate silvering curls encase her round face, contrasting starkly with the black lace of her gown. Her small hand remains a chaste weight on his arm as she guides him into the heart of the harbor, humming all the while.

"What can you tell me about this Air Pirate Talos?" he inquires when she stops.

In truth, he'd rather the silence plagued by information they've already thrashed out than his pathetic labored breathing. He sends a mental prayer of thanks to Rama, patron god of Siro, for the wooden planks that make up the harbor. They're much kinder on his improving injury than the uneven cobblestones that constitute Alba's busy streets.

"Not very much, I'm afraid." The duchess taps a gloved finger to her chin. "Jerold met him while traveling for the queen, as he did you. You've no need to fear, however; Talos calls himself an adventurer now. Jerold assured me his pirating days are long over, and exaggerated in the stories, besides." Before Kamil can question why an "adventurer" requires so much privacy that he's unable to meet them at the Althea estate, she points to a spot over his shoulder. "Ah! And this, I believe, is our ship, Mr. Ramses."

"So it seems." Kamil shifts to observe the vessel they've halted in front of.

It's old and battle scarred, a long gash marring the otherwise beautiful face of the painted mermaid at its figurehead, its torn blue— almost black—sails dancing behind her like wings, but Kamil feels no surprise. After all, whatever else he may be, madman or immortal, this Talos is legendary. Up until recently, Kamil considered him a mere folkloric hero, but Jerold had relayed otherwise—had given him his hope back. Why shouldn't the ship suit the man?

A lowered bridge awaits them. With the duchess's aid, Kamil hobbles aboard. They meet a young boy on the main deck with hair as dark as Kamil's, but chopped jagged and short, goggles strapped on top.

Soot streaks his olive-toned cheeks and his unorthodox outfit: a black corset worn like a vest, brown woolen breeches, short gloves, and muddied riding boots.

The boy crosses his arms and says, "I'm Shui and this is the *Galatea*," in a distinctly feminine, rankled voice. "Captain told me to take you to him."

"Thank you... Miss Shui." This earns Kamil a dirty look. The duchess gapes at his side, scandalized into silence by Shui's appearance. The three of them begin their trek across the deck, Shui scouting ahead. It's evident she doesn't appreciate playing guide to them. Gritting his teeth into a courteous smile, Kamil asks, "Where has the rest of your crew gone, Miss?"

Shui shrugs a bony shoulder. "Some are belowdecks. Most went into town. It's been a while since we docked in port. Gotta get supplies, don't we?"

"Yes, I suppose you do." Kamil's hazel-eyed gaze flicks past her.

In spite of Shui's boorish demeanor, the *Galatea* appears to be a well-maintained craft. The wood below their feet gleams, freshly mopped but no longer moist. That adorning the decks, forecastle, and mainmast also seems sturdy, and new layers of indigo-blue paint, to match the sails, complete the airship's careworn yet preserved façade.

Kamil wonders if Captain Talos wanted to make a good impression on them, but he's diverted from the absurdity of the thought by all the weapons that suddenly surround them: sabers, rifles, revolvers, grenades, crossbows, and cannons, all wiped down and sparkling, at once gorgeous and terrifying.

Shui shoots him a sly glance over her shoulder. "You're looking a little green, mister." The arch of her eyebrow and the way she titles him are both condescending, her sneer, more so.

The duchess, at last regaining her bearings, pats Kamil on the arm. "It *is* called a gun deck, my dear, and the good captain has to protect his crew from legitimate pirates somehow, does he not?"

"Of course," says Kamil, but he cannot conceal a grimace.

It seems even she is better versed with weapons than he, but then, she's wife to the vice admiral of the royal navy, while he's a pacifist philosopher. Kamil feels cold sweat break out once more beneath the verdant frock coat he wore to meet Captain Talos. He wishes he could loosen the bow tie at his neck, but both of his hands remain otherwise occupied.

Although he grits his teeth against the throb it causes in his foot, relief washes through him when they climb down a ladder into the gallery, leaving the gun deck behind. A line of doors and windows pockmarks the walls on either side of them. Only a raised hatch, to enter the hold, ruins the smooth surface of the ground below Kamil's feet.

"The captain's quarters are through here." Shui gestures toward a door feeding into the stern, closest to the ladder. Kamil offers another silent thanks to Rama for the propinquity of the location as she knocks loudly. "I brought you those peacocks you asked for, Captain!"

"Peacocks?" huffs the duchess, quietly indignant, her painted lips pursed behind the veil.

Before Kamil can respond, they hear a booming voice shout, "Bring 'em in, Shui."

She wrenches the door open at once, and they see the profile of a man facing a table piled with strange gizmos and gadgets, a cloth draped over most. His long brown duster coat nearly brushes the floor behind him, slit so they can see black tweed breeches and leather boots within its undulating bulk. A darker brown bomber hat, common among aviators, sits on his head. When he turns, its earflaps and the hem of his coat swish like the wings and feathers of some great bird.

"*Y-you're* Air Pirate Talos?" Kamil blurts out, jaw dropping open.

The duchess blinks in surprise as well, and Shui sniggers into her palm. Captain Talos, meanwhile, frowns. Vivid strands of red hair brush over his forehead into huge blue eyes, bright as a cardinal's. Freckles dapple his pale cheeks and nose, but like Shui, much of his features are obscured by soot. One possible source of his griminess is the boiler exhaling steam beside a small bookshelf to his right.

His mouth crooks into a grin. "I prefer 'adventurer.'"

"But tales about Talos have been told for *at least* a century. I've read some myself," says Kamil, more to himself than the man. Everything he's heard of the elusive and illustrious Captain Talos, he now turns over in his mind, growing more and more bewildered. The Duchess of Althea had claimed her husband met the man over a decade ago and that they'd been trading supplies—primarily adamantine, the rare "living metal" Jerold's men could never find themselves—ever since. "*You* can't be more than a boy."

"*I* can't be more than a couple years younger than you." The captain crosses his arms, appraising Kamil and the duchess. "I suppose I understand your confusion, though. Truth is, it was my master who your vice admiral met—the previous Captain Talos, Shui's grandfather. It's less a family name than an earned title."

He juts his chin at Shui, and there must be some hidden signal in the motion, because she salutes and beats a retreat from the cabin. A few notes of whatever bawdy tune she's whistling carry back to Kamil's ears, a mockingly upbeat backdrop to the vestiges of tension in the air.

"Who are you, then?" he whispers, dread building like an attack in his pounding heart. He barely feels the duchess squeeze his arm or her apologetic assertion that she hadn't known what they'd encounter aboard the ship.

Captain Talos bows low at the waist, his smile slanting into a smirk. "I'm but a humble tinker, Mr. Ramses, but rest assured, more than enough for the services you require, so long as your purse's as pretty as your face."

"We can pay." The duchess's brown eyes shine in earnest.

Ever since his arrival in Alba, she and the vice admiral have treated Kamil with unparalleled hospitality, much in the manner parents would a long-estranged but dearly loved son, and a warm burst of affection gushes through Kamil's body now, a shield against the ice he unearths in Captain Talos's fair blue eyes.

"No!" He scowls at the crimson carpet decorating the cabin, plush beneath the heel of his boots, if blotted here and there by soot. "We were wrong to come here, Your Grace. Whoever this... *boy* is, he's not the man we seek, and I won't waste a single penny on this travesty he's fashioned. Let's go."

He begins directing her out of the room. Although her hoary brows furrow, she puts up no resistance. They're past the threshold of the door, almost to the ladder, when the captain's disparaging chuckle reaches Kamil's ears. He turns back to find the man leaning against the table, arms crossed.

"I see how it is," he says, upper lip curling into a sneer.

Kamil glances between him and the ladder, then inquires "And how is that?" against his better judgment.

Captain Talos shrugs. "Just that you're a stuck-up fop, like every other lord and lady in this land, too good for an urchin's piss even when you're on fire."

"I-I beg your pardon!" Kamil's cheeks grow hot. Beside him, the duchess inhales loudly, but the rage that sings through his veins deafens him to it. "I am *nothing* like you say, Captain. I came to Camlaan to *help* the Altheas and other reformers improve the quality of life for commoners, the way I helped Siro's king. I lost a *limb* to that cause, and you think me some sort of wastrel?"

Captain Talos simply arches a fiery eyebrow at his rant. "In my experience, Mr. Ramses, there are no *good* rich men, but some are smart. Are you?"

He extends his left arm to push up the rightmost sleeve of his coat, undershirt and all. For the first time, Kamil notices that only his right arm is encased in a kidskin glove that roughly reaches his elbow. Captain Talos brings its hand to his lips, teeth catching in the material around his middle finger. He tugs off the glove with a deft jerk of his head.

A gasp escapes Kamil at the sight. The glow of the gas lamps hanging along the walls alights across Captain Talos's revealed arm. It glints gold, solid in some areas, gears and spiraling mainsprings perceptible in others, a work of art observably hammered from the adamantine his crew has won renown for seeking out.

Kamil draws near enough to it to see the minutiae of the detail work: small, shiny nail plates shimmer on each finger, their distal edges and cuticles silver, knuckles and joints rising above them, leading to a slender wrist perfectly proportional to its flesh-and-blood counterpart. He doesn't dare touch it, afraid it'll fall apart.

"I can help you," says Captain Talos, more reserved now, "but only if you give me a chance to."

Kamil looks away from the clockwork limb, up into pale blue eyes, and finds himself unable to break contact. He hadn't realized they'd gotten so close—hadn't had the sense to, after the captain's revelation—but now he can see the gossamer red lashes that fringe each orb, protracted and plenty.

The duchess, whom he had released to examine the automaton, clears her throat. "We will pay, won't we, Mr. Ramses?"

"Yes," answers Kamil.

Her subsequent laugh trickles, watery but full of resolve. "I'll have your bags brought up, then."

Captain Talos finally breaks Kamil's stare to tell her, "Worry not, milady. I'll take good care of him. I'm an old hand at this." Here, he flexes his mechanical fingers and winks, earning another, gigglier laugh, despite mistitling her. "In but a fortnight, I'll have a nice new prosthetic for our lovely Mr. Ramses here, and you can ferry him off to a proper doctor to get it fitted, all right?"

"Yes, please don't fret over me," Kamil says, facing her. She crosses the distance between them and allows him to take her hand. "I'll be out of the hospital and back at your estate before the vice admiral returns."

Brown eyes glossy, she nods. "Jerold wouldn't have sent you to Captain Talos if he suspected for a second that you'd come to harm. Please don't tarry, dear. We can discuss your philosophies with Queen Blodwyn as soon as you are well."

Stroking his knuckles one last time, she relinquishes him, gifts Talos with an amiable smile, and exits the cabin. Soon after, Shui ushers the harried driver of her carriage to Kamil. The man leaves him his two small bags and ducks out, Shui loping behind him. For the first time, Kamil and the captain are completely alone.

Talos clears his throat. "Well, suppose I need to take a gander at that 'limb' of yours, eh? I'd wager it's a foot. You've been limping something awful since you got here." He makes a sweeping gesture toward the bed. "Take a seat, Mr. Ramses, and show me what we're dealing with."

Kamil frowns at him but does as directed with as much dignity as he can muster. He lowers himself onto the mattress and leans his cane against its frame before glowering down at his booted foot. When he glances up, Captain Talos nods encouragement. He sighs and bends to cup the arch of his heel in his palms.

Pain lances through his leg at once. Clenching his teeth, Kamil tugs hard, but the leather in his grasp feels slick as the scales of the lizards and snakes common in Siro's deserts, too slick to hold, and soon his eyes smart with humiliating tears. He stops and shuts them, breathing harshly.

It hurts. It hurts *so badly*. How could he have been naïve enough to, even for a second, trust it was getting better?

He hears footsteps, dull on the carpet, pad over to him, the swish of cloth, creaking leather, and then a surprisingly kindly "Here, let me."

When he opens his damp eyes, it's to the sight of Captain Talos kneeling between his legs, his hands a cradle for Kamil's boot. He doesn't immediately yank it off. Instead, his blue eyes travel to meet Kamil's, reassurance in their pastel depths. Their gazes remain locked as he finally eases it off, and inwardly, Kamil marvels at the gentleness his prosthetic arm is capable of.

The faint odor of rot soon pervades the room, cloyingly sweet, but Captain Talos doesn't react with disgust. Above his ankle, Kamil's foot seems fine. Below, a stump of flesh resides, puckered, shriveled, and atrophied beneath a fresh bandage spotted sparingly with blood. Kamil stares at it, expression impassive, dead to the gruesome sight. It had been worse, after all, before the foot was amputated: a veritable canvas of greens and yellows and purples, his toenails cracked and black. He should feel lucky that the doctors of Alba had at least managed to save his leg, once he left the accursed boat that brought him to their land, but a familiar bitterness begins to creep into his heart. It never would have happened if he had just remained in Siro.

"Hey, buck up." The captain's voice shatters his growing melancholy. "You'll survive this, milord," he says, tapping the metal of his index finger against the bony swell of Kamil's ankle. It makes a muffled, tinny sound but doesn't hurt at all. "If a ruffian like me can do it, so can you."

Kamil finds himself matching the man's teasing grin. "I suppose you, of anyone, *would* understand how I feel. But I am not, dear Captain, a lord."

"Ah, of course. My apologies." Talos's expression doesn't falter in the least. Quiet elapses as he inspects the injury. After a few minutes, he carefully releases Kamil's foot, rises, and dusts himself off.

"Well?" asks Kamil, still seated, picking at the hem of his frock coat with nervous fingers. He's a little unsure, in fact, how he'll get off the bed without making a fool of himself, but Captain Talos's smile bolsters his courage.

"Mr. Ramses, with my help," the man says, "I'm certain you'll be waltzing like a prince, sweeping all the pretty ladies off their feet, in no time at all."

Kamil laughs. "You should be careful before you promise such things. To be truthful, I was never very fortunate in either of those categories even in my prime."

"Oh?" The captain's eyes widen a fraction, a formidable feat considering they're already his most prominent feature. He chuckles. "Well, you get some rest, and I'll see what I can whip up."

"Rest?" Kamil repeats. "Here?" A pointed glance at his stump of a leg has him flushing. "Oh, you really don't have to desert your quarters on my account, Captain—"

"Who says I'm leaving?" asks Talos. This time, Kamil's eyes grow round, but the man's guffaws interrupt his indignant sputter. "I'm just pulling your leg. Your stuff's already nice and snug here, so you may as well cozy up too. Besides, I can do my tinkering just about anywhere."

"Oh." Kamil blushes brighter. "Um, thank you, Captain. Truly."

"Don't mention it." Talos picks up Kamil's boot and lopes toward the door but halts there for a second, squinting over his shoulder. "You look like the bookish sort. If you'd like, you can poke through my shelf. You'll certainly be here long enough to fall prey to boredom. Call if you need anything. I'll be back to get a plaster of your leg in the morning."

Before Kamil can do much more than nod, he stalks off. Kamil wilts onto the surface of the captain's bed. It smells of him, of oil and metal and smoke and something more distinct than that, something poignant and musky. Because the sheets are so soft, Kamil doesn't care that they'll wrinkle his clothes unrepentantly. He closes his eyes and allows the black oblivion of sleep to overtake him.

His dreams tick a clockwork lullaby.

OVER the course of the next week, Kamil and the crew of the *Galatea* fall into a semicomfortable routine. When he wakes each gloomy day, he doesn't bother changing out of the simple *thawb* he'd brought along from his homeland, similar enough to the nightdresses worn by Alban gentlemen to avoid issue or comment.

Although he wipes himself off frequently with a washcloth, he's convinced he's begun to smell quite ripe after the first few days, but no one comments on his rather pitiable state, and slowly, his wound resumes healing. Someone from the crew arrives every morning to escort him into the mess hall. Even having met Shui, he's surprised to find there are men *and* women aboard the *Galatea*, and that most aren't native to Camlaan. He even starts to befriend some. The captain, however, rarely joins them for meals.

"He's working like a dog on that fake foot of yours," Shui informs Kamil with a sneer when he finally works up the courage to ask after the man. "You'd best be grateful. I can barely get him to eat or sleep as is."

Kamil feels his ears burn. He has to remind himself that, appearance notwithstanding, Shui is a lady and essential to his own needs. "I *am* grateful, but it isn't as if he won't be paid handsomely for his services, Miss Shui. Please don't patronize me."

She just snorts and retreats to accomplish her duties as first mate, leaving Kamil in the care of the amicable, always mirthful medic, a man with umber-dark skin and a fluffy cloud of gray-black hair, from a kingdom neighboring Kamil's own—a kingdom, like his, of heat and foliage and life. They bond over this, reminiscing together in the captain's cabin as Ayzize applies poultices and fresh bandages to his foot, mitigating Kamil's discomfort with relaxed talk.

"I left Siro but a few months ago," Kamil explains, "but I miss it more every passing day."

Tying the excess strips of Kamil's bandage into a neat little bow, Ayzize releases his foot so he can right himself, then offers him a sympathetic smile. "The illness mustn't help." His accent lilts, almost nonexistent, his usage of Camlaan's tongue elegant and musical, but it merely serves to remind Kamil how narcissistic he must sound.

"I apologize for my selfishness, Ayzize," he says, his smile self-deprecating. "Here I am, blathering on about my paltry woes, when you must have been away from Emwòd for many years yourself, much longer than I."

"Please, Kamil, don't trouble yourself." Ayzize beams at him. His eyes are warm and silvery, crinkled beyond just the corners, a sign of his advancing age. He uses Kamil's name like a familiar, a *friend*, and that above anything puts Kamil at ease. For so long, he's been Mr. Ramses, when at home he was only Kamil. It's nice to have that again. "I've had many an adventure aboard the *Galatea*, and we're always traveling, so I visit my motherland more than sufficiently. The captain and crew, however... *they* are my family."

Kamil ponders this, frowning. He has six sisters himself, and his mother, at least, is yet alive, clucking worriedly after his affairs as often as she's able to despite the distance between them, keeping up with him via dozens upon dozens of letters, which he receives and sends even aboard the *Galatea*, thanks to the crew's frequent supply runs into town. Although he loves this about her and longs for her hearth, he sees the serenity and contentment in Ayzize's expression and doesn't apologize anymore, cognizant that it will go unaccepted.

"Captain Talos," he says instead. "Why doesn't he ever join us in the mess hall? He visits me before bed often enough, to take measurements and ask questions of me, but I.... Is he really so occupied, or has he been avoiding my company?"

Ayzize rumbles a melodic laugh and rises, smoothing out the velvety material of his long two-piece robe, more colorful than Kamil's *thawb*. "I assure you, I've known Rory many years, since he was but a boy, but never have I seen him avoid an issue, even when it may have been wisest. Don't let him vex you." He inclines his head at Kamil and, still chortling, ambles out of the room.

Kamil gawks after him, mind jumbled with thoughts. *Rory*. It suits the captain, a slip of a name, rolling off the tongue, a herald to glee and grins like his upbeat personality. "Rory.... It's a nice name," he decides and promptly feels very chagrined.

In an attempt to distract himself, he cracks opens the book he'd left on the bed, caressing its careworn pages and imagining Captain Talos doing the same. It's a book of fairy tales. Most of the books on the shelf are, save some on the topics of aeronautics and automatons. Generally, he finds them all fascinating, an insight into Talos's guarded mind and interests, but now, the words smudge together, shirking his focus.

Against his better judgment, he sets it aside, laces up his boots, and makes to stand, bracing against the carpeted ground with his cane. Once in the hall, he realizes he doesn't know where the captain has relocated to. "Captain Talos," he calls out, propping his shoulder against the wall closest to the cabin to take some of the weight off his recovering foot. "Are you there, Captain?"

A barrage of thumps reverberates below before the hatch a few feet from him, the entrance to the hold, pops up. Talos pokes his head out, sans his favored bomber hat for once, and grumbles, "What do you want?" Wisps of smoke smolder around him.

"Oh, er...." Kamil gawks at the man. He looks paler than Kamil's ever seen him in what insubstantial sunlight streaks through proximate portholes, the bluish bruises ringing his eyes and his slightly too-long red hair providing palpable foil for his sickly pallor. "I came to check your progress" is the excuse Kamil ultimately selects, and he feels it's an appropriate one since he hasn't really been privy to what the captain does with his prosthetic in private, "but now I can't help wondering, which of us is truthfully ill? You look horrid, Captain."

An owlish blink greets his statement. It soon morphs into a rakish smirk. "Are you concerned about me, Mr. Ramses? How quaint."

"No," retorts Kamil, quick and curt. "I simply question your ability to provide what I'm paying you for, if you're liable to fall asleep at any given moment."

He regrets his scathing riposte when the man flinches, but the countenance, like the rest of the captain's most vulnerable expressions, soon transforms into a mischievous grin. "Come down here, if you can. I've got something brilliant to show you." He ducks back into the hold.

Kamil doesn't move at once. He wonders if being forced to climb down yet another ladder—something he hasn't had recourse to do, luckily, since his first day on the airship—is punishment for his previous cheekiness. He barely knows the man, after all, so what can he really discern about his capacity for cruelness? Kamil sighs, grits his teeth, and commences his excruciating journey, too prideful to yield.

Halfway down the four-rung ladder, he feels hands at his hips, which aid him along the remainder of the route, and he's glad for a chance to compose himself before he turns to face Captain Talos. He doesn't wear his solitary glove anymore. The adamantine surface of his mechanical arm glimmers despite the dimness, crossed with the other in front of his chest.

Something flits between them and away, so swift that Kamil twists instinctively to get a glimpse of it: a strange birdlike creature, spiky feathers and beak agleam, chirping high and singsong. It darts behind one of several boilers and vanishes from view, but other fantastical sights remain: model boats in bottles; shelves stocked with nearly as many books as the Ramses' home library; worktables like the one in the captain's cabin piled with clockwork contraptions, from tiny animals to timepieces, some asleep, many in motion.

"Did you…." Mouth an O of astonishment, Kamil cases the room. "Are *all* of these yours?"

Captain Talos scratches his head at Kamil's display of awe but nods. "Like I said, I'm a tinker, and damn good, in my humble opinion."

"Not to mention modest," says Kamil, his tone dry. He's smiling, though, and the captain beams in reply. A toy mouse scurries past them, back gray as its breathing brethren, but steely and without fur. It chases the bird till it once again abandons its sanctuary behind the boilers, and the red glow of burning coals chases their clever little bodies out of sight. Kamil regards the mechanical creatures and their inventor. "Although I suppose you have no need to be. Your work is… breathtaking. The best I've ever seen. You must be something of a virtuoso, Captain."

"Awww, shucks." Talos's freckled cheeks blush pink, a pleased smile appending to the characteristically sardonic set of his mouth. "Thank you, Mr. Ramses. I didn't figure you for the complimenting type, to be honest."

"I believe we've misjudged one another," Kamil says. He's relieved by the levelness of his voice, and furthermore, glad his own swarthy complexion doesn't allow for such a vibrant, visible reaction. It would only do him a disservice in the courts of politicians and queens and, of course, his own king. But on Captain Talos, who cuts such a daunting figure, it's oddly endearing. He clears his throat. "Yes, you're rather talented. You've been as privileged with my commission, I hope?"

"Course I have." Talos wanders over to a table at the very end of the hold and picks up the object at its center. It's small, but larger than the bird or mouse, and a darker burnished gold than his arm, silver coils punching out. "What do you think?"

Kamil stares, unable to speak, breath caught in his throat. Talos smiles, not unkindly, and tips the prosthetic foot closer. Like his arm, the detail work is exquisite: the delicate arch of the Achilles tendon, the swell of the sole, the near-luminous toenails. Most of it runs opaque, the rest vaguely transparent.

Tears smart Kamil's eyes. "It's beautiful. Thank you *so much* for expending such effort on my behalf."

"Well, uh, you're gonna pay me for it," answers Talos, faint discomfort tainting the cocky tilt of his smirk, "so I reckon it's a fair trade."

"I'm still grateful," Kamil tells him sincerely. Rather than admit that such a masterpiece merits any price, he places a hand on the second rung of the hold's ladder. "I should go and allow you to finish your work in peace. But do remember to rest and dine, Captain, or you may force me to pay you another visit. Miss Shui, Ayzize, and I are very concerned."

"Wait!" A call halts him midascension. He turns to find Talos looking as surprised as he feels, before he replaces his mask of disaffection and shrugs. "If you'd like, Mr. Ramses, you can pore over the books shelved down here as well. They're older than I am, from many a distant land, and perhaps less... whimsical than my personal collection."

A shred of his preceding discomfort seems to return, but Kamil proffers him an understanding smile. "Thank you, Captain. I shall take you up on that offer, I think, but to doubt your taste in books would be to grievously insult my own, so please refrain from doing so in the future."

"W-was that a joke?" asks the captain after an instant of startled silence. When Kamil's smile doesn't flicker, he bellows a laugh in his oddly deep way. "Well, you may have luck with the ladies yet, even if you never learn to waltz. They're sure to love a man with a keen sense of humor, handsome even in his bedclothes, who's willing to lose a limb for the causes he deems worthy."

Kamil offers him a deadpan look. "Please desist from mocking me and return to your work, Captain, or I will have Miss Shui come to wrangle you."

"As if she would," Talos says but doesn't appear convinced by his own vehemence. He grins. "Good day, then, Mr. Ramses."

"Good day, Captain," replies Kamil, facing the ladder to hide his smile.

HE DROPS in on the captain regularly after that, and more astonishingly, the man deigns to visit him.

It isn't common by any definition. Talos has a surprising amount of work ethic for either a pirate or an adventurer, but Kamil comprehends why. They're on a deadline, and while the power is in his hands to extend it at will, as much as he finds the captain's company unexpectedly enjoyable, it doesn't stave the pervasive feeling of loss he's had since his foot was amputated. He desires his personal autonomy more than anything.

And yet, a telltale smile tugs at his lips when Captain Talos swaggers into his temporary quarters one night, two glasses in one hand and a bottle held against a stack of cards in the other. His balance is impressive, but then, he has such adroit fingers.

"Wanna spread the broads?"

Kamil nods and accepts one of the glasses. It radiates heat and an herbal smell, its liquid contents a murky white. "What is this?"

"Rice wine from Shui's grandfather's storage." Talos takes a sip of it and smacks his lips. "Someone has to drink it, don't they? Old man's been dead awhile now and Shui's more a beer girl."

Kamil takes a sip as well. An explosion of scorching sweetness ruptures across his taste buds. He relishes in the taste as they kick off their game. They play and drink for almost an hour in easy quietude. Only after the bottle is half-finished does Kamil say, "He must have held you in high regard, to make you his successor."

"I suppose you could say that." Talos doesn't look away from the cards as he speaks. "In a way, he was like a grandfather to me too. I was pretty young when I joined his crew."

"Oh?" Kamil leans forward without meaning to, till he hits the table the captain had dragged between them with an embarrassing, overeager "Oomph."

A smirk meets his unsubtle efforts. "Curious, aren't we? Makes sense for you scholarly gents. But yeah, he picked me up off the streets of a woebegone city like Alba. I was apprenticing in a shop making automatons for rich patrons, and even then, I'd wager myself better at it than the maestro's son. It's probably why he hated me so much, but Captain was impressed with me from the get-go. You should have seen him, how spitting mad he was at the maestro, when between one of his visits and the other, I lost my arm. Stole me back to his ship right then and there. Raised me like his own and taught me his craft. No one ever beat me just for fun after that." The open dismay on Kamil's face must unnerve him, because he stops and shrugs. "Don't look so down, Mr. Ramses. It's the way of the world to step on those beneath you, and orphaned strays scrape the bottom of the barrel, but me? I'm king of the skies now, thanks to him, and how many of the men who hurt me can say that?"

"I hope none at all," answers Kamil with a fierceness that startles him as much as the captain, who blinks at him. Kamil clears his throat and inspects his cards. A painted queen regards him, regal and lovely, and seeing her, he's more eager to meet Queen Blodwyn than ever. When he does, he can change things, so Captain Talos will feel as safe atop the earth as he does amid the clouds. "You may call me Kamil, you know," he says, keeping his eyes trained on hers.

A minute of silence ticks by. Kamil hopes dearly, sorely, that the captain will smile, like sunlight dispersing a storm, and permit him to call him *Rory*, at last; but no, the man's eventual retort is atypically reserved. "Perhaps I may, but I shouldn't. I won't." He tosses down a card that trumps Kamil's and wins a trick, but defeat isn't the origin of Kamil's mortified blush. The rest of their game slips away sans conversation. At its end, Talos says, "I've finished your automaton."

"So early?" Three days of the fortnight deadline remain.

"Yes." The captain nods, earflaps bobbing. "I've already sent ahead a message to your hostess. You won't be in my uncultured company much longer."

"I don't think your company uncultured at all," Kamil says, "but thank you."

Captain Talos nods again. He exits with a bow that, for once, doesn't feel mocking, his "Good night" polite.

TWO mornings hence, a carriage arrives to whisk Kamil off to the hospital. He expects Talos—*Rory*, his traitorous mind now often supplies in a wistful sort of way that, frankly, nettles him to reflect on—not to show his face, but sees him in the midst of a disgruntled Shui, a misty-eyed Ayzize, and others of the crew whom he'd managed to befriend during his short sojourn in their company.

Gaping, he watches Talos break away from the meager contingent, looking daisy fresh and clean for once, his vibrant red hair wet and curling beneath his hat, a bag, presumably to hold Kamil's commission, slung over one thin shoulder. He smiles at Kamil and motions toward the bridge, before which the Duchess of Althea's hired driver stands, looking somewhat uncomfortable. His carriage is visible far below on the cobblestone streets hugging the wharf.

"May I escort you, Mr. Ramses?" the captain inquires. Without thinking, Kamil snaps an agreement. Talos's overly pleasant demeanor doesn't slip in the slightest as he says, "Thank you."

They follow the driver beyond the dock. Although faded pain ruins Kamil's first real breath of fresh air in two weeks, he refuses the captain's aid. In any case, the throb of his leg isn't quite as agonizing as it had been when he first arrived aboard the *Galatea*. He forgets the pain entirely after entering the carriage, whereupon he catches sight of the duchess for the first time in as many days, and they clasp hands companionably, looking each other up and down, she in another black gown, he in his most comfortable coat, hair braided down his back, below a top hat so the perpetual breeze won't upend it.

"You're looking so energetic, my dear," she exclaims. "It does me well to see such color in your cheeks!"

His face aches with the force of his smile. "I feel rejuvenated simply by virtue of having seen you, Your Grace."

Captain Talos climbs, unnoticed, after them. From his seat beside Kamil, he frowns at the two of them, eyelids hooded and brow furrowed, before a leer overtakes his chill-reddened lips. "If I didn't know any better, I might think this to be a lovers' reunion, but you make for an odd pair."

"C-Captain!" Kamil sputters, inwardly fuming.

But the duchess merely laughs. Her gaze, sharp and dark, latches on to Talos's arctic blue eyes. "It seems you, too, have grown attached to our lovely Mr. Ramses, Captain, if you're willing to see this through."

Talos reddens and looks away. "Yes, well… don't mind me. I'm just here to see what Alba's hospitals are looking like these days. Ayzize would string me up by my laces if I missed such a golden opportunity."

For the rest of the trip, he focuses on the view rolling past their windows. Kamil has to admit it's beautiful, this scenery. The sky above, rather than an abysmal gray, has lightened to a shade of blue suggestive of the captain's eyes, clear as crystal, flecked here and there with grays and greens and the rare purples. The sun sparkles across grass and stone and homes, a coin-bright spotlight on even the beggars who wander the streets. And yet, while participating in animated conversation with the duchess, Kamil finds himself staring at Talos through his peripheral vision. Always, he drags his gaze away using main force. Always, it's to find the duchess watching him, inquisitiveness and amusement warring in her round, vivacious face.

It's a relief to reach the hospital, a drab Romanesque mansion evocative of a castle, topped with pointed towers that stab into the air like arrowheads. When he and the duchess step out of the carriage to meet the young woman awaiting them at the entrance, dressed in the white-capped garb of a nurse, Kamil expects Captain Talos to stay behind. For a few seconds he does linger but eventually chooses to trail them in, appearing at once curious and detached. He remains reticent as the nurse explains the procedure of the operation, her voice a low and serious bass uncommon to most women.

"The wound should, by now, be well enough for surgery. You've stopped bleeding, haven't you? Although adamantine permits more independence than generic prosthetics post-attachment, the method of application can be relatively painful, and the risk of working with such an organic metal is, like a heart or a kidney, that it may ultimately reject you."

"Can it do that, truly?" inquires Kamil on a rush of nervous breath. "I-I know it will hurt, and I don't care, but if it fails after all this...."

Talos reaches out and catches the hand atop his cane. He gives it a single squeeze before his arm returns limply to his side. His fingers are cool and metallic, solidly supportive, for those transient few seconds. "It won't fail. *You* won't fail. You're not a delicate flower like most rich men, Mr. Ramses. You're *strong*."

He sounds completely sure of himself—of *Kamil*—and Kamil envies him that confidence. With less conviction, he says, "Well, the captain's work is masterful. Hopefully that will help my cause."

"I'm certain it will," the Duchess of Althea chimes in.

She, opposing Talos, doesn't release the hand she holds. Kamil thinks of the contrast between her skin and Talos's, her fire to his ice, and offers her a feeble smile. Sensing the unspoken request in it, she picks up his conversation with the nurse and probes for feedback in his place until the doctor, a harried older man, scurries into the vestibule, a twisted handkerchief in his grasp.

"The room you requested is prepared, Your Grace," he says, sparing Kamil a brief glance. "We are equipped to begin."

"Yes, of course, Dr. Addams. Come along, dear."

They head toward the hall leading out of the lightly furnished antechamber. Kamil waits to hear the tattoo of Talos's boots and, upon doing so, lets the muscles in his shoulders and back loosen minutely. He knows the captain won't stay long, and he knows he shouldn't expect him to. They will likely never see each other again after this day, and furthermore, he was merely a client to Talos, like those before his days on the ship whom he'd spoken of resentfully, but if only in his heart, Kamil admits he wants Talos by his side. His mouth puckers firmly shut, however, because he refuses to request such kindnesses of Talos, to seem even weaker in the eyes of so contradictory a man.

His resolve almost succeeds. They reach the room reserved for him, small but homey, with large windows decked in frilly, open curtains he suspects the duchess had a hand in picking. Though the bed at its heart does little to impress, he realizes he wouldn't have wanted it to be much larger, regardless, because he's grown so intimate with Talos's diminutive cot. If he could spend a fortnight in that, he can survive the remainder of his recovery, postsurgery, in this. There are no bookshelves like Talos's, though, and Kamil's throat clenches at the lack of them. He makes a silent promise to beg some off the Altheas. Perhaps they'll find a few *not* about weapons and war. Perhaps they'll even find some fairy tales....

"Please, Mr. Ramses, be seated." Dr. Addams addresses him for the first time, dissolving his stupor. He does as the man bids, and the new position leaves him facing the others from the bed. Near his hand lies a dressing gown, ostensibly for him to change into, but the doctor hasn't stopped speaking. "We will begin the procedure without delay, of course. Nurse Hildegard discussed some of it with you, yes? You will be anesthetized with ether now, and by the time you stir, the limb will be attached. It may take a week, in all, to see if it works as it should, at which point you will begin rehabilitation at the Altheas' estate. Isn't that so, Your Grace?"

"Yes." The duchess presents Kamil a wavering smile and says, solely for his benefit, "You will be fine, dear. It's as Captain Talos said: you are strong."

"Thank you."

She disappears then, with Talos and the others at her heels, to afford him some privacy while he changes. Only Nurse Hildegard reenters once he's finished, a vial in hand. She removes its stopper, brings it to his nose, and says, "Take a deep breath, Mr. Ramses. As deep as you can."

The incisive smell of ether wafts into his nostrils, stringent and chemical, yet at the same time somewhat saccharine. His ears pulse for a moment, and then it feels as if a balloon is expanding in his head, filling it up with air. His mouth dries, a bitter, cottony taste filling it. He hears his own voice, a faraway entity that pleads with Hildegard to see if the captain has left, and to call him in if he hasn't, but at this point, Kamil's happy and high, uncaring of his earlier pledge not to seem hungry for the man's attention.

When Talos walks in, a blur of white and red with the barest hint of blue, Kamil imagines some fondness in his eyes, even as an exasperated sigh meets his ears. Talos touches his hand and, unlike earlier, doesn't release it. "You really are annoying, you know that, Kamil?"

It's the first time he's ever used Kamil's given name, and Kamil means to smile, but Morpheus refuses to spare him another second, another witty utterance, so he shuts his eyes and succumbs to the effects of the ether, retort lost on the tip of his heavy tongue.

His dreams glint and glimmer, sun too red, sky too blue, pain a distant haze, Talos's hand growing more temperate by virtue of his unyielding, human grasp.

EVERYTHING aches.

Blinding lights hit Kamil's twitching eyelids, adding to the thrum in his temples and the fever that sears through his veins. His body would feel miles away, he suspects, if not for the prickly tingling of his arm or the steady throb beneath his knee. Kamil takes a deep breath and pushes stifling blankets off his torso.

He has to grind his teeth to keep from emitting more than a groan at the motion, but soldiers through his discomfort to sit up as far as he can. That's when he notices the bird on his otherwise bare bedside table. It's a beautiful blood-red thing, utterly inert though no cage keeps it in place, and its immobility is why he doesn't immediately recognize it.

Down in the hold, with Captain Talos, it had been flying, wings constantly spread, metallic beak poised to sing.

Propped against the headboard of his tiny hospital bed, he reaches out toward the bird. Its wings begin to flutter, ever so slowly, at his subdued touch. He gasps at the sight, and the cool of it against the pad of his fingertip, evidently metal, its tiny head, crowned in spiky vermillion feathers, revolving to watch him.

"Rory," he whispers, because who else could create so charming a thing? Just then, there's a knock at the door. Hoping it will be the captain, he says, "Come in!"

Instead, it's Nurse Hildegard. She beams. "Ah, you're awake at last! It's been nearly two days." He returns her smile awkwardly, then glances back at the bird, which looks between them with its bright, beady black eyes. Noticing the subject of his interest, she continues, "Pretty, isn't it? Your captain friend left it for you. A parting gift, he said."

"Parting?" Dread displaces the last bits of fogginess from Kamil's head.

Nurse Hildegard scrutinizes his ashen face with some concern but nods. "Yes, Mr. Ramses, he and his crew have left Alba, from what I've heard. Her Grace tried to convince him to stay for a while longer—for your sake, I gather—but he claimed imperative business to attend to elsewhere. Evidently, they disposed of their assorted adamantine and need to procure more at once, and Alba, as you now, isn't rich in such resources."

"I see." Kamil trains his eyes on the bows of his legs below what remains of the blanket. He doesn't want to look at Hildegard or the bird, doesn't want to mull over her words, nor the possibility of the captain's departure, but…. "I was naïve to expect anything else, wasn't I?" A bitter, self-deprecating smile shapes his mouth.

Nurse Hildegard doesn't immediately speak. He presumes she's pondering ways to cheer him up, and observes the exact moment she gives up on the prospect, her shoulders in their white ruffled apron strings drooping, her budding smile wary. "Would you like to see your foot now? It's rather more useful than a toy bird, I think."

Her words are a slap to the face, allowing him to forget, if only momentarily, all his many woes. "Oh yes! *Yes*, I very much would."

Her smile becomes more genuine at his obvious enthusiasm. She dashes to his bedside and, with nimble fingers, tidily strips off his blanket, leaving it bunched at the foot of his bed, under his feet. He has to bend forward to follow the brown line of his legs past his dressing gown's hem, but the dazzling flash of his automaton catches and holds his gaze with ease. He isn't the only one, he soon learns when the bird takes wing to land on his ankle, just prior to his prosthetic foot.

In many ways, it resembles Talos's prosthetic arm: silver and gold and pellucid gem. There's a distinct lack of the latter, nonetheless, so the illusion of skin seems more concrete than it had with the captain. And yet, were they together, he and Kamil would be a matching set. But the chances of them ever getting together again are nil, so Kamil comforts himself with the fact that Jerold arranged for them to meet at all. He wouldn't have this opportunity otherwise.

"Lovely, isn't it?" asks Hildegard. This time, he hums in acquiescence. She extends her gloved hands to him. "Shall we see how it holds up?"

"Let's." Kamil slips his naked fingers around the cloth of hers.

It still feels strange, he thinks distractedly. In Siro, while women cover up in their sweeping saris and petticoats, hair hidden by scarves, they pay so little mind to hands, even garnishing them in bangles and henna and rings. Nurse Hildegard's are comparatively plain but strong. They hold him steady as he slips off his bedsheets and fights for balance, legs nearly giving away beneath him at the tenderness of his fresh wound. He scares off the bird with their tremors. His foot holds, however, and while it's faint, the chill of the marble floor seeps into the sole—both soles—and all pain is lost to the sting in his eyes. Although he laughs, airy and anxious, tears track down his cheeks.

"Should I fetch Dr. Addams?" asks Nurse Hildegard, alarmed by the display. Another difference on the subject of Camlaan: that its men prize stoicism, abandoning sentiment to women, in a way the men of Siro do not. Perhaps Talos's motherland was the same, Kamil thinks, remembering his unwillingness to show weakness.

He shakes his head to clear it, his long hair a tangled curtain from the days he's spent unconscious. The bird comes to rest on his shoulder. "No, no, I'm fine. Absolutely fine." And for the first time in months, in spite of his wrinkled gown and snarled hair, in spite of whatever toil lurks on the horizon, he is.

"I should update him, in any case," Hildegard says. "The doctor will want to check up on you, and Her Grace wouldn't be pleased if we didn't send word to her posthaste. She left not long ago, in fact, to freshen up. She's been very apprehensive."

Kamil nods and allows her to help him seat himself on the bed once more. He watches her go, thinking of the duchess. He'll be happy for her company, himself. The thought of her sitting at his bedside, waiting for him to regain consciousness, fills him with pleasant, bubbly warmth, like a hot bath after a day of labor. Besides, he expects she'd like to confer on his rehabilitation and, the floor yet glacial below his wriggling toes, he knows they both desire for it to happen as smoothly as possible.

The next week passes in a rush of probing doctors, nurses, vague sensitivity, an energetic little avian attendant, and the Duchess of Althea's maternal hovering. He writes letters to his mother and sisters, as always, and spends a Herculean amount of time asleep, recuperating lost strength. Each day, he walks farther and farther on his feet, feeling like a newborn fawn, until he's scoured every inch of his small room and has begun taking short treks in the halls of the hospital, where he visits fellow patients.

Finally, a carriage arrives to convey him to the Altheas', and his grueling rehabilitation commences. If nothing else, the exertion makes it easier to forget a certain red-haired, blue-eyed captain, though he permits the bird, a creature he'd been tempted to call Rory but had chosen to name Aurae instead, to take command of his chamber as it pleases. In spite of its love of exploration, it rewards him by never flying too far, always remaining a call away.

Months roll by. The Duke of Althea, vice admiral of the queen's navy, comes home. Kamil hasn't seen him since the preliminary days of his illness, when he was bedridden and delirious at the Althea estate, the duke and his wife guiltily checking in on him like fretful parents. Compared to the duchess, the vice admiral is a solemn, remote man, but Kamil met him first in Siro, and Jerold has done so much to make up for what has happened to him since that before long, they are at ease in one another's presence once again, conspiratorially discussing their imminent meeting with the queen.

That day, too, comes and goes. It isn't until an additional two months afterward that Kamil and the duke exit the Houses of Parliament, drive past streets in less of a state of squalor, and discover an unexpected guest at tea with the duchess, awaiting their homecoming. Although the man has his back exposed to Kamil, his red hair, bare of its hat and curling at the nape, plainly divulges his identity.

He turns to bequeath Kamil his familiar impish grin as the duchess says, "Isn't this a wonderful surprise?"

Kamil snaps his jaw shut but manages a nod of concurrence. "W-what are you doing here, Captain?"

"Well, don't look so eager to see me," answers Talos, arching a fiery brow. He inclines his head at the vice admiral, who recovers his decorum enough to hide his puzzlement at the stranger's presence and return the gesture.

"Let's give them some privacy, Jerold," his wife says, coming forward to take his arm and steer him out.

Talos heaves himself out of his chair with a dramatic sigh of relief. "Thank goodness. Shui's more a tea gal than me. I'd have waited under a tree for your carriage, but either your duchess has got the vision of a hawk, or I'm less impressive a hunter than I thought."

"Is that what you are?" asks Kamil. "A hunter? Does that make me your prey?"

While he must, at last, be snapping out of his daze, he still feels far away from this moment, unsure whether it's reality or a dream. Since their parting, the latter has undoubtedly transpired more than often, so enmeshed with even his waking thoughts that it's almost a fairy tale in its own right. He'd just never dared to hope it would ever earn a happily ever after. It may not, even now.

The captain shrugs. "Not really. Although it's quite rude to make fun of a man's analogies when he's not half as educated as you."

"But no less intelligent!" Kamil's fervor brings a blush to Talos's fair face, remindful of the red feathers on his mechanical bird. Abrupt anger assaults Kamil at the sight. He compresses his fists and, more caustically than before, demands, "What are you doing here? Don't play me for a fool, Talos."

"I wouldn't do that," Talos says. All traces of his playful smile have vanished. He glances toward a window, as he did in the carriage when the duchess teased him about caring too much. The sight only invites more ire from Kamil, but Talos deprives him of the opportunity to translate it into yelling. "A little birdie told me you were heading back to Siro soon. I've never been there myself, but I heard tell it's beautiful."

His gaze roams to meet Kamil's, a wistful urgency in its oceanic depths, though his tone retains its swaggering quality. "I was thinking, since you're likely sick of the sea after your last trip, you might, with me, take to the skies?"

"Captain…?"

"Free of charge, of course," Talos adds hurriedly. "And, uh, you needn't call me that, really. You said once, aboard the ship…. Well, you can do as you please."

"What would *you* like me to do?" Kamil inquires. "To accompany you? To call you Rory?"

Talos's mouth twists to one side. He looks very unsure of himself, very helpless and lost and young, but while Kamil wants to spare him that, he also wishes him to be honest, to not mask any and all of his weaknesses from him, if only the once. At length, Talos says but a word: "*Yes.*"

And then Kamil's fingers are in his red hair, palm framing his freckled cheek, their lips a lattice of soft, amorous flesh. Kamil can't remember who instigated the first move but can't bring himself to care. Using his free hand, he cages Talos's metal fingers in his own, and all the while murmurs a mantra of, "Yes, Rory, yes, yes, yes, beautiful Rory."

"Kamil," Talos says between kisses that leave them breathless, "I-I want to stay with you, if that's okay? For as long as you'll have me. The ship's meant to be Shui's, anyway, and even if she doesn't think she's ready, she'll be a better captain than me. I've been telling her so forever. When she's finally settled, maybe I can set up shop in Siro, sell some of my trinkets?"

Kamil hears a throat clearing. They break apart, panting and wild-eyed, to the Duchess of Althea surveying them, the set of her face unreadable, her eyes inscrutably dark, her powdered features indistinctly red. She resembles, in this moment, the hawk they had joked about, and Kamil knows he doesn't solitarily feel like a field mouse.

"My lady," he starts to say, just as she breaks out into a beaming smile.

"Shall I presume Captain Talos is staying the night, then?"

Kamil and Talos—*Rory*—exchange a fleeting look. Kamil clears his throat and takes Rory's hand. "Yes, my lady, and... thank you. For everything you've done for me."

She waves away his gratitude with an effortless flick of her wrist. When she retreats, still in obvious good spirits, they pick up where they left off: whispering about their future together, leaning so close that a single motion, a single tilt forward, can coax them to kiss again if they desire it.

They meet each other halfway.

ANKA GRACE has been making up stories for as long as she can remember. In high school, she began putting them down on paper, regaling her friends and family with them, and she's never looked back. She knows she made the right decision by majoring in literature and creative writing in college, because reading and writing are her two true loves. Tea and coffee are a fair third and fourth.

Anka's personal mission is to create diverse casts of characters wherever possible. Growing up, she felt estranged from the characters in even her most favorite books, because so few were like her. She tries to do her part now so that her readers won't feel the same way. In addition to diversity, Anka loves all things fantastical—dragons, fairies, jinn, kitsune—so expect to see those and other mythical creatures popping up in her works.

Anka is available on Twitter (https://twitter.com/gracefullyanka) and Tumblr (http://gracefullyanka.tumblr.com) to answer readers' questions and rock out. She lives in New Jersey with her close-knit family.

SCREWS

R.D. HERO

"YOU'RE doing me quite the favor, Bellhouse."

Julius Barnes trailed several feet behind his father, gaze to the ground, barely paying attention to the conversation taking place ahead of him. Pleasantries had already been exchanged, Julius had already proved he could string two words together, so his responsibility in this endeavor had already been fulfilled.

"Think nothing of it, Amos," John Bellhouse said, his voice magnanimous, his glossy shoes tapping on the floor.

Julius tuned them out, gaze drawn up when he could just feel them nearing the end of the hallway. He heard clanking and yelling and deep laughter, and just for a moment felt a little tremor of excitement before the usual dull apathy washed over him again. "We'll stop by to the office. You can leave the boy out on the bench," Bellhouse was saying, Amos nodding along, worrying a bowler hat in his hands, before shooting Julius a pointed look.

Rolling his eyes, Julius followed them through an enormous arched doorway, industrial in its square, simple design, and suddenly all the sounds Julius was hearing were amplified. Despite the shouts and cranking of machines, Julius kept his face down, his gaze on his father's shoes, lip curling at the dust being kicked up around him.

"So here she is, the main floor," Bellhouse said with an expansive wave of his hand. "Built a year ago. Quite sad to leave the place downtown, but hanging on for nostalgia's sake was eating into business." He crossed his arms, clearing his throat proudly, and glanced at Julius and Amos. "You know, people come in from across the ocean to see how I've set up this place. Of course, they also want to see the world's first mass-producing screw factory too, for the sake of witnessing history."

Julius couldn't contain a less than subtle snort. As if to cover it, Amos laughed loudly and said, "Truly, you have the mind of a forward-thinking businessman. I'm hoping it will rub off on Julius here. His head is in the clouds lately."

"Mhm," Bellhouse murmured, nodding. "The folly of youth."

"Yes, indeed," Amos said, and they stood there in shared commiseration. Close to scowling, Julius kept his face down instead.

"Well, this way," Bellhouse said, and Julius followed their feet for a few yards until they stopped again. "You can just stay here, lad. Your father and I have a few things to discuss."

There was a hand on Julius's shoulder. "Just stay put, all right, Jay? Don't cause trouble."

"Yes, Father," Julius replied with a sigh, shrugging off the hand. How was he supposed to get up to anything in a *screw factory*, anyway? Honestly, though, he was tempted to leave. This whole farce was purely his father's making, and Julius had had no say in it—in fact, he objected adamantly.

His father disappeared with Bellhouse into a small room, and Julius took a seat on the mentioned bench. Finally, he glanced around this supposed beauty of a factory. And what he saw was alarming.

As in, it was a very close replica to most of his favorite wet dreams.

Hands clenching into trembling fists, eyes wide, Julius stared at the work-hardened, sweaty bodies of the men scattered around the factory. These men were wearing rugged, dirty clothing and all of them had rough stubble shadowing their faces—faces either lined with intense concentration or laughter at something another said. One man had an arm up, looped over a gigantic stack of metal rods, carrying to the end of the room, and another man was stretched out across some cutting machine, rowing the lever toward his body and then back again.

Pursing his lips, Julius glanced away. There was nothing to admire about these men—they were all probably criminals and definitely illiterate.

A shadow fell over Julius, pulling him from his frustrated thoughts. "We're leaving, Julius."

"Yes, Father." Standing, he kept his eyes on the ground again. There was no point even looking.

"You'll be back bright and early tomorrow," Amos said, guiding Julius out by the shoulder. "John has agreed to take you on for at least six months."

"Six months?" Julius breathed, face jerking up to look at his father. "As... a bookkeeper or something?"

His father let out a low chuckle. "Oh no, Julius. You'll be making screws."

IN THEIR modest home, a small duplex apartment a few streets from city hall where Amos worked, Julius was sitting down to dinner with his family.

"Julius isn't speaking to Daddy," Mary Barnes said. Julius narrowed his eyes at his sister.

"Is that so?" Helena Barnes replied lightly, setting a delicious-looking roast down on the table before taking her own chair at one end, with Amos sitting quietly at the other. Julius watched them shoot a private look at each other, and his chest tightened with irritation.

"I just don't see why I have to do this," he said, tapping his spoon on the table, eyes cast down. He hadn't planned on complaining, and wanted to prove to his father that he wasn't a child, but this was simply *unfair*. "I'm nineteen years old. I should be going to school."

"And I agree with that," Amos replied flatly. "A law school."

Exhaling, lip jutting out, Julius sank in his chair. "Forcing me into indentured servitude will not crush my spirit, Father."

"Oh ho." Amos laughed. "Now it's that I want to crush your spirit?"

Julius took an angry bite of his cornbread. "What else does it mean to cast me down with the great unwashed?"

Perhaps he had crossed a line. His father was appraising him disapprovingly, food forgotten. "Listen here, Julius H. Barnes. I didn't spend all this time getting cozy with the worst kind of politicians to make sure you had opportunities at graduation for you to throw it all away for some ludicrous—"

"It is *not* ludicrous," Julius snapped. "Was it ludicrous when Marlene Dawes found a way to harness steam power for flight? Was it ludicrous when Alfred Howser constructed a steam engine powerful enough to safely run a two-story city bus? There is so much more to be done, to be invented, and I—"

With a slam of his mug, Amos cut Julius off. "Those are two people out of how many would-be inventors, Julius? It's the same odds as panning for gold!" He paused at a stern look from Helena and sighed. "Anyway, Julius. If you want to go to that damn engineering school, then you'll pay your own way. If it's really your dream, then you must be willing to work for it."

As Julius was unable to think up a valid retort to that, his scowl only deepened. "Fine," he spat.

He was too embarrassed to look at his mother, so he stuffed his mouth full of food and childishly ignored the conversations going on around him.

AT 5:00 a.m. sharp (an ungodly hour, in Julius's opinion), he stood, shifting from one foot to the other, waiting at the gate. By then, several men had already gone through carrying lunch pails, but none had stopped to query about the lingering boy.

He wasn't sure where he was supposed to find John Bellhouse and had been under the impression that he was rarely at the factory anyway. *Well*, Julius thought, licking his lips, *I'll most certainly ask the next man who comes along.* There was no reason not to; it wasn't like these men would pull out a knife and stab him.

And yet when the next man appeared from the corner, walking toward the factory, Julius's voice caught in his throat.

He wasn't any taller than Julius, but he had that overall thick, muscled look men got from manual labor, with his sleeves rolled up and his shirt tucked in at a trim waist.

And he was actually looking at Julius as he walked up, which was a first. "You lost, kid?"

"I know exactly where I am," Julius snapped back, shoulders squared.

The man cocked an uninterested eyebrow. "Uh-huh."

He tried to shoulder past Julius, who started opening and closing his mouth, torn between admitting he hadn't the vaguest idea where he was supposed to be going and not looking like a complete dunce in front of this....

Julius gulped. *This man who looks like a wartime propaganda poster brought to life.*

"Excuse me," he finally managed to work out. The man stopped and glanced over his shoulder, waiting. "Actually, if it isn't too much trouble...."

"Spit it out, boy." The man sighed.

Rankled, gritting his teeth at being called *boy, kid,* by this man, the man he couldn't stop staring at, Julius shook his head. "No, never mind."

The man shot him one last dubious look and shrugged. When he had disappeared into the factory, Julius exhaled a shaky breath, and his cheeks felt a little hot despite the snow covering the ground. Well, no matter; that man was clearly not a member of polite society. He could barely grunt out more than two words, after all! It was alarming that Julius had to mix with these degenerates, and he would make quite sure to avoid them if possible, especially that... man.

Reaching his limit with the cold, Julius decided to just search out John Bellhouse, assuming he was there.

As it was, Bellhouse did come to the factory rather often, to show it off to distant relatives and old school friends. Julius knew this because John Bellhouse told him so as they were walking down the familiar hallway to the main floor of the factory, not a few minutes after Julius had run into him at the entrance.

"You could have come right inside," Bellhouse said amiably. "I'm not quite sure what Peavey will do to the both us if I bring in the new hire late."

Julius was still working the chill out of his fingers, huffing a warm breath against his palms, and thought to ask who Peavey was but deduced he would most likely learn soon enough. "I was surprised, Mr. Bellhouse, by the hours your factory keeps."

With a chuckle, Bellhouse nodded. "Indeed, dawn to dusk. It's a boon that we house the workers ourselves. God only knows how many we would lose if they were free to carouse about town after curfew."

"These men have a curfew?" Julius replied dryly, tickled by the image of a schoolmarm, lantern in hand, walking down a row of cots to make sure all these gruff, dirty bruisers were in bed.

"And if they want to keep their posts, they'll stick to it," Bellhouse said, his friendly face betraying any attempt at sounding stern. "Not that we are slave drivers. Oh no, they are given a half day every week."

"That sounds more than generous," Julius said. "Surely the city is better off without this riffraff mucking about anyway."

Clearing his throat, Bellhouse paused. "Yes, well, don't worry, Julius. I know how you must be feeling about this whole endeavor, but your father has your best interest at heart."

Julius sincerely doubted that, but he didn't say anything and just murmured a response, keeping his expression impassive. They were at the large, open square entrance to the main floor of the factory anyway, and once again Julius felt a slight pickup to his heartbeat, his mouth feeling dry. Through the entryway, he made a quick pass of the room with his gaze, but there was no sight of that man from the gate.

And then he grimaced, mentally berating himself for even looking.

"All right, then," Bellhouse said lightly. "I have some business to attend to, so if we could just—ah! There he is."

An older man than Bellhouse and his father was walking toward them, his pace hindered by what must have been a bad leg, with the way he was limping. His craggy face was set in a scowl. "Bellhouse," he barked, "this—"

"Yes, Mr. Peavey, this is the boy I was talking about," Bellhouse replied, patting Julius's back.

Peavey's eyes narrowed. "The boy for the lathe?"

"Uh, well," Bellhouse said, and it sounded like he tried to laugh, but it came out too self-aware. "Yes, but if that doesn't work out, you can shift one of the other men on to the lathe, and Julius here can do something less complicated."

Snorting, Julius crossed his arms and stepped far enough away from Bellhouse to feel like he wasn't under some cloak of protection. "I am certain I can handle anything that is considered *complicated* in this establishment."

Peavey considered him, lip curled. "Is that so, lad?" And then without waiting for an answer, he turned to John. "Well, it's your factory, Bellhouse."

"Fantastic," Bellhouse replied, either oblivious to or ignoring the disdain in Peavey's voice. With one last pat on Julius's shoulder, he nodded to the two of them and then strode over to the office, disappearing inside.

The moment the door shut, there was a long, drawn-out sigh from Peavey, and Julius turned to look at him with a frown. "It's not like I want to be here any more than you want me to."

"Boy, I have queries stacked up ceiling high from men who need a job to support their families, and yet I had to give up a prime spot to a brat like you," Peavey growled, his face turning red. "The last thing you should be doing right now is acting like you've just been condemned, because if that's the attitude you take, then that's exactly what this is going to feel like," he finished, jabbing a finger at Julius's chest.

Cheeks heating, Julius slapped the offending hand away. "Don't touch me with that dirty hand."

"Dirt—" Peavey spluttered, his eyes going wide, mouth working as he tried to say something, and Julius just watched him until he started to raise his hand.

"Hey, boss," came a low, rough voice. Julius recognized it immediately and froze. "There's a double order—not sure if they intended that or not."

The man from the front gate was there, was somehow angling himself between Peavey and Julius before either of them could say anything, and Peavey was already deflating. Julius stood behind the man, gaze drawn down the strong line of his back, confrontation with Peavey almost completely forgotten. "I have the order slip over by the loading deck, if you could take a look," the man finished.

Exhaling, Peavey shook his head. "Yeah, all right. You deal with *this*, Hooley." He stomped away, toward the machines and men at the other side of the factory.

Julius watched him go, glad he didn't have to interact any further with Peavey. But then the scent of sweat and smoke hit him, his gaze moving back to the man standing so closely next to him, and Julius could see the very beginning of collarbone, a hint of chest under a grimy work shirt.

"Getting on the wrong side of Peavey would be a mistake, kid."

Blinking, Julius quickly tore his gaze from the man's chest and looked up into brown eyes. "He was assaulting me."

The man's lip curled with wry amusement, and Julius nearly lost his breath.

"You're a little peach, huh," the man said, walking away from Julius, who quibbled for a second before scampering forward behind him.

"Excuse me?" Julius replied, trying to sound indignant even as he rushed to keep up with the man.

The man laughed—*at Julius.* "You bruise easily."

"What?" Julius was beside himself by that point, talking to this man who smelled like hard work and tobacco and dirty things, but all he was doing was making fun of Julius.

"That ain't so bad," the man said. "You're a little soft, but John Bellhouse is too, yeah? Soft men always seem to do well."

"I was proficient at track and field, I would have you know," Julius replied with as much dignity as he could muster, but all it earned him was an amiable chuckle. His face was flushed red by that point, he could just feel it, so he made sure to keep behind the man—Hooley, he had been called. "Is Hooley a first or last name?"

"Last," the man replied. "First is Hank."

"Hank," Julius repeated sedately. "Hank Hooley."

Another low chuckle. "Don't wear it out, kid."

"I'm nineteen, I would have—"

"Me know, yeah, yeah, I get it."

Julius felt his stomach drop, eyes widening, but then Hank glanced over his shoulder at him, smiling. "Nineteen, huh?"

Oh *God*, like Helen brought about the fall of Troy, certainly that smile could devastate history. Julius would make a bumbling Paris, however, with the way he was just gawping at Hank like an imbecile. Hank simply raised his eyebrows and turned back to face the way he was walking.

They were down a hallway Julius hadn't seen the day before; it went to the opposite direction of the factory, near the back. After all that, it hadn't occurred to him to ask where Hank was taking him, and now of course he couldn't get one word out. He had never been so tongue-tied in his life, not even when he met Maeve Halstrom, the inventor of the more efficient, small steam engines used on wheelchairs and velocipedes.

So he practiced, in his head, the things he could say to Hank Hooley and cleared his throat. "Yes, nineteen. At sixteen I won the Woolcott Award for young excellence and innovation in the steam field, at the Woolcott Society of Inventors."

He heard a slight exhale. "Sounds fancy."

"I invented a—well, it was the schematics—" Julius's enthusiasm was flagging as self-consciousness took over, and his gaze flicked across Hank's shoulder to what Julius could see of his face, trying to suss out if he saw interest, or boredom, or irritation….

Hank glanced at him suddenly, and their eyes met. "Schematics for what?"

"A very precise watch," Julius replied breathlessly, eyes close to watering with how dumb that sounded. As if Hank Hooley cared about millionths of a second.

"Ah, yeah," Hank said. "Those shiny little devils rich men keep in their coat pockets, huh? I inherited one from a grandfather, but the damn thing doesn't even work, so, who knows? Maybe I'll pawn it off or something."

"I could fix it," Julius replied quietly.

Hank didn't respond, just shot Julius another curious little smile and then nodded toward the door they were approaching. "This is the supply closet for the workers. You can't wear what you're wearing in the factory, got it?"

Glancing down at himself, Julius cursed his Sunday best. Of course it was the wrong thing to wear to a factory—he had seen the men's sturdy pants and simple cotton shirts already; he should have known better! And now Hank Hooley was going to think Julius was even more of a soft peach than he already did.

Seeming oblivious to Julius's misery, Hank pulled the door open and beckoned Julius inside, where there were shelves upon shelves of folded pants and shirts, all similar to the ones the men in the factory wore. "We're each given two sets, and when those wear out, the next set is taken from our wages, although I don't suppose you'll be here long enough to need to worry about that." Hank pulled two shirts and two pairs of pants and tossed them to Julius, who caught them with a jerk.

"Where do I get them fitted?" Julius replied, holding one of the shirts up to his chest, the others tucked under the crook of his arm.

"You serious?" Hank replied. Julius looked up to see him staring skeptically at Julius.

"No," Julius replied quickly and as levelly as he could. "That was a joke."

"Mhm." Hank ran his hand over his hair with a sigh, nodding back toward the hallway. "You change, and then meet Peavey back on the floor. He'll show you what to do. I guess we'll find you a bunk after shift."

Julius clenched the clothes in his hands. "A bunk?"

"Yeah." Hank was already looking bored with this entire endeavor. "Where you think you're gonna sleep?"

"I was going to go home…," Julius replied.

Hank snorted at that, shaking his head. "Peavey won't stand for that, kid. Anyway, no more dawdling. I've got work to do." And with that, he slid past Julius and strode down the cramped hallway.

"So I told her, if she really wanted to move out here with the kids, she'd be living in a hutch in the slums. Better to stay out in the country."

Julius observed the group of men sitting together on a bunch of shipment boxes at the edge of the dock that lined the factory, nodding and murmuring in commiseration for the man with the lonely wife. They were all eating from their lunch pails and watching the ships go by and drinking what Julius heavily suspected was ale. He stood back from them, shifting from one foot to the other.

He was specifically staring at the empty spot next to Hank Hooley. Well, great men never hesitated, so he walked as swiftly and determinedly as he could, then plopped himself down on the box not a few inches away from Hank.

Silence descended on the group. And then one of the men laughed and said, "Well, looky here, Hooley."

Hank was curved forward, his head tilted to Julius as he stared at him sideways. "Where's your lunch, kid?"

Reacting involuntarily, Julius flushed at the sudden attention from Hank and glanced away, stuttering. "I ate it already." Which, at that moment, was when his stomach chose to growl.

There was a light snort next to him, and then an apple entered his field of vision. He stared at it for a moment and then snatched it up, taking a large bite. "So," he heard Hank say, "how was your first shift?"

Julius glanced around and saw that all the men were waiting for an answer. Truth be told, Julius's body was aching in protest of all the manual labor he had done in the past few hours, which mostly consisted of lugging large amounts of metal rods from one side of the factory to the lathes, where they were being cut down to thousands of identical screws.

"It was tolerable," he said resolutely. This neither seemed bad nor pleasing, each man just nodding in neutral affirmation.

"You were a little slow," Hank replied, "but it's your first day, so no problem there. You'll get stronger and faster."

Well, that had never occurred to Julius. He had been so wrapped up in hating every single thing about his father's command that he work at the factory, he'd never stopped to consider the benefits... such as building himself up to look like these men... and then maybe Ha—the men would respect him.

But that was a diversion from his dream.

"I do not intend to remain trapped here much longer," Julius said. "My sentence, if you will, has an ending date." He only needed his father to see how committed he was, and then Amos Barnes would most certainly pay for Julius to go to the Inventor's Academy.

"A sentence, huh?" Hank replied idly, taking a bite of his meat pie.

Julius swallowed with a gulp, his eyes going wide. He heard a few sniggers. But he ignored them, telling himself that what Hank Hooley thought of him would never matter in the long run. "This is the work of the uneducated."

He could almost sense the humor from the group evaporate, and Hank's eyes on him, considering and appraising him. "That so?" Hank said finally, taking another bite of his pie.

A tense moment passed, everyone focused on their food, but Julius could feel the animosity directed toward him. He narrowed his eyelids, trying to keep steady, eating the apple in slow, measured bites, but he could feel tears pricking at his eyes. "Excuse me," he muttered, sliding off the box, and walked as quickly as he could without running away from the men.

Inside the empty factory, he dawdled, thinking to himself that he should just go home. These men hated him, Hank hated—

"All right, kid." The words were said in a tired sigh.

Julius clenched his fists, his lips pressing together in a tight line. "I am not a child. You don't need to console me."

He turned, and Hank entered his field of vision, then leaned against one of the large machines. "Console you?" He laughed. "Oh man, kid, you've really got things wrong here."

When Julius just dropped his head even more, Hank sighed again. "Even though you're a right ponce, my buddies and I, we're gonna try and let you into the fold, you know? But if you're going to act so condescendin' to us, then you can go and fuck yourself."

Eyes widening at the crude language, Julius jerked his face up, his mouth dropping. Hank smiled at him. "You think you're better than us because you can draw up all those *schematics* and build steam engines." Pausing, Hank considered Julius.

"Let me ask you something," he said. "What do you think holds all your fancy machines together?"

Julius blinked once and then involuntarily glanced around at the factory.

"That's right," Hank continued. "Without us, all your plans and your inventions would come to nothing but a pile of scraps."

After a second, Julius licked his lips and said, "I apologize."

This earned him a nod. "Now come on back outside. I may have some of my meat pie left for you."

"WELL, there's the academy, and then there's the society," Julius slurred, waving his hand about. "The society only inducts you as a member once you've proven yourself adept and able to contribute to the growth of knowledge."

One of the men, Tom, sitting on the bunks with him took a sip of rum and said, "Huh, so even if you did get to that school of yours, you still might not make it as an inventor."

"I don't need the society to be an inventor," Julius replied primly. "There was Jacoby Hannigan, you know. He was a free agent and did quite well in the industry." He sniffed, shifting his pillow out from under his leg and holding it to his chest as he drew his knees up. These cots were not fit for human use, especially ones who worked all day such as he had.

"Never heard of him," Tom grunted.

"'M sure he invented the steam toilet or something," Hank said from beside Julius.

"Hah!" Tom said. "What would that do, heat your ass before taking a shit?"

Julius's face scrunched with disapproval. "Certainly we can be gentlemen in our conversations."

Snorting, Hank reached over to ruffle his hair. "Sorry, peach, didn't mean to burn your delicate ears."

Julius pushed the hand away, his cheeks heating, about to admonish Hank even more when the door to their bunk opened and another man popped his head in. "Peavey's gone to Ankcham for three days," he said, his eyes shining with delight.

Glancing around, Julius tried to suss out what that meant. Hank and Tom had started to grin too. In fact, Tom was already on his feet and rooting around in a dilapidated chest he kept at the foot of his cot. Julius only became more curious when he pulled out a pretty well-kept vest and clean shirt.

Tom glanced over at Hank and Julius. "Come on, lads!"

Julius felt a hand slap his back. "You go on with them and have fun. They'll take care of you."

"Ah, come on, Hank," Tom whined.

Hank shook his head. "I'm too old for this." He laughed. "I need to sleep."

"I'm not going," Julius said quickly. Tom shot him an exasperated look, so he said, "This is the hardest I've ever worked in my life. I'm dead tired."

With a shrug, Tom pulled on his clothes. "You're missing out, kid. We could really show you the town."

When the door shut behind him and silence fell, Julius realized he had somehow found himself alone on a bed with Hank Hooley, who was just as sloshed as Julius was. Clearing his throat, Julius kept his eyes on his toes. "So, do you have a missus back in the country?"

"Who said I was from the country?" Hank replied idly.

Julius looked at him. "Do you have one in the city?"

"No, I don't," Hank said with a sigh, reaching over to set the bottle on the ground and then leaning back against the wall, folding his hands behind his head. "What's with the questions?"

"No particular reason," Julius replied, his eyes drawn down the line of Hank's body. In his school days, in the showers, Julius had seen awkward bony bodies and pudgy bodies and strong bodies on the more physically adept of them, and all of those had their advantages and places in Julius's fantasies, but none had ever stopped him dead in his tracks like Hank Hooley.

And it wasn't just the masculine vision of that strong, stubbled jaw going down to a tempting collarbone, or the thickness of his arms and chest, or those brown eyes that were both warm and intelligent.

Julius couldn't figure out what it was that made his mouth go dry. Maybe it was everything. He was besotted.

Curving his spine, Hank winced at a pop. "I don't get how those guys can go all day and then all night," he muttered.

Julius opened his mouth to respond, and nothing came out. He inhaled and then tried again. "I know the tension points. I could help work out some of the stiffness."

Hank glanced at him, eyebrows rising. "What?"

Gathering himself, Julius replied, "I could rub your back. It's known to relieve the tension from working all day."

"Uh," Hank said, considering him, "sure, why not?"

Well, Julius had already gotten this far. "Take your shirt off."

He heard a chuckle and a low "Yes, sir" as Hank sat upright to pull his shirt off, giving Julius a full view of his naked chest and belly stretching upward. Julius had to choke down a moan at the visible trail of curls leading down past the waist of Hank's pants. Never had he felt so blessed in his life.

"Like this?" Hank asked, turning his back to Julius and crossing his legs.

"Y-yes," Julius stuttered, his hands shaking. He rested back on his knees, his gaze roving every inch of naked skin he could see, wishing he had some reasonable excuse for having Hank pull his pants off as well.

"Well, get on with it."

Julius flinched, his heart threatening to pound right out of his chest. Gathering himself, he reached forward and rested his palms on the hard slopes of Hank's shoulders, and they were so warm. Very slowly, Julius rubbed his thumbs up, his eyes trained on the crease of skin they created. "Okay," he said softly.

He actually did know how to do this; his mother was a fan of home remedies, and joint stiffness and backache was something she had many books on. So, holding his tongue between his teeth, he started kneading at the points he knew would make Hank moan.

And he did. It was low and luxurious and seemed to surprise him, because he stiffened up immediately, his head turning slightly to glance at Julius. "Well, damn." He laughed.

Julius didn't know if he expected anger or what, but this was better. "That felt all right?"

"It felt pretty darn good, kid. So don't stop."

Nodding, Julius continued, working down Hank's spine. The muscles under his hands were stiff, and with each little moan they loosened from his touch, making his own breathing heavy. He could feel the strain in his pants, but he couldn't bring himself to worry about it, all his attention focused on Hank.

When Hank was basically a drowsy puddle, leaning his weight back against Julius's grip, Julius slowly shifted off the bed and gently let Hank down until his head was safely resting on the pillow. Julius grabbed the blanket, tucked it around Hank, and then risked running his fingers through Hank's hair.

Finally, as he was standing, the full impact of his arousal hit him, and his entire body flushed. He stumbled out of the bunk room, headed for the toilet.

JULIUS spent his twentieth birthday at the factory. That was two months after he started working there.

At six months, on a visit to his parents' house, he didn't understand the surprised looks they shot him until he passed the hallway mirror and saw his own reflection. No longer was a scrawny schoolboy staring back at him. He still wasn't as built up as the other men, but his entire body was so much more substantial, and he got stuck staring at himself with pride and wonderment.

During dinner, the talk was set around light subjects until Amos Barnes finally set his fork down with a clatter, his face tight with frustration. "Just how long are you going to be stubborn about this, Julius?"

Julius, with spoonful of soup still in his mouth, stared at his father. He swallowed and then asked, "Stubborn about what?"

"I thought you'd last, hell, maybe two weeks," Amos ground out. "But it's been months! You're wasting your life."

Julius glanced around at his mother and sister, who were both also watching him with curious expressions. "These were the terms you dictated, Father," Julius said slowly. "If I wanted to go to the academy, I had to pay for it myself."

"You—" Amos barked, but then he stopped. "Well, you're right about that."

"He is following through, darling," Julius's mother said.

With a rough sigh, Amos shook his head. "Well, I don't want you mired there forever—there is no way to explain it to the relatives. I will go to this academy of yours. If it is as reputable as you claim, I will consider subsidizing your tuition."

"Thank you, Father," Julius replied, his tone sedate. Suddenly, his dream of going to the academy was a lot closer than it had been before. He knew the meager wage earned at the factory meant he would never be able to go there, not for years, but he had found he cared less and less about that each day he spent working with Hank Hooley.

But he bit his tongue and smiled, and the talk around the table became light again. His thoughts were elsewhere.

"THAT'S great, kid," Hank said absentmindedly, his eyes cast down on a checklist he was going through for an order about to be shipped off from the dock.

"It would mean I would stop working here," Julius replied, his arms full with a box of square drive bolts.

Hank's eyebrows pinched in concentration for a moment, and then he looked up at Julius. "Seems you're trying to ask me something."

Staring back, meeting Hank's eyes, Julius wanted to say *yes*, he was asking whether Hank would care if Julius left, if he cared that Julius was there. Would he miss Julius? Did he enjoy these months they'd spent together, working and living? What did he think of Julius? Had he caught the way Julius had more and more openly stared at him, to the point that the other men had to have noticed by then?

But Julius just shrugged. "I did not expect it to happen this quickly."

"You like working here?" Hank asked, returning to the checklist.

Julius watched him. "I like working here with you." He thought he caught a minute pause, but then Hank was back to walking down the line of the shipment.

"Put that box here," Hank said, pointing at an empty space, his voice sounding a bit rough. His face was turned away from Julius, who carefully set the box down and then stretched his arms up, working out the kinks in his back.

He happened to glance at Hank and froze. There was a slight tint of red on Hank's cheeks. "Do you like working with me?" Julius blurted, his arms dropping.

Hank's gaze jerked to him, but then he turned his head again and started stomping back toward the factory door. Julius quickly followed suit, his mind racing. He had never seen Hank look flustered before, *ever*.

"You didn't answer," Julius pushed, easily matching Hank's pace, watching him closely.

Hank's lips were pressed tight together, his hands balled into fists. "Cut it out."

This reaction only bolstered Julius and made him walk closer to Hank, trying to gauge Hank's reaction to that. They were nearing the factory, and Julius felt his time running out—the moment would be over and he'd never get a straight answer.

At the last second, he grabbed Hank's wrist with a jerk and pulled him out of view of the open door, hidden behind the wall of the factory, pushing him up against it. Their eyes locked, and Julius saw the trepidation in those usually confident brown eyes. "Please answer."

"What does me liking to work with you have to do with anything?" Hank replied, his voice a low growl.

"You know what," Julius replied forcefully. He wondered if Hank was going to pretend he didn't, pretend he hadn't noticed the way Julius followed him around and latched on to every word he said. But even then, Julius had always figured it was a one-sided infatuation. "Please, Hank, if there is something here… I won't ever leave!"

Hank blinked at that, his lips parting. But then his expression leveled out, and he glanced away from Julius. "I don't know what you're talking about."

Roughly dropping Hank's wrist, Julius scoffed. There was a crushing weight in his chest, unhappiness drawing the color out of everything, and he didn't know what he could say to fix it. He didn't want to have a tantrum, but he couldn't help striding away, fueled by rejection and anger.

"SO YOU'RE just gonna sulk?"

Julius ignored Hank and kept reading the little penny pulp novel he had found on Tom's bunk, lying on his stomach with his face away from the bunkroom door. He heard a low sigh, and then Hank stepped into the room and shut the door. "You should just go with the rest of them," Julius said tightly. "It's not every week Peavey is gone."

"Yeah, yeah," Hank muttered, settling down on the cot opposite Julius. "Listen, kid—"

"Julius, not *kid*."

Hank inhaled, sounding amused, and sighed again. "Julius. What kinda thing are you trying to say by ignoring me? I ain't worth talking to unless you get a fuck out of it?"

Disbelieving, Julius sat up and glared at Hank. "I'm dealing with a shattered heart here!" And when his gaze landed on Hank, he froze, because Hank wasn't wearing his shirt, and the buttons of his pants were undone, and he looked ripe for the plucking, leaning back on his elbow as he rested against the wall, one leg bent up and the other hanging off the edge of the cot. His hair was wet from the bath.

Julius didn't even try to hide his hungry gaze, tracing each detail carefully, his mouth practically watering. "I want you so badly."

"I know," Hank breathed, his tone beleaguered. "Never thought I'd have to be dealing with some young buck sniffing after me at this age."

"You've been with men before?" Julius replied, unable to quell the slightly hurt warble to his voice, despite the warmth in his chest at being called a *buck*, which somehow implied more masculinity than he had ever afforded himself. It made him run his hand down his own arm, reminding himself how much he had changed.

Hank's response was an amused, curled lip and a cocked eyebrow. "I ain't a coy little virgin, that's for damn sure."

Considering him, considering the way he was staring at Julius and the way he had spread his bent leg out a little, framing his crotch, Julius had to get up. It took less than a full stride to reach the other cot, and then Julius dropped to his knees on the ground, staring up at the delicious vision that was Hank Hooley.

Julius reached forward and circled a loose hand around Hank's ankle, keeping his gaze matched with Hank's, but Hank wasn't betraying any emotion.

Slipping his fingers up, Julius nudged under Hank's pants leg, caressing the warm skin. "I was too nervous to even speak the first time I saw you." Hank snorted at that, but Julius could see the faint red tint on his cheeks. "You were the only one who bothered to say something to me, with me looking like an idiot out at the gate."

Hank observed him silently for a moment, eyes hooded, and then he drew his other leg up and spread them even farther. Julius's breath caught when he reached down to start rubbing at his groin. "You gonna help me with this?" Hank asked.

Like a shot, Julius was up, pushing forward to crowd a laughing Hank against the wall, his cheeks flushed with nervous excitement. "Please let me," he mumbled, holding his hand over Hank's. Their faces were so close, and Julius dipped his to press against Hank's neck, breathing in. "God, I want to so badly."

"Want to what?"

Julius let out a little whine of frustration, swatting Hank's hand away so he could do it himself, rubbing against the hard outline. "You know what I mean."

"I don't," Hank replied, his voice dancing teasingly. "You're gonna have to say it."

Julius broke, shoving himself against Hank, running a shaking hand down his muscular thigh. "I want to fuck you, Hank! *Please.* I want to fuck you. I do, please...."

"All right, all right, quit whining," Hank said. "I get it." He gently shoved Julius away—maybe with some trouble—and huffed an exasperated breath. "Help me get these off."

Julius nodded adamantly, grabbed the waist of Hank's pants, and jerked them down, pulling Hank onto his back in the process. With a chuckle, Hank obediently lifted his hips so Julius could tug them off and over Hank's knees, and then Julius was stuck with an eyeful of Hank's cock, thick with arousal.

He looked up to meet Hank's eyes and saw the headiness there too. Leaning forward, Julius pressed a featherlight kiss against Hank's lips. His chest nearly burst.

This time, Hank shoved him violently away, and Julius fell back with a shock, wondering what was wrong—but Hank was staring at him, face flushed, eyes blazing as he dropped around lengthwise on the bed, reaching down to palm his cock. Julius watched the display, Hank jerking himself with a broken, rhythmless pace. "Julius...."

That woke him up, and he quickly straddled Hank, bending down to get his fill of licking at Hank's nipples, pinching them, and then running a hand up and down Hank's belly, Hank's legs rising up on each side of him.

"Get your fucking dick out," Hank breathed, his eyes shut.

Julius agreed with that sentiment. The strain at his crotch was painful by that point, and he nearly ripped the buttons away, fumbling to undo them. Hank was shifting beneath him, moaning with need.

Pulling his cock out, he slid back and wrapped his arms around Hank's thighs, pulling one leg up at a time to rest on his shoulders, and then that delicious, muscular ass was exposed to Julius, within his reach.

"Bastard," he heard Hank moan. "Don't you *dare* stick it in yet."

"What?" Julius breathed, his voice high. "What do I do?"

"Spit in your goddamn palm and soften me up."

Julius tried to think through the mechanics of that, and he thought he knew what Hank meant, so he gathered the saliva in his mouth and spit in his palm. Reaching down, he slicked Hank up, a rush of lust shooting up his spine when his fingers brushed against Hank's hole.

Hank was panting, pushing against Julius's hand. "Like that, yes… like that."

Dipping a finger in, Julius pushed against the tightness. He slipped a second finger in, curling them and spreading them, earning deep, throaty cries from Hank. "Can I do it now?"

He saw Hank's throat roll in a swallow, and then, "Yes."

With a resolute breath, Julius brought his hand to his cock and pushed his hips forward to rub at Hank's opening before shoving in completely. Hank arched up with a gasp. Julius made sure he had a better grip on Hank's legs, and then he started rolling his hips slowly, breathing evenly and trying not to lose all reason too early.

He couldn't tear his gaze away from Hank, watching that man, that epitome of *men,* writhing wantonly beneath Julius, fingers gripping the sheets. He started pushing his hips forward to meet Julius's thrusts, licking his lips. "Harder, Julius."

Julius complied with the order, snapping forward roughly, leaning his weight forward to bend Hank nearly in half, the cot creaking and jerking beneath them. Hank's hand was on his cock, moving in time with Julius's thrusts.

Feeling Hank tense up, Julius watched his face closely, watched that tremor of the final crest, the way Hank was striving for it, and then all the tension broke and Hank's expression smoothed out with release, his come spread across his chest.

Julius wasn't far behind. He had lost all semblance of control, fucking Hank with as much power as he possessed, driving forward deeper into the heat and tightness, the buildup pushing him to thrust even harder. "Christ," he grunted when he came, his head dropping as he was overwhelmed with pleasure.

He stayed like that for a moment, breathing slowly as he tried to savor every feeling.

Hank's legs slid down, Julius slipping out of him. Not really thinking, Julius gripped Hank's hip and turned him slightly so he could get a good look at the slick come dribbling out, at Hank's ravaged ass that Julius had just claimed.

Looking up, Julius checked on Hank, expecting annoyance, only to see that he had dropped an arm over his face, his lips parted in docility.

After a breath, those lips quirked up. "What are you doing?"

Julius ran his fingers over the stretched hole, pushed in. "I, uh… I like looking at what I did to you. Sorry."

There was a faint laugh. "I get it," Hank replied. "I know what you mean."

Figuring he had played enough, Julius let Hank's hip down and crawled forward, resting his weight on Hank, leaning up on his elbows so he could get a good look at Hank's expression. "Why did you let me do that?"

Brown eyes met his. "'Cause I want you to leave."

Julius felt a crushing blow to his heart and his face crumpled. Hank must have seen that, because he smiled gently and reached up to palm Julius's cheek. "Come on, kid, I ain't heartless. I want you to leave and invent all those steam things you've been blathering on about. You're smart enough to do it."

"I don't get you," Julius replied miserably.

Hank sighed. "I didn't want you following me around forever. You got the fuck you wanted, and now you can leave."

That was it, he really did believe that Julius only wanted…. Well, what had Julius done to prove otherwise? "I don't want to leave," Julius said softly. "I love you, Hank."

Hank's eyes flashed at that. "I don't need some kinda useless love from a kid, got it?" he said gruffly, breaking eye contact.

Letting those words sink in, Julius nodded. But he wouldn't let Hank get his way, because Julius could see the regret on his face. "If I come back here, rich and famous from inventing something amazing, and you're tired from all these years of backbreaking factory work, and I offer you a life of leisure from that point on, will my love still be useless?"

Hank looked up at him with surprise. "Now, kid, that is not what I was aim—"

Julius covered Hank's mouth with a grin. "I mean, I would have to leave first and go and follow my dream and all that. But I don't believe I would be truly motivated to do that unless I had someone special waiting for me at the end of it."

He felt the hot breath of a sigh against his palm. Hank closed his eyes and then grabbed Julius's wrist and pulled his hand away. "Can't say I'd turn down something like that."

A sense of elation quickly started to spread through Julius's veins. "I get to see you before that, though! I get to come and talk to you."

"Yeah, yeah," Hank replied, squirming in protest under Julius's weight and then elbowing him to one side. "Now let me get some sleep."

"What?" Julius cried, closing his arms around Hank to pull him close, "After all that, and you're just going to sleep?"

Hank let out a small laugh. "Christ, boy. That's exactly what we're both going to do. We've got work in the morning. Ain't no time for any more flowery talk."

"Flowery talk," Julius echoed flatly. He dropped his head.

Lip curling up, he sighed in defeat and hunkered down next to Hank, figuring he had a few more minutes until he had to go to his own cot. He chose to spend it tracing a small line down Hank's stubbled jaw to his neck, overjoyed with the thought that he was now allowed to touch him.

He wondered how long it took for Hank Hooley to confess love. Maybe just as long as it took to become a famous inventor, or maybe it was something that would never happen at all. Either way, Julius felt pretty secure with his arms wrapped around Hank. Wouldn't be that long before he could buy Hank a home, and they'd live there together, and Hank would probably keep calling Julius *kid,* even if they ever adopted one of their own.

Julius grinned widely at that, burying his face against Hank's neck. He'd grow up more, and Hank would respect him, and they would live in equitable harmony.

It would be a good life.

R.D. Hero lives a life completely dedicated to m/m. When she isn't spending time sifting through multitudes of yaoi looking for the rare perfect one, she's writing slash online. Once in a while, if she has to, she goes out into the real world to do unsavory things like "college" and "socializing." Mostly though, she prefers to stay in her cave with her boxer, Brandy. You can find her at http://www.rdhero.com.

THE CLOCKWORK HEART

KIM FIELDING

THE metal barrow was still nearly empty, only a few broken bits clattering about in the bottom. Dante Winter stopped and gave the glowering sky a long, considering look. Did he have time to attempt a bit more collecting, or should he hurry back to his home before the downpour began? It was his empty purse that decided him. He hadn't been eating well, and the rent was due in a few days. If he didn't find some items to refurbish and sell soon, he ran a real risk of finding himself homeless.

He felt ill at the idea of being out in the world without his small refuge.

Thunder rumbled ominously, but his determination paid off when he sifted through a small heap of refuse and discovered a clockwork mermaid the length of his forearm. She was filthy, but Dante could tell the parts were finely wrought by a master's hand. It had likely been an expensive device when it was new, intended primarily to sit on a shelf and be admired. But someone had got hold of her—a child, perhaps—and treated her roughly. The gears no longer turned, stilling the motion Dante could see in his mind's eye: the tail fluttering smoothly and her arms and head moving in synchrony. One piece of the tail fin was missing, much of the brass was corroded and dented, and most of the enameled colors had been scraped away from her face and scales.

Dante turned the find over in his hands, inspecting it carefully. Yes, he decided. It would take many hours of work, but he could restore her. Annette Swan, whose shop specialized in expensive toys with nautical themes, would pay well for such a bauble. Dante could earn enough for another month's rent at least.

He set the mermaid gingerly in his barrow and gave her a gentle pat. "I'll have you better than new in no time at all," he said. "You'll find a much finer home than a rubbish heap."

Smiling, he turned the barrow around and headed toward home. But he hadn't gone far when it occurred to him that the mermaid would look especially nice with some adornments. A zinc chain about her waist, inset with bits of colored glass to simulate jewels. Maybe a matching chain around her neck. He tried to ignore the idea. Thoughts such as this had led to the falling out with his father, who had a solid reputation for producing well-made, inexpensive watches but had no patience for his son's impulses to add bits of decoration and whimsy to the timepieces.

But pleasing his father was no longer a consideration, Dante reminded himself. So he turned the barrow aside, toward a large mound of broken glass. He wouldn't need much—just a few tiny bits. He already had some small lumps of zinc in his workshop.

The first fat drops of rain began to fall as he sifted through the colored shards. He used his arm to push his untidy strands of hair away from his face, then poked cautiously at the sharp rubble. He always wore gloves when he was collecting—he couldn't afford to injure his hands— but the leather wouldn't withstand the most dangerous splinters. He had no trouble finding dark-green glass, but it took considerably longer to unearth the precise shade of blue he was hoping for. He didn't have any luck at all finding red, but then he hadn't expected to. Red glass got its color from gold and was therefore more expensive and rarer than other hues.

Well, his mermaid would do well enough with sea colors. He needed to hurry up—his clothing was soaked already and he was beginning to shiver.

He kept his head down as he pushed the barrow between piles of debris. Cold rain ran under his collar and mud squished into the holes in his boots, chilling him even more. He longed for his hot stove and kettle, and he wondered if he could manage to find enough food in his cupboards for a stew, or at least a decent soup. Probably not. But he was so wet already, he might as well make a detour to the butcher shop to beg a marrow bone. Mr. Poweders was occasionally willing to grant him a small amount of credit. And the greengrocer—maybe he had a few sprouted potatoes or wilted carrots he'd be willing to spare, a tiny onion or two. Dante closed his eyes and shuddered, picturing himself interacting with so many people all in one afternoon. Perhaps he'd make do with tea and dry biscuits instead.

His eyes were still closed when he tripped over something, nearly landing headfirst in his barrow.

Normally the refuse was kept in neat enough piles and the passages between them were clear. In fact, before Mr. Abernethy had granted him access to the rubbish heap—a privilege for which Dante paid five sovereigns annually—Dante had been required to promise to keep everything tidy as he scavenged. But now something was sticking into the pathway. It took Dante a moment to recognize it was an arm.

For a brief moment, his heart constricted as he imagined a corpse among the rubbish. He pictured his mother very clearly as he'd last seen her: sheets and nightdress and skin equally white. But no, that had been almost ten years earlier, when he was hardly more than a boy. And the arm in the mud before him glinted dully from bits of metal.

He pushed the barrow to the side and crouched for closer inspection. It was a mechanical arm, and although it was sheathed in synthetic skin, the covering had been torn in several places, revealing a delicate structure of metal and wire.

A wise man would have stood and hurried away. But Dante was not wise, and there was something about the arm that made his throat feel tight. Perhaps it was the way the fingers were bent and hooked into the mud, as if in an attempt to claw free of the pile of garbage.

Dante began clearing the rubbish away.

Although the rain was sheeting down, making his grasp slippery and his body tremble, he was able to move the garbage quickly because the pieces were mostly large: a broken wicker chair, some warped sheets of tin roofing, a staved-in trunk. Soon he had excavated enough to see that the arm was attached to a body.

"A golem!" he exclaimed, although he wasn't truly surprised. The human-shaped automatons were terribly expensive, and the few people wealthy enough to afford them usually kept them safely indoors, sharing them only with their closest friends. But he was aware golems existed, and he'd caught sight of them twice in his life: one being led by a leash down High Street by its owner, and another displayed in a shop window in a part of the city far too good for the likes of Dante. He'd never seen one so closely.

This golem was in very poor condition. Its limbs were twisted grotesquely, its skull slightly indented on one side. One eye was gone and the other—an unnatural but beautiful shade of lavender—stared sightlessly. Its skin was ripped in many places. Its hair, long strands of indeterminate color, was hopelessly snarled.

Dante shook his head over the waste of it, of someone destroying such a wonderful piece of craftsmanship.

And then the golem moaned.

Dante's feet slipped in the mud as he scrambled backward, and he narrowly avoided falling. He could see now that the golem's torso was moving ever so slightly, its back rising and falling as the bellows of its lungs moved in and out.

Good Lord. If he were able to repair the golem, how much could he sell it for? It might be too damaged to salvage, or fixing it might be beyond his skills. But if he were successful, he wouldn't have to worry about rent and food for a year at least. Maybe longer. He could afford new boots and some better tools. He could buy a warmer coat.

Dante—tall, broad shouldered, heavy boned—was built more like a laborer than a craftsman. He was naturally muscular despite his poor diet and uneven exercise. His father used to make disparaging remarks about his size, as if Dante had grown so large just to spite him. But today Dante was glad for his strength because the golem was as heavy as a man. It made another noise as Dante set it in the barrow, a sort of drawn-out groan. Broken gears shifting, maybe. He made sure the mermaid and the other small items he'd collected weren't crushed under the golem's weight, and then he set out for home.

DANTE'S home was small, crowded, and messy. It was really more a shed than a house; not so long ago it had served as storage and as a repair shop for his landlord's steam carriage. But the landlord had bought two more steam carriages—larger, grander models—and housed them in a more spacious garage. This old building had stood empty until Dante worked up enough courage to ask if he might rent it. Although Mr.

Sainsworth was wealthy, he was never one to turn down a few more coins, so he'd acquiesced willingly enough.

It had taken only a bit of work to make the place habitable. Gas lanterns were already installed, as were a sink and stove. An outhouse stood a few yards away. Sometimes Dante missed the large copper tub he'd enjoyed in his parents' house, but he made do with the sink and a few towels. He'd scrounged an old iron bed that needed only a few repairs, a slightly wobbly table, a pair of unmatched chairs, and a few pots and pans and the like. He'd bought the cheapest mattress he could find—something his back sometimes regretted—and a few linens. The building already came equipped with an enormous workbench and several sets of shelves.

His home was a bit dreary. He hadn't bothered to decorate it, having neither the money nor the time for such frivolities. But today it didn't matter, because all he craved was some warmth and dry clothing.

He parked the barrow in its usual corner next to the workbench, lit the stove and lanterns, and began stripping. His boots were completely sodden, so he set them as close to the stove as he dared. He hung his wet clothes on the line near one wall. As he waited for the kettle to boil, he toweled himself off and tugged on his spare set of clothing. It was in as poor repair as the other.

Finally, he poured himself a mug of tea, grabbed a hunk of stale bread and his last bit of cheese, and sat at the table.

He could have lived more comfortably if he'd chosen to work for others. He was skilled at his work; even his father had admitted that. But his soul had been ground away with each day spent under the old man's critical gaze, creating or repairing one featureless timepiece after another. So he'd left. He'd obtained a position in a master craftsman's workshop, assembling delicate jewelry and clockwork toys for the very rich. But even there he hadn't been allowed to use his imagination—everything was made to his employer's orders. Besides, he felt uncomfortable being surrounded by the other men and women who worked there. At first they tried to chat with him, but his responses were awkward and stilted, and soon they ignored him instead. *Standoffish*, they'd said. *Thinks he's too good for us.*

So now he was on his own, with no master and no judgmental coworkers. He could repair things however he fancied, as long as he could find the proper components. He didn't yearn for wealth or recognition; if he could afford only a few more comforts, he'd be quite content. A man like him needed little more.

The tea was good, hot enough to burn his tongue. It warmed him from the inside out, and his belly was satisfied by the bread and cheese. He stood and stretched, then ambled over to the barrow. After turning up the flame in a nearby lantern, he considered his options.

The golem looked even more pathetic in the strong light, its body folded into an untidy heap in the barrow. Dante cleared a space on the bench—an effort that took him some time—then lifted the golem and arranged it supine along the surface. Its chest was moving, making a rattling wheeze with each intake of breath. "Why *do* the golems breathe? It's not as if they're living beings." He stroked his bristly chin. "I expect it's to make them appear more human." The golem's maker had made other efforts toward realism as well: flat brown nipples, a shallow navel, a soft plump penis nestled above a pink scrotum. But aside from the messy tangle on its head, it was hairless. And of course with its current level of damage, with its innards showing quite clearly and its form twisted into impossible angles, it was very clear the golem was nothing but a broken machine.

"Ah, but such a clever machine!" As Dante cleansed away the mud and grime, he marveled at the workmanship. The automaton's skeleton was of some alloy that was both light and strong. Ingenious pumps worked fluids through a mechanical vascular system. Where a man's heart would be, the golem had a compact engine. Dante made an incision in the skin and was delighted to discover that the engine still functioned, beating as steadily as his own, but he couldn't work out what fueled it.

He knew the golem possessed a mechanical brain as well, some kind of device that permitted it to learn simple commands and perform certain tasks. He was tempted to take a peek inside its head, but he suspected he wouldn't understand what he saw. Alchemy and magics, according to the rumors. Those were the things that made golems work.

"Damn," he said after more inspection simply turned up more mysteries. He rubbed his eyes wearily. He wasn't going to be able to repair the golem—its workings were beyond him. His dreams of prepaid rent and warm coats faded away. He consoled himself with the thought that maybe he could at least use some of the golem parts in another project.

He'd work on the mermaid instead, he decided. He reached for the golem, intending to store it on one of his shelves with the other broken bits and pieces. But when he touched it, the golem made another sound—a tiny whimper. It turned its head slightly and *looked* at him.

And gods help him, but Dante saw emotion in that single lavender eye. Fear. Pain. Despair.

Golems were machines, and machines did not possess *feelings*. In fact, sometimes Dante fancied himself a machine as well, cold and unemotional, incapable of love or joy. More than once he'd dreamt of splitting open his own skin and finding nothing but clockwork.

"Can you understand me?" Dante asked quietly.

The golem tried to answer, but its jaw was broken and the sounds it made were too garbled to be words. It nodded twice, very slightly.

It was horrible. Nothing so mangled should be capable of movement, let alone… thought. Consciousness of a sort. Dante felt as if he might be sick. He grabbed a dusty sheet of canvas from the nearby shelf and quickly draped it over the golem. He'd work on the mermaid. At least he might earn a bit of money from that.

He cleaned the mermaid carefully. Free of grime, it looked better already. He pulled his stool to the bench, settled his magnifying lenses on his nose, and reached for his most delicate tools. He'd fix the interior mechanisms first and then worry about the decorations. With great care, he removed a few of the metal plates to expose the gears that moved her tail.

Usually when he worked he lost all sense of time and place. It was as if his mind and body ceased to exist, or perhaps shifted to a different plane of existence, and the tools became extensions of his fingers. Very often he'd finish a project and find the stove gone cold, his back and legs horribly cramped from hours of sitting.

But not this evening. Yes, he managed to repair the tiny clockwork so the mermaid's tail moved sinuously, and he even began the more laborious task of working on the bits that controlled her arms and head. But he never became completely immersed in his work. His gaze kept straying over the lenses of his spectacles to the canvas-covered form on the table, even though the lump was silent and unmoving. There was a *presence* in his home now, and it made him very uncomfortable.

Finally, he made a small noise of frustration and disgust, and he set the mermaid aside. If it hadn't still been raining hard, he would have gone for a walk. Yes, it was well past dark, but he frequently walked for miles at night. The later the hour, the fewer people he would encounter—people who looked askance at his shabby clothing or, worse, attempted to speak to him. He never knew quite what to say in response to idle pleasantries. It was as if everyone else in the world had received a script but his had been misplaced.

Frowning at his forced incarceration, he heated another kettle of water. He didn't make proper tea this time. Instead, he added a bit of crumbled dried mint to his cup, as well as a few chamomile flowers. He hoped that might help fight off the rawness he was feeling in his throat. "Can't afford to become ill," he muttered. He drank the concoction too quickly and burned his tongue again.

He was hungry, but there was no point dwelling on that. He stripped off his trousers, coat, and shirt, leaving only his threadbare long underpants and undershirt and his thick woolen socks, which needed darning. He doused all the lanterns except the one beside his bed, then climbed under the quilts. He opened his sketchbook and began to draw the mermaid as she would look once he completed the repairs.

The charcoal pencil flew over the page, rapidly tracing the sleek lines of her body, the details of her face and hair, the jewels Dante planned to add. But he didn't stop drawing once the mermaid was complete. He added a sandy sea bottom dotted with shells and fronds of greenery. A small school of fish materialized over her left shoulder. They were fanciful, quite unlike any of the drab creatures the fishmongers sold. Off to the left and far in the background, he sketched a few lines suggesting an ancient shipwreck. And there—just barely visible at the edge of the page—was a large tail fin. A merman swimming away. The mermaid's friend, perhaps. She looked as if she were engaged in a playful pursuit.

"Stupid," Dante said when the drawing was complete. His sketches were of no use whatsoever. His father used to tear them to pieces when he found them. Dante should probably do the same. But he didn't. In fact, he found himself smiling slightly at the pencil mermaid, sharing in her happiness.

He set the notebook and pencil aside and reached for the lantern. But just as his fingers touched the switch, he thought he heard a noise.

Not the rustle of the mice that occasionally ventured into his home in search of crumbs. This was more like a whimper. It was so quiet he could almost tell himself he'd imagined it. Maybe it was just a gust of wind.

But he was a poor liar, even to himself. "Damn it all," he growled as he shoved away the blankets and climbed out of bed.

The workbench was cloaked in shadows so thick Dante could almost feel them. The room smelled of dust and damp and mint. The rainfall had slowed and was making a steady dull pounding on the roof. Oddly, Dante's heart was pounding too—*thud-thump, thud-thump*, like a gear slightly out of balance.

His hand was uncharacteristically clumsy, so it took him a moment to light the lantern. And even then he simply stood for a moment or two, staring down at the canvas.

"It's only a machine," he said. He'd never hesitated over a machine before. He was confident around engines and devices, secure in the knowledge that if he didn't already know what made them run, he could work it out quickly enough. But now….

"Enough!" he said sternly in his father's voice, and he tugged the canvas away.

The golem's face had once been beautiful, with broad cheekbones, a long straight nose, and a full upper lip. Now that its hair was dry, the strands glowed rust-red in the lantern light. The golem had impossibly long eyelashes as well, even on the lid over the crushed and empty socket, and tiny lines had been artfully made near the corners of its eyes and across its forehead, so it resembled a human face rather than a mask.

The golem looked at him. Dante could discern its pupil contracting and dilating minutely as the golem's gaze continued. What wonders of optics had been created for this toy?

"Do you *want* things?" Dante hadn't meant to speak and was startled by his own slightly hoarse voice.

The golem blinked twice and then nodded.

"Do you want to…." *Live* wasn't the right word. Dante rubbed his head. "Do you want to exist? Or I can… can end you."

The golem's eye widened and the fingers of one hand curled.

"Do you want me to try to repair you? I'm not certain I can."

The golem tried to speak. Dante was fairly certain it said *please.*

With a sigh—but also with a certain amount of strange excitement racing through his nerves—Dante reached for his tools.

THE rain had stopped. The sun shone weakly through the high windows of his home, illuminating the dust motes dancing in the air. Dante set down his tool and stretched his cramped back and shoulder muscles, then rubbed his sore fingers. "I can't do any more right now," he said.

He'd been speaking to the golem as he worked. He usually mumbled to himself, little half-intelligible phrases of instruction about what to do next. Sometimes praise or curses, depending on how the repairs were going. But this night the golem had been watching him—listening to him—and it had felt natural to offer a brief explanation of what he was about to do. "I'm trying to straighten this bit of metal here" or "This tubing needs unsnarling." And he'd discovered that if he didn't give warnings, the golem would moan in seeming pain as Dante prodded its workings. Its limbs would shudder with tension and its wheezy breaths would speed up. But if Dante *did* explain, the golem was... calmer.

Now it lay on his worktable, arms and legs newly straightened. Dante had soldered patches onto its broken skeleton, had straightened the pneumatic system so it now ran smoothly, had improvised replacement parts for missing or broken gears. Another solid day or two of work might bring the golem into reasonable working order. But he couldn't do much for the damaged skin beyond some clumsy stitching to hold the tears together. He couldn't replace the missing eye. And he couldn't repair the caved-in portion of the skull, at least not without great risk of destruction to the engine housed inside—the engine that allowed the golem to move and think and feel.

"I'll never be able to sell you," Dante said. "I've wasted all this effort." But the effort didn't *feel* wasted. Not when the golem looked at him.

Dante's stomach was so empty it felt inside out, and his eyes were gritty with exhaustion. But instead of climbing into bed, he lifted the golem into his arms, carried it across the room, and settled it on his mattress. It looked more human there than on the workbench, which was unsettling. Dante pulled a blanket up to its chest. "Do you sleep?" he asked.

The golem regarded him silently. Dante hadn't yet fixed its jaw.

Shaking his head at his own foolishness, Dante walked to the stove. He swayed on his feet as he waited for the kettle to heat. His eyelids were heavy. Perhaps he should invent a machine to prop them open.

Two mugs of tea did little to placate his hunger or alleviate his bone-deep fatigue. But they warmed him, at least, and his fingers obediently did his bidding as he turned again to repairing the mermaid.

ANNETTE SWAN pursed her lips at the deep shadows under Dante's eyes and the scruffy growth of his whiskers. But she took the fabric-wrapped bundle from him anyway and set it on her glass-topped counter. She carefully unwrapped the folds of material to reveal the mermaid. Just enough sunlight came in through the shop's front windows to make the toy's glass jewels sparkle.

Mrs. Swan still hadn't said a word, but her pale eyebrows rose slightly. Dante hoped that was a good sign.

"Did you make this yourself?' she asked.

"No. I found it and repaired it."

"But the jewelry, was that original to the piece?"

Dante felt his cheeks warm slightly. "No."

She lifted the mermaid and peered at it more closely. After a few moments of turning it this way and that, of prodding at it here and there, she turned the tiny key located in the mermaid's flowing metal tresses. Dante had impulsively added a tiny bit of blue glass to the key, thinking it made the protuberance look more like an ornament and less like a piece of machinery. The mermaid's tail fluttered and her arms and head moved. The motions were pleasingly smooth and the inner gears were inaudible.

Mrs. Swan nodded and placed the toy back on the folds of cloth. "How much do you want for it?"

Oh, Dante *hated* this part. He was absolutely no good at haggling. He always felt as if he were being unreasonable in his demands *and* being cheated, both at the same time. But he needed the money very badly. After a quick glance around the shop, where he knew all the shiny baubles would bring high prices from wealthy customers, he straightened his back.

"Fifty sovereigns," he said.

This time, Mrs. Swan's brows rose even higher. "Fifty?" She was a tiny woman about Dante's age—and probably half his weight—but she carried herself with such confidence that he'd always been slightly terrified of her. In the past, he'd likely have backed down at once.

But not today. "Yes." He kept his tone very firm.

She regarded him with the same serene calculation with which she'd considered the mermaid. He tried not to squirm, and he hoped she couldn't hear the gurgles of his empty belly. Finally, she gave him the tiniest of smiles. "All right. Fifty it is. One moment, please."

Dante swallowed a groan of relief. He felt slightly faint, and not just from lack of sleep or food. Fifty sovereigns was far more than he'd ever earned from a single piece. It would be enough to keep him fed for some time and to buy a few incidentals besides.

Mrs. Swan left him at the counter as she disappeared into a back room. When she returned a few moments later, she held a red cloth bag. "Would you like to count it?" she asked, holding it out to him.

"No. I, um, I'm sure you...." His words ground to a halt as his cheeks burned. He was fairly certain she was teasing him, and he didn't know how to respond.

She chuckled lightly and pressed the bag into his hand. "It's because of the jewelry," she said. "You took a nice piece and made it truly special. It'll fetch a good price. I hope you bring me more like it soon."

"I... I'll try." He tucked the heavy purse into his inside coat pocket, the one that didn't have a hole in the lining.

"Perhaps you might have some rest first, though."

"I... um... yes."

Mrs. Swan tilted her head at him, that little smile still playing at the corners of her lips. "Or perhaps you'd prefer a good meal first. I was going to have dinner soon myself."

Oh good *Lord*! Was she flirting with him? Dante's face went a new shade of scarlet. "I... have to go now...."

"Of course. Good afternoon, Mr. Winter."

He stumbled out of her shop and down the street.

Dinner was an excellent idea, he decided after a few blocks. Something hot and filling. But not here, in this neighborhood where all the shop windows displayed expensive amusements for the wealthy and where passersby viewed his scruffy appearance with some alarm. So he turned off the main street onto a smaller one, and then a smaller one still. He passed under rows of brick and stone buildings, each towering four or five stories above him. There were pots of red flowers in the windows, but also lines hung with laundry. Children raced about, laughing, finding him not worth their notice, and the smells of food wafted temptingly from kitchens. This was not far from the house where he grew up and where, presumably, his father still lived.

A few more blocks and the surroundings grew shabbier. Not as shabby as him, perhaps, but definitely many notches below Mrs. Swan's neighborhood. Slightly grubby shops sold home goods, used books, and vegetables. Steam rose into the sky above a few larger buildings, which no doubt housed fabrication workshops of one kind or another. There were no steam omnibuses in this neighborhood, nor hackneys for hire. Just tired-looking people walking home from work.

Dante found a restaurant that met his needs: cheap but clean and not too crowded. He sat in the shadows of the back, letting the other patrons' conversations wash over him as he ate a decent hunk of beef with potatoes and green beans and drank a pint of satisfactory ale.

He thought about Mrs. Swan, who'd been widowed very young by the same cholera epidemic that took Dante's mother and sister. Mrs. Swan was pretty, with a heart-shaped face and with ash-blonde hair she kept elaborately coiffed. She was friendly to him and didn't seem to mind his social ineptitude too much. Not only was she apparently rather well-off, but she owned a shop that made the perfect showcase for Dante's work—and she appreciated rather than reviled his attempts to make his pieces more decorative.

If Dante were different, he might try to court her.

With his stomach sated but his mind slightly troubled, he paid his bill and left. It was dusk, and a rare westerly breeze had cleared the air of coal smoke, bringing instead a faint tang of salt from the sea. Dante felt the unfamiliar weight of the coins in his purse, and instead of walking back home, he headed in the opposite direction, toward the river. He deliberately kept to the side streets, avoiding the crowds on the busier thoroughfares. Finally he came to a street he knew well and to a familiar row of pubs.

He'd visited these pubs quite often when he still worked for his father. The False Rose. King Edward's Arms. The Cat and Mouse. Each was much like the other—dark, redolent of sour ale, filled with silent men exchanging sidelong glances. Conversation wasn't expected. Was, in fact, almost discouraged. You paid your coppers for a pint and took a seat, and when your wandering gaze locked with someone else's, you each gave small nods. Separately, you'd walk to a long, gloomy hallway at the back, where an attendant held his hand out for additional payment. You found an empty room, you removed as little clothing as possible, and you fucked. The act was so mechanical and passionless that even while he plunged in and out of another person's body, Dante always imagined himself a clockwork figure of one man screwing another.

Probably Mrs. Swan would not want that on her shelves.

He skulked on the street corner, watching as a tall man entered The Cat and Mouse. A moment later, two men left the Rose—one older and sporting a neat gray beard, the other very young and pretty. They were talking quietly with each other, laughing lightly as they walked. Neither glanced at Dante as they passed.

Instead of entering one of the pubs, Dante turned away. But although he was so tired he was numb, he didn't return home. He walked with intent to a neighborhood not far from Mrs. Swan's, where couples rolled slowly down the street in their private steamcars. The tops had been removed from all the steamcars so the occupants could take careful note of who was wearing what and accompanying whom. If they noticed Dante at all, they curled their lips slightly in distaste before looking swiftly away.

The shops here had tall, broad windows displaying extravagant suits and dresses, crystal vases and bowls, breathtakingly expensive necklaces and earrings. It was in this neighborhood that Dante had once seen a golem on display. It had been posed like a classic statue, but its violet eyes had followed the movements of passersby.

There were no golems visible tonight. One shop had a child-sized steamcar, as elaborate as the fanciest real ones and, according to the sign, fully functional. Another shop sold exotic pets: dogs with fur dyed in candy-floss colors, chattering monkeys, sad-eyed fairies with jewel-toned wings. Dante shuffled past all the bright windows and turned onto a narrower, slightly less grand street. He stopped in front of a window in which swaths of rich fabrics were draped in appealing array. He took a deep breath and went inside.

Two gray-haired women stood at the long counter. They gave him twin scowls of disapproval, but he tried his best approximation of a winning smile as he approached them.

"Yes?" demanded the shorter woman imperiously.

"Um, good evening. I… I need some fabric."

She narrowed her eyes. "For what purpose?"

"Er…." He swallowed. "I make toys. I'm working on a sort of, uh, doll right now, and I need something to simulate skin. Please."

Her icy glare didn't thaw, but the other woman looked thoughtful. "The fabric must look like skin, but must it also feel like it?"

"As much as possible, yes. But I'd like it to be fairly… sturdy. I don't want it to tear."

"Silk," she said confidently. "Upholstery silk. It's very strong but smooth to the touch." She was already moving out from behind the counter. Dante trailed in her wake as she led the way through a forest of fabric bolts. The material came in every imaginable color and pattern. Some of it was brocaded in gold or silver, while others had intricate scenes embroidered on them. He wondered whether the work was done by hand or by machine. *Could* a machine produce something so beautiful and complex?

The saleswoman stopped in front of a densely packed shelf. "What precise tone were you looking for?"

Well, that was a good question. Although he'd spent many hours working on the golem, he'd paid little attention to the exact shade of its skin. "Um… something like my skin, I suppose."

She wore a pair of lenses on a chain around her neck. She put them to her eyes and peered at him for a moment, then turned to scan the shelf. Her hand hovered indecisively before she grabbed one of the bolts and held it next to Dante. "Yes. Will this do?"

He reached over to touch it very gently. It did feel a bit like cool skin. "I think so."

The fabric cost him a shocking amount of money, but he smiled anyway as he walked home.

THE golem was exactly where Dante had left it: on his bed, the blankets tucked up to its armpits. But it turned its head to watch Dante as he entered the building and removed his outer clothes. It even tried to smile a bit. Dante was surprised how pleasant it was to come home to someone—no, he reminded himself sternly. Some*thing*.

"I can't work on you tonight," Dante announced a bit petulantly. "I'm far too tired. I need to sleep."

The golem blinked at him for a moment. And then, to Dante's utter shock, it rolled itself off the bed, landing on the hard floor with a thump and a moan.

Dante rushed over. The golem had pulled the blanket with it as it fell and was now wrapped like a museum mummy. It took Dante a few awkward moments to unwind the blanket. He examined the golem anxiously for fresh damage, and he was relieved to find none. "Don't undo all the work I've done on you!" he scolded.

Now the golem looked distressed. It tried to raise onto its knees—for what purpose Dante couldn't imagine—and he pushed it back down gently but firmly. "Just stay there. Don't... don't *do* anything."

The golem froze.

Dante sighed before tossing one of the blankets over the troublesome thing. He wasn't sure why he bothered. Wasn't as if it could get a chill. But it *looked* cold, huddled naked on his unswept floor.

"Oh, you are a fool," he grumbled. And then he got ready for bed.

HE SLEPT later than he'd intended. When he woke up, the golem was right where he'd left it, curled up next to his bed. It smiled tentatively at him as he sat up and rubbed his eyes.

Dante left the golem there as he performed his morning ablutions and ate a hearty breakfast. He couldn't remember the last time he'd managed sausage and eggs, and today he even had some lovely sliced tomatoes and two thick slabs of toast. He was glad he'd stopped at the grocer's on the way home the previous night. His mood was uncharacteristically light as he carried the golem to the workbench.

"I'm going to fix your jaw first," he said, which made the golem smile crookedly.

Repairing the jaw took a long time, as did the broken bits of the golem's fingers and feet. But when he was done, the golem could wiggle its digits freely, and its mouth opened and closed without causing obvious discomfort. As it turned out, the silk fabric was not a very precise color match—it was a few shades lighter than the skin—and the stitching that held the patches was more uneven than Dante liked.

He took a break for a very late lunch, chewing on an apple and some cheese while he stood beside the bench, giving his work a critical view. The limbs were straight and the gears moved well. The damage that remained, although quite extensive, was mostly cosmetic. He thought the automaton should work all right, even if it looked terrible. "Can you speak?" he asked.

"Yes, master."

Dante was so taken aback at the sound of the golem's voice that he barely noticed the honorific. He'd expected the golem to sound like a machine, perhaps creaky and stilted. But it didn't. Its voice was deep and warm and very human.

"What's your name?"

The golem smiled. "Whatever master wishes."

"Well, yes. But didn't you have a name before? With your previous... owner."

The smile faded and the golem looked away. "He called me Puppet," the golem whispered.

Dante winced and wondered if the machine could truly feel shame. "Well, that won't do. How about...." He stroked his whiskers as he thought. "Talon! It's perfect."

"Talon?" The golem seemed pleased by the name, if puzzled.

"A mythological figure. A living statue created to protect an island and a goddess."

Oh. When the golem smiled like *that*, he was almost beautiful, despite the devastation to his face. And when had *it* become *he*? Perhaps that happened with the giving of a name.

"Thank you, master. I like it very much," Talon said.

"Good. But don't... don't call me that."

"What shall I call you then, sir?"

"My name is Dante."

"May I move, Dante?"

"You…. Of course. I'd like to see how well you're functioning anyway."

"Thank you." Slowly and deliberately, Talon sat up. Dante stepped back as Talon swung his legs over the side of the bench and began to stand. His knees buckled, and Dante darted forward to catch him before he fell. After a moment or two of steadying, Talon was able to stand on his own.

At which point he swiftly dropped to his knees and bent his back in a deep bow. "Thank you, sir. Dante. Thank you."

Dante felt his face grow warm. "For…. Don't…. For what?"

Talon remained on his knees but straightened his back to look up at Dante.

"Good Lord!" Dante exclaimed. "You can cry?" Because Talon's eye was shining and a trail of moisture ran down his cheek.

"I can cry. Thank you for rescuing me. For repairing me."

"Oh. Well… it's what I do." Dante shifted his feet uncomfortably. "Stand up now. Let's see how well you're working."

For at least an hour, Talon moved about obediently while Dante inspected him. A few gears required adjustment, but in the end Dante was reasonably satisfied. Talon had a slight limp that Dante just couldn't fix, but Talon said he was free of pain at least. In fact, Talon seemed very happy indeed, until he walked to a corner of the large room and caught a glimpse of himself in Dante's ancient frameless looking glass.

"Oh!" Talon exclaimed. His legs wobbled and he nearly fell.

Dante rushed to his side. "What? What's wrong?"

Talon stared at his reflection. "I didn't realize…. How can I serve you like *this*?" More tears dripped down his face and he fell to his knees again, this time in despair rather than gratitude.

Dante's mouth was dry and his stomach heaved. He'd known how golems were used by their owners. He'd heard the jokes and innuendos, and he knew it wasn't out of a preference for detail that golems were designed to be anatomically correct. He'd always been mystified why someone would get pleasure out of fucking a machine. But now that he'd spent some time around one of those machines and knew what Talon was like, sex with him seemed much more like rape.

Dante set a hand on Talon's shoulder. "I've work for you to do here, if you like."

Talon twisted his head to look up at him. "Work?"

"I… I'm sorry I can't do a better job repairing you. You're very complex and I haven't the knowledge…." He swallowed. "Could you… could you perhaps help with my domestic chores? This place is a mess. My clothes need mending. My shelves have become terribly disorganized."

Talon scrambled to his feet and wiped the tears from his cheek. "You'll keep me, then?"

"Of course. If you like."

Talon folded his arms around Dante.

People rarely touched Dante. He couldn't remember receiving hugs when he was a child, and he'd never managed to form a close friendship with anyone. Even on those occasions when he'd visited the False Rose or a neighboring pub, the contact between him and other men had been limited to what was necessary. There had been no caresses, no gentle strokes, no lips pressed to neck or shoulder.

Dante stood there awkwardly, not returning Talon's embrace. But he couldn't help noticing how their bodies fit together. Talon was a few inches shorter than him and somewhat more delicately built. He didn't feel like a machine, and when he rested his head on Dante's shoulder and sighed, he sounded very human.

When Talon pulled away a moment later, he looked quizzical. "I'm sorry, ma—Dante. Do you prefer if I don't touch you?" The corners of his mouth turned down and he glanced away. "I disgust you."

"You don't. I'm just… I'm not very good with people."

And now Talon looked back, surprised and delighted. Who knew a machine could be so mercurial in mood? "People? You view me as a person?"

"Er… yes, I suppose so. In a broad sense…." But Dante didn't get to finish his thought, because Talon was laughing. If an automaton could cry, it was no great wonder he could laugh as well, Dante thought. But Talon's happiness turned out to be infectious, so that soon Dante was chuckling as well. Good Lord, when had Dante last laughed?

Still grinning broadly, Talon reached up to stroke Dante's cheek. "Thank you. You can't know.... Well, thank you. I will serve you well, I promise. Anything you ask of me."

Dante took a half step back. "I think... what I'd ask of you now is that you get dressed."

Talon had to wear Dante's spare set of clothing, which was too large for him. And he'd obviously never worn clothes before, so Dante had to help him. Afterward, Talon spent a long time staring at his reflection in the looking glass, bubbling with amazement at how much he now looked like a man, at least if one overlooked the devastation to his face. Dante discovered his own cheeks were aching from the unaccustomed smiling.

Talon had never performed any household chores before so Dante had to demonstrate, but Talon learned very quickly. He asked a thousand questions—not just what and how, but also why, and every time Dante satisfied his curiosity, Talon's joy grew a little more. Dante had the sense that Talon had rarely been indulged this way by his previous owner, that his first master had preferred to order him about instead. But Dante was having *fun*. Huh.

While Talon apparently possessed an inexhaustible store of energy—from a still-undiscovered source—Dante did not. The hour grew late and the mattress grew ever more tempting. Finally, when Talon was considering how he might reach the high windows to clean them, Dante shook his head. "Not tonight. I need to sleep."

"Oh! Of course! I'm sorry." Actually, Talon didn't look especially sorry. He grinned impishly, as if he'd been planning to keep Dante awake all night.

Dante looked around the room. "I can't afford to buy another bed for you just now...."

"I can't share yours?"

"I don't think.... That's not a good idea."

"When it's dark, you won't see how ugly I am. You can imagine—"

"No!"

Talon flinched at the harsh tone, so Dante made an effort to calm himself. "I won't use you that way," he said.

"Why not? It's what I was made for. I belong to you and you can do whatever you wish with me."

Dante was not in the mood to explain ethics and morals to an automaton, especially when he was a bit fuzzy himself on the matter. "What I wish is to go to sleep. You can take a blanket and find a place for yourself on the floor. I'll buy you something more comfortable when I've enough money."

Talon nodded obediently. He watched silently as Dante readied himself for bed—seeming slightly alarmed when Dante left to use the outhouse and then relieved when he returned. And when Dante stripped to his underclothes and climbed into bed, Talon curled up on the floor right next to him.

Dante was smiling as he doused the lantern.

IT WAS a very strange thing. Dante had spent his life in solitude, and yet he adjusted quickly and comfortably to constant companionship. Perhaps because Talon was a machine, albeit a very human one. Dante had always felt relaxed around machines.

Talon turned out to be excellent company. He worked very hard at cleaning; soon their home was immaculate. He organized Dante's shelves of materials so the bits of metal and wire and glass were laid out in much more sensible order. Not only did that save time, since Dante didn't waste minutes searching for that piece of something he knew he'd stashed *somewhere*, but Dante also rediscovered things he'd forgotten he had collected. And he found himself more readily inspired, his creative indulgences flowing much more easily from mind to fingers.

He sold two more pieces—a reworked scuttling crab with a jeweled shell to Mrs. Swan and a watch with an intricately engraved case to a shop specializing in timepieces. His purse was fatter with coins than ever before. He paid three months' rent in advance, filled his cupboards with dry goods, and bought Talon a suit of clothes and a mattress of his own. Talon wordlessly insisted on placing his mattress as close as possible to Dante's, and he positively preened in his new outfit.

Talon also learned to cook, even though he didn't eat. He was no great chef, and occasionally his choices were startling or even inedible, but most of the time his meals were at least as good as anything Dante could have managed. Besides, cooking kept Talon busy, and he was always truly delighted to watch Dante enjoy what he'd prepared.

Oh, Talon had his annoying traits too. He talked. A lot. And while Dante didn't usually mind, the constant chatter could irritate him when he was trying to work. Still, he rarely asked Talon to be quiet, because Talon was so clearly thrilled to have the freedom to speak. He never explicitly told Dante that his former master had rarely permitted him to talk—in fact, he very rarely mentioned his previous existence at all—but that was the impression Dante received.

Talon could be a bit of a mother hen. If Dante worked too long, Talon would gently ease the tools from his fingers and pull him away from the workbench. He'd make Dante eat or exercise or sleep, whichever Talon deemed appropriate for the time. And if Dante tried to leave home with his hair uncombed or his face unshaven, Talon clucked at him, sat him down, and groomed him. "You're so very handsome," he'd say as he untangled Dante's curls. "If you'd only make yourself more presentable and smile more often, you wouldn't be so lonely."

"I'm not lonely," Dante would answer, and for the first time in his life those words were almost true.

One afternoon, Dante laced on his boots.

Talon abandoned his sweeping to rush over. "You've a rip on your sleeve. Let me try to sew it."

"You needn't bother right now. I'm only going to the rubbish heaps. I need to begin a new project or we'll be broke again soon."

"Oh." Talon glanced quickly at the door and then away. He hadn't been outside even once since Dante had brought him home.

"Would you like to come with?" Dante asked.

Talon's eye went wide but then his face fell. "People might see me."

"They might. I sometimes pass a few between here and there. Is that a problem?"

"I don't want.... I'll bring shame on you."

"Why on earth would you do that?" Dante asked in genuine puzzlement.

Talon brushed his fingers over the ruined part of his face.

And for once, it was Dante who initiated a touch. He retraced the path of Talon's fingers with his own, gently brushing over dented skull, missing eye, badly patched skin. "I am not ashamed of you," he said truthfully.

Talon kissed him.

Dante was taken entirely by surprise and froze in place—which didn't deter Talon at all. Talon simply tugged Dante's head down so as not to have to strain upward, then wound his fingers through Dante's hair and held on tight. Of their own accord, as if some hidden mechanism had been activated, Dante's arms rose and wrapped around Talon. Talon's tongue teased at Dante's lips until he opened them, and then slid inside. Talon tasted slightly metallic, like blood, and his tongue was amazingly soft and agile. Dante wondered for the first time what it was made of, and then forgot that thought immediately when Talon pressed tightly against his body.

After a moment, Dante pulled back slightly. "You can... you can...." He cleared his throat.

Talon laughed and pushed his hips forward so that his arousal was even more evident against Dante's. "I am fully functional. I can *want*, Dante. I want you. I can feel you wanting me back. Please?"

For a moment, Dante considered saying yes. Good gods, he wanted to. But then he shook his head and moved back. "I can't. We can't."

"Because I'm not real?"

"Talon, I think you're more real than I am. But you can't... you can't choose freely, and I won't take advantage—"

"But I do! I have. You've never forced me to do anything. I told you. I *want* this."

"You want this because you were made to."

"So were you! Perhaps you weren't built in a workshop like me, but humans are made to want one another, to yearn for friendship and touch and sex and love. You can't stop yourself from needing those things any more than I can."

"I can! I don't *need* anyone. I told you from the start, I'm no good with people. I have nothing but a clockwork heart."

Talon's answer was almost a whisper. "Even a clockwork heart can love."

Dante shook his head and went to fetch his coat.

THEY were silent as they walked to the rubbish heap. Dante was slightly in the lead, while Talon followed, pushing the empty barrow. The sky was its usual pewter gray, smelling slightly of sulfur and smoke. As he commonly did, Dante chose a dirt and cinder path along a dried-up creek bed. They saw nobody except for a shriveled old man walking a flop-eared dog. He didn't look at them as they passed.

Mr. Abernethy lived in a tiny shack at the entrance to the rubbish heaps. Dante rarely saw him, although he suspected the other man often watched him from inside. Today, though, Mr. Abernethy appeared in the doorway, pipe in one hand and bottle in the other.

"Who's that, then?" He jerked his pointed chin in Talon's direction.

"My... assistant."

Mr. Abernethy squinted for a moment and then shrugged. "Assistant, eh? Coming up in the world." It wasn't clear whether he was mocking Dante.

"A little," Dante replied.

"But you're still clawing through rubbish."

"Because sometimes I find a real treasure there."

With another shrug, Mr. Abernethy ducked back into his hut.

Dante led the way to some of the likelier spots. At first, Talon only watched as Dante sorted through the debris, casting most things aside but placing a few bits and pieces in the barrow. But then Talon seemed to get in the spirit of things, and he began going through the piles too. Sometimes he'd hold something up—a bit of metal, a broken something—and Dante would say yea or nay. Talon had a good eye and managed to find a few items Dante might have overlooked—a nearly intact panel of stained glass, a wooden box full of bearing balls. It was nice to work together, Dante concluded. And the barrow filled more quickly too.

They were heading to the exit when Dante slowed and then stopped. Talon halted as well. "Did you see something, Dante?"

"No. It's only... this is where I found you." He pointed at one heap of cast-off wreckage that wasn't much different from any of the others.

"Oh."

"The most valuable thing I've ever discovered here."

"But I'm worth nothing. Nobody would buy me."

"You're worth everything, and I'd never sell you." Dante cleared his throat and looked away.

Talon let go of the barrow handles and moved to Dante's side. They looked at the rubbish. After several long minutes, Talon sighed. "Master was nothing like you. He was cruel. It didn't matter how obedient I was or how hard I tried to please him. I think it made him feel powerful to make me feel weak."

Dante settled his arm on Talon's shoulders. "I'm sorry."

"He never saw me as anything but a toy. And when he grew tired of me... well, he was like a petulant child. He broke me. And then he threw me away." Talon's voice grew quieter, hoarser. "I don't know if I can die, Dante. I thought I'd be here forever. Alone." He made a choked sound and turned to burrow his face into Dante's shoulder.

Dante stroked Talon's copper hair. "I will never throw you away. Stay with me as long as you want. You won't be alone."

Talon responded by sobbing and holding him tight. Dante's own words echoed in his ears. *Won't be alone.* Gods, maybe Talon was right. Maybe even Dante could need.

Dante remained lost in contemplation as they returned home. This time they passed several people, each of whom gave Talon startled looks. The first time it happened, Talon flinched and ducked his head. But Dante kept his back straight and head up, and he looked into the eyes of each person, daring them to say anything about his golem. His Talon. None of them did, and soon Talon was walking taller as well, as if Dante's pride had spilled over to him.

Back at home, Talon helped put away their new supplies. "Would you like me to make you dinner now?" he asked when they were done.

"Not yet. I want to get started working."

"What will you make next?"

"I'm trying to decide. I could repair those opera glasses and they'd sell for quite a lot, but I'd have to buy a set of lenses first. Maybe I should fix that folding knife. It won't fetch more than a sovereign or so but should be a quick job."

As Dante stroked his chin in thought, Talon padded across the room to the bed. He picked up Dante's sketchbook, leafed through it for a moment, and carried it over. "Why not make this?" he asked, holding the page for Dante to view. A sailing ship floating through the waves, with three sails, a jaunty flag, and a figurehead of a warrior. A sea monster's giant tentacles were reaching up, ready to grab the hull.

Dante flapped a dismissive hand. "That's just... something I imagined. A frivolity."

"But it could be really spectacular! You could make the ship rock back and forth so it looks as if it's moving through the waves. And the tentacles could appear and then disappear."

That was exactly what Dante had imagined. "I don't make things, Talon. I'm only... a repairman. I find broken things and I fix them."

"You're more than that! You *create* things!" Talon slammed the sketchbook onto the workbench and took a step back, arms spread wide at his sides. "Look at me! You took a broken golem—a heap of worthless garbage—and you turned me into a *man*. Not... not a pretty man, but a real one. You can damn well make a stupid toy boat!"

The gears of Dante's heart moved quickly and the bellows in his chest rushed air in and out. Electricity zipped through the wires of his nerves. And then an amazing thing happened. He looked at Talon and saw a man—an imperfect man, but very beautiful—and at the same time the metal and glass inside Dante softened. Became bones and muscles and hot, salty blood.

Dante became a real man too.

With a wordless cry, he lurched forward and scooped Talon into a tight embrace.

What followed after that was no less of a revelation. To make love instead of simply fucking. To play with Talon's body, finding what would make Talon gasp and moan, and to experience Talon doing the same to him. To ease into welcoming tightness—not as his partner lay splayed against a wall, but in his own bed—and to look down at a face that had become familiar and beloved. To see a single lavender eye fill with tears of happiness, and to lick those tears away and find them sweet, a balm to his soul like mint tea and chamomile to a sore throat. To find every bit of his lover's body beautiful, patches, dents, and all. To hear his lover say he found Dante beautiful too, and to know Talon meant it, no matter how flawed Dante was.

Afterward, they lay naked together in the bed Dante vowed they would share from then on, and they traded soft secrets as the night bloomed. Talon said he would like to learn to read, and he thought maybe he would like to see more of the world than the tiny bits he'd been afforded so far. He said he'd overheard his old master talking about passenger ships that sailed through the sky. Talon wondered what it would be like to see the world as a bird does.

And Dante vowed he would no longer simply fix things. With the confidence Talon gave him, he would let his imagination roam freely, and he would create things. Wonderful things, with all the gorgeous, useless bits of ornament his heart desired. And maybe he'd become wealthy from his work but that wouldn't matter, because as long as he had his hands, his tools, and Talon, his heart would be content.

His beating, warm, loving, loved, *human* heart.

KIM FIELDING is very pleased every time someone calls her eclectic. She has migrated back and forth across the western two-thirds of the United States and currently lives in California, where she long ago ran out of bookshelf space. She's a university professor who dreams of being able to travel and write full time. She also dreams of having two perfectly behaved children, a husband who isn't obsessed with football, and a house that cleans itself. Some dreams are more easily obtained than others.

Kim can be found on her blogs:

http://kfieldingwrites.blogspot.com

http://www.goodreads.com/author/show/4105707.Kim_Fielding/blog

and on Facebook: https://www.facebook.com/KFieldingWrites.

Her e-mail is dephalqu@yahoo.com, and she can be found on Twitter at @KFieldingWrites.

THE GOLDEN GOOSE

MARK LESNEY

TWO burly footmen chased me through the house, and I had no choice when I reached the dead-end corridor. I popped out the fourth-story window to the screams of the household and barely missed falling to my death. Although temporarily blinded by lace curtains, I managed to catch the rusting waterspout beside the open window. It paid to be prepared and know the turf.

I held on to temporary salvation, safe for a moment, but at the expense of half the skin on my left palm and a nearly torn-off shoulder.

I didn't like the way the spear-point iron railings looked up at me from far below as they hungrily circled the larder stairs. I clung in desperation while the squared-off piping began to buckle with my weight.

I stank like a French pissoir, all my fine plans of daylight robbery undone by a pug-faced chambermaid who had forgotten to empty the grande dame's pot. How was I to know the lass would try to manage it in secret while the rest of the household staff was dealing with afternoon tea?

Her timorous creeping had outdone my own much-practiced stealth and all my preparations. We slammed into each other in the hallway as I tried to make my silent getaway. She screamed. I cursed. The rest can be expected.

Stale lady piss was a chilling damp across my shirtfront. Thank God the dame had not done worse in the middle of the night!

But my offended nose and sense of dignity were the least of my problems as one of the footman half threw himself out the window, the other apparently grabbing his legs, as his companion tried to reach me from above. The whistle of the local bobby began to shriek from around the street corner. It was like an opera performance of the Wild Hunt—a cacophonous symphony chorused with the ululating cries of the upset household just above me and the noisy crowd gathering below.

This was not the great triumph of criminal mastery it was supposed to be. I pictured tomorrow morning's *Times*—"Joshua Clarridge, Thief, Killed in Robbery Attempt, see page 17"—as I slipped three feet lower, clinging like a roach to the bending drain.

I joined in the chorus of howls from below as a loud thwacking pain convulsed my shin, a raging blow racing up through my thin trousers. Looking down, I met the enraged glare of the dame, her golden wig atilt, white forelocks poking from underneath, above her horsey face. She flailed up at me from the window just below, deadly with a silver-tipped umbrella that she swung like a hardwood staff. If she'd been ten years younger, her blows might have shattered the bone. Had she not been so out of breath with her exertions, her hollow wheezing might have joined the musical performance in banshee screams.

What damnable luck! I'd ruled out the chance of a midnight raid when I found out by flirting with the aging bootboy that his mistress had trouble sleeping and kept her gaslight on at dark. It had cost me two half-pints in the local pub, and enduring his bad breath, but the information had been solid gold.

Afternoon tea, then, was the next best choice—the perfect time in most fine households for a daylight robbery. The upper floors were habitually emptied of all servants as they attended to other duties. And in this case I had been assured that the lady herself never climbed back up the painful stairs once she went down, especially when a midday meal was being served. She was even having company today. Unwittingly, the local reverend, looking for a handout and a bellyful of sandwiches and sherry, had obliged me in my plans.

No one should have been the wiser. The grande dame's ruby necklace, earrings, and her fabled pearls all mine—my life's triumph of criminal design. Unfortunately, though, as generations of housebreakers before me realized, midafternoon was the worst time to get away when things went wrong.

Gawkers had gathered by now in the narrow cobbled street below, blocking the road to carriages. A cab man, his hansom stuck, was pointing me out in laughter to his fare. Ordinarily sedate matrons shouted for the bobbies to hurry up as I clung to my ever-tilting perch, completely visible to the crowd below, like some aerial Punch and Judy show. Only instead of a copper, it was a titled hag whomping on me, and with an umbrella in place of a truncheon. Every inch I descended made me a better target for her blows.

If I fell, I was a dead man. If they caught me, I was a dead man.

"It'll be the gallows for you, sonny!" the gap-toothed judge had gleefully promised me on my eighteenth birthday as he gaveled me down for fifteen years in Newgate Prison. Only one of which I served. I took the opportunity to make myself very friendly with a fat old guard who was convinced I'd run away with him to France when he got me free.

Poor sod. They took him up two days later at the boat train to Calais, after I'd completely disappeared. But if they caught me now....

I surveyed my chances, looking madly around for possible escape. Other bobbies from neighborhoods nearby had joined my local nemesis, and their wailing whistles echoed with his. Those interfering bluebottles would turn the corner and I'd be done with for sure.

So with gritted teeth and a prayer to the gods of luck and thievery, since shinnying down would do no good, I twisted and pressed my thin-soled shoes against the brickwork of the house, taking aim as best I could. Then I pushed off with all my might, clinging to the piping as the bands that held it to the house all snapped at once when their rusting bolts broke free. I flew backward, out of reach of the flailing umbrella, propelled to my final destination with the drain I clung to.

The blow was stunning when it came, and I lost hold of the pipe as it struck the wooden slats of the fence across the narrow street. I was summarily deposited on the other side, hidden from the main street in a dead-end alley between two houses slightly less prestigious than the one I'd just been robbing.

I plopped deeply into the local night soil collector's cesspit. Softer than the hardpan dirt of the rest of the alleyway, to be sure—but was an unbroken back truly an acceptable trade-off for the smear of human waste upon my teeth?

Coughing and choking, I limped my getaway, hobbled by the pain of the grande dame's umbrella, bruised but at least unbroken. Any moment the alleyway would swell with my pursuers. It wasn't as if my location was a secret. Half of London was applauding as I fell.

They wouldn't even need dogs to track me. The human nose was quite sufficient for this stench. I had to get away or find someplace to hide.

It was merest accident that led me past a particular one of the endless nine-foot privacy fences that blocked the back gardens of this too-rich neighborhood from its narrow alleyways. I heard the sound of scuffling—surely blows on skin—as I stumbled by it. I might have continued on, but I swear there was a plaintive cry for help suddenly silenced.

In for a farthing..., I thought as I backtracked and scrambled up the wood. I had to get out of the alley warren anyway, or I'd be caught for sure. The tiny warp of the fence slats wasn't enough to see through, but it still gave purchase to the cross boards, making just enough of a ladder for one as nimbly trained as I. Still, I bashed my shin in the same place as the dame's rain of blows in my final push to the top of the wall, and I almost cursed out loud.

From such a short height it was an easy, rolling fall into the spectacularly planted garden. Though I landed on some particularly thorny roses whose dried canes should have definitely been pruned last season before they snapped and dug their splinters in my side.

Combat had nearly finished as I crept upon the scene, peering out in secret from behind a large oak tree I could use if I had to get back over the fence in a hurry from this side.

The apparent winner was by far the less appealing of the two.

The thickset man pressed his forearm into the younger man's throat, crushing the life from him. As he lay on the ground, the victim's face was starting to purple. There was no choice and I stepped out from my hiding place, intent on stopping murder if I could.

Then, unaccountably, the brute sat up, straddling his unconscious foe. He pulled at the young man's clothes, snapping buttons on his trousers, and rolled him over, exposing white buttocks to the harsh glare of the afternoon sun.

Then he suddenly he started pawing at his own trousers.... Well! There was, of course, only one action a gentleman thief could take.

So I darted silently forward across the well-rolled grass, changing course only enough to snatch up a small branch of kindling from a pile by the large stable shed in front of which the two combatants had struggled.

The workman, for such he seemed in his rough-spun shirt and his dirty trousers, took no notice of me. He was too busy struggling in frustration, as his lust grew greater than his coordination, though he managed as I tiptoed closer to unbutton his own trousers and slip down to just his pants. Given his looks, even I didn't want to see the results when he finally got them off.

So I pictured the assailant's head as a somewhat large and lumpy cricket ball and, rushing forward, gave one mighty swing. It was a very different sort of smack compared to what I was used to, and the range I got wasn't very far. But it served to stop the intended insult.

With a howl of pain, the brute struggled up from his victim, shook his scraggly mane, and rose up, looming above me like a yeoman Hercules. Or perhaps a Cyclops, for my blow had nastily bashed his right eye closed.

One look at his raging face and massive frame, and I did the only thing possible—I up and ran as fast as I could, darting past him through the gaping door of the large shed. If I couldn't fight, then maybe I could slam shut the door and bar it from the inside.

That wouldn't help the prone half-naked young man on the gravel drive in front of the stable shed, but I couldn't help that now. Other than providing a distraction.

My pursuer was almost upon me, and there was no bar to seal the door. I looked madly about the gigantic shed, too frightened to be amazed at the mass of whirling gears and bursts of steam that filled the building, leaving no room to run, much less to hide.

The Cyclops was screaming at me now and I couldn't help but look backward at his fury. As he crossed the threshold, he suddenly fell on an uneven sill, his trousers dropping down about his ankles, for he hadn't properly buttoned them up again. Seizing the moment as he struggled with his clothes and tried to rise, I leaped over him and grasped up my trusty branch from the ground where I had dropped it.

I kept whacking at his head until he stopped trying to get up and the small branch snapped into splinters in my hand.

He wasn't quite dead, since his chest still rose and fell, and he wheezed spittle through his broken teeth. But he wasn't likely to get up for at least a while.

So I turned then to his victim, who was already struggling to his own feet, somewhat worse for wear. The young man refused the touch of my assistance, shoving me off with a cry that I recognized as fear of an additional attack.

I backed away a few steps and surveyed my rescued laddie in distress.

As the purple fled from his features with the paleness of approaching shock, they showed up bruises that had not been visible before. I could see he was a proper gentleman of twenty-odd or so, just a few years younger than me. And quite handsome of face and form—not that I was lacking in that area myself.

The garb he wore, though made for laboring, was not that of the working class, but had a vest, well-worn, with rows of pockets, the whole of best tanned leather. The torn shirt beneath it was made of the finest Irish linen, if I were any judge of quality (which I assure you I was, having worked in a dolly shop for six months of my misspent youth, taking in pawned goods that were mostly thieved).

The young man's disheveled trousers were also of the finest leather, though covered with chemical stains and evidence of burns. And the pants peering from beneath them were smooth and finely stitched, even as they were still slightly down, revealing a tantalizing glimpse of pubic hair and more. The pale root of his masculinity, barely revealed by his dishabille, nestled in a radiant thatch of red-gold that trickled upward. Because it was a view he was not voluntarily providing, I forced my eyes away out of courtesy with some regret.

His shirt was still torn open and the rivulet of his red-gold hair stopped its climb at the center of his belly. Too soon for my tastes, but it was still quite pleasing to the eye. As was the rosy aureole of a nipple that peeked out coyly through a rent in his shirt. It graced a surprisingly muscular chest, given the slightness of the young man's overall frame. In height he only reached my nose, and I was not considered a tall man, at least by most.

From beneath an equally radiant but slightly fairer crop of tousled red-gold hair, his deep-brown eyes widened at my unabashed gaze.

I averted my own eyes, at least somewhat, as with both hands he finished hoisting up his trousers with some alacrity. He also pulled shut his torn shirt with one clutching hand to achieve an awkward sort of modesty. When his face met mine once more, it held a faint rose of embarrassment, which was far more appealing than the purple bruise it had become while being strangled.

There was a sudden gurgling noise and a whistle of steam behind me. A grind of gears started, then stopped, with a sound like tearing metal.

"Good God!" the young man shouted as he ran by me, still buttoning his trousers with both hands. He darted around his still-supine assailant and rushed into the shed.

I whirled to watch him as he thwacked and prodded the strange machinery with a small wrench and a screwdriver that appeared instantly to hand from his waistcoat pockets. The great hulk of metal and glass grunted and gasped and hissed in complaint at his attentions far more than the man that I had bludgeoned had done for me.

"Grab that! Hurry!" The young man looked over his shoulder in a panic, urging me forward to help. "Give it to me!"

While looking at his excellent form from closer by, I pondered what I could safely grab without a summary rebuke, when he quickly pointed in sheer frustration to an unattached knob-like device just out of his reach. He wildly turned a many-spoked metal wheel, which threw off sparks into the air. "Shove that in the hole," he ordered, pointing toward a darkened orifice beside him.

I could only imagine…. "Or the mercury chamber is going to explode. It'll kill us both and poison the whole neighborhood!" he cried.

I obliged with alacrity, despite my total sense of unreality at everything that was occurring.

As soon as he calmed the great machine, his shoulders slumped in sudden exhaustion. He mopped his brow and face with a handkerchief, then turned to me. He doffed his shirt and vest in the steaming heat that filled the shed. There was sweat dripping down his face and neck and a fine line of perspiration traced its exquisite way down the curvature that began on each side of his upper thighs, the pair of which embraced a taut, lean stomach.

His sweat formed two rivulets that inched down toward the groin and the red-gold hairs lurking there above his trousers in a way I would gladly emulate with lips or tongue.

"Thank you for saving my life. Or at least preventing Nate from…. Well, whatever. I can't believe he really meant to kill me. Not after what he said.

"I'm Gordon Phillip Dennis. The Viscount Dennis, if you're into meaningless titles, by the way," he said, reaching out his hands to firmly clasp my own.

"And you have not only saved me, but saved this neighborhood, and helped me save my great design." His lopsided grin, a bit too wide for his fine features, was the only thing not perfect in his face. It was as if a chiseled statue from the Metropolitan Museum—Winged Mercury or Apollo—had come to life. One that had deep-brown eyes and thick curled lashes instead of empty orbs.

If a white rabbit in a waistcoat had suddenly appeared and invited me to tea in the company of a sweet young girl and a dormouse, it would have seemed quite normal in comparison to the events in this strange garden. Was I even in the heart of London anymore? Had I hopped the fence into another world?

And if I hadn't, then where were the police? Because if I survived whatever was going on with this machine and this man, then the jewels, among other things, were still bulging in my trousers. Beyond these garden walls, half a hundred people from the street, not to mention two footmen, a butler, a chambermaid, and the dame herself, could recognize my face.

So I had no choice but to play along with this mad fellow. Viscount, indeed! But perhaps I could find refuge with him—he was a fine young man, after all—until the hue and cry broke off. And he was right: I had saved him from a fate far worse than death, and I was helping with his damned machine. He owed me something.

There were other considerations, equally important. Along with his fine clothes and even finer face, I had finally noticed that his garden and this huge stable shed in it were fronted by a remarkably great house, more suited for the country than the center of the city. It was finer by far than the grande dame's own. If I could manage an invitation to go inside—the house, I mean—there were so many possibilities in store.

It took the better part of another hour to get his strange invention to settle down completely into a purring hum and just the occasional spit of steam. In the first fear of deadly blasts and poison gas, we were both too busy to notice his attacker had awakened and made his escape. Because when we finally turned to where he had lain, the fellow—Nate, he'd called him—was gone.

"I need a drink," the Viscount Dennis said, moping at his forehead again with his kerchief. He tossed it to me as if I were to mean to do the same. It was very nicely monogrammed and made of silk. Which meant, of course, that it was ruined. Even I knew silk wouldn't wash.

"Come up to the house; there's still ice in the kitchen, I think, and there's something I need to tell you about that bastard."

But I think I saw more than he realized as we entered to the great hall from the back door of the mansion. I saw too many dark square outlines where paintings must have hung for generations and now were gone. And surely the few remaining sticks of furniture in the hall and the one or two rooms I glanced in as we passed were not a fair representation of the mansion in its prime.

There was not a single scrap of present wealth, by any stretch of the imagination. It too much held the hallmark of the cash-strapped nobleman, who'd sold everything that wasn't nailed down or visible from the street, to pay the upkeep on his house and property.

That was not good at all, and I revised my plans. The likelihood of there being anything of portable worth seemed very small. But if I could just persuade this viscount that he should keep me around a little longer, this great house would be the perfect place to hide until the coppers gave up their pursuit. Who'd look for me here?

And the service was quite good. If a little odd.

I'd never been waited on by a full-fledged lord. Except, perhaps, for that one time in that brothel where I'd stayed....

He poured us both a cool cider from a great tan jug. The pantry was a small room, of oppressive dark-stained cherrywood, and I noted that any sign of family silver was long gone from the empty sideboards along its walls.

As he sipped his cider, the viscount looked me up and down, as if really seeing me for the first time. I smiled and tried to look my most personable, and desirable, if that might work.

Then he sniffed. And his face crinkled.

"My God! It's you! You stink!" he said. "You need a bath!"

And he grabbed my mug, slammed it down, and whisked me up the stairs.

I assumed that Viscount Dennis was treating me as he himself was used to being treated by long-dismissed manservants as he came up behind me and wrapped a huge white fluffy towel around my naked, dripping form. The reek of my person had led to his insistence on the immediately doffing of my clothes. Once he had filled the tub with steaming water, pumped by hand using some contraption I had never seen before in any bathroom, he waved me into the water, seeming not to look behind where I stood in my birthday suit. And unfortunately stank.

He'd fled my unabashed nakedness as soon as he filled the tub. But not so quickly as he hadn't had the chance to take things in if he wanted to.

Now, looking in the full-length mirror in front of which I stood, wrapped all in toweling, I finally caught his gaze. Viscount Dennis, or Gordon, as he now insisted I call him, glanced quickly away, though it hardly mattered. For even though I was presently swathed in a modest manner from my nipples to the toes that peered up and wiggled conspiratorially at me from the sodden floor, had he wished to inspect the property, he'd had plenty of time once again to see all he might wish to see while I was rising from the bath.

And more so, especially with the rapid and uncontrollable tenting of the towel that occurred when his arms crossed under mine to knot it at my breastbone in what was, perforce, an intimate embrace. If this was what manservants did for their masters in stately homes, it was something I could aspire to. With the right servant.

"I'll try and do something about these wretched clothes," he said and plucked them up from the floor in his small but muscular hands. For a moment I was in a panic, until I spied my unopened purse placed with my pocket watch and my kerchief near the porcelain basin on its stand. It would have been awkward had he looked inside and found my booty.

Still pretending not to glance in my direction, Gordon held my clothes at arm's length as he fled the room. I could just smell their pong from where I stood before the foul scent vanished along with my handsome benefactor. I myself now smelled of lavender soap. Not a scent I would have chosen, but it was better than it had been.

"Well, well." I nodded to my counterpart, who grinned at me from the mirror. Opportunity knocks. A golden goose was far better than a sack of stolen banknotes, if you knew what you were about.

He came back soon enough with clothes from some departed servant—not the unlamented Nate, of course—and I found myself a dashing rascal in an underfootman's garb. I hadn't had a proper suit this fine since I was thrown out of Cambridge.

But far from improving our relations, my appearance in servants' livery seemed to put me in my place. For he abandoned me at table after plopping down a ripe wedge of cheese, some tinned beef and stale bread, and more of the cider for my supper. I looked out the back windows to watch for him, but he didn't return from his precious shed until it was time for him to escort me to a big four-poster bed in some room upstairs—fine enough, but unfortunately not his own.

"There are bedclothes and more blankets in the cupboard there should you wish," he said. "And we have an indoor toilet next to the bath at the end of the hall. Sleep well. And thank you again. In the morning we will try to sort things out" was all he said before he left me again to my own devices. Although disappointing on the one hand, that still left me the opportunity to ply my trade.

Perhaps one of the greatest benefits of being a house thief was the ability to assuage my overwhelming curiosity. Not being a member of the aristocracy, or in fact even possessing any sort of household of my own, I was fascinated by the details of the secret world of these strange creatures who floated above the hoi polloi like angels in their vaulted heavens. Locked drawers and jewelry chests were an affront to these sensibilities, and the moment I saw them, I longed to set things right.

Yes, there was a thrill to discovering some valuable bauble secreted in its hiding place, waiting for my touch. But I confess, I was even more delighted when I stumbled upon a cache of letters or a neatly scribed diary bound in leather or velvet and sealed with a tiny keyhole that proved no match to my deft skills. I was too fastidious to break such delicate locks, feeling a strange debt to those I considered my hosts, even though I was not quite an invited guest within their homes.

These types of treasures were rarer than jewelry, and I never took them away with me. But if the night was young, I would take the time to creep into a shadowed alcove and use my black lamp to quickly scan their secrets. And if they proved too lengthy and too interesting, and if time grew quickly toward the dawn, there were several occasions that I put them carefully back, remarking on my place, and returned the following night to continue their fascinating tales of sorrows, loves, debauchery, greed, violence, or speculative philosophy.

Now, I must admit there were other housebreakers among my kind who valued these treasures too, above all others. Not for their fascination, but for the perfect blackmail that absconding with them made possible. Such a sordid business was beneath me, though. I had no wish to profit from these secrets, merely an overpowering desire to know the depths and loves and follies of my fellow man, with whom I had so little contact. For I worked by night and slept by day, trapped by economic circumstance in a stratum of lowly companions whose manner and intellect could never fill my needs.

Besides, successful blackmail required a partner, someone willing to confront the client and even more willing to bash in heads if necessary. Not to mention the fisticuffs the cornered might lash out with, should they truly fear their secrets might escape them. I'd heard of one too-cocky blackmailer shot by a pretty little pistol held by a visiting American girl when he'd tried to sell her back her letters to a lord.

The incident with that fellow Nate notwithstanding, my penchant for violence was very small.

But tonight I was in a position where my guilt would be obvious, should my rifling be discovered. Otherwise, I might have left one of my special calling cards in my handsome host's desk, as I often did when the secrets I uncovered in a locked drawer or vanity proved particularly juicy, entertaining, or tempting to a less highly moral character than myself.

The cards I usually carried on my midnight adventures were embossed by my own tiny printing press (as these were not the sort of things you could have run off safely in the hundreds at a local shop. Not if you were leaving them behind in a house you robbed.). My cards were of the finest paper stock and bore a simple message on their face:

This place is not secure. Beware of blackmail.

—A friend.

It was the least I could do in payment for an evening's entertainment. I must admit I did once drop off a particularly vile journal, anonymously, on an unwitting police sergeant's desk at a particularly busy time of day so no one noticed. For the benefit of the law, I made sure it came complete with a few harmless letters from a nearby desk that had the crest of a well-known noble house and the villain's signature to boot, stuffed among the incriminating pages to provide comparison.

The lovingly described rape and murder of two prostitutes, sealed up forever in the family crypt, was something even I could not ignore. But I found out later that the idiot coppers returned the lot unremarked to the high-ranking scion, as if they had been some luggage from the lost and found they'd discovered.

It was a lot harder getting hold of them again from their new hiding place and putting them on the desk of the editor of the *Times*—who I assure you had as much curiosity as I. They were used to great result, though I am against capital punishment as a rule.

By philosophy, as well as by profession.

So it was with little surprise and much delight that I crept up in the middle of the night and sorted through half a hundred daguerreotypes of handsome men that were secreted in the bottom drawer of the desk in my current host's study. It was not the most remarkable collection I had ever seen in my wanderings and, in fact, was comparatively innocent. The subjects of the life studies were engaged in fairly mundane activities, for the most part, just with less than the normally requisite amount of clothes.

And only a few showed any obvious sign of excitement in their roles as gardeners or stable hands or footmen. I smiled at the thought of my host's apparent attraction to the lower orders, for there was scarcely a lower order than myself at the moment. And to my credit, if I were being totally honest, I was far more excitable than some of those portrayed.

So I studied my host carefully over morning breakfast as he served me again with his own hands, there being a total dearth of servants in the place.

"I have a proposition for you," he said as we sat across from each other at a table laden with a less than opulent fare. I was now again in the long-gone footman's hand-me-downs, my own clothes deemed irreparably damaged from the dual insults of my battle with Nate and the earlier contents of the chamber pot.

I couldn't disguise a snicker as a thought unaccountably crossed my mind. The clothes I now wore reminded me suddenly of one of the more pleasant photos in his collection. I tried to look nonchalant, and I forced down my breaking smile as he looked up at me, puzzled, then focused his eyes back down upon the morning *Times*, which he devoured with more interest than his food.

"The damned bankers are at it again," he swore and threw down the paper suddenly. "They are destroying civilization and enslaving the common man! I can't wait any longer!"

He looked at me as if awaiting comment. Not knowing what to say, I stayed silent and just stared into his eyes. He shrugged it off and carried on.

"I need your help with my experiments. With that lout Nate now good and finally gone, there's no one left. And I am critically close. So close, in fact, I've moved forward the schedule and the workmen will be coming tonight instead of next week. The machine is obviously not safe here anymore. I don't know what Nate was up to before I discovered him in the shed and he attacked me. But I think he sabotaged the machine. It never did that before....

"I have been remiss in risking the safety of my neighbors. I see that now. And now that Nate has formed some sort of mania about me, I can't risk staying here in case he returns. I can better finish the final preparations at the wharf anyway. And the ship is all but ready. I can finish things in the next few days. If you will help me."

I didn't need to hide my smile, for it vanished in my total amazement at this tangential train of conversation to what I'd conjured. "Help you? Assistant? I don't know the first thing about machines...."

"You knew enough to take instructions yesterday when someone else might have panicked. You behaved well and helped prevent catastrophe. Above and beyond all that, you saved me from death or even worse, had that fellow had his way. Even if those weren't two of the most sterling recommendations I can think of, I don't have any choice. You're the only one at hand. And I can't do it all alone.

"There isn't much money left to pay you, though I can manage some. But there is food and clothing and lodging. Given your gauntness and pallor, I assume you haven't been eating very well. Am I right? I mean no offense. I really do need an assistant. And you seem strong enough and fairly formed. It's better than going to prison, too, I imagine...."

"What do you mean?" My face grew taut. I felt my hands gripping at the table edge.

"Maybe I seem a dreaming fool to you, both in my choice of previous assistant and in taking you in so blithely without question. I am not so absent-minded to miss the fact that you leaped over the wall into my garden just minutes after the din of police whistles announced that a criminal was at large. You were the last amazing thing I saw before Nate strangled me into unconsciousness. I thought I was having an hallucination, until I awoke to find that you had saved me. But whoever you are, perhaps you will be willing to help me with my great work. If you refuse, I will of course give you the chance to leave before I summon the authorities. I owe you that." His handsome face was strangely less appealing when it looked so very smug.

I sighed.

"What is this great work?" I asked, resigned.

"I've no time now to explain." He stood and told me to join him in the garden shed when I was ready.

"And by the way, certain parties will be grateful at the anonymous returning of their property. I just thought that you should know." And he pulled the back door shut behind him.

That noble bastard! Rather than follow after, I quickly ran upstairs. And, of course, why should I have been surprised? For when I pawed under the mattress in the room he had assigned me, I found the purse I had hidden there was empty. All the precious jewels I'd stolen at such cost the day before were gone.

There was nothing I could do but stay on and help the madman—if I weren't willing to murder him. Which I almost was.

So I joined him silently in the garden shed, where we spent hard hours dismantling his machine and packing its glass and metal pieces into wooden crates, following some preset order based on numbers etched into the equipment and writ in chalk upon the boxes. They made no sense to me, but it helped me follow his orders without question. Which was good, because he refused to answer any but just pointed, lost in some inventor's reverie, or perhaps just too much enjoying his power over me. I myself refused to attempt more conversation.

But at last we were done. And as we rode through the darkness in a hired carriage following the wagon packed with all his boxes to the river, he finally deigned to tell me everything.

"You have been remarkably uncurious as to the nature of my device," he said, sounding almost disappointed.

"I had other things to think about, as you well know," I countered angrily.

"Now, now, none of these petty concerns will matter once I've destroyed the world," he said to calm me down.

"Destroyed the world?" I prayed I heard him wrong. Prison or assisting a madman with Armageddon. It was a sorry choice, if true.

"Only the bad bits," he said. He seemed quite amused at my dismay. "Just capital," he added.

"Not London, surely!" I exclaimed. "Washington, perhaps, or Paris?" I suggested as more reasonable substitutes.

"No, not capitol! Capital! The monetary system!" he half shouted in frustration, shoving aside his thick blond hair that kept falling in his eyes.

He babbled on and on about the banking system and how it was ruining the world... so I stopped listening. Happily there was no time for him go on further about how labor and not capital should be the wealth of nations, as the cart pulled up to the wharf and we were soon working like madmen on the coal scow to reconstruct his great machine, part of it above decks, where it attached to a giant furnace already constructed there. Several coalmen stood waiting and began to stoke the furnace to bright flames when he gave the sign.

Finally, we attached the other end of his device to piping that led to the cargo hold.

I balked a moment as we stood belowdecks above a gaping hole that plunged down into darkness. For the life of me, I had never seen a ship with a hole in the bottom of its hull, and I wondered why the sea wasn't boiling up and we weren't sinking.

Gordon started climbing down a ladder of iron rungs set in the side of the plunging hole. I refused to follow until suddenly bright light blazed from below, brighter than I'd ever seen in my life indoors. So I went down. He pointed to a row of glowing glass tubes set on opposite sides of what I realized now was the inside of a giant metal sphere crouched below the coal scow underwater.

"I've harnessed limelight from the theater, safely in these glass tubes. A thin stream of oxygen flows through with added lime, piped in from above to keep the flame going. They have to be waterproof in case we spring a leak. That's why we don't have any of those new electrics. Nasty things, electrocuting people right and left! A little water and... well, you can imagine. But ignore those. This is why we're here."

He beamed like a new father at a device that hung delicately poised above a metal orifice in the floor. Twelve thick iron bars protruded out from a great gear in a circular design, each several inches apart from the other. There was a spiral of copper wiring around each one, almost sealing them from top to bottom, except for an inch or two of naked iron on either end. They surrounded a crystal orb the size of a small child's head. It was three-quarters filled with mercury and held in place by a silvery rod that pierced its center. Thinner glass rods, also filled with mercury, passed through holes in the gearing and led to coiled, flexible piping that snaked over the floor and plugged into the wall of the great metal sphere in which we stood.

Feeling a crick in my neck, I stood up to my full height, unaccountably having been crouching all this time. It was as if the weight of the water I knew was all around me had been pressing in. The metal arching of the central roof of the sphere, which held the hole from which the ladder rungs descended, was still some four feet above my head when I stood tall.

Despite its size being larger than several rooms I had lived in, I suddenly felt very much enclosed. Of course, Gordon gave no sign he noticed my discomfort.

"This device"—he pointed to the crystal orb and its surrounding iron rods—"when lowered through this self-contained air lock into the ocean, will collect gold from the seawater by means of this special accumulator of my design. The iron rods will spin in a merry chase around it, driven by steam created from the very water by which the device will be surrounded. The silver rod—solid white-gold platinum, by the way—will continue to energize the mercury in the globe as the essences are used up to collect the gold from the seawater pumping by—directed by great hoses under the water.

"It's all fueled by the boiler heat from above. Once started, we'll sail slowly back and forth along the coast. We have to keep moving because the concentration of gold in seawater is so very low that we will quickly exhaust any local area we are in should we remain stationary.

"Protruding some fifty feet below our submersed steel container, this crystal accumulator will ride beneath the waves, collecting flecks of gold like children plucking blossoms from a meadow."

"Gold!" I exclaimed. All was forgiven him! "We'll be rich!" I used the excuse of my unbounded joy to seize him up in a manly embrace and dance him round and round, with chest and loins pressed tight together in joyous camaraderie. Unfortunately, doing so meant I tripped over the piping and pulled it free.

Gordon pushed me aside in fury as the mercury poured out and he dove for the metal tubing I'd dislodged in our merry twirl. It took nearly two hours to deal with the spill that resulted from my untoward display.

Sadly, it was especially disappointing for the accident occurred just a minute into our dance, during which, I swear, he expressed his own firm delight at my exuberance.

"Damnation!" Gordon exclaimed over his sphere, which had shifted from an impressive display of silvery glow to an empty husk of glass.

"Surely you can fix it!" I cried, the loss of vast quantities of gold being harvested from the sea suddenly taking precedence over my fear of his disdain.

"I don't know if I have enough activated mercury left in reserve. The stuff you spilled is useless until I purify it again from whatever contaminants it picked up from the floor and until I apply the recharging process."

"You'll fix it. I know you will," I said. "And we'll be—you'll be rich again. On top of the world! I just know it. I have full faith in you."

"Rich!" He stood full height and looked at me in amazement. "You still think of riches? We're meant to destroy wealth, not create it! Haven't you been listening?"

Damn, how could I have become caught up with this madman! Why couldn't he be a harmless little Fabian socialist? Instead he was a rabid revolutionary, Shaw's Superman in form but not in mind. He had been serious in his ranting! I had tried not to believe….

"Can't we enjoy the gold a little first? Set ourselves up? Just a small self-sustaining estate. Nice house with good facilities. A deep well, perhaps a nearby stream with a corn mill? And if there's not going to be any money left in the world after you flood the market with gold, a very big garden for barter? And chickens. I love eggs. And surely they could be traded. And what about jewels? We could buy a lot of jewels!" I said, forgetting for a moment that this man before me had brazenly returned my own ill-gotten gains to their owner.

How many potatoes for a diamond? I suddenly wondered. Perhaps potatoes would be the new money? The Irish would be rich then. We'd need a big farm, not just a garden!

"We'll set ourselves up first, and then we can destroy the monetary system at just the right time. Bring down the world of the bloated plutocrats!" I pleaded.

His scowl of disgust was his only answer.

Only my hope that I could persuade him to turn aside his mad scheme, at least for a year or two, once we had collected enough gold, persuaded me to continue on. That and the thought of the shining red gold and other assets held behind his tightly belted pants. And his smile, when he used to smile. And his eyes. And, well… there were too many things about him. I was becoming a womanish fool, for heaven's sake!

It was just the want of pleasure, surely. And profit, of course. There couldn't be anything else between two men. The chase, the "kill," the parting—a hunter's passion. That was how I'd always seen it.

Finally, like Cleopatra's barge of old, our coal-topped scow sailed its ungainly way down the Thames and to the sea. We settled at last in a prechosen position about a half mile from the nearby English coast.

"The accumulator works best at higher pressure for some reason," he explained, finally exhausted by my endless questions. I figured, anything just to get us talking again. "It's a delicate balance with the quartz, though, since for safety's sake it can't go too deep or it might shatter. This should be perfect," Gordon said as I helped him turn the crank to lower the device into the sea.

We had our bit of excitement four cramped days later, most of which we spent in that damned metal coffin together. Eating and sleeping. Talking.

We really hadn't had much choice. Other than the tiny captain's cabin, far more cramped than this, the coal scow held no suitable accommodations. Its decks were crowded with great mounds of the black ore, wooden crates, and the giant furnace. The coal men slept uncomfortably in the chill Channel air beneath spreading canvas. They took turns keeping the furnace stoked so the ship could continue its slow but steady movement up and down the coast.

They had to have been more miserable than us, but it wasn't heartlessness on the part of my companion, I was sure, just the casual thoughtlessness of the upper classes for the comfort of the lower. For all his revolutionary fervor.

But at last the first stage of the experiment was over. The accumulator was retracted from the sea and a hot jet of air dried its surface by a unique series of tiny steam-powered bellows gauged to provide just enough force to evaporate the water but leave the gold still clinging to the quartz. As the water dried, I scrambled to look and thought for a moment that I caught a golden reflection. Then I looked closer as the sphere drew farther upward.

"There's nothing there!" My shout echoed throughout our metal home.

Gordon smiled at me. "Au contraire," he said. "Oh ye of little faith!"

He placed a piece of finely polished ceramic tile beneath the suspended orb and reached over to turn off the apparatus. The vibration of our tiny submarine compartment suddenly stilled and I realized there had been a dull continuous sound our whole time underneath the waves that was only really noticeable now that it was stilled. With a tiny watchmaker's brush, he dusted the surface of the globe. And kept on dusting. In several moments I could see the faintest golden haze floating down to the ceramic, a fine dust—like a gilded memorial to the maid's day off.

"Pure gold!" Gordon said, barely above a whisper.

"Pure bollocks!" I replied, but scarcely more than a whisper myself. If I raised my voice, I was afraid the added wind would blow any hint of our success from sight.

Gordon's great brown eyes widened at my reaction.

"Four damnable days in this bathtub a dozen feet beneath the sea. And you show me this—enough gold to gild the edges of a single volume of *Martin Chuzzlewit?*"

"Well, you have to think economies of scale—obviously the two of us will never upset the gold market by ourselves, but when I publish the patent there will be hundreds of these ships, thousands, milking the sea of its vast golden treasure day and night, year after year, bringing the Bank of London and Wall Street to its knees!"

That's when I realized that he was completely, barking mad.

I tried my best to explain it calmly, lest he should have a stroke once he figured out the truth.

"Gordon, the sandwiches and the ale we picnicked on these past four days cost money. This... this gold... could hardly make a shilling's worth. Have you seen the cost of coal? You've used up half the pile we've got up there! Sailing round and round, not to mention running your machine! The workers' food and salaries! The captain's wage!

"And my God, it suddenly occurs to me—where did you get the thousands of pounds for this contraption, not to mention gallons of pure of mercury and a platinum bar the length of my forearm?" I was shrieking now like half a madman myself.

"My father owned some unentailed land in the country that came with the title and some very nice paintings from my grandmother, who was a favorite of Gainsborough.... I thought, after this is done, money will be useless. So there was no reason to hold any back.... And with the furniture, and the silver, and grandmother's jewelry...."

And this was the man I'd fallen in love with! And indeed, I realized in my horror at that moment that I truly did love him. Like a woman loves a man. I wanted to be with him forever. He was not a golden goose—just a simpleminded one. The most naïve and silly, good-hearted person I had ever met. The smartest man perhaps in all the world... but still a goose.

"You have to see that none of this will ever work," I said.

His shoulders sagged.

"I know," he said. "I'm sorry. I knew two days ago when I just couldn't contain myself. When you said you'd go mad if you didn't get a few hours' air up top. I brought the accumulator up just to have a quick look. I was so excited.... But I didn't even turn the magnet off. I could see in an instant how badly I had failed. The orb should have been coated with almost a half inch of gold after fourteen hours, by my calculations. But it looked just like this." He waved his hand. "And I knew then it would never work." He sighed. "I'd done something wrong. Some variable...."

"Hellfire and damnation!" I interrupted his self-pity. "Why did we stay down here cramped so tightly for four long days? Two days more after you knew! This has been a total misery!"

Then his face paled and he brushed aside his matted hair, which was really the only thing in the entire sphere that resembled the metal we sought.

"Has it really been so bad?" He raised his eyes to look directly into mine. "I figured you'd realize soon enough that I would never turn you in to the police. No matter what. And I'd spent all my money. There was no reason for you to stay...."

I was about to answer when we were rudely interrupted by an angry shout down the tube that led to the coal scow up above.

To my astonishment, I recognized the bellow. Somehow Nate had followed us and boarded the ship! It gave him great delight explaining to us that he was in complete control above. That our crew couldn't help us now.

"Come up!"

"So you can kill us, or worse?" Gordon shouted back with commendable bravado.

"No killing. Your crew are safe up here, with us. We'll put you all in a life boat and just sail away the scow. No one hurt. Everybody safe and sound," Nate said quite pleasantly.

"Let me talk to the captain, then!"

There was a long silence from above.

"The stokers?" Gordon pleaded.

"Damn you!" Nate shouted down. "Now we've got to do this the hard way!"

"The machine doesn't work!" Gordon shouted up to our tormentor in one last effort to save our lives.

"They said you might say that. Well, never mind. I could wait until the need for food and water drove you to surrender, but my employers are not very patient, and they feel themselves capable of analyzing anything you came up with if they get their hands on it."

"Don't you be coming down here!" Gordon cried. "Or sending anyone else! I've got a pistol! And I'll shoot. You know I will." I looked at him, fully aware we were unarmed. He shrugged.

"You should have liked me better, Viscount. I might have spared you this… had you been more cooperative before. I found your secret cache while copying your plans and knew you wanted it! Oh well, this shouldn't damage things too badly. That's what they said…." His voice faded and suddenly we heard a massive clanging. The light disappeared from the shaft above. I was about to stick my head up to look when Gordon pulled me back violently, just in time to keep me from being smashed to the floor by the force of seawater rushing down the tube.

"He's shifted the outlet hose to the mouth of our exit," he said. "The water we were pumping through the accumulator to help extract the gold is rushing down on us instead."

As if knowing how we were going to drown would somehow make it better—a scientist to the end. I rolled my eyes. There was no way we could climb up the only exit with that torrent pouring down.

"Can't we stop the flow?" I asked.

"It would take me at least ten minutes to unscrew the panel and reroute the steam from the pumps, if I even had the tools. We have maybe less than five." The water was already to my waist and creeping to his breastbone.

"Can you swim? And are you very brave?" He was grinning wildly in the flashing lights, and somehow I grinned back.

"If he's got the hose pointed down, then that means the hatch must be open!" he shouted above the din of rushing water.

He half scuttled, half swam to the side of the compartment farthest from the accumulator. He struggled to pull open a panel, reaching as far above his head as he could manage. Then he darted back and pulled me through the water toward a lever hidden within.

"You're taller than me—got longer arms. I won't be able to reach this and still keep to the pocket of air as it grows smaller and smaller. And we have to keep breathing as long as we can. You must wait until we are almost smothered and then pull the lever. Hold on to me and follow through the water, kicking like mad as if your life depended on it, for it surely will. I know my way through the dark in here like a blind man. I built every inch of it myself. If you miss the hole while we're spinning around, you'll be doomed."

"Dark? Spinning round?" I tried to keep the terror from my voice.

"When you pull that handle, pneumatic bolts will pop around the descent pipe and propel our sphere from its attachment to the ship. A plate will automatically seal the opening in the hull to keep the ship from going down. It's a protection in case of a storm so bad the scow might overturn. We would, of course, have evacuated there to safety.

"As for us, in one quick moment the sea will rush in, forcing out the last of the air, and the pressure will be equalized. If we are fast enough and can hold our breaths, we should be able to get out of the tube and swim to the surface before we sink too far and the press of the water kills us, or we're too far down to make it on one breath, or the tube spins round and embeds itself in the ocean floor, blocking our escape. Any such consequence is possible, since I haven't calculated all the parameters. But it's the only way…."

He looked at the panic on my face. "Oh, buck up, man! They say drowning's not so bad a death, but I am not in any hurry to test it out and this water is too damned cold to die in! We'll be fine! We'll show that bloody Nate a thing or two!"

His brave words barely hid the panic in his voice.

"Just remember when we exit the tube, if you can't tell the way up, then exhale as small a bit of air as you possibly can. The bubbles will show the way skyward. So swim like mad in their direction. And hold your breath until you want to die! And longer, because I won't lose you now!" He paused and started paddling, his feet no longer touching floor.

"We'll worry about Nate and any of his confederates when we reach the surface. I'm hoping they'll be too confused to think to look for us in the water. It's a slim chance," he said with utter honesty. "But it's all we have."

I nodded and grasped the lever with one hand and his coattail by the other as he dogpaddled to try to keep his head above the water. The bubble of air shrank quickly and reached my chin. Suddenly he darted forward and, grabbing my face while paddling, he kissed me violently on the lips, then pushed away.

"Breathe deeply," he ordered through my shock and the salty taste of the seawater from his lips. He pulled my hand to his belt, his frightened face illumined in the flickering limelight. "Remember to hold on!" he shouted, then sputtered, now totally submerged. He pushed up wildly. We had less than a cubic yard of air between us when he cried "Pull!"

I nodded and gripped his belt the tighter with my left hand. I yanked the lever with my right. It didn't move. I yanked again as water covered my lips, then panicked as nothing happened.

Instinctively, I spun completely around and pulled the recalcitrant lever with both hands, the metal cutting into my skin as it jerked into position.

There were deafening pops of pressure thumping through the water in assault upon my ears as the sphere suddenly shuddered. Then we began to spin around. The limelight snapped out as the last thin cables attaching us to the ship broke free. We were tumbling down in darkness.

As I held my breath and waved my arms madly through the black water, I didn't have the slightest idea where to go. I'd lost my grip on Gordon when I let go to yank the lever with both hands.

I pushed off the floor, or ceiling, or sidewall of sphere, flailing into knobs and perhaps a chair. There was no way or time to find escape in the darkness, and I knew that I was dead. Then something tugged my sleeve and a hand grasped mine, pulling me backward like a doll. Then I was shoved forward and what might have been upward, my head smashing into the sidewall of the exit tube. It was the most blessed pain I'd ever felt.

Knowing suddenly that safety was beyond and that Gordon had given up precious seconds of breath to try to save me and was somewhere trapped behind me, I madly kicked the water and pulled at the stair rungs, trying to get out, to get out of his way.

Suddenly I tumbled through free ocean, flailing my arms, in utter blackness. The metal sphere was gone, presumably slipping ever downward to its doom. Gordon must have gotten out! But there was nothing I could do for him, nothing I could see.

Desperately fighting panic and the urge to breathe, I managed to let loose a few bubbles from my mouth—and almost choked at the sudden urge to breathe it caused.

I couldn't see the bubbles in the dark, but felt them crawling up my face toward my right ear. I knew then that I was swimming parallel to the surface on my side, and I adjusted course toward what I prayed was open air.

At last, blood pounding in my ears, I saw above me a vast silver mirror, as if made of the same mercury that had filled Gordon's mad device. I pierced through and in the brilliant moonlight gasped new life into my lungs. I saw the coal scow almost a hundred yards away, a floating shard of light against the horizon, between me and the outline of the coast less than a half a mile beyond, its cottages on the cliff side showing tiny squares of light.

There was no way anyone on that ship could see my insignificant head and shoulders, awash upon the waves this far away. For a moment, I am ashamed to say, I was so intent on breathing and on my own miraculous survival that it took me several seconds to realize Gordon was nowhere to be seen.

I almost cried out, when hideous gasps broke close behind me, like a damned soul torn from its coffin trying to seize back life.

When I swam up to him, Gordon looked at me in relief.

Then damned if he didn't roll his eyes upward, showing white. In a sudden faint, he slipped gently back beneath the waves. I barely got to him in time or he would have disappeared again into the sea, a permanent companion to his damned machine. I cupped his white head in the moonlight, keeping it afloat while I paddled on my back. I headed as quietly as I could to the only hope we had left. With Gordon unconscious, I had to reach the ship. I dared not try for shore.

Already the cold water was draining me too quickly. I was shivering, and if my shakes became uncontrollable, I would be unable to swim myself, much less keep Gordon's head afloat. We had to get aboard the coal scow. Or die. And even if we made it there, I didn't give much for our chances with Nate in full control, our own crew dead.

"We're so close to shore," I whispered once Gordon awakened. Somehow I'd managed to push him up and over the low side of the scow and to clamber up myself. We hid behind one of the great piles of overflowing coal that filled the decks. "Can you swim it?"

He shook his head. "It's too cold. I'd never make it. I'm too small to keep from freezing. That must have been why I passed out when the rush of panic left me. When I saw that you were safe. If we can steal a rowboat and smash the engine, we can get away."

"That's too much of a risk, getting to the engines," I said. "We'll steal the rowboat and set the scow on fire. They'll have to abandon it, but by the time they do, we'll already have made our getaway."

And so we did.

I regret, though not deeply, what happened next.

As we watched from a safe distance, Nate and his gang of two other murderers, unable to fight the flames, struggled to launch the single lifeboat we'd left them. Then the raging fire we'd started by smashing a single lantern against the furnace reached the pile of crates that clustered on the stern.

Gordon had forgotten, or had chosen not to tell me, that there was a large stock of quite volatile chemicals in those boxes.

The explosion filled the night.

We rowed toward shore.

He babbled as he shivered. "If I'd ended the experiment right away, and you knew it was a failure, you'd set off to London as soon as we landed, leaving me for good. I am not rich anymore.... Just the house and what's left of the furniture. Nothing to offer someone like you.

"Thank God the captain and the stokers had no family.... How would I have made them recompense? How could I have led them to their deaths?" I think he was beginning to cry.

I continued to row in silence, parallel to the shore. I could see, and more easily hear in that strange way that voices carried across the sea, that a crowd from the village was gathering on the beach. The now dwindling fire behind us must have been quite a sight when it first exploded. I didn't think we'd want to answer any questions, so I rowed on.

"A good opinion you have of me...," I said quietly, so my voice wouldn't carry.

In his misery, Gordon just huddled and wrapped his arms around himself tighter. Neither of us had anything left to say.

But once we safely reached land and before we began our hike to find the nearest road, I loomed over Gordon and, before he could say a word, shut his mouth with my own. He grabbed hold of me then, as if we both were drowning still.

Two weeks later, in our tiny steerage cabin, heading toward America, he proved he was not so naive as I had thought him after all. Or at least not after I showed him the whats and wherefores of the doing. We lay naked together in my lower berth. This time, cramped quarters seemed perfectly all right.

Even if Nate was no longer a threat, his employers might figure out we'd survived. Once we hopped a farmer's cart, then caught a train to London, we had risked going to back to the mansion. We quickly picked up what we could—which was very little beyond clothes and luggage, for Gordon had indeed spent all his ready cash and everything portable on his vast experiment. Then a cab to Euston Station, and the train to Liverpool. The day after we arrived there, we managed two berths in steerage on White Star's *Teutonic*.

A change of name and continent—or at least my companion's well-known moniker—seemed our only option.

"How will we live?" Gordon asked me. "If I try to capitalize on any of my known inventions, or contact my bank, which still has a few hundred pounds left in my account, the powers that were after us will know that we survived. They'll never believe my invention didn't work. If only I had a stake—I could become an inventor again and create things no one would ever associate with the dead Viscount Dennis. But it's not to be." He sighed.

I rolled over him, delighting in the slide of my naked skin against his, to grab at our clothes, flung haphazardly on the floor in our eagerness to reach a state of nature once we were finally alone. Luckily the other two berths in our cramped steerage cabin—or third class, as the White Star Line insisted on calling it—were empty. Our original partners in the tiny room—scarcely a two-foot gap between the bunks—had been a pair of brothers from Lithuania, one of whom spoke a little English. A surprisingly small bribe and a cheap watch I had filched while shaking hands with a crewman was all it took to split them up to other cabins, leaving us our privacy once the ship had sailed.

As Gordon watched in mild bemusement, I fumbled in his trousers for the small cache of money we still had. I waved the pound notes in his face.

"Once we use this to show the Americans at Ellis Island that we're not paupers, we're going to spend some on the finest New York clothes. With whatever's left, we'll set up in the fanciest hotel we can afford. You'll be Lord Such-and-Such as far as the colonials are concerned. And I will be your manservant.

"With such a title, no one would think it odd that you were selling off some of your inheritance to a reputable buyer to pay some unfortunate gambling bills—you're Jack the Lad, you know. They'll give you a far better price at a jeweler's than they'd ever give the likes of me at a pawn shop. Especially if you casually mention that your bride-to-be was in the market to bejewel her trousseau."

"But I don't have an inheritance left, and I hardly think you'd like it if I suddenly came up with an American bride!" he countered.

"One night, maybe two of us in a fancy American hotel in the richest city in the world.... I think you can count on having an inheritance to hand." I rubbed my thumb and fingers together right in front of his nose. "You may be a damned good inventor—I'll take your word for it after the sphere—but I can assure you that I'm a damned sight better thief! Though I'll need a new set of lock picks. That will take a bit of cash...." I pulled one bill from the wad and scooted over to slide it into my shirt pocket.

"And later, while you're hobnobbing with the proprietor of the slightly less than top-notch jewelry store, I could explain in private to a pert little counter girl how the bride would likely insist on helping to design all her own jewelry. And she'd bring her father along. Who really has the money. If truth be told... you're not all that rich yourself. But that's all right. These American fathers are so casual in their spending when purchasing a title for their darling daughters. I'll be a little drunk. Indiscreet with all your secrets. Rumors will fly! I'd be surprised if the greedy proprietor didn't call on you the very next morning, offering you the run of his shop and a superb price on your inheritance, whatever that might turn out to be. I'll try for diamonds, though. They seem to favor diamonds in the States. Diamond Jim Brady and all that." I babbled on, too excited at the prospect of getting back in the game to let him speak a single word.

"We'll rebuild your fortune despite you, after all!" I promised him and climbed back onto his smooth chest to nibble at his aristocratic nipples before he could complain.

But we'd not be rebuilding his damned underwater sphere. And somehow I would have to steer him from trying to destroy world capital again. There had to better way to save the world than to plunge us into financial disarray.

"Now who's the golden goose?" I asked him, playing with his nether parts with great familiarity. Gordon's eyes glowed wide in the dim electric light shining through the door slats from the corridor beyond.

Instead of making socialist complaints, he rolled me round and pushed me down beneath him, nuzzling his face against my lower back. Then he showed me again all he'd learned these past few nights of voyaging. And there were one or two new things—quite unexpected— that made me think I must have missed the best of his daguerreotypes in my midnight prowl.

Or maybe once he got a handle on a subject, as it were, he could quickly learn to improvise. He was a genius, after all.

But I carry on too much. And we still do—the new Lord Such-and-Such and I.

MARK LESNEY spent too much time in grad school, has had sequential careers as a scientist, university professor, science writer, medical writer, and editor, but really only wants to spend all his time writing fiction. He is a cat person and is addicted to reading and to role-playing, simulation, and adventure computer games. He varies wildly from INTP to INFP depending on circumstance, mood, and current career. All of this should be enough information to mimic his persona in an RPG character or programmable killer robot.

SPINDLE AND BELL
AUGUSTA LI

I.

A BOOT with a dinged copper wing tip jabbing between Spindle-Reed's hip bone and rib woke him, as it did most nights. The boy sat up and scuttled backward until the wall of the tiny cupboard aborted his escape. He blinked his watery eyes and shielded them against the sickly yellow light beyond his space with his forearm. Slowly, on his hands and knees, he crawled out of his cubbyhole and the pile of tattered, dirty clothes that served as his bed and into the larger room.

"Ugly little mutt, i'n't he?" Ivor Lardweller said, jabbing an elbow toward Spindle as he flopped his fat ass into a rickety chair and reached for the gin bottle.

"Aye," his associate agreed, scratching at a floppy tit beneath his unbuttoned leather waistcoat. "You're a generous man, Ivor, showin' 'im Christian charity." They clinked their dented tins cups together in a toast.

Spindle knew it was true as he took the steel plate Ivor slid across the floor. He gulped down the slice of hard bread but ignored the two strips of bacon. He didn't like it—it tasted dead, like he gnawed on the stiff body of an alley cat lying beside a heap of garbage. He really wanted his special milk, and he eyed the green glass of the bottle from the chemist that sat on Ivor's desk. Finally, after Spindle had choked down the dry bread, Ivor poured the clear liquid into a dirty glass. He dumped the milk on top, splashing some across the table. The substance at the bottom reached up, extending tendrils into the thick creamy fluid, their ends curling like the tentacles of some forgotten sea creature. Spindle licked his lips—saliva flooding his mouth and his fingers twitching to get a hold of it.

"You have it, you ugly fuck," Ivor said, holding the concoction out to Spindle, who eagerly took it and gulped it down.

"Ugly little fuck," Ivor's associate echoed as if he'd never heard anything quite so witty or brilliant, sipping his gin and smoking a cigar, his spittle darkening the end to the color of black coffee.

Spindle knew it was true. His ancestry was like a waste bin, the Irish, Chinese, Gypsy, Ottoman, maybe Jewish, and probably even Faerie so muddled together and rotted and spilling into one another that no one wanted to pick through the slimy refuse to sort it out or see if the mess hid anything valuable. Spindle doubted it did. He was lucky Ivor cared if he lived or died—that Ivor gave him the special milk.

As long as he had the special milk, when he woke and before he went to sleep again, Spindle would be all right.

He slurped it down, swiping away the clotted liquid collecting at the corners of his mouth with his tongue, as the sense of serenity flowed outward from his belly. Spindle's muscles relaxed, and that weird sense that it would all work out covered him like a soft, accepting cloak. His belly unclenched and his vision grew soft and hazy, lending the little flat with the haze of stale smoke hanging below the ceiling, its stained walls and peeling paper, and its clutter of illicit goods an almost dreamlike beauty.

Spindle set the empty glass on the tabletop as he stood. He fastened the brass closures on his brown leather vest. Ivor and his friend had started playing a game with a deck of dog-eared cards and mostly ignored him as he slid a slender dagger into its sheath on his belt. He carried it in case he got into trouble, but he'd never had to use it and doubted he ever would. Because he could go places very few others could, he would likely always manage to escape.

In his bare feet, he picked his way across the dusty wooden floor, weaving between the chests and crates piled into irregular towers. He took his mask from an iron hook on the pitted plaster wall. He checked the filters at the ends of the two cylindrical tubes near the bottom, and confident they'd last another night, he slipped it on and inhaled the familiar scents of rubber, leather, and his own sour breath. He'd had the mask as long as he could remember, and over the years it had taken on the shape of his angular face. He tightened the strap that ran between his eyes, over his forehead, and through his spikes of straight black hair to connect with the one wrapped around the base of his skull. Then he slid his bulky brass goggles on over the top and made his way toward the small window on the opposite side of the flat—the one covered in sheets of oiled cloth and so tiny only Spindle could contort his body enough to pass through it.

Spindle expected Ivor to say something about the improvement to his face now that he'd donned his gear, as he did most nights, but the two portly men were too engrossed in their game to pay him any attention.

Old Ivor often said only a lunatic would walk through Seven Dials after dark. From the roof, Spindle looked out across dwellings as ill proportioned and deformed as many of the residents—himself included—all made from burned bricks covered in decades of filth. People congealed in the mazes of irregular streets and alleyways, children playing with marbles in the gutters, men in every stage of inebriation staggering in and out of public houses, puking across piles of trash, or facedown in the refuse covering the road. Tonight, a group of ruddy women shouted obscenities as a pair of them brawled, tearing strips from each other's filthy dresses, while the others stood watching and taking bets on who would win. Some of the people had masks like Spindle's, but not many. Most just covered their faces in stained and tattered rags in an attempt to keep the disease floating on the air at bay. Spindle didn't see anyone who'd contracted the sickness, but they would have likely been driven off by force at the first flecks of blood on their lips.

He moved across the rooftops, gripping the shingles with his long toes, along Great Andrew Street, toward the affluent area between St. James Park and Victoria Street, where he'd been successful in finding things for Ivor before. Spindle stayed to the shadows and out of the sight lines of the policemen in their stiff blue uniforms and the state-of-the-art masks they'd been issued. Ivor had given him a few pointers before he ventured out—how many years ago? Eight? Ten?—and Spindle had figured out the rest. He spotted a block of houses and looked left and right. Seeing no one, he sprinted to the corner and leaped, catching the blocks at the edge of the tower five or six feet above the walkway. He shimmied easily up rounded outcroppings, his nimble fingers and toes finding purchase in the quarter-inch grooves of mortar between the ivory-colored blocks. He scrabbled up the horizontal walls as easily as the spider Ivor often compared him to and soon found himself on the multileveled roof.

The upper class and well-off had installed air-filtration systems not long after the sickness came. They'd sealed off their homes, quite literally avoiding breathing the same foul air as the Irish, the foreigners, the Gypsies, the Faeries, and the poor—everything Spindle held within his lanky limbs and golden-brown skin. The devices on their rooftops extended as far as he could see—some resembling the bellows in blacksmiths' shops, others ribbed rubber tubes pumping up and down within glass canisters, forcing the outside air through elaborate sieves and screens before it entered the homes of the wealthy. Steam, produced by coal furnaces and massive copper water tanks, fueled most of the machines, and the white vapor mingled with the oily black smoke obscured the London skyline, turning the streetlights and porch lamps to orange smudges.

The force of the fans on the rooftop where Spindle stood smashed his gnarled hair flat to his scalp and sent the tines flapping behind him. Sometimes a door leading to a ladder—for use by the servants who shoveled coal into the furnaces—allowed an easy entry into the buildings. Tonight, Spindle found the iron doors locked, so he went to the edge of the roof and stood with his back to it, holding on with his feet as he folded his body backward until he could grip the windowsill below him. He searched for unlocked windows; on the fourth and fifth stories of these luxurious flats, it wasn't unusual, and he had no trouble breaking through the wax or rubber seals the rich felt so confident would keep the diseased air out.

Within a few hours, Spindle had filled his pouches with coins and jewelry—more than enough to please Ivor, escape a whipping, and earn his special milk. He knew he should go home, but he loved the freedom of London's rooftops beneath the moon, going wherever he chose, the wind in his hair, the fog beading to sparkling droplets on his forearms, and the moonlight resting on his shoulders like an encouraging hand.

Everyone else was too afraid to come out into the open air, especially at night, especially in the fog, because of the sickness.

Spindle felt like London was all his. He had a few more hours of darkness, and so he decided to explore the block of flats across the street. The building was modern and impressive, all gray stone, iron balconies, and arched windows. With a backflip, Spindle launched himself across the street and landed on a third-floor terrace, looking in a set of French doors while supporting himself upside down on his hands. Just then, the wind pushed a clump of clouds away from the moon, and a square of silvery light fell across the front of the building and shone in through the glass. Spindle twisted himself right-side up, crouching with his heels and palms on the narrow edge of the wrought-iron rail.

He tilted his head and stretched his neck, his compulsion to get nearer to what he saw beyond the glass doors unexplainable.

A boy lay on a bed, the thick white pillows billowing like clouds around his head. His skin looked white and perfect—like the Chinese dolls Spindle had seen for sale in a shop—against the down-filled linen. He had the palest yellow hair Spindle had ever seen, almost as light as the bedclothes it curled across, and his lips, slightly parted in sleep, were plump and full, just slightly pinker than the rest of him. Spindle stared; he couldn't seem to turn away from such beauty. But more than the pleasing aspect—that of a cathedral angel—held his attention. For some reason, watching this young man sleep filled Spindle with peace, almost like he'd drunk his special milk, but without the disorientation. His vision of this boy was as sharp and clear as a diamond, and he couldn't tear his gaze from the radiance. The boy not only seemed to reflect the light, but to glow with his own luminescence.

Spindle didn't know how long he perched on the iron railing before the beautiful boy's eyes opened. He flinched when he noticed Spindle outside his window. Spindle couldn't imagine what the boy thought, seeing him in his mask and goggles, his black hair sticking up like the feathers of a rumpled crow. The white-gold angel boy recoiled for only a second before getting out of the huge bed with a great effort. As he opened the doors, wax fell in elongated chunks to the parquet floor. Warm sanitized air rushed out to engulf Spindle.

"You might as well come in," the incandescent creature in the ivory nightshirt said as he turned away from the doors. "I have the sickness already; I can't get any more doomed than I already am."

Spindle knew he should run. He recalled all Ivor's warnings about the horrible things that would happen to him if he was caught. It would take only seconds to stand, drop backward, and catch the edge of the rail below with his hands, but....

Spindle stood and balanced on the thin iron bar on the ball of one foot before pushing off, flipping in the air, and landing a few feet from the resident of the huge white room. He looked down at his soot-and-grime-encrusted toes against the pale, immaculate wood—as if he needed reminding he didn't belong in a place like this.

II.

"ARE you just here to rob me or do you plan to kill me too?" The young man didn't seem as troubled as he should by either prospect. "Well? How in God's name did you get up here, anyway?" He stepped around Spindle and looked down, then left and right. Maybe he thought Spindle had used a rope or something. The damp air seemed to aggravate his condition, and he started to cough, stumbling backward until he could grasp his bedside table to stay on his feet. Doubled almost in half, the man groped with his unoccupied hand until he clutched a lace-edged handkerchief and pressed it to his lips. In only a few moments, it was saturated with blood. The man opened a drawer, found another white cloth, and wiped his mouth. Unable to stay on his feet, he sat on the edge of the bed.

Spindle tilted his head to the side, but of course he couldn't answer through his mask; his model was too old and heavy to permit understandable speech. Why was he still here?

"What's your name?" the young man asked.

Spindle unbuckled the strap bisecting his hair and let his mask fall slowly to hang around his neck. He slid his goggles up to pin the chaotic spines of his hair back. As fast as he could, Spindle grabbed a kerchief from the neatly folded stack in the open drawer, flicked it open, and pressed it over his face, both to protect himself from the disease in the room and the sickly air coming in the open window, and to hide his ugliness. As stupid as he knew it was, he had to talk to this boy—he *had* to.

"If you thought I was going to kill you, why in the hell did you open the window?"

The boy looked up until their eyes met. By the light from the gas lamps burning on the walls, Spindle could see they were a soft blue-gray, muted, like the sky on one of those days when it couldn't decide whether or not it wanted to rain. There was pain behind them and in the way his full lips curled down at the corners. "I don't get a lot of callers. Are you going to tell me your name?"

He shouldn't…. "Spindle-Reed."

The other man laughed a little until it made him start coughing and he had to dab at the corners of his mouth again. "That's... interesting." He used the heavy wooden bedpost to haul himself to his feet and extended his hand. "I'm Belenus Wilfred Hastings. I would love to tell you my friends call me Bel—at least, I have always imagined they might, if I had any."

Spindle stared at the offered hand, extended in greeting, as an equal. He took it—the skin was cool and smooth, the bones beneath as fragile a dove's—shook, and said, "Glad to meet you, Bel."

Bel smiled, petal-pink lips parting to reveal a flash of white tooth. He gave Spindle's hand a small squeeze before collapsing on the bed again. "So, Spindle-Reed, if you're looking for a place to burglarize, I'm afraid you've chosen poorly. There's little here besides old books and some equipment that's worth less than the metal it's made of if you don't know how to use it."

"Is it just you here?" Spindle asked, taking in the massive high-ceilinged room, twice the size of Ivor's flat, maybe their whole building. Between the white marble columns, soothing portraits—seaside views and vases of flowers—hung on the walls. Fire burned in all three inglenooks.

Bel looked suspicious, his thick-lashed eyelids bunching and creasing. "Why do you want to know?"

"'S a big place for one person, 's all."

"Would you mind?" Bel gestured to a silver pitcher and some glasses on a table across the room. Spindle fetched him water, surprised when Bel took it from his dirty, foreign hands and drank. "Thank you. If I answer your questions, will you stay for a while?"

It was Spindle's turn for distrust. "Why?"

Bel sighed, the rattle in his throat reminding Spindle of paper crumpling. "Well, if I can be assured my murder isn't your intention, it will be nice to have someone to talk to for a bit. I haven't seen a soul besides the servants in days, and they can't talk to me through their masks when they bring my meals and turn the bed down."

A quick glance over his shoulder told Spindle at least a few hours of darkness remained. "I can stay for a while. Talk." He didn't know what made him want to, but something did. He didn't get to talk to others much either. After all, who would he discuss anything with—Ivor? His savior and caretaker had warned him others would run screaming if they saw his hideous face, so Spindle no longer tried to approach them, though he longed to fiercely sometimes, as he stayed hidden and watched them from the shadows of the crooked chimneys. Maybe that was what he'd recognized behind Bel's eyes.

"Won't you sit down?" Bel indicated a pair of upholstered chairs in front of the closest fireplace, and without being asked, Spindle took his elbow in case he felt weak again and they crossed the room and sat down. "You might as well take that cloth off your face. The particles that cause the sickness are small enough to move through it. In fact, I doubt these filtration systems or even your mask will save you, but they are making a lot of money for the people who design and build them."

"How do you know?" Spindle asked. "Are you a doctor?"

"I wanted to be," Bel said wistfully. "Back when my parents allowed me to leave this suite of rooms."

"You're a prisoner?" Spindle asked. He could think of worse fates than being a prisoner in a place like this, with servants bringing meals and running his baths, chairs so soft Spindle felt like he sat in the palm of an angel.

Bel laughed a little, cautiously, as if afraid it might trigger another coughing spell. "I'm sure they don't see it that way. You see, I'm a unique case. Most of the people who get sick are dead within a few weeks, months at the longest, but I contracted the disease at thirteen. I've had it for almost five years. Mum and Dad think if I stay here, in the purified air, resting, away from the foreigners and Faeries they think started this plague, I might stay alive. I know they're wrong, but I suppose it's a natural reaction for parents. Still—" He looked out the large window, and the moonlight reflected off his eyes.

A thousand questions and statements shouldered and jostled their way toward the forefront of Spindle's mind, and the one that made it to his lips first surprised him. "There must be something they can do."

Bel's smile creased the corners of his eyes, and for some reason that made Spindle's heart flounder a few times. "You—you're sweet, but I'm afraid not. I have been looking for a cure, and I'm getting close, but it's too late for me. I'm certain it will only work if administered at the very onset of symptoms."

The fact that Bel assumed Spindle understood those big words, that he didn't talk to Spindle like a simpleton who barely knew the language, was one of the nicest things anyone had ever done for Spindle, and he felt sure Bel didn't do it on purpose. It just never occurred to him to presume Spindle was stupid because he was poor and dirty and his skin was brown. What an unusual young man. Then his words wriggled past Spindle's distraction. "There's a cure?"

"Take that cloth off your face," Bel asked in a way that made it sound very important to him. "I can't promise you won't get sick, but I can promise that scrap of linen won't prevent it."

"It isn't that." Spindle sunk into the chair and curled forward, as if he could make himself small enough to disappear. "My face will frighten you. I'm—"

"Let me see." Bel rested his pale, almost weightless hand on Spindle's shoulder, met his gaze, and smiled, and in that moment, Spindle would have done anything he asked. He let the handkerchief flutter into his lap.

When Bel gasped, Spindle turned away in shame. "I-I know how ugly I am. I'm sorry. I tried to warn you."

Bel moved his hand across Spindle's shoulder, up his neck, and to his chin, which he cupped in his soft palm and turned Spindle back around to face him. Spindle's cheeks felt scalded under Bel's scrutiny. "Ugly?" he said in a whispery voice. "You—I have never seen—You're *beautiful.*" He ran his fingertips up Spindle's cheek, down his nose, and touched his lower lip in the center.

"You're having me on," Spindle said, grabbing his wrist. The delicacy of the bones defused his irritation, though, and he loosened his grip. "That ain't nice."

"Haven't you ever seen yourself?" Bel asked. He moved his fingers into Spindle's hair, to the edge of his ear, and Spindle stiffened. Of all his features, he hated his ears the most, both of them large, long, and spade-shaped, one bigger than the other and folded over at the tip. "Spindle-Reed, you're... wonderful to look at. Truly."

"You were saying you can cure yourself," Spindle said, to change the subject and hopefully quell the acrobatics of his stomach and even out his stumbling heartbeat.

"Myself? No. Others... perhaps, although not yet."

If it was true, this fragile boy would be the hero of the age. "How?"

"The other doctors have it wrong," Bel said. "They're looking to industry, manufacturing and machines, some modern miracle, to save us.

But it's going to come from nature. Let me explain. When I got sick, I started studying furiously. At that time, I couldn't accept that I was going to die. For a long time, I couldn't fathom why some people got sick and others didn't. I guess I wanted to know what I'd done to deserve affliction. There were pockets around the city of people who exhibited preliminary symptoms but recovered. Why, I wondered. What could be different? I won't bore you with my process, but after many years, I determined that it was the water. The people in those small areas weren't getting their drinking water from the systems of reservoirs and aqueducts the city installed back in the fifties, but from the small old wells in the squares. Some of those wells have been there for centuries.

"I had to bribe my servants to bring me samples of the water, but I found a common thread, finally: a particular species of mold living on the stones of the wells and getting into the drinking water. Assuming those people drank that water every day, they would have ingested the mold shortly after becoming infected. In the tests I've done, the mold attacks the infection without harming healthy cells."

"Wait," Spindle said, "you figured all that out at what, fifteen?"

"Or sixteen," Bel said. "I've always been a bit of a prodigy, I suppose."

"So, if someone gets sick, they can just drink from one of those wells and be healed?" It sounded too good to be true to Spindle. "Why don't you just drink it?"

"I tried, of course," Bel said, resting his hand on the back of Spindle's neck and looking far away. "My infection is too far along. As for the rest, there simply isn't enough water for every sick person to drink. I've been working with the doctors at the Royal Hospital and corresponding with the Royal Swedish Academy of Sciences, trying to devise a way to replicate the mold, to refine it and make its healing properties more vital."

"And when that happens," Spindle said, "you can take it and be cured."

"I... I suppose only time will tell. I don't want to talk about the plague anymore, if you don't mind. It's been my constant and often only companion for five years. Will you help me to the window?"

Spindle stood and bent down so Bel could drape an arm around his shoulders, and together, they made their way to the window. The moon had gone down, and the buildings of London stood black and indifferent against the jaundiced, artificial light. "Tell me about what it's like out there," Bel said, putting nearly all his scant weight on Spindle. Spindle, with his long limbs and hard, wiry muscle, was strong, so he didn't mind.

"It's just London," Spindle said, realizing he could smell Bel's hair, minty and herbal, his skin, and the clean fabric of his nightshirt. "What do you want to know about?"

Bel sighed with unabashed longing. "Everything. The gin houses and brothels. The ladies in the parks. The men working down on the docks. The shops selling birds in cages. The steam-powered omnibuses. All of it."

So Spindle began talking, telling Bel everything he wanted to know and answering his many questions. Soon, Bel grew too tired to stand and they sat on the edge of his huge bed, and not long after he had to lie down. Spindle kept telling him everything he could think of, because it made Bel smile and Spindle liked that. Before he realized how much time had passed, he noticed a wash of diluted pink creeping up from the eastern horizon. He needed to get back to Ivor and his special milk; he was beginning to crave it acutely, and soon it would start to hurt. "I should go."

With a great effort and a hand on Spindle's shoulder, Bel hoisted himself up and brushed his cool, dry lips across Spindle's forehead. "Spindle-Reed, thank you. If you want—well, I'll leave my window unlocked tomorrow night."

When Spindle made it back to his nest in the closet, numb and merry after his milk, instead of the obscure images of walking on a rope, learning to bend in half, or swinging from a bar high above a net that usually flitted around in his half-sleeping mind, his thoughts just kept returning to that kiss.

III.

SPINDLE no longer minded so much when Ivor woke him with a kick or a tossed ale bottle, because a new night had become something to look forward to. Life, in the past few weeks, had become more than forcing himself to eat, getting valuable things for Ivor, and drinking his special milk. Now he woke with an eagerness to visit Bel, to speak with him and bring him interesting things he had found. Spindle now had something he'd never even known he wanted: a friend.

"You know," Bel said, "a lot of those old wells have been filled in with concrete." They were lying in his bed, angled so the crowns of their heads rested against each other, and Bel had his palm stretched across the strip of skin between the bottom of Spindle's vest and his trousers. "It makes me think. If they'd managed to fill them all in, we never would have discovered the mold. The irony is, they did it to prevent the spread of disease, all in the name of progress. In the name of progress, the cure to this disease could have been lost. I think of all the fields they're leveling to build factories and towns, all the forests they're clearing in the Americas for farmland, and…. What if there's a flower, or a leaf, or a tiny mushroom that only grows one place in the world? If it's destroyed, we could lose something so valuable. People will die when they could have lived. Then again, there are things we've discovered that we probably shouldn't have. Spindle, are you an opium addict?"

"I don't know what that means, Bel."

Bel sighed—no irritation, just… Spindle wasn't sure. Weariness, maybe—and rolled to his side and propped himself up on his elbow with a great effort. "You're already getting impatient. You want to leave me, go chase the dragon."

"What? No." Spindle told the truth—he loved being with Bel—but he was noticing a thirst for the sweet, special milk Ivor would give him in exchange for the string of pearls, jade tiepin, and gold watch he'd found.

Bel leaned in. The tip of his nose nestled into the divot above Spindle's upper lip as he took a small sniff. The breath he exhaled filled Spindle's mouth, the air cool against his teeth and gums, and though it tasted sweet, Spindle detected a hint of the dead taste that made him avoid Ivor's greasy greenish sausages.

"I smell it on your breath," Bel said. "I know the smell. When I first got sick, my physicians gave me laudanum for the pain. For a few weeks, I drifted in and out of sleep, unable to distinguish dreams and visions from consciousness. It was like… being under warm water. But after a while, I decided, if my life would be, um, abridged, I wanted to experience it in all its pain and glory. I stopped taking the laudanum, and you can too. Does this Ivor you've told me of give it to you?"

"Ivor takes care of me," Spindle said through a clenched jaw. "He took me in, and if he hadn't, I'd have nowhere to go. Who else would want me? Who else would care what happened to me? I'd be dead in the street if not for him. Maybe worse."

Bel clearly couldn't support himself any longer, and he collapsed onto the pillow, his fingers wrapped around Spindle's neck and his lips moving against the shell of Spindle's deformed ear. "I know, love, I know. Right now, nothing else seems as important as, what did you call it, your special milk? But it's a brutal mistress, and this Ivor is using it to control you. Don't you see? He makes you steal for him, and he knows you will, and that you'll always come back, because you need what he has. Tell me it isn't true."

"I—" Spindle didn't know how to answer. He'd really only heard one word, and after that, the swish of his heartbeat in his head had flooded the rest. "Love?"

Bel flinched, and even it seemed to tax him. "I… did not mean to presume. I beg your pardon."

Spindle clamped his stinging eyes shut, gathered Bel's light, bony body to him so Bel lay across his chest with his head tucked beneath Spindle's chin, and burrowed his face against the top of Bel's head until Bel's white-gold curls spiraled between Spindle's lips. "You. You do not have to beg anything of me. I'll do anything you ask."

With a wheezed-out giggle, Bel asked, "Why?"

"I've never had a friend before. I like it."

"So do I." Bel nestled closer, his skin cool but sweaty. "God, I envy you, Spindle. Your freedom. The time you have. You can go anywhere you like, do anything you like, and you don't have to try to pack it all in to however many weeks or months you might have left. You must feel like the world is at your feet."

"It's just London," Spindle said. He couldn't quite express how, with Buckingham Palace, Westminster Abbey, Piccadilly Circus, and all the rest at his disposal, he'd never found anything more wondrous than he had in this stuffy little room.

"Just London," Bel said on a rattling exhale.

"You're tired," Spindle said. "I shouldn't be keeping you from sleeping. I should go so you can rest." He moved to sit up, but Bel clutched his leather vest in the weak grip of his fist.

"No. You have been a godsend. My days are numbered, and I want to spend as many of them as I can with you."

Spindle felt like all his blood had turned to the kind of dirty ice the puke and horse piss froze to over the filthy cobblestones of Seven Dials. "Me? No, Bel. You're close to finding the cure. You're going to get better, save hundreds of lives, and live to father a few dozen grandchildren. And then you'll look back on your nights with the grubby Irish-Chinese-Faerie and wonder what in hell you were thinkin'."

"I'm sure you're right." Bel stroked his hair, but Spindle still felt his reassurance was meant to comfort Spindle and not himself. "But not about that last part. If I live eighty years, I'll never forget you or regret a moment we've spent together, so please don't say such things about yourself."

Spindle still had a hard time believing Bel wasn't teasing him, about to call him a twisted imp or an ugly mongrel, same as Ivor and everyone else. "Those things are true, Bel."

"They're not, and hearing them hurts me."

"Tell me what I can do."

"You have to get away from the opium, love," Bel said. "It won't be easy, and it won't be pleasant, but you'll be a slave to it until you do. I want to be able to think of you free."

Spindle, with the craving for the milk tightening his gut and making his hands shake, ignored Bel's wisdom. "No. I mean, what can I do for you?"

Bel, though he tried, couldn't quite lift his head, but he tilted it back so he could look into Spindle's eyes. "Do you mean it?"

"More than anything."

"I want to go out into the city, see London, experience London. I want to drink gin and rebuke unfortunate women. I want to see markets and eat a greasy pie. I… I want to breathe free air, Spindle. Just once."

"London is filthy and cruel, people trampling each other over a scrap."

Bel sighed with obvious longing. "Yes. Chaos. Survival, as Sir Charles Darwin might define it. People living, interacting, making, and destroying. Real. Not like this... this artificial farce. Not even the air is real here. Spindle... will you take me? Just for one night? Before—"

Since Spindle couldn't bear to hear Bel's next words, he interrupted. "Won't it tire you out? Make you sicker?"

Bel shook his head, his gilded curls brushing Spindle's neck. "It's a fair trade. I want—*need* this. Will you?"

"Aye, I will, Bel."

"When?"

"There's something I have to do first."

Bel made a soft affirmative noise and rubbed his cheek against Spindle's chest. Spindle reached across him and cradled the back of Bel's head in his hand until he knew Bel was fast asleep. Then he gently rolled Bel to his back, tucked the ivory down coverlet around his shoulders, got out of the bed, kissed Bel on the forehead, and left through the window with the unspoken promise of returning as soon as he could.

IV.

INSTEAD of returning to Ivor, Spindle made his way to a tavern in the Saint-Giles-in-the-Fields district, as far from Seven Dials as he could get. At just after dawn, the Leper's Refuge was empty except for a large man snoring facedown on a table in the corner and the large pockmarked proprietress with the checkered rag tied around her mouth and nose. Spindle's hand shook as he dropped the pearls and the gold and the mother-of-pearl pocket watch on the bar in front of her.

"I need a room for three days."

The woman, spilling out of her plaid bodice like lumpy dough, eyed Spindle with scrunched brows. "Ain't sick, are ye?"

"No. Just tired. Just in need of a place I won't be disturbed." He added an ivory cufflink to his offering.

"No Faeries."

"I ain't." Spindle dropped the other cufflink with a soft clink. "A Faerie would just englamour you into a free room, aye?"

"Aye," the woman said, eyeing the pile of riches worth more than two months in the dilapidated death trap. It was probably enough to buy the building and all its furnishings. "Three days?"

"Three days. Fresh water and a few loaves of bread." Spindle slid her the pilfered jewelry and she slid him a key.

"Upstairs. Second door on the right."

SPINDLE lay on the straw-stuffed mattress, sweating, stomach cramping so hard he cried out loud. He retched until he'd emptied his stomach, then leaned over the edge of the bed to gag up nothing. Then he curled in a ball and trembled until the agony gave way to sleep. He woke up to more of the same, then fell unconscious again.

Go to Ivor, some part of him whispered. The voice grew more insistent the longer he lay in pain. *Give him what you have. Kiss his boots. End this. Nothing is worth this.*

He might have done—he wanted to more than he'd ever wanted anything; he just wanted his milk that would let him sleep without his heart tripping and his stomach trying to shit itself out—but Bel... Bel was worth it, worth this, worth anything, and so Spindle bit the filthy sheets and seized, hacking and hurling though there was nothing left to come up. He twisted and turned, unable to get comfortable, his back throbbing above his hips. His neck and head hurt, hot and swollen as if infected. He heaved toward the chamber pot filled with his feces and sick up before rolling away and gathering the thin quilt between his knees. Though it was fetid and close, he shivered all over and tried to make some valid excuse to go to Ivor and get the milk....

Just one more time, and then....

Then I'll stop. Not now. Fuck! This hurts! But Bel....

Bel wouldn't mind once more, would he? Bel could wait a little longer... maybe.

He had made Bel a promise. He'd never promised anyone anything before, and though he'd had no parents to teach him right from wrong, he knew promises must be kept.

Bel. For Bel he could hurt.... For Bel, he could do anything....

V.

ON THE evening of the third day, just before sunset, Spindle woke to a different world. Gone was the warm, hazy sense of stumbling through a dream; everything looked crisp, the edges sharp and defined—frightening and dangerous but gemlike in their clarity. Though Spindle still missed the feeling the special milk gave him—still craved it—it was liberating to know he didn't have to rely on it. If he didn't want to, he didn't have to go back to Ivor. He could go anywhere he wanted, and he planned to.

First, food. Spindle hadn't eaten in three days and it felt like longer. He felt like he'd never really eaten. He'd certainly never felt as ravenous as he did now. He hurried to dress, went downstairs, slipped the big proprietress a pair of earrings that made her cold eyes light up until she was almost beautiful, and ordered eggs, potatoes, baked beans, an eel pie, mushy peas, toast with cheese, and even a few pieces of bacon. He'd never known food could taste so good, and he managed to finish most of it before leaving.

The shops and stalls around St. Giles sold only secondhand items: much-mended clothing, worn-out boots, rusted pans, and chipped china. Spindle had hoped to find a decent coat, maybe a shirt and tie, so he'd look nice for Bel. He wouldn't have minded something a little worn or patched, but all the garments he found on the racks were moth-eaten, dry-rotted, and they smelled worse than his leathers. He sighed and moved on to the next stall: a lopsided little shed containing bins and shelves full of machine parts in no order whatsoever, just thrown and piled together. Spindle shifted through the greasy shafts and gears, not in search of anything in particular. The shop's owner, a gaunt man wearing heavy goggles over a dirty bandanna, watched him from a stool as he chewed a toothpick with his few remaining teeth. Something shiny caught Spindle's eye, and he lifted it from the chaos: a discarded piece of a steam-powered spinning machine, with a steel rod about as long as his finger that tapered to a point, a segmented brass whorl near the top, and a little hook at the end. A spindle. On a shelf nearby, he found a silver bell a little less than an inch high. He bought them both, along with a delicate chain, for a penny.

Just as the last few rays of sooty sunlight retreated from St. Giles, Spindle finished attaching the spindle and bell to the chain, each with a little copper ring. He smiled at what he'd done. He liked making things, hoped to do it again sometime soon. He'd never realized that about himself when his universe had consisted of only drinking the special milk and passing the hours until he could have it again. He'd have to thank Bel, and he didn't think the necklace would be nearly enough. Maybe it would make up for Spindle's attire. If he'd wanted to spare the time, he could certainly find a suit in one of the houses near Bel's. He did, however, stop at a pump in a square and wash his hair, body, and teeth as best he could. The lack of opiates in his blood had awakened more appetites than just for food, and he didn't quite understand the fluttering in his belly, but he wanted Bel to find him... pleasing.

SPINDLE found Bel in high spirits after he climbed the turret at the corner of Bel's building, flipping to the rail in front of Bel's window, pushed off, landed on his hands, and walked over into the room. Bel, dressed in a dark-blue suit with long tails and satin lapels, hurried to take Spindle's face in his white-gloved hands and kiss Spindle at the corner of his mouth.

"You're here," Bel said with a bright smile, drawing all Spindle's attention to the plumpness of his lips and the way his cheeks bunched up and his eyes crinkled at the corners.

"You're dressed." Spindle had only ever seen Bel in his nightshirt. He liked the way the suit accentuated Bel's lean frame, and he ran his hands down Bel's arms, his waist.

"I've been dressing every night," Bel said, his hand still on Spindle's cheek, "in case you came back. You look well. Healthier. That reminds me! I got word today that the Swedish scientists isolated the mold that destroys the infection causing the sickness, based on my notes and the samples I sent them! What's more, they've successfully grown it in their lab! An elixir that will cure the sickness can't be far off!"

That smile—straight white teeth between swollen pink lips.... Spindle couldn't resist. He leaned in and pressed his mouth to Bel's, tilting his head so their lips could intersect. He ran his tongue along Bel's lower lip, the edge of his teeth, until Bel's tongue ventured out to meet him, uncertain but needy. Spindle wound his arms around Bel's waist and pulled their chests together. Chinese fireworks erupted behind Spindle's eyes as they dared and explored, and his heart wanted to shoot like a bullet from his chest. Other things happened to his body, things that made him circle his hips and grind against Bel's thigh. Why had he waited so long to do this? How had he not wanted this the first night he'd watched Bel sleeping?

They separated from each other's mouths but still clutched each other's clothing, panting against each other's wet lips and grinning. Then Bel's smile dropped away and he wouldn't meet Spindle's eyes. "I don't want to give you false hope. The new developments are promising, and they'll save thousands, but for me—"

Spindle pressed two fingers to Bel's lips, as if by stopping the words he could stop what they would say. "I have something for you." He reached into one of the many pockets of his leather trousers, uncurled Bel's fingers from his hip bone, and placed the necklace in his palm.

At first, Bel seemed confused, his fair eyebrows high on his forehead as he looked from the necklace to Spindle and back again. "I— a spindle and a bell."

His eyes sparkled, and he kissed Spindle again before slipping the chain over his head. It looked startlingly elegant against his dark-purple tie. "It's beautiful. Thank you. I'll treasure this, keep it close to my heart even while I sleep. Are you going to take me out?"

Spindle's voice failed him, caught somewhere between his throat and his mouth, so he just nodded and sniffed. After a few moments he recovered enough to say, "You'll have to hold on to me so I can get us down. Can you do that?"

Bel burrowed his fingers into Spindle's unruly hair and rested his forehead against Spindle's. "I'll hold on to you for all I'm worth."

VI.

THEY rode an omnibus to the East End, along with the washerwomen, factory workers, and high-end prostitutes returning home after visiting wealthy clients. Bel marveled at it all, but Spindle was nervous. He noticed the glances Bel got in his expensive suit; the others noticed he had money and he was weak. If they tried anything, Spindle would have to defend him. The idea made Spindle's blood flow a little faster. He dared anyone to challenge them. It would feel good to stand up for Bel, to do something worthwhile for once.

It was Saturday, and the streets were clotted with men and women going in and out of gin houses, public houses, dancing halls, and smoking dens. Spindle kept an arm locked firmly about Bel's ribs, kept Bel close and safe. Bel wasn't the only gentleman of means to enjoy the city's more vulgar diversions, but with his youth and beauty, he attracted attention. Their lack of masks also drew some suspicious glares, but Spindle couldn't reconcile being uncomfortable—or hiding Bel's face— if it wouldn't do them any good. He wasn't the only one to appreciate Bel's classically handsome features. Bel'd already been propositioned by more whores, male and female, than Spindle could keep count of. Each time, his pale cheeks colored a little and he muttered a too-polite declination. Spindle was so proud to be with him, a startlingly lovely young man—and everyone noticed—who wouldn't even speak harshly to the lowliest unfortunate.

When Spindle arched a brow at Bel after they'd escaped an especially tenacious professional lady, Bel only said, "Everyone deserves respect. All people. She's just trying to feed herself the only way she can."

Spindle grinned. "You're an odd sort of gentleman, Bel."

Bel fondled the necklace Spindle had made. "Anyone who would do less is no gentleman. Besides, writing someone off as unworthy can be a terrible mistake. After all, I thought you had come to rob me, and you've turned out to be the best friend I've ever had. If I'd dismissed you because of your brown skin or your Faerie's ears—both of which I find... absolutely alluring—I wouldn't be here with you tonight, and that would be quite a shame."

"Aye." Spindle squeezed Bel's tiny waist tighter. He wished he had Bel's talent for saying exactly what he felt so prettily. He wished he could tell Bel how much it meant that Bel walked beside him without shame, has arm hooked with Spindle's.

Bel pointed to a line of people standing in front of a corner building, and they joined the queue, paid a penny each, and went inside and found seats. A scandalous French film—a courtesan and her patron—flashed in grainy shades of gray shot through with white lines like forks of lightning, but Spindle couldn't look away from the light strobing against the planes of Bel's face and open mouth.

"Oh, oh my." Bel gasped when the film concluded. "I had no idea."

Spindle wove an arm behind him to support him as they walked. Outside, the summer air reeked of old ale, garbage, piss, and human sweat. He thought about the brief bit of cinema. "Well, it's a part of life, innit? Men and women... uh, relations."

"It's a part of life that shouldn't be public," Bel chided mildly before coughing discreetly into his kerchief.

Spindle wasn't sure. He'd found the film awkward and a little nauseating, but he knew in this part of London, sex was a transaction, same as selling ale. "What now? A drink? A dance? What do you want to do?"

"All of it," Bel said, looking back and forth, clearly finding some wonderment in the filthy distractions of the East End Spindle couldn't recognize. "I want a piss-warm ale from a public house, and I want to dance to an off-key song played on the pianoforte. I want to see the clockwork animals in the mechanical circus, and... and then I want to rent a room above a cheap tavern and... and spend the night with you, Spindle. That is, if you want that."

"I do," Spindle said. He wanted to lie in a bed by Bel as he had so many times, but in such a different way. A way where he could feel Bel's porcelain skin beneath his hands, beneath his body. Feel his skin slowly color and heat, feel more of that enticing hardness he'd noticed against his back in Bel's flat. He leaned in to whisper next to Bel's hair. "I want to lick every inch of your skin."

Bel chuckled. The black centers of his eyes nearly eclipsed the blue-gray and his cheeks turned almost cranberry. "Maybe we should skip the rest of it, then."

"No. I want to give you everything you'd hoped for."

"You foolish man," Bel said, smiling up at Spindle. "You are all I ever hoped for. If there's one thing I want before—Spindle-Reed, I just want you. Please, find us somewhere, anywhere, we can be alone. Tonight, I'm free, and I know what I want to do. I know you don't want to hear this, but I may not have another chance."

Heart racing, Spindle caught Bel's hand and led him up the street. They passed a troupe of Chinese acrobats, in red silk costumes that stirred something almost forgotten in Spindle, but they didn't pause to watch. The past, remembered or gone, didn't matter. Tonight mattered. There would never be another tonight, and Bel wanted him, and they were free, with all of London spread out before them like a buffet dinner. In spite of all the possibilities, all Spindle wanted sprawled in front of him was Bel. He had wasted so much time already because of Ivor and his stupid milk, and he didn't want to squander another second. As soon as they found a public house, they paid for a room and staggered up the stairs and locked the door. Clothes came off and they fell into the straw-stuffed mattress, making love to the background sounds of drunken singing and street brawls, sickly gaslight and pristine moonlight pouring through the dirty little window.

Despite Bel's illness, they lay together three times, maybe more, if one counted the satisfaction hands and mouths could bring. Bel seemed to want to pack all his life into that stolen evening of absolute abandon, and Spindle could deny him nothing. Spindle let Bel sleep against his chest until the sunrise illuminated the dirty streets, and he had to rouse his—his love, his Bel—and urge him to dress so Spindle could take him home.

Bel looked tired in the silty morning light, and Spindle felt guilty. "You're worn out. I shouldn't've kept you up all night."

Bel, dressed now, rubbed his face up the side of Spindle's. "Hush, my love. Please. It was the most amazing night—everything I've ever wanted. You, you were brilliant. You set me free. For one night, I got to be a man. Not a sick man, just a man. And not because you brought me here, but because that's how you think of me—not as frail and infected. Last night, you were with me as a man. You weren't concerned about my health and I... I needed that so much. Thank you."

"Fuck, Bel! I-I love you." It was a pitiful response, but Spindle had nothing else to offer.

"I love you too. Thank you for letting me experience love. No one should have to die without knowing love, the way it can make everything else unimportant…. You, when I look at you, nothing else matters. When I look at you, I'm not dying, I'm just starting out, and it's just the two of us, and the world is beautiful and full of possibility. Can you even comprehend what you've done for me? What you have meant to me?"

Spindle didn't know what to say. He just gathered Bel into his arms and held him tight, unwilling to let death or anything else try to steal him away. *Let it try.* "I have to take you home, don't I? I have to give you up."

Bel laughed against Spindle's neck, his lungs rattling like bottles breaking in the street. "The staff will be bringing my bland breakfast and useless medications within a few hours." He coughed, pulling away from Spindle to clutch the windowsill as he scrubbed at his bloody lips. Spindle rubbed what he hoped were soothing circles between Bel's prominent shoulder blades.

"And you need to find your cure," Spindle said. "And then, when you're well, I'm going to make your every dream come true. I'm going to make sure you're happy for the rest of your life. Every single bloody day will be better than the last."

"Of course, Spindle. Of course it will."

They took the omnibus back to Victoria Street, and Spindle tucked Bel into bed, kissing his forehead after he gathered the coverlet under Bel's chin. His beautiful face was pale and pinched with pain. Spindle knew Bel had overdone it. He pinned a lock of golden hair between Bel's small, round, perfect ear and promised him he'd be back soon. He didn't think he could survive more than a day. Bel had hooked him in faster than the special milk, and he made Spindle feel a hundred times more wonderful.

VII.

THAT night, Spindle visited a few of the expensive flats around Westminster Abbey and the Houses of Parliament. In addition to money and jewelry, he wanted clothes. He wanted a proper suit, complete with shiny shoes, a tiepin, and cufflinks, so Bel would be proud to walk beside him. Despite his skin and ears, if he had the right clothing, they could go to galleries together, to a respectable theater, places suiting Bel's station. There were so many possibilities, now that his days weren't measured by waiting for Ivor's poisoned milk. He still craved it a little, thought to have just one more dose, but the fear of disappointing Bel dissuaded him. What a gift Bel had given him, getting him to give it up and regain control of his life. Spindle doubted he could ever repay him, but damn it, he'd try.

By morning, Spindle had a whole new wardrobe along with pockets stuffed with jewelry. He made his way back to St. Giles, so he could sell what he'd pilfered. He'd need to rent a room tonight, and hopefully Bel would be with him. Already, after only a few weeks, Spindle couldn't imagine his life without Bel in it. He wasn't a simpleton, despite what others might think when they looked at him, and he knew he'd never be a gentleman and live in an expensive apartment like Bel, or with Bel, for that matter. Their time together would always be secret and stolen, but Spindle couldn't help imagining it as he sat eating a kidney pie, perched on a section of crumbling brick wall, watching the steam trolleys chug past. Bel would find the cure to the sickness; he would be honored as a champion, as he should. Maybe they'd put up a statue in St. James Park. Bel would still want to be a doctor, Spindle knew. Healing and helping others was as woven into his being as the gold threads were woven into Spindle's stolen cravat. His golden hair would turn silver, and lines would crease his ivory skin, but his gentle blue-gray eyes would always look out at Spindle just as they had last night, full of trust, longing, and appreciation. Without judgment or shame. The way Bel looked at him, like he counted on Spindle to fulfill his every dream, scared Spindle a little. No one had ever depended on him for anything more than pocketing loose earrings or bending in half backward. It was... flattering, validating, to be tasked with something like Bel's happiness. Spindle couldn't bear the thought of shattering the absolute faith in Bel's eyes when he looked at Spindle.

Lost in his musings, Spindle didn't notice Ivor and his four hired thugs approaching until it was too late to run. One of the men grabbed his elbow, and another pressed a knife to his ribs.

"Well, well, well, me lad," Ivor said, his voice muffled by his mask. "Whorin' now, are ye?"

"What?"

"We seen ye last night, Spindle-Reed, you and your *foin* gentleman. What he sees in such an ugly fuck is beyond me. I guess if you can suck his cock like you suck down the milk I give ye, I might understand."

"Ugly little fuck," one of the other men said, and then he grabbed his crotch.

"He says... Bel says I'm beautiful."

All of them laughed, the cruel sound distorted by the filters through which they sucked air, and then Ivor spoke again, all false sweetness as he fondled Spindle's neck and cheek. "Ain't I been good to ya, lad? Ain't I given ya a home and regular meals when any sane and sober man would have kicked your Chinaman-Faerie arse into the gutter where it belongs? Yet I took ye in, and I asked so little for me efforts, for me Christian charity. You ungrateful little fuck."

"Leave me alone," Spindle said, struggling against the man who held him and eying the dagger Ivor insisted he attach to his belt. "You turned me into an addict, and I don't want no more of your help! Let me go!"

Ivor laughed, his big belly bouncing. "It don't work that way, me lad. Way I see it, you owe me for years of room and board. Whatcha got in your pockets, Spindle, lad?"

"Nothing! Let go of me!" Spindle twisted and freed himself from his captor, drawing his knife at the same time and pointing it at the group of men. "Leave me alone!"

"Ah, me boy," Ivor said as the big thugs closed in. "I'm afraid you're mine. I *made* you, I *bought* you, ye ugly little fuck. I made ye to bring me shinies, and that's what you'll bloody do!"

"No!" Spindle leaped back, getting behind the crumbling wall, and swept with his dagger. His steel cut through dirty cloth, dirtier skin, and white fat. Ivor doubled over to clutch at the oozing gash, and Spindle drove the knife into the back of his neck, pulling when it caught against something inside, and stabbed down again, and again. Ivor fell facedown on the filthy cobblestone, and Spindle ran while his cohorts stood stunned. When he reached the shoddy building at the end of the alleyway, he scuttled up the wall, ran across the roof, and tucked into a flip at the edge, landing lightly on the shingles across the street. Running along rooftops and dodging chimneys, Spindle soon put enough distance between himself and Ivor's thugs that he felt confident to drop to the street, make his way to a bench beneath a linden tree, and sit down.

The shops here sold new merchandise, and the ladies wore white dresses and elaborate hats with dainty little masks that matched their attire. They leaned in to whisper as they passed Spindle, and he noticed Ivor's blood on his vest and bare arms, and he hurried to find an air filtration pipe to climb into and get out of sight.

Watching the Sunday strollers from the rooftop of a cathedral, clinging to one of the grotesque sculptures adorning its eaves, Spindle realized Ivor was really dead. The man who had sheltered him, fed him, and claimed to care about him was gone. Spindle was free, but he really was on his own, and he was afraid. He flipped to his hands and pushed off, his body forming a backward arc above the street until he landed on the next building. He'd make his way to Bel. Bel would say something; Bel would know what to do.

VIII.

Since it was still daylight, Spindle crouched on the roof across the street from Bel's building, the ruckus of the filtration machines drowning out every other sound. He watched as maids in gas masks stripped the linens from Bel's bed and pulled the lace curtains from their rods. Men wheeled in barrel-sized metal waste bins and emptied the contents of all Bel's cupboards and drawers into them. Soon after, a regiment of young girls entered to scrub the floor and walls. Bel's books, notes, and diagrams went into rubber-coated canvas sacks. They brought pails and mops to clean the floors, and when they finished, they'd sanitized everything—removed every trace of Bel's presence in the rooms that had been his home and prison for so many years.

After twilight fell and the servants vacated Bel's chambers, Spindle crossed the street and stood in the room he knew so well. It smelled of ammonia, and it was cold. Bel was gone, Spindle knew, really gone. He went to the bed, but the servants had stripped away even the pillowcases that might hold the fragrance of Bel's hair. Spindle stretched out across the bare mattress, his fingers working against the fabric as the tears ran into his mouth. They'd washed him all away; not even Bel's scent remained in the room he'd been confined to, and Spindle wept, burying his face in the astringent-scented feather pillow. God, even Bel's scent was gone. They'd erased him, made it as if he'd never lived between these walls.

It was Spindle's fault—he'd kept Bel up all night and worn him out. And now, now Bel was—God, was he really gone? Gone forever? Spindle buried his sobs in the pillow. He couldn't do it without Bel, couldn't be strong without Bel behind him. God, this couldn't be true. Bel couldn't be gone; he was too good, too genuine—

It should have been him. The world needed brilliant doctors like Bel; it didn't need another crossbreed sneak-thief. It should have been him, and Spindle would have taken Bel's place, but it was too late now.

As Spindle lay sobbing quietly, replaying in his mind the many nights they'd just sat and talked, recalling every word they'd said to each other and all those he had wanted to say but never had and never would now, he would have given anything for one more day, one more day to make Bel happy and show Bel how much he loved him. As his thoughts turned to that magical night in the East Side public house, Spindle thought how good it would be to have some of his special milk. It wouldn't take this pain away, but it would numb it; it would numb him to everything. Besides, what did it matter now? Bel wasn't waiting for him anymore, and he never would again. He couldn't disappoint Bel now, any more than he could please him. It would be easy to get something, even without Ivor. Spindle could find some jewelry, or he could do some acrobatics for a few pennies. Then he could go to the chemist's or one of the Chinese smoking dens.

Why not?

But he couldn't; he knew that. It would be like taking the gift Bel had given him and tossing it in the gutter. Bel had given Spindle a whole lifetime of freedom, and Spindle had given Bel a single night. It was a piss-poor trade, Spindle knew, but the least he could do was appreciate what Bel had done, hold it close to him, and protect it no matter what.

He sat up and looked around the room, as cold and sterile as one in an asylum, and wondered what they had done with Bel's necklace. Would they have—Spindle choked on a sob as the words formed in his thoughts. Would they have buried him with it? More likely, they would have tossed it in the nearest bin. The cast-off spindle and fragile little bell would have looked worthless to anyone but the two of them. But together, those two mismatched and discarded baubles had made something beautiful.

Where had they laid him to rest? Spindle would find out, so at least he could visit him, make sure Bel wasn't as alone as he had been in life. If only there was something more he could do. He decided he'd live his life as Bel had hoped: free and happy. Maybe then, if Bel was looking down, seeing Spindle might make him smile. He had loved being able to make Bel smile.

Spindle rose from the bed. There was no reason to stay or to ever come back here. Before he left, he rifled through the crumpled paper, pens, bits of broken glassware, unwanted clothing, linens and books— everything they would burn to prevent Bel's disease from spreading— until he found the little necklace and slipped it into his pocket. Then he went to the window, stood on the rail, and let himself fall, chest-first and legs arched backward, toward the darkened cobblestones below. At the last moment, he caught the first-floor balcony with his toes, dropped onto his hands, walked over, and sprinted into the thickening shadows.

IX.

FROM the small balcony of his flat, Spindle looked out on an entirely different London. Though it had only been a year and a half, all the steaming, chugging filtration systems were gone, and windows and doors stood open to the warm early-autumn evening, allowing voices, fragrances, and music to pour into the night. On the streets of his semirespectable district, ladies and gentleman strolled arm in arm, laughter spilling unhindered from their bare faces. Spindle knew London was still far from perfect, but it was a damn sight better than it'd been with everyone scared to death and coughing up blood.

Spindle looked over his shoulder at the fair-haired young man sleeping soundly in their bed, smiled, and then slowly stripped off his tailed coat, shiny leather shoes, trousers, tie, waistcoat, and shirt. He tossed them into the bedchamber and stood in nothing but his old, snug leather trousers, the necklace he'd made—the first one and the most important—cool against his bare chest. Then he picked up his leather satchel and slung it over his shoulder.

It had been over a year since Spindle had done any contortions or acrobatics, but his body remembered how to bend and stretch as easily as it remembered how to breathe, and moving along the rooftops, he soon made his way to the Royal Hospital.

They'd recently built and dedicated an entire wing for the study of infectious diseases: a sprawling new building with a hundred beds for those who couldn't afford treatment, and a glorious dome crowned with a cupola. Eight buttresses supported it, and a marble angel stood at the base of each one. Spindle easily scaled the wall to reach one of them—Gabriel, he thought, because of the trumpet—and jumped atop the angel's head. Even for him, it wasn't easy to shimmy up the smooth marble spine, and it took him an hour of exertion to reach the crown and the huge bronze statue atop it. He looked up at the smooth face, and the clouds parted to allow a shaft of moonlight to fall across it, and Spindle's heart cramped. None of the people who idolized this man, who owed him their lives, knew how he had suffered. Spindle knew, and his heart hurt for his lonely hero.

"Evenin' Bel," he croaked out. "I miss you, love."

Spindle sat at the statue's feet and let his long legs dangle down. "I wish you could see how London looks from up here. I swear I can see forever. I'm sure you'd marvel over it. I wish I could have carried you up here so you could look down over everything. So, I-I'm sorry it took me so long to visit, but I've loads to tell you, love. They found a cure for the sickness, all based on the work you did. You saved thousands of lives, and I hope you know that, wherever you are. As for me...."

Spindle cleared his throat and scrubbed at his cheeks. "Me? Well, I can't complain, I s'pose. I hope you'll be proud to hear I ain't been near the laudanum, even though I still want it, all the time. I make jewelry now, from things I find, and I'm doing all right; got me own flat and everything, and... and I met someone, Bel. I hope you don't mind. His name's Nathaniel, and he plays the violin. He's a good man, and he loves me, but... but fuck, Bel, he ain't you. He—Nathaniel knows there's a part of my heart he can't ever have, that part that'll only ever be yours, but we have an understanding, and we have a life, and it ain't half bad, Bel. That's what you do, right? You live. I thought a lot about it, and I knew that was what you'd want me to do."

For a while, Spindle just watched the twinkling lights of the city and let his tears fall silently against his bare chest. His memories of Bel were growing hazy and distant, like a dream upon waking, and when he looked at the statue's placid face, he thought, but couldn't be certain, that the sculptor hadn't got the nose quite right. It was a beautiful statue, but it didn't have blue-gray eyes.

"I-I came to thank you, Bel. For everything. Everything I have is because of you. Even Nathaniel, because you taught me how to love and not be afraid to feel things. I—everyone knows about all those people you saved from the sickness, but only I know about how you saved my life. Fuck, Bel. I wish I could have told you all of this while you were still alive, but I just wasn't used to talking to people, you know?

"I wish I could have told you more, done more for you, but I have one last thing I'd like to do." Spindle dried his face on the back of his hand, drew a halting breath, stood, and opened his pack.

He took out a small gas-powered torch he used to make jewelry, and then he pulled the necklace from his pocket, climbed up, lodged a foot between Bel's hand and his hip, and draped the necklace over the statue's head. Using a few strips of solder, he attached the chain, and then he melded the spindle and bell to the statue's chest, letting them melt right into Bel's heart. He was crying softly by the time he'd finished, and he brushed his lips against the cool bronze mouth of the statue. "Keep 'em close to your heart, love, 'til I can join you. I love you, Bel."

Weary and feeling worn thin, Spindle scuttled down, dropped to his haunches, and sat with Bel awhile longer. Leaning his head back against Bel's knee, he lost himself to memories for a long time, until the first glimmer of light roused him. He stood and stretched, climbing up to give Bel's cheek a final, loving, regretful caress before packing up his things. "Bye, Bel."

Slowly, Spindle made his way home. Nathaniel would be waiting with toast, jam, and coffee. He'd want to kiss Spindle, and maybe more, before Spindle made his way to his workshop and Nathaniel went off to practice with the symphony. It was a good life, as good as it was going to get, and Spindle would live it—for both of them.

AUGUSTA LI is the author of several short stories, novellas, novels, and yaoi manga scripts, created either on her own or with her partner in crime, Eon de Beaumont. Gus and Eon are also artists and are currently hard at work on many manga and prose projects. They would love nothing more than to see the yaoi/BL genre flourish in the West. Video games, manga, and anime have been huge influences on Gus's work. Xbox Live calls Gus away from work far more often than it should.

Visit Gus at http://www.BooksByEonandGus.com or keep an eye out at anime conventions and Goth clubs around the East Coast.

Untouchable

Layla M. Wier

FEDERAL Agent Agamemnon Rawson didn't have an office. He kept a hole-in-the-wall room above a business I realized was a bordello as soon as I walked inside. I don't mind women but they don't turn my head, and some of the girls were clockworks anyway, with empty eyes and painted porcelain faces, turning their sightless stares on me. I kept one hand tight on my briefcase and the other on the .38 Colt under my arm as I edged up the narrow stairs. I knocked on his door.

"Come in," said a rough voice, so I did.

It was January, 1930. In Chicago, a hundred miles away, some unknown kid named Eliot Ness had just put together a task force to strike at "Scarface" Capone, king of the Chicago booze trade. I didn't know that then, of course. I was a newly minted federal agent myself, and my orders had been handed down straight from the United States District Attorney himself.

Rawson wasn't to know it, of course.

I stepped into a room that might easily have been the crib of one of those working ladies downstairs. Or maybe a prison cell without the bars. An iron bed frame with a thin mattress, a ladder-back chair with a washbasin on it, and a gas ring for cooking were the only niceties.

But there were books everywhere, and every kind of book under the sun: dime-store paperback potboilers, the latest works of the literary-salon darlings, translations of French and Russian writers, and heavy volumes of Shakespeare and Milton with thick cream-colored paper and cracked leather covers. You couldn't take a step without having to kick a book out of the way.

Rawson sat on the bed with a book open beside him, his place neatly marked with the classified section of the *Tribune*, and a double-barreled shotgun in his lap. I knew him because he looked just like the pictures I'd been shown, a rawfaced and rawboned man in his forties. He wore his hat indoors, and a clean shirt with suspenders; a black greatcoat lay folded over the back of the chair.

"I'm Agent George Aldis, sir," I said, hands spread to either side of me. "You're expecting me."

"Am I?" he said in a voice that was milder than I expected to come from his big, hard frame.

"The Prohibition Bureau sent me down, sir. I'm to work with you on the Sweet Pea Osborne job."

"Identification?"

I reached for my pocket, very slowly; his hand twitched on the shotgun. I flipped out my shiny new ID.

Rawson snorted. "How old are you, Aldis?"

"Twenty-six, sir."

"Twenty-six. Hell." Rawson took his hat off and ran a hand through his hair—light brown, streaked with gray, a good deal longer than Bureau standard. Then he rose and shrugged into his coat.

I must have stepped back, because he stopped and looked at me, really looked at me, for the first time. His face was craggy, bony jaw unshaven. His eyes were a striking, clear gray. I wouldn't call him handsome, but there was something about him that drew my attention, even then, before I knew him at all.

"Are you afraid of me, Agent Aldis?"

Telling the truth seemed unwise, but so did lying to that gimlet stare. "Well, back at the Bureau, they say—" I cut myself off, but his eyes were like steel.

"Oh? Go on. What do they say about me back at the Bureau?"

I'd gotten myself into this. So I gave him honesty. "They say you have no heart, sir."

"Is that what they say? Perhaps you should see the truth of it, then."

He unbuttoned his greatcoat and began undoing his shirt. My face heated. He couldn't know about that part of me. No one knew; I'd never have passed the Bureau's exhaustive background checks if I hadn't been scrupulously discreet. "I don't think this is necessary—"

"As your senior agent, I'll tell you what's necessary, Aldis."

Rawson pulled back the shirt to reveal a ruined devastation of scar tissue. A part of me wanted to recoil; a larger part was drawn, compelled. His chest was a cracked and seamed wasteland, pink scars running in all directions from a steel plate, about eight inches in diameter, embedded in his chest and slightly offset to the left.

When I held my breath, I could hear a soft, steady ticking that I had presumed to come from a clock somewhere in the room.

Forgetting myself in my curiosity, I stepped closer, peering at the inset steel plate with fascination. The exact mechanism by which it was held to his flesh was difficult to determine, though I could see bolts or rivets ground off flush with the polished surface. At a guess I would say it had been bolted in and the flesh allowed to grow around it.

"How do you wind it?" I asked and then looked quickly to his face, clamping my jaws shut. "Sir, I'm sorry. Professional curiosity, that's all—"

Rawson looked neither offended nor amused; his stubbled face was stonelike, impassive. "Some secrets are best kept for security reasons, Aldis." He began to rebutton his shirt. I forced myself to tear my gaze away, granting him privacy to cover himself.

"It's exquisite work," I said, staring fixedly at the corroded gas ring with a cold coffeepot sitting atop it and trying not to listen to the small rustling sounds as he arranged himself properly again. "On par with the very best arts of the German doctors. Who was your physician?"

"That's my business." I risked a glance to find him all done up again. "Have you eaten yet, Aldis?" he asked me as if nothing had happened.

"No, sir. I just got into town."

"Driving?"

"Train."

"Let's grab a bite, then."

Before we left the room, he tucked a book into the pocket of his greatcoat—a habit so practiced it was automatic. A gleaming, well-oiled .45 revolver went in the other pocket.

RAWSON had a car, an ancient Locomobile steamer with an electric refit, but he left it parked and we walked to a neighborhood diner. The sky was the flat gray of a Midwest winter, and the sharp wind made me turn up my collar.

"You're gonna need a decent coat," Rawson said, holding the door for me. A blowsy waitress smiled at him in a familiar way, and he angled straight to the farthest booth in the back. He sat with his back to the wall. "Where you in from?"

"Los Angeles," I admitted.

"Movie star country," he drawled. "The Wild West. Lotta crime out there?"

"There's crime everywhere."

Rawson took his coffee black and ordered a steak nearly raw. I had the meatloaf. While we waited for our food to arrive, he studied me with those too-sharp gray eyes. I felt like I was being taken down to my parts: the Bureau regulation haircut, my new Sears suit, the slight bulge under my jacket where I carried my piece. I wondered if he was making a mental file for me: George Leon Aldis, age twenty-six, five foot eleven, one hundred sixty pounds, blue eyes, brown hair. It's what I would have done. I'd read his Bureau file cover to cover, but seeing him in front of me was something else. I couldn't help cataloging all the little things that weren't in the file: the way he laid out his knife and fork neatly beside his plate, his pressed shirt contrasting with the scuffed shoes. After the waitress poured his coffee, he added a small dollop from a silver flask. I pretended not to notice and lit a cigarette to cover the sharp smell of illegal rotgut. I offered him one; he shook his head.

His file said he'd had no relationships at all in the past fifteen years. No girlfriend, no close friends in the Bureau, no known associations outside it. All Rawson did was work. And, apparently, read. His file said he was a voracious reader but hadn't mentioned how wide-ranging his interests.

"Earlier, you said it was professional curiosity that made you wonder about me." His voice was casual. "What exactly is your background, Aldis?"

"I studied medicine and engineering in college."

His eyes narrowed a bit. "And now you're with the Bureau?"

"It was the problem solving that always appealed to me," I tried to explain. How could I tell him, when I could hardly justify it to myself, that cutting into human flesh with my scalpel appalled me, let alone some of the abuses that went on under the guise of legitimate medical research? Terrible creations like the sex-doll clockworks in the bordello, or women with gear-driven butterfly wings to suit rich men's fancies. Huge clockwork war engines destroying cities during the Great War. Capone's goons with guns and knives for hands—

Men with clockwork hearts, perhaps, who walked around like any other men. I could hear Rawson's heart ticking quietly, now that I knew what to listen for.

"Anyway, the case," I said, getting back to business. "You've been pulling surveillance on the docking tower up at Kankakee."

Rawson nodded. From the seemingly bottomless pockets of his greatcoat, he brought a stack of photographs and handed them to me. He had nice hands, I couldn't help noticing—long graceful fingers, marked with scars, but nimble. The elegant beauty of those hands, so much at odds with his gunslinger persona, wasn't in his file either.

I'd already seen the photos, but I looked at them again anyway. Sometimes you miss things the first time.

Airspace over Chicago is crowded, and the capricious weather around the lake plays havoc with airships, which are just big balloons, after all. So a lot of the major freight lines unloaded at Kankakee, transferring their cargo to trains that rolled on up to Chicago. "Sweet Pea" Osborne's shipping company was one of Capone's supply lines for moving bootleg booze out of the Midwest.

"Trouble is, I don't think the Kankakee tower is the hub they're using," Rawson said.

I looked up at him sharply. "It has to be. All the supply chains from both directions lead there."

"I'm just telling you what I've seen. They bring in a lot of empty barrels, but I haven't yet seen 'em put on a full one."

I opened my briefcase and pulled out a map marked up with Osborne's shipping routes. "Well, they come in with a load of empty barrels, so they must be going somewhere after that. Where do they go?"

"You think I haven't thought of that? I followed a few of 'em as long as the roads went the right way. Other times I stationed myself fifteen miles south and picked up their trail for a ways from there. Either way, same result." His incongruously elegant finger traced one of my red-marked lines. "They go to St. Louis and Indianapolis and wherever the hell else they're scheduled to go."

"You think Osborne's a dead end?"

"No," Rawson said flatly. "Capone's using him to move booze; I'd stake my career on it. I just haven't figured out how." The corner of his mouth tucked up in a grim smile. "Guess that's what you're here to help me figure out. Partner."

WE SAT surveillance on the Kankakee docking tower for three days.

You get to know a man on a stakeout; you can't help it. You learn all his little habits, the interesting ones and the annoying ones. Rawson didn't have many of either. He divided his attention between the object of our surveillance and a paperback novel—he went through four of them in the three days we watched the tower, alternately scribbling notes in a dog-eared notebook. By the second day, I broke down and picked up one of my own. We didn't play cards or talk, except brief conversations when one of us left to pick up food or sleep.

And yet, I still felt I knew him after those three days. I knew that he drank strong straight coffee at all hours of the day and night, often laced with something I wasn't supposed to know he had in that little hip flask. I knew he liked red meat, didn't eat anything green, and had a quick, almost shy smile that came out when he didn't think anyone was looking.

And I knew how he wound his clockwork heart, though I didn't say anything about it. I'd been supposedly napping beside him when he did it, but actually watched him from under my cracked eyelids. There was a little panel in the brushed-steel surface of the thing that slid back cleverly to reveal a small winding knob. After three days in Rawson's car, I'd stopped noticing the ticking. It was a steady background counterpoint to my life; that was all. On the infrequent occasions when I wasn't near him, I found myself straining to listen for it.

His file had been absent any mention of the heart, though everyone knew about it from office scuttlebutt. I knew it had to be documented, so it must be at a higher level than I had access to.

"Agamemnon, huh?" I said as we watched tiny little guys in dark coveralls scuttling around the base of the tower. "Your folks must have loved the classics."

Rawson grunted. He was buried in his novel again. He glanced up at the tower, then at his watch. "Time for your check-in, isn't it?"

I thought I'd been discreet about that. It wasn't easy finding a pay phone while fist-in-glove with another agent.

Rawson snorted. "Look. I know you're here to report back to the home office on me. You're a mole, a plant, a stoolie. And what's more, I don't blame 'em. The only funny thing is it took so long for it to happen."

"Agent Rawson—"

"Are you listening? I said I don't give a double damn. I work on my own and I never pay much attention to the rules. I'm exactly the sort they'd suspect of double-dipping. The only reason they keep me around is because I get results. You're here to keep an eye on me. That's all right. Assuming you're sending reports upstairs and not to Osborne's bunch, that is."

"I'm honest," I said. At his wry look, I amended. "About that, I mean. I'm not on the take."

"I know," he said, and when I gave him a careful look, he said, "If I thought you were tipping off Osborne, I wouldn't have said anything." One hand touched the pocket where he kept the revolver, in a meaningful kind of way.

I wasn't sure whether to take that as a serious threat or not. One thing I did know, though: Rawson was reading me as intently as I was reading him. More than once I'd caught him watching me, the same way I watched him when I knew he wasn't looking.

It wasn't only his loyalties that I wondered about, and it wasn't only for my reports that I examined him. That broad mouth was so much more mobile and expressive than I'd realized, as I learned to read its nuances. The jawline, with its two-day growth of stubble, wanted to be touched. And most particularly, the clockwork heart, in its steel case—what I felt wasn't the engineer's urge to take it apart, but rather, the desire to lay my hand against it, to feel that steady ticking through my palm and down to the core of my being.

And that was exactly what I couldn't do. Couldn't even give a hint. What I contemplated, in my weaker moments, was exactly the sort of impropriety that would get a man sent packing from the Bureau, unless he had highly connected friends who could hush it up for him. I didn't. I was a small, unprotected fish swimming in a very large pond. Over the past few years, I'd never managed to learn not to feel these things, but at least I had learned not to betray myself when I did.

I wasn't sure why Agamemnon Rawson, of all people, had awoken my interest. It was made up of equal halves intellectual curiosity and a pure animal compulsion I hadn't felt for anyone in years. I wanted to touch him; more than that, I wanted to feel him push me back into the seat, his weight on me, his stubbled jaw scraping across mine—

I shuddered, closed my eyes, pushed it down. When I opened my eyes again, his level gray gaze was upon me, as if I fascinated him more than his dime-store novel.

RAWSON was right about the Kankakee tower, not that I'd doubted him. No longer than I'd known him, I could tell Rawson wasn't a man to say a thing if he wasn't sure of it.

But that left us spinning our wheels. "It doesn't make sense," I said over coffee in Rawson's favorite diner. We were both warming our bones after another cold night in the car. Outside the lead-colored sky spit small, hard flakes of snow. "They offload the empty barrels and put them on a train for Chicago. Then they put on a few crates of legitimate cargo, but nowhere near enough to fill a ship that size. And off they go." I pulled out the map again. "You're sure they don't stop anywhere near Kankakee?"

"Sure as I can be," Rawson said. "I tailed one damn near all the way to St. Louis."

"Are you sure it was the same one? Maybe they swapped it." Dirigibles were big business in the Midwest, where the wide flat spaces had seen docking towers spring up at every grain tower and cow town.

They couldn't move freight as efficiently as railroads, but they were faster and weren't limited to just the places that had train tracks laid. Some said the automobile would take over eventually, but I didn't see it happening unless the roads got one hell of a lot better and electric engines grew more efficient. Big, slow-moving cargo ships in every color of the rainbow were a common sight over the cornfields, winter or summer.

"I know how to keep a tail," Rawson said flatly. "Even if it's in the air."

I raised my hands in a wordless apology. "Okay, what if the load's already on the blimps when they come into Kankakee? Seems a bit circular, coming in with the full barrels *and* the empties, but Capone's a canny one. If he knows we know about the Kankakee depot—"

"It'd be a good way to throw us off the scent," Rawson agreed, a light in his pale eyes. "Then we waste our time chasing them all over creation, trying to figure out where they're loading it. Meanwhile they drop off the empty barrels, send 'em up to Chicago, and fill up again."

We pored over the map. The possible sites were endless, all the more since we didn't know how close to Kankakee they might be loading.

"They have to get the full barrels to the dirigibles somehow," I said. "Either trucks or railroads. Kankakee's on the main rail line to Chicago; we need to look for either a spur line or a good road that could handle a lot of loaded trucks."

"I wouldn't put my money on trucks. Out here in corn country, people would notice a bunch of trucks going out to the same spot all the time." Rawson shrugged. "But a train stops at a siding to offload some freight—no big deal, happens all the time."

So we were looking along railroad tracks. To make it harder, there wasn't necessarily a road going to the site. In fact, the more I thought about it, the more sense it made. The train came in and dropped off its load. The airship came in and picked it up. Then it flew on over to Kankakee, unloaded the empty barrels and any extra hands who'd been on board to handle the pickup, and went on its way. Capone knew full well that the loading and unloading points, along with the breweries, were the most vulnerable part of his operation. Getting it off the road system made it hard for us to find or raid.

Hard, I told myself, didn't mean impossible.

WE FOUND it by working backward. Rawson's notes were a mess, organized by a system that made sense only to him, but he'd written down just about everything that had happened since he'd been sitting on the tower. So we knew which flights came in with empty barrels every time, which had them sometimes, which never had them at all. In addition to that, now that we knew what we were looking for, we noticed that some of the supposedly unladen airships flew low and wallowed in the air. It could mean leaky gas bags—you get that a lot on older models—or tricky air currents, but it could also mean they'd been loaded somewhere else. I bought a clean map and we started marking the routes of the low-flying ships. Pretty soon we had a solid picture of which flights were likely hauling booze and which weren't, and nearly all of these came in and out through a certain swatch of airspace.

Then Rawson showed up with two horses he'd gotten from God knew where.

"You're kidding me," I said.

"If we're right, it's the only way to get where we're going."

We worked a regular grid, riding along railroad tracks south and east of Kankakee. In this flat country we could see trains coming a long way off, more than enough time to ride out into the cornfield, far enough so they wouldn't spook the horses, and watch them blow by with a good head of steam as they rolled on down toward St. Louis and Memphis. We always tried to leave ourselves enough time to get back, have a meal, and get a roof over our heads before dark. Rawson might be fine with rolling out a bedroll in a cornfield somewhere, but I wasn't about to unless I had no choice. The horses were stabled nearby with someone else in Rawson's wide-ranging array of local contacts.

It was cold, miserable work. Rawson didn't seem bothered by the chill, but I hunched in the warm coat and boots I'd bought at his behest, blowing on my frozen fingers and thinking about sunny beaches somewhere far south of there.

One thing about the days on horseback, though—Rawson couldn't read in the saddle (at least, not for any length of time), so it gave me an opportunity to draw him into conversation. Mostly I talked about myself: the all-American childhood, going out for sports but finding more interest in quiet, bookish pursuits. I'd always loved taking apart clockworks to see how they worked. Human bodies fascinated me as another interesting kind of puzzle.

"What changed that?" Rawson asked.

"People bleed," I said. Dissecting corpses in medical school had convinced me I didn't want that kind of life. I'd become drawn to other sorts of puzzles.

I drew out Rawson's life in bits and pieces. He'd spent a number of years working in Kentucky and Tennessee, the boot-scraping of Prohibition agent assignments. "The Mafia's a cakewalk compared to backwoods Tennessee." He'd served in the Great War, something he talked around rather than about, and of the time before that, all I could get were occasional snatches of stories about his days as a small-town sheriff, the son of the sheriff before him.

I knew the bare bones of this from his files, but I enjoyed hearing it from him, embellished with all the details dry paper couldn't relate. One thing he would never tell me was what had happened to blow a hole through his chest. I didn't push him on it. He'd tell me or he wouldn't. I knew full well it wasn't my business. I owed my superiors an honest report, but I didn't owe them a piece of a man's soul.

"So how's your report on me coming along?" he asked me as we rode side by side under a sky so blue it was almost white. After days of low gray clouds, threatening blizzards that never came, the weather had cleared off and the day was almost pleasant. Puddles gleamed like mirrors along the steel rails. "I still have a job; must be favorable."

"Just passing along what I see." What I didn't mention was that I hadn't sent back a report in days. I could tell myself I'd been too busy and too tired when we rode back in the evenings to find a pay phone. Certainly it was what I'd tell anyone who needed to know.

We stopped by the railroad tracks to eat sandwiches, wrapped for us that morning by the waitress at the diner. The sky was tinted bloody, the cold closing in behind the sun. The horses lipped unenthusiastically at dead grass. "Night's coming on," I said, wrapping up our trash. "Better be getting back." It would be full dark by the time we did, and fiercely cold.

"A little farther," Rawson said. "Moon's almost full, and it'll be clear."

I groaned and mounted. "There's nothing out here, just like the last ten places we checked. You know something I don't?"

"I got a hunch, that's all."

We rode along the railroad tracks in the deepening dusk. I hoped Rawson knew what he was doing and the horses didn't lame themselves out here in the dark. It would be a long, miserable walk back to town. With the sun's setting, the cold had deepened; the air hurt to breathe. Every stubbled cornfield was glazed in a layer of frost. Our horses' hoofbeats rang on ground frozen like iron.

We slowed to a plod as the twilight lengthened into night. The moon had just risen, winking at us across the silvered fields.

"Look," Rawson murmured, his low voice carrying to me on the still, cold air.

A dirigible floated over us. I wouldn't have seen it if he hadn't pointed it out to me. Normally they're lit up like Christmas trees but this one was running dark, illegally so, a blot against the stars.

We reined in the horses and watched it drift over us. The rural night was so still and quiet that I could hear the low throb of its steam turbines and the shouts of the crew as they trimmed it. A light flickered here and there when someone opened a door or window.

"Night," Rawson said as we traced its slow descent. "The loading had to happen at night. Otherwise someone would've seen it, even out in this country. A ship's not small, and Illinois's flat as a table."

"Some coincidence we're right nearby when it comes down."

"Not so much." He was smiling now, a quick sideways tug of his mouth in the moonlight. "Figured they made the exchange at night, so I made sure we hit the likeliest locations once it turned clear."

"You could've mentioned it," I muttered as we urged the horses forward. "That's part of what having a partner is about."

"I'm used to working alone." He pointed across the cornfields, following the path of the airship. "Look there."

A light winked against the night. The great, silent bulk of the ship was making straight for it.

We urged the horses to a canter. The railroad tracks ran straight and silver in the moonlight. The light winked again, and this time I recognized that the structure beside the tracks, a pale skeleton under the moon, was an abandoned grain elevator.

We crossed an old road, overgrown with weeds, and reined in behind a row of gnarled oaks. Rawson passed me a pair of binoculars. I could just make out a man covering and uncovering a lantern at the top of the structure, flashing signals to the dirigible as the crew cast down lines. A two-man crew on the ground made them fast. Beside the tracks, barrels were stacked in neat lines, awaiting loading.

Rawson dismounted and tethered his horse.

"Wait, what are you doing?" I whispered. "We should take some pictures and head back to town. Come back with a crew, stake it out until the next time they take on cargo, and raid the place."

Rawson's shotgun was strapped to the saddle; he pulled it free and checked the load, his breath smoking in the moonlight. "You get a bunch of agents tramping around out here, half of 'em in Capone's pocket, and these boys'll shift the route somewhere else. We know their method, but it ain't much good if we don't know where. We can't stake out every grain elevator in Illinois."

"This is insane," I muttered, sliding off my horse and touching the weight of my .38 under my arm. "What are you planning to do? There must be a dozen men over there. Rawson—" He was already heading down the tracks, his long legs eating the ground. I had to jog to catch up. "This kind of thing," I whispered fiercely, "is exactly why they put a watchdog on you. You know that?"

"So stay back and watch."

The fields around the elevator were overgrown, giving us ample cover despite the brilliant moon. We were close enough now that I could hear the men talking to each other—shouts and curses and exhortations to hurry. The airship bobbed gently at its moorings like an overgrown child's balloon. Its steam engines, damped down, smoked gently.

"Do you have a plan?" I whispered as he checked the load in the shotgun.

"Depends on whether I can count on your help or not."

I stared at him in the moonlight, the wide-brimmed hat and the long black coat swirling around his legs. His heart ticked softly in the crystal-cold air. He was a figure out of myth, the last of the gunslingers, and I knew I'd long since passed the point of no return on a whole lot of things. I drew my pistol. "Tell me where to go."

HE TOLD me to stay put and wait for his signal and disappeared into the night, ignoring my fierce whisper of "What signal?" behind him.

The cold was vicious, creeping down the collar of my coat and over the tops of my boots. I crouched and shivered and fought the urge to stamp my feet to warm up. They'd loaded more than half the cargo. Rawson better make his move soon, or they'd cast off the moorings and leave us standing useless in the Illinois night.

Then a shot erupted over the heads of the loading crew. I glimpsed Rawson by the glare of the lanterns, with that ludicrous coat billowing out and the shotgun pointed at the foreman of the loading crew. "Nobody move!" he bellowed. "This is a federal raid!"

I stood up and shouted, "You heard the man! You're surrounded, boys. Guns down and get on the ground."

Most of them did it. These guys weren't high-level gangsters; they were just teamsters and airship crew in Capone's pocket, and most weren't even armed. Rawson hopped up onto the dirigible's loading ramp, and I realized he meant to take the whole thing: crew, airship, hoodlums, and all. Crazy bastard.

I tossed my prisoners ropes from the barrels and got them started on tying each other up before they had a chance to realize there were only two of us.

One of them decided to be a hero, though. He made a dash for it while my attention was focused on the others and started cutting free the mooring lines, bellowing, "Feds! Cast off! Cast off!"

"Get on the ground!" I yelled at Hero Boy, but he pulled out a little semiauto and popped off a few shots at me. I ducked behind a silo.

Moored on some lines and free on others, the airship rolled ponderously to one side. The steam turbines began to fire up; some idiot up there, panicked by the gunfire, was stoking them before the big old bird got clear of the grain elevator. The stern of the dirigible began to rise, while the nose was still tethered. She pivoted slowly and gracefully. I could see what was about to happen, but there was no way to stop it. The entire great bulk of the thing came around and the stern hit the grain elevator, crumpling slowly and inexorably into the huge structure. Rusty sheet metal and splintered support beams avalanched down. The side of the dirigible was stove in from stern to midships.

The stern, where the turbines were—and the coal fires that powered them. This was about to go real bad, real fast. "Rawson!" I shouted and jumped onto the loading ramp where I'd last seen him.

The lower cargo hold was a mess, with unsecured barrels rolling everywhere as the ship slewed on her mooring lines. I glimpsed Rawson on one of the catwalks, easy to recognize by his wide-brimmed hat and billowing coat.

There was a massive crunch, and I looked over my shoulder to see boiling water and steam cascade down the side of the grain elevator. That had been one of the boilers for the turbines. An instant later, a flash of fire raced up the side of the steeply tilting dirigible just as momentum popped loose the last of the mooring lines and she floated free.

Modern airships used helium for lift, rather than the highly combustible hydrogen of their predecessors; however, the doped and painted cloth containing the gas could still go up like a Roman candle if the wind was right. The pilot abandoned ship, flinging himself over the side of the gondola into the cornfield below us. We were off the ground now, drifting without direction.

"Rawson!" I yelled, and he turned my way. "The ship's on fire! Let's go!"

Hearing me, Rawson jumped to the level below, and just as he did, a hood wearing the trademark pale gray fedora of Capone's gangsters hove up on the catwalk above him with a tommy gun. I fired but missed; he was too far away. Rawson swiveled around and the shotgun roared.

With my attention on them, I didn't even realize I was in danger until the same pistol-toting goon I'd chased on board popped up from behind a rack of lashed-down barrels not fifteen feet from me. He had me before I had him. The gun wasn't loud, nothing but a quick series of pops. I felt no pain, just an impact like someone kicking me in the chest.

My gun fell from my numb fingers and I tumbled backward into the cornfield below. I guess it must not have been far to fall. I didn't feel myself hit. Above me, the flaming dirigible was impossibly huge against the stars as she cruised over me, wounded, trailing mooring lines. She went down in graceful slow motion in the middle of the cornfield. Flame climbed her side. I couldn't raise my head, but I could feel the wash of heat.

Something dark blocked my view of her crumpling, burning shape. "Hey," I slurred. "I was watchin' that."

"Shut up, Aldis." Rawson's hands, the long graceful hands I'd admired, were doing something out of my sight. It hurt. I cursed him good and long.

He barked a short laugh. "Never heard you cuss before. Didn't know you knew how."

I lay back against his chest. He'd wrapped his coat around me. I could hear the ticking of his heart. It seemed to falter, slow one minute, skipping beats, then faster the next. It was me, I realized, fading in and out, losing time.

The pyre in the field lit everything up bright as day. I could smell its charred-plastic stink. My head was tipped back; I couldn't see the flames anymore, but I could see Rawson's face, a grizzled study in black and orange.

"Someone's bound to see that," Rawson said. "Can't miss it. We'll have help out here before you know it. You still there, Aldis?"

"What happened to the bad guys?" I wanted to know. The words came out garbled, but he seemed to understand.

"Some got tied up, some got dead, and some just lit out running. Course, since the sheriff's department is sitting around with their thumb up their ass, looks like the prisoners'll have time to untie themselves, run off into the cornfields, and marry some nice farmer's daughter before we get help out here." He gave me a little shake. "Hey, Aldis, why don't you take some of the conversation? I can't get you to shut up most of the time."

"Tell me," I said. My mouth tasted like metal. "Tell me how you lost your heart."

Silence. I wondered if I'd stopped being able to hear, but I could still hear the muted roar of the fire. Then Rawson said, "It was back in the war. This isn't in your files anywhere?"

"Not in any files," I mumbled. "That I saw."

"Well, I did a lot in the war that they don't want me to talk about. You guessed it was German work; you were close. Swiss Germans. They're the best with clockworks, always have been. Got my chest blown out, got it patched back together so I could go back and run more dirty jobs for my country."

He rocked slowly on his heels, staring into the fire. I wasn't sure if he knew he was doing it, but it was nice. I let it carry me away, that and the whiskey-rough growl of his voice. "They wanted me to stay on after the war, you know. Foreign service. I told 'em fuck off and go to hell. But I never made it out, not all the way. Being a lawman, it's in my blood. My daddy was a sheriff—I tell you that?"

"In your file," I whispered.

He snorted a laugh. "Yeah. Guess so."

"Think I'll get one?"

Rawson seemed to come back from whatever long-ago place he'd gone to. "One what, Aldis?"

"Clockwork heart."

"You dumb sonofabitch," Rawson said. "You got a heart already. Works just fine. A steel heart's for a stone-cold steel bastard like me."

"You're not as cold," I said, and the words came out slow, measured to the pace of his ticking heartbeat, "as you want everyone to think."

The ticking was like a lullaby. It stopped and started and skipped beats, but I knew that was all me. His heart was a metronome, never faltering or pausing as long as it stayed wound. Good Swiss engineering. That steady ticking followed me down into my dreams, keeping time.

Maybe the lips that brushed mine were only a dream too.

I WOKE doped to the gills on morphine in the hospital in Kankakee. Those early weeks are a blur; the only thing I remember clearly is that Rawson was there a lot of the time, reading beside my bed or helping me sit up for tasks too intimate and unpleasant to talk about.

"What are you getting out of this?" I asked him one time. I was feeling a little better, propped on pillows where I could look out the window. I wasn't expecting an answer, let alone an honest one, but to my surprise, after he read a few more pages of his book, he gave me one.

"Maybe because it woulda been nice if someone was there for me."

Out there in the world, the war with Capone went on. Rawson vanished for hours or days, came back smelling like gunpowder and the clean scent of cornfields. He read aloud to me from Dickens and Zane Grey.

It snowed outside my window.

My boss came down to talk to me. He asked me a lot of questions about the report I'd compiled on the incident, especially the reason most of it was in Rawson's handwriting—I'd been too weak to hold a pen, so I'd dictated it—and then a lot of questions about Rawson, most of which I didn't answer. We ended in a shouting match. I started out the department's darling for taking out a major link in Capone's southbound supply chain and ended up being put on report for the first time in my career.

"Happens to me all the time," said Rawson, who'd overheard a lot of it.

"It's stupid," I fumed, staring out the window. A silver dirigible drifted by, high and serene above the frozen cornfields. "Half the men in this organization are rotten, looking the other way and pocketing fat wads of cash from Capone. We all know it. So what happens? They fix on the honest man and shove him to the curb for not obeying the rules."

Rawson shrugged. "It's how the game is played. You'll get used to it."

"I'm tired of playing that game, and I sure as hell don't want to get used to it." I sank back against my pillows, exhausted from my outburst. Then I looked at him. "You said you're a lawman to the core. You ever think about serving the law in a different way?"

"You mean go back to being sheriff? It's crossed my mind," Rawson said. "At my age, though, with my"—he tapped his chest—"infirmity, they won't consider it."

"That's not what I was thinking." I closed my eyes. Easier to talk to the darkness behind the lids. "I'm thinking about quitting. Going freelance."

"Most private eyes I've met are scum," Rawson said. "Out for a quick buck, that's all."

"It doesn't have to be that way," I said, still with my eyes closed. "Maybe it's a chance to do what we do, but with fewer rules and more options. No steady paycheck, it's true, but with a partner you can count on at your back."

"Partner, huh." Rawson's voice was low and speculative. I opened my eyes and found him watching me with that steady gray gaze that seemed to take in everything.

"The government has a lot of rules," I said. "The civilian world… not so many. And who gives a damn what private eyes do? Everyone knows they're not respectable anyway."

I wasn't sure if he'd get what I was driving at. Maybe that kiss in the cornfield had been a dream, after all. But he rested a hand on the edge of the bed and leaned in, unblinking, his pale gaze holding me.

This time I was wide-awake to enjoy it, and I did. We explored each other's mouths as carefully as if we were collecting evidence for a case. He smelled like leather and gun oil, and the hand that came up to cup my chin was callused but gentle.

He was the one who pulled back, finally, looking at me with a kind of soft wonder. "See, I knew you had a heart," I said. I laid my hand on his chest, like I'd wanted to do from the beginning. I could not just hear it but feel it, a steady and comforting vibration, no different from a flesh-and-blood pulse when it came right down to it.

He covered my hand with his own and bent in for another kiss. Our afternoon passed in that fashion, measured by the steady ticking of his heart.

LAYLA M. WIER is the romance pen name of artist and writer Layla Lawlor. She was born in a log cabin in rural Alaska and grew up thirty miles from towns, roads, electricity, and cars. These days, she lives in Fox, a gold-rush mining town on the highway north of Fairbanks, Alaska, with her husband, dogs, and the occasional farm animal. Their house is a log cabin in a birch and aspen forest. Wolves, moose, and foxes wander through the front yard. During the short, bright Arctic summer, Layla enjoys gardening and hiking, and in the winter, she writes, paints, and draws.

Website: http://www.laylalawlor.com

Blog: http://laylawier.wordpress.com

Twitter: https://twitter.com/Layla_in_Alaska

SWIFTSILVER

BELL ELLIS

SEAMUS was sixteen and had been Demolo's apprentice for ten years when he first made swiftsilver. It was purely by accident, a tincture of Naman's compound accidentally titrating into a heated crucible of silver nitrate, but the accident was magical in a way. After a cloud of odiferous smoke and a dizzy moment, Seamus found that the crucible contained a small quantity of something resembling quicksilver—a cool silver-colored liquid. But quicksilver was its own pure substance; that much he knew. He had added no quicksilver to this.

The liquid was light and beautiful and by all appearances purest metal, yet an amalgam. Seamus tested its conductivity and found it astounding; he heated and cooled it and it retained its liquid form. It seemed immutable once created. He wondered whether it was a slow poison, as was quicksilver; but weeks of handling it yielded no ill effects. He wasn't sure what uses the substance could be put to, but in its own way, swiftsilver was a tiny miracle to him.

He never told Demolo; he kept the swiftsilver in a tiny casket in his sleeping nook. It was an infraction large enough to merit dismissal—not that Demolo would ever dismiss Seamus; he would merely punish him forever. But that infraction was nothing compared to his ensuing misbehavior: Seamus continued trying to create the substance, slyly hiding his efforts from his boss.

Three more years passed before he succeeded again.

IXTHIOCOPOULOS TENET (Thio to his friends, not that he had many) was whizzing through the sky in his latest modified aircar when disaster struck.

This was nothing shocking. Disasters were always striking Thio. He had a habit of doing unnatural things such as playing with fire, toying with steam valves, building contraptions out of sharp and hazardous materials, and yes, whizzing through the air in flimsy metal cars, hardly more substantial than carts. Thio was, in fact, deciding to call them "aircarts" rather than "cars" as he rapidly fell out of the air in one of them.

The cart shattered and scattered, while Thio stayed mostly together. He collected a couple of souvenirs from the accident: one broken arm and a furiously-scribbled set of notes (the arm that broke wasn't his writing arm, fortunately or perhaps unfortunately) detailing everything that might have gone wrong.

He decided he needed to seek out a good alchemist to judge whether he was using an inefficient form of fuel. The idea of seeing an alchemist occurred to him because his crash landed him directly in front of the door of one.

The emerging alchemist didn't seem very happy about that. He charged through the door, leaving it swinging, a dusky-olive-skinned young man with a neatly combed widow's peak and black eyes so sharp they seemed to cut right into Thio's face.

"What the blazes are you *doing*?"

Thio drew himself up straight, neglecting his notes and smiling. "I beg your pardon. I was simply testing my latest design in aeronautical—"

"You've broken the signboard!" The young man pointed sternly up at the board, now cracked through the middle and dangling haplessly from one chain. It said:

Demolo
Expert Alchemist and Apothecary

The last word was cracked in two: "Apot" and "hecary".

"So I have!" Thio said contritely. "So I have. I assure you, it won't happen again. I never crash in the same spot twice."

"Whyever crash in the same spot *once*?" spluttered the alchemist. "Demolo is going to be furious with me!"

Thio paused, confused. "Who is Demolo and why would he be furious with you for my crashing?"

The young man sighed tightly. "Because Demolo would be furious with me for a cloud crossing the sun on the wrong day of the week, that's why. Are you injured?"

Thio smiled again, brilliantly. "I appear to be in fine shape, excepting the fact that I think I have broken my arm." And then he fainted.

THE flyer—Seamus couldn't think of what else to call him—seemed wildly out of place in the apothecary wing of Demolo's shop. Seamus had carried him to a couch and laid him there haphazardly, the young man's long limbs stretching to the floor on one side and the wall on the other. Whoever he was, he was a mess, scratched and bleeding in a dozen places, bruised and swelling in a dozen others. His arm wasn't hanging right either, and Seamus suspected the young man had been right about it being broken.

Aside from his injuries, the flyer had a cloud of messy blond hair, clear green eyes (presently closed), fine features, freckles, and the cut of his clothing said he came from money. Under other circumstances, Seamus would have found him handsome. Even in this particular circumstance, Seamus couldn't help looking at the man with a mixture of envy and mild hopelessness. Despite his unconsciousness, there was something dramatic and exciting about him. Something Seamus would never have or know.

Demolo burst into the shop unceremoniously, his gray beard swinging as though in a high wind, and he howled, "And what has been done to my beautiful shopfront?"

Seamus sighed. "This man crashed into it."

"Can I not leave the store in your charge for a paltry two hours without mayhem resulting? Seamus, I continuously expect your youth to mature into wisdom and I am as continuously disappointed! When I took you in, yes, when I graciously took you into my home, I knew somehow that it would mean years of pain and trouble, I knew it and yet I did it.

And here we are. Again I am forced to endure the results of your carelessness!"

Seamus merely nodded and kept silent. He knew the formula of the speech by now; first it would be all alarm and shouting, and then a long and droning recitation of Demolo's generosity in taking Seamus in as a child ("Off of the street, where you would doubtless have starved!"), followed by a lamentation on the harshness of life ("I grow old and yet my life will never have peace in it!"), and then the ensuing acceptance of his fate ("But I am too kind a man, always, and continue to tolerate you...."). It would be long minutes of haranguing before Demolo would finally get to the point of telling Seamus what he wanted done to fix the problem.

In fact, Seamus was nineteen and might be expected to know what to do about a problem without being told, now and then. He knew, for instance, that the wreckage in front of the shop needed clearing and that the spilled reeking substance in the yard would need to be quenched with wood shavings. Also the signboard needed to be taken down, glued, and repainted. But he hadn't dared to do a thing until Demolo came home, wouldn't have dared to do any of those things without specific instructions. To act on his own would mean a whipping or worse. Years of that punishment had toughened Seamus's skin considerably, and he no longer minded the pain, but to be whipped like a child stung his dignity.

Seamus had a lot of dignity.

Even carrying the unconscious man into the shop was an infraction, but Seamus hadn't been about to let him languish in the street. Some things Demolo would simply have to work around.

Demolo was finally capping off his lecture with "I can never trust you again, Seamus, never again. My work is simply too precious...," when a voice broke in.

"Why be angry at him? I'm the one who broke the board!"

Seamus started and stared at the unconscious young man, who was no longer unconscious and was grimacing in pain. But his eyes were blazing in indignation.

Demolo simply stood silent in shock.

The young man struggled to sit up. "Do you have an answer for me? Why are you angry at him? He was very upset about your signboard and told me so. He was as upset about it as if it were his own shop! And then he saw that I was wounded and brought me inside (thank you, friend), and I say, I'm in need of an apothecary, is there one on the premises who does other things than flap his great boring mouth?"

Demolo glared at the young man, but he could see as well as Seamus that he was facing a gentleman, and he didn't dare to yell back. "My... apologies, sir. Of course I intend to assist you within my humble capacity. I was merely waiting for you to wake."

"It would have been a noble favor if you had set my arm while I was fainted," retorted the young man. "But as it is, I'll take what help I can now."

Seamus, meanwhile, was standing very, very still. He had never in his life been defended by anyone, and his chest and stomach felt tight and achy, as though filled with bubbles. He knew his face was red. He wasn't sure whether he was embarrassed, but the slightly hopeless feeling he had toward the young man blossomed into something stronger, something like awe.

He wished he had defended himself. Surely the flyer despised Seamus for simply standing there and accepting the unjust accusations.

But when Demolo went to the back to gather his herbs and the materials for a splint, the young man looked up at Seamus with a smile and a wink. He said, "My name is Thio, and I'm in need of a good alchemist to help me with my experiments. Will you help me?"

Seamus said, "Demolo is the alchemist, not me."

"But you're the adventurer. I can see it." Thio's eyes seemed slightly mad, but even that madness was alluring.

Seamus suddenly felt it would be worth ten whippings a week if he could continue to see Thio. This was by far the most interesting thing that had ever happened to him. "How can I help?"

"I knew it!"

"You knew what?"

"I knew I'd find it here!"

"Find what here?"

Thio smiled. "The answer."

Seamus wanted to ask what Thio meant by that, but he kept quiet. He had a sudden, strange feeling Thio might be right; there was an answer here, a big one, and Seamus didn't need to know what it was to know he wanted to find it out.

IT TOOK Thio's arm ten weeks to mend to the point where he could fly again, which was considered a blessing by his neighbors, but the time did not pass him idly by. He spent most of it pestering Seamus, who was bemusedly willing to be pestered.

Demolo disapproved. "Why are you neglecting your work, Seamus? Is it that young man? Has he been distracting you yet again?"

"He pays," Seamus said. Money was one of the few things that would shut Demolo up. And money was something Thio seemed to have; he brought it to the shop in quantities that would shame a silk caravan, and with it he would bring orders for solvents and solutions, medicines and magic, enough to keep Demolo in business for years. Seamus privately suspected Thio was donating Demolo's services to half the city's indigents. Thio never told. But he continued to keep Demolo busy so he could accost Seamus and prattle on about his latest inventions... and the inventions of others.

"They're calling it a combustion engine, and it's the very latest thing. Haven't you worked with kerosene yet? They've just started refining barrels and barrels of the stuff, down in Holsland. I've been mixing it with different things and burning it; Father uses it for lamp oil, of all the unimaginative things! He has no vision. Me, I'm *made* of vision." Thio laughed. "All vision and no substance, that's what Pa says."

Seamus would look at Thio's notes and point out mathematical errors and errors of logic (there were many). Thio was never offended when he was caught in a mistake. He would thank Seamus merrily and then plunge off into some new, error-riddled theorem.

"The wings are bowed, see, like the ribs of a ship. But also like the interior of a church, which is what gave me the idea of creating these sort of buttresses with the hinges on them.... Talk about flying buttresses—these ones truly fly!"

Seamus tried his best, but even he couldn't get most of Thio's inventions off the ground. The trying was fun, though. Thio was irrepressible. He laughed off burns and injuries, was delighted by explosions, and scoffed at failure. Seamus, who had always worked intently and cautiously, meticulously planning for and avoiding errors, was both scandalized and exhilarated by Thio's devil-may-care process. But then, Thio had never had Demolo ranting and raving about his smallest mistakes for hours on end.

Seamus lost sleep trying to keep up with both Thio's work and his usual workload. He tried his best, but even he was exhausted finally, and his temper flared one day as Thio tried yet again to attain the proper mix of saltpeter and kerosene for a slow-burning torch. Seamus was convinced that without a solid binding agent, the exercise was useless. Thio kept trying to keep the mixture fluid. In the midst of bickering, Seamus finally swore, swept the beaker off the table, and knocked over the burner, watching in satisfaction as their experiment went up in smoke. *It needed the wooden surface. I was right.* He turned to Thio, pointed at the burn spots on the floor, and said, "That's what I think of your theory!"

Thio, for the first time, seemed wounded. "But Seamus, you were so close to success. I can't accomplish this without you."

Seamus looked into Thio's hurt green eyes and felt ashamed. "I'm sorry, Thio. I don't think I should do any more work today; I'm... I'm too weary. I'll make mistakes."

"Weary? Have I been wearing you out, then?" Thio smiled. "I'm told I do that to everyone, nobody can keep up."

"It's not that." Seamus scooped some sand out of the sand barrel and covered the spots on the floor, keeping himself busy so he didn't have to look into Thio's eyes again. He didn't know how to tell Thio what the real problem was. Seamus was simply too busy in general: he had to assist Demolo in all his orders, but he was also responsible for cleaning the shop, for cooking the meals, sending out the laundry, taking and delivering orders, answering letters, tracking the financials, and a dozen other things. "I like working with you, Thio." He felt his face redden as he said it and hoped it didn't show. "But Demolo needs my attention as well."

"Why don't you quit and work solely for me?" Thio asked.

Seamus stared, but Thio's eyes were full of earnestness. Seamus said, "But that's out of the question."

"Why?"

"Because...." Seamus stopped. *Because Demolo can't do without me.*

"Think about it, would you? Honestly, Seamus... you may be the first person I've ever met who can keep up with me." Thio grinned. "I would consider that invaluable. A better service even than your mastery of chemistry."

Seamus blushed even redder.

THE one thing that could put Thio into a positively foul mood was inclement weather. Explosions became troublesome when there was a danger of getting wet, and most forms of precipitation were anathema to flying, even when the most flying one did was to plummet out of the sky.

He glared out the rainy window and pouted like a child. It was cold enough to be icy outside, and that meant anybody of good sense was indoors. Thio disdained most forms of good sense, but even he wasn't going to risk one of his contraptions on icy cobblestones.

Strangely enough, Seamus seemed to be in an excellent mood. He hummed as he stirred his concoctions and made his careful, precise notes; his steps were light as he filed away packets of herbs and powders and did the inventory. Thio still wasn't entirely sure just how much Seamus did at the shop, but it seemed to be nearly everything. His shoulders were typically hunched, as though he were carrying a weight with him at all times. But today they were firmly straight.

Demolo isn't here today, thought Thio. *That's why.* And the rare sight of Seamus smiling almost made the rain worth it.

Almost.

"What are you making?" Thio set himself on the sofa, lounging. None of the furniture in the place felt big enough for him. Then again, sometimes the world didn't feel big enough for him either. He thought one day he might split the seams of the world....

"Nothing interesting," Seamus said lightly. "Mixing a zinc oxide ointment for rashes. I've been told it can be used as a paint." He held up the mixing knife coated in the bright white substance. "Pretty, isn't it?"

"It's as white as a cloud, which is to say, it's almost blue." Thio grinned. "You're right, it's nothing interesting. Tell me something interesting!"

"You are."

"You flatter me, but I have no interest in myself at the moment."

Seamus ducked his head slightly, that faint smile of his still on his lips. Thio was fascinated by Seamus's smile. It seemed to want to hide, as though it were afraid of being called out or punished. And just now, Seamus was on the verge of saying something, but also on the verge of deciding not to. Thio sat up.

"What is it?"

Seamus laughed softly. "I have something I find interesting, but I doubt you will agree."

"Show me. Quickly, before I die of boredom. I'm in dire need of stimulation, my dear friend."

Seamus rolled his eyes. "Come with me."

Thio followed Seamus into the rear of the shop and then up the stairs into the living quarters. This was an inner sanctum; Thio had never been upstairs before, and he nearly bounced with curiosity as he mounted the steps. The room upstairs seemed hardly worth his anticipation, though. It was small and dark and dusty, and the rough bed in the corner was unmade.

"You live here?" Thio asked, keeping his voice carefully neutral.

"Oh no. This is Demolo's room. I'm back here," Seamus said, opening a tiny door in the corner. "Sorry, I'm afraid there's scarcely room in here for two...."

Thio peered inside Seamus's room, which seemed no larger than a closet. A small window looked out upon the rainy street and seemed to usher the cold into the room rather than blocking it out. Seamus had a cot (neatly made) in the corner, stuffed with straw, the blanket threadbare. He set his lamp down on the floor and rummaged around in a small pile of objects by the cot—obviously his personal belongings, and very few they were indeed.

Thio felt as though he were seeing his friend for the first time.

He had known Demolo was not wealthy, even as merchants went, but he had not realized what that meant in terms of Demolo's apprentice. Seamus's life was humble below Thio's imagining. And just the thought of spending cold winter nights beneath such a paltry blanket made Thio shudder. There wasn't space for a stove.

His dismay quickly turned to anger, and he opened his mouth to vent it, when something stopped him. Seamus had turned around and was holding in his hands a tiny box of dark stone. It glinted in the dim light. Seamus said, "It might be better if I showed you in more light, but if Demolo comes home...." His eyes finished the sentence with a worried look. "Best I show you in here and then put it away as soon as possible. I do not need to add that you shall tell nobody about this?"

Thio put a hand to his lips. "Silent as the grave."

Seamus opened the box, and inside was a small quantity of silver liquid.

"I call it swiftsilver."

"Quicksilver?"

"No, it's not the same substance. This is something new."

They looked at the swiftsilver together, poked and prodded it as Seamus talked about its origins, and finally Thio asked to hold it in his hand.

Seamus gave him a pained look. "You won't spill it?"

"Upon my honor."

Seamus, with excruciating care, tipped the swiftsilver into Thio's hand.

Thio was immediately shocked. "It's light! Quicksilver isn't light as this."

"Quicksilver is thirty times the weight of an equal quantity of water. Swiftsilver is actually lighter than water, per volume." Seamus peered anxiously at the tiny glimmering puddle in Thio's palm. "Perhaps you'd better put it back now."

Thio held his hand out to the tiny stone casket, but before he could pour the precious fluid back into it, the sound of a slamming door downstairs startled them both. Demolo had apparently returned early and was in a bad temper. The door was doubtless bruised.

Meanwhile, Thio was staring in horror at his empty palm and a scattering of faint silverish droplets across the floor.

He looked up to Seamus's eyes, half-afraid of what he would find there, and saw a stunned woundedness that would soon be heartbreak. Thio felt his stomach sink. He knew now that the swiftsilver was Seamus's one treasure, the only thing he owned of any worth at all. It must have meant the world to him.

Thio began to say something, anything to somehow mollify the disaster, when suddenly Demolo's voice was raucously calling just behind them. "And what now? Who is in the house? *Seamus!*"

Seamus's face, still stricken, filled with alarm. "It's only Thio, sir."

Thio said, "Ah, Demolo, I had been waiting for your arrival. I have new orders for you." He had learned the fastest way to quiet Demolo was to mention money.

But Demolo seemed different from his usual, ignorable self. His eyes were blazing with rage, and his face was red. "Get out, whelp."

Thio stood straight, unsure of whether Demolo was talking to Seamus or to himself, but either way he was affronted. "I beg your pard—"

"I said *out!*" Demolo shouted. "Out with you! No more orders, no more of your filthy coin and your smug face in my shop. How dare you... how dare you engage in.... *Out! Out* of my rooms, *out* of my shop, *out* of this neighborhood or I'll be rid of you with Prussic acid! You pestilence! *Out!*" He punctuated each word by shoving Thio down the stairs and toward the door, and Thio was too surprised by Demolo's sudden energy and fury to resist. He couldn't understand it; what was so special about the rooms above the shop that Demolo would explode over Thio being in one of them?

Demolo tore Thio's vest in the furious motion of throwing him out the door and capped his astounding performance by screeching "You'll never see him again!" and slamming the door.

Thio stood in the street, in the cold rain, stunned and angry. So whatever this was, it had something to do with Seamus. And he suspected he knew what it was. *The old fool. He* would *think that.*

Not five seconds had passed before Thio was scheming up ways to see Seamus again. He never liked following orders, much less orders delivered so rudely. But there was more to it. He hadn't realized just how dear Seamus had become to him until this moment: the moment when it was threatened that they might never see each other again.

Thio didn't intend to let this go without a fight.

SEAMUS huddled in bed that night, trying desperately not to weep like a child. He felt a dull, heavy feeling in his chest, and his throat was tight, and everything in the world was gray and miserable and wrong.

It seemed in one fell swoop he'd lost his entire world. First, the swiftsilver, gone forever; he couldn't even think of that without closing his eyes and trying to imagine it away. Then there was Thio, driven out, never to return. Seamus found he couldn't think of that either. It hurt too badly to contemplate. Thio, who laughed and joked and shone like the sun. It would be like eternal night now.

But that wasn't all. Demolo seemed to have gone mad somehow. Instead of haranguing Seamus or having him re-sort all the herbs or clean the grates with a scrubbing brush, instead of beatings or howlings, Demolo had simply given Seamus a look of utter disgust and gone to bed without another word. Something in his eyes said that Seamus had done something so wrong he wasn't even worth correcting. Seamus had failed in some way, so deeply, so profoundly, that no whipping could cleanse it.

Seamus realized he hated Demolo, *hated* him. And yet Demolo was the only parent he'd ever had, and the only companion he might reasonably ever have from this moment forward, and the thought of losing even the dregs of Demolo's regard made Seamus feel cold and dead inside.

All of it was like being dead.

He woke to the dawn's light and rose to prepare the morning meal. He found Demolo had risen before him and prepared his own food, and seeing this was a new hurt where Seamus thought no more hurt was possible. Demolo refused to speak to or acknowledge Seamus throughout the day, and Seamus was minutely grateful that he knew his duties too well to require instruction, but with the passing hours, more of his innards seemed to wither and die. By the end of the day, he was shuffling about like a man asleep.

He went to his bed, feeling more alone than he ever had in his life, and saw again the empty stone box where his one treasure had been. Seamus fell into bed and tried his hardest to be dead.

Half through the sleepless night, he heard a faint rapping on his window.

Seamus startled up from his cot, staring. He couldn't see anything through the thick glass and the muck it was covered in, and the window wasn't made to open. Cautiously, he tapped back.

The rapping was repeated, surer of itself this time. Seamus thought, *Thio.*

More quietly than he had ever done anything in his life, Seamus crept from his room and passed by Demolo, who was fortunately snoring loudly enough to wake the entire street. Seamus snuck downstairs and went to the back door of the shop, thinking perhaps Thio had broken into the back garden and climbed up to Seamus's window.

But when he emerged, he didn't see Thio clinging to the wall outside the window. What he saw was a massive, rounded, stretched canvas, lightly pressing against the house. It took him a moment to make out the basket beneath it, and the flame; and then he realized Thio had somehow got hold of an air-balloon boat.

"Halloo!" he cried softly.

"And hello to you too!"

A rope landed at Seamus's feet. He had never climbed a rope in his life, but he saw there was a loop tied at the end, so he gamely put his foot into it and stood in preparation to be heaved up. He didn't doubt Thio could lift him; Seamus was thin as a reed and Thio had already proven to be surprisingly strong despite his wiry limbs. It was still a shock when he rose from the ground, carried up to the basket in short, efficient tugs. Seamus reached out and felt the warmth of Thio's hand around his own. It sent a thrill through his entire body.

Thio helped Seamus into the basket and embraced him bodily, and Seamus was shocked again. He realized he could breathe, and his heart could beat, and somehow, against the odds, he felt alive again. Seamus laughed.

"Hush now, or you'll wake the old geezer before we can make good our escape." Thio grinned and stepped back to turn up the heat lamp. It flared, and in moments the two were rising above the roofs of the city.

Seamus felt as though his heart would burst; he had gone from utter despair to utter joy in the space of minutes, and with each tick of the clock he felt freer. He laughed again, gazing out at the city from the air. It had never seemed more beautiful. The lights of the windows spangled the darkness like gleaming jewels on black velvet, and in the distance he could see the silhouette of the graceful lines of the roofs, backlit by a tinge of violet in the faraway sky. "Thio, this is magnificent!"

Thio threw out his arms, which nearly tipped the basket. "Now do you understand why I must fly?"

"Absolutely!" Seamus cautiously put his arms out too, as though he were flying. "It's the pinnacle of existence, isn't it?"

"Great minds think alike, Seamus."

IT TOOK Seamus mere minutes in the sky to become his more usual dour, careful self again. He turned to Thio and said, "Thio, I'll have to be back before dawn. If Demolo catches me out...."

Thio was thunderstruck. "Back? Why go back at all?"

Seamus's dark eyes went wide, as though the idea had never occurred to him. "But where would I go?"

"Come and work for me, as I said before!"

Seamus chuckled bitterly. "You are joking, as you were before."

Thio indignantly drew himself up, nearly tipping the basket. "I am as far from joking as the sun is from the moon. You want out of your place. I want you with me. I see no issue here that a simple relocation wouldn't neatly solve."

"Thio," Seamus said in a pleading tone, "you can't be serious. What work could you possibly have for me that I can't do in the shop? I belong there. You see that, surely. And... and...." He paused, struggling for words. "Demolo... needs...." He stopped in distress.

Thio put a hand on Seamus's shoulder and frowned. "Demolo needs someone to heap abuse upon, and do you know something? He can easily find someone else. I need you to create alchemical compounds and to heal my fractured bones when I crash. That means you and you alone. And anyway... Seamus, why care what Demolo needs or wants? Hasn't he gotten enough from you?"

Seamus looked at his hands. "Perhaps you are right. Demolo hates me now, anyway. He acted all day as though I didn't exist."

Thio felt a fresh wave of anger. He had come to realize how sensitive Seamus was, and to know Demolo had found a new way to hurt him made Thio's blood burn. "He's an old fool and a cruel one. Seamus, I... I would forbid you to go back if I could. You're your own man, of course, so I can't." He shook his head. "That you should care what Demolo thinks, or needs, or feels. Faugh!"

"I was mostly confused," Seamus said softly. "What had I done? I don't believe he saw the swiftsilver. He was so angry...."

Thio nodded. "Ah. Well, as to that... he seemed to think you and I were... er...."

"Were what?" Seamus asked with perfect innocence.

Thio coughed, feeling himself redden. "He seemed to think we were corrupting each other, unless I miss my guess." He smiled and shrugged. "As I said, a fool."

"He seemed to think we were... what?" Seamus was still just as confused.

"Seamus. Surely you've...." Thio stopped and realized that, no, Seamus hadn't. Ever. "Don't you know anything about...." But that was a dead end too, he realized. Seamus didn't know a thing about it. Not one thing.

Seamus appeared baffled into bewilderment, and his eyes were growing frustrated. "No, I don't, or wouldn't, or haven't, or... what have you. What? *What?*"

"Surely you've heard talk or... or tales...."

Seamus stopped, appearing to make the connection. He shook his head, his face blank. "But we're two men."

"Yes," Thio said, quietly. "To some, that doesn't matter."

Seamus kept staring at Thio. Finally, he whispered, "Help me to understand."

And Thio, face-to-face with such utter innocence, did the only thing he could think of.

He kissed Seamus. He took him gently by the shoulders, leaned in, and gently but thoroughly kissed his lips.

They parted in silence.

Seamus whispered, "I've never known of such things." His eyes were large and full of something Thio couldn't quite interpret and couldn't ignore.

Thio cleared his throat and said, "Well... I've known little enough myself. But I at least know what they *are*. Enough to know that... Demolo thought that we were doing that. And other things. In your room." Thio's face felt hot, and his lips were tingling. It was a terribly exciting feeling.

Seamus took a half step toward Thio and said, "Would that...?"

"Would that?"

"Would that have been so very terrible?"

Thio found himself short of breath. "Yes...," he whispered, moving forward. "One of the most terrible things on this earth." They kissed again, and this time it was as though they knew each other this way, as though their bodies recognized what was going on.

"I don't believe you," said Seamus softly. "I think this must be one of the most wonderful things on this earth."

Thio felt a familiar stiffening in his trousers, and he reached down to adjust the almost painful swelling; his hand brushed the front of Seamus's trousers as it reached its destination, and Seamus gasped in shock. Thio said, huskily, "I believe that you're a wiser man than I am. I have believed that since I met you. But... please believe me that... I wouldn't...."

"You wouldn't?" The tone was verging near hurt.

"I wouldn't... I would... I.... Damn and blast it all!" Thio swept his arm around Seamus and drew him tight, kissing him fiercely. He reached down and rubbed his palm roughly against the swollen outline of Seamus's member, feeling Seamus cry out against his mouth. Thio pulled away slightly so he could watch Seamus's face as Thio's hand unbuttoned him, slid down beneath the fabric, found Seamus and gripped him firmly....

Seamus threw his head back and his mouth opened soundlessly as his body responded. He panted, struggling to breath, his legs thrusting up against Thio's as Thio continued to handle him; he clung to Thio's shoulders, the basket swaying beneath them as his gasps turned slowly into grunts that shuddered into moans.

All too soon, he spasmed several times in Thio's grip and released his ecstasy, as they drifted high above the roofs of the city, alone, and wild, and free.

"WHAT? I did tell you my father was important."

"You didn't tell me he was Baron Tenet of Lessings!"

"I didn't think I had to! How many Tenets could there possibly be in this town?" Thio grinned. "Anyway, it's only a title. I think we've been to Lessings all of... twice."

"*Only* a title." Seamus shook his head ruefully. "Bestowed by a mere king, I suppose? Who was just the tiniest bit royal?"

"Only slightly royal indeed. The ministers have all the power these days anyway."

Seamus rolled his eyes.

Thio spread his hands. "What?"

"Your life is astounding. Do you know that?"

"It is now." Thio put a hand on Seamus's shoulder and smiled warmly at him. "We're going to be doing stupendous things together, my friend."

Seamus had to stop himself from physically leaning in to Thio's body, and then realized he didn't have to stop himself after all; he leaned in, pressing himself to Thio's warmth, feeling the energy almost palpable, thrumming through his skin. They stood together like that for a moment. Seamus said softly, "Stupendous things like the thing we did in the balloon last night?"

"Stupendous would be to fly to the moon. What happened last night would be better characterized as sublime," Thio said authoritatively.

That isn't an answer, Seamus thought, but it made him feel good nonetheless.

They had coasted into the courtyard of Thio's father's estate in the wee hours of the morning, the balloon a ghostly second moon descending from the sky to land in the garden, gently crushing a small patch of columbine flowers. Thio had extinguished the lamp, leaped out, and beckoned Seamus to do the same. They'd had to quickly drag the basket out into the path to keep the canvas from deflating in the wrong direction and smothering the laurels as well.

Seamus had been nervous about entering the house, but Thio had simply walked in (the outer gate of the courtyard was apparently locked, but the door of the manse was not) and led Seamus up the stairs and into a chamber that seemed to have been specially prepared to receive him. Seamus had walked into the room in a kind of shock. There was a curtained bed, a table, chairs, a thick furry rug, and a fireplace, all illuminated by a gently glowing gas lamp. He had never experienced this kind of opulence and didn't quite know what to do with himself, but when he had turned to Thio for some kind of help or guidance, his friend had disappeared. Seamus's first night in the manse had been a fitful one.

But he had woken to Thio's voice calling him, and that had made up for it. The breakfast—sausages, eggs, mince pies, fresh bread with honey and jam, and tea with fresh cream—had also made up for it. And now he was exploring the library, Thio at his side. Seamus wondered if he was still asleep after all and dreaming.

The rooms of the house were enough to intimidate and overwhelm him, but finally they descended to an underground level and entered a room where he immediately felt at home.

Thio gestured grandly around and declared, "Welcome to my laboratory!"

Seamus gaped at the sight. The room was massive, stone walled and floored, filled with half-built machines, tools of all sorts, tables covered in the detritus of experimentation, and shelves and shelves and endless shelves filled with....

"You've been *storing* all of it?"

Thio threw back his head and laughed. "My plans have come to fruition! Welcome to, well, I should say now, *your* laboratory."

The shelves were filled with chemicals, powders, glasses and vials, tubes and stoneware and metalware, samples of elements and jars of preserved organic tissues. It was nothing less than the full catalog of items Thio had been purchasing from Demolo for months.

Seamus felt almost a panic. He looked at Thio, trying to understand.

Thio put a hand on Seamus's shoulder, smiling gently. "Yes, it's all yours. Seamus, I want you to come in here and do wonders."

Seamus shook his head. "Thio... I'm not sure I'm capable of wonders."

"I don't believe that for a moment, but if you never achieve wonders, then I want you to come in here and do forgettable nonsense. And Seamus, I want you to create swiftsilver again."

"I need to sit down."

Thio helped Seamus to a chair and table nearby, and Seamus carefully cleared away the bottles and vials, sat down heavily, and put his head into his arms on the table. He tried to breathe.

It was like a dream, but even his sleeping mind had never dared to dream anything this marvelous, this grand. And he thought, *How like Thio. He's either lost in the heavens or plummeting toward his doom.* Seamus wasn't sure which this was, this grand gesture of... of.... Seamus groaned aloud, unable to think of anything to compare it to.

"My dear friend, what on earth could be troubling you?"

"I'm unaccustomed to the miraculous."

Thio paused. "You'd best get accustomed to it quickly."

"I'm realizing this."

IT TOOK some moments for Seamus to compose himself to the point where he could examine the riches on the shelves around him, and Thio waited, watching to see whether his friend would recover. Thio hadn't expected Seamus to wilt so dramatically. He couldn't seem to anticipate Seamus's reactions to things, which was a problem, because Thio in general was a force in the world to be reacted to.

Seamus grew sober as he examined the materials around the room, and suddenly he gave Thio a sharp look that was reminiscent of Demolo in a bad mood. "Thio, I am sorry to see that these are hopelessly misplaced and in no kind of recognizable nor useful order. Did you simply randomly place everything as you bought it?"

Thio tried to look contrite. "Oh dear. I did try to keep track of what I had and what I hadn't, but no, it would take a true alchemist to sort through all of this."

Seamus sniffed. "Well, you'll have to settle for me." And he began to look around, busily.

"What are you looking for?"

"A pencil, if you please."

Thio located a metal pen and a scrap of paper, and Seamus began to rapidly make notes as he walked around the room, inventorying all the tools of his trade. Thio suppressed a laugh of pure delight as he watched Seamus exchange his dismay for busied irritation, an irritation Thio knew was half made up of pleasure. He sensed Seamus would always be happiest when there was a problem to be solved. That made the two of them a sensible pair, as Thio spent half his life causing problems in need of solutions.

"Shall I leave you to it, then?"

Seamus didn't answer. He was too busy muttering, "Acids next to alkali… good heavens…. The sodium needs to be packed in oil…. Is he trying to explode the entire house? Saints preserve us…."

He spent the rest of the day wrestling the laboratory into some semblance of a pleasingly ordered state, excepting one short break during which he permitted Thio to drag him to dinner, even though Seamus wasn't particularly hungry. He had even less of an appetite when Thio cheerfully informed him that Thio's father would be at dinner. Seamus's eyes grew wide, as though he was in the presence of a great calamity, and he stopped in his tracks. "The Baron of Lessings is... is... at *dinner*?"

Thio paused, puzzled. "The Baron of Lessings has been known to eat dinner regularly. Almost every night, in fact."

"And I'm supposed to... eat with him?" Seamus's voice rose to nearly a squeak on the last word.

"Well, I confess it's a little irregular, but since I've made it clear to him that you are to be treated as a friend and *not* a servant—"

"I'm not a servant? But you hired me!"

"Well, yes, in *name*.... Will you please stop stopping? You're about to yank my wrist out of its socket. Seamus, I didn't bring you here to be an underling and I don't consider you one."

Seamus kept walking but looked completely baffled and alarmed, a look that remained upon his face for most of the dinner, to Thio's disgust.

Thio's father, of course, barely noticed. "And here's the young man my son has brought into our house from off the street." It was close enough to something Demolo might have said that Thio winced internally, but Lord Tenet's eyes were kind as he said it, if officious. Then again, they were always officious. "I must thank you. I've seen a few of his designs since he began to perform his experiments under your guidance, and one might almost call them practical. I even espied a bit of prudence, here and there. All your doing, I expect. You appear to dampen his insanity oscillator."

Thio brightened, surprised. He hadn't realized his father had been paying so much attention to the changes. In fact, he hadn't realized his father paid attention to his work at all.

Seamus merely stared for a moment and then mumbled, "Thank you, Lord Tenet."

Thio's father left the topic alone for the rest of dinner, merely discussing a few matters of state with his son. He wasn't a great talker at the best of times. Thio spent most of the dinner regaling Seamus and his father with tales of the wondrous things he intended to accomplish. He suspected both members of his audience had similar dubious opinions of his schemes, and the notion pleased him for some strange reason.

They returned to the laboratory, and a few hours later, Thio had to drag Seamus away from it again in order to prepare for bed.

THIO escorted Seamus to his room again and appeared to be about to leave when Seamus caught his sleeve and held it. "Thio."

Thio stopped. "Whatever is it, my friend?"

Seamus dropped his head slightly, his cheeks burning. He tightened his grip, unable to determine what he should say.

Thio took a step closer. He said sympathetically, "Seamus, you'll grow accustomed to this place in time. It's merely a house. Perhaps a bit large, a bit grand, but merely a house, where a father and son live. Maybe you don't realize it, but it's been a house filled with a great deal of aloneness."

"Are you alone?" Seamus smiled a little. "I thought that I was."

"You, my friend, are in the best of company. As am I. And we need our rest if we are to prepare for stupendous events on the morrow."

"But...."

"But?"

Seamus, cautious as he had always been, felt if he didn't somehow take a chance, he would suffer for it the rest of his life. He kept his gaze fixed on Thio's sleeve, unsure what might happen if he met his eyes, and said the one word on which his entire world hinged: "Stay."

Thio was quiet, but he didn't go.

Seamus felt it wasn't enough somehow; he hadn't yet found the word that would work the magic he wanted. "Stay with me. You have been alone. I have been alone. Haven't we endured enough of that?" He finally looked up into Thio's eyes.

Thio looked more serious than Seamus had ever seen him. "Seamus... this seems dangerous in a way that even our experiments are not."

Seamus moved closer to Thio, their breath mingling. The air felt warm between them. "Thio, I would fly, even at the risk of crashing. My only fear is that you don't want to... with me."

Thio's eyes, always slightly crazed and filled with energy, were strangely soft. "Then you have nothing to fear." And he kissed Seamus.

It was like their first kiss, the same power pulsating between their mouths and filling their bodies; Seamus felt his heart pound and his mind cloud over. His hands twitched, wanting to—he did not know what they wanted to do, but they wanted to touch, and to hold, and…. He realized he wanted to do to Thio what Thio had done to him. He hesitantly let his hand slide down between their bodies and….

Thio gasped and groaned, low and deep in his throat, and pressed closer.

"I know that I want something, but I don't know what it is I want." Seamus let his lips brush over Thio's, aimlessly, hungrily. "Tell me, Thio, what do I want?"

"Let's go into the bedchamber."

They met on the bed, hastily undressing, and Seamus let his gaze linger over Thio's body as it was revealed. He had always heard the poetry of women, how beautiful their bodies were; women were a mystery to him, but couldn't men's bodies be beautiful too, he reasoned? Thio was tall and slender, his muscles elongated and graceful, his skin golden, his hair golden, his eyes nearly amber in the light. He looked as effortlessly supple as a leopard.

Seamus hoped his own body wasn't too embarrassing. He leaned forward hesitantly, reaching out, and he stopped, waiting for Thio to object. Thio didn't. He tilted his hips up invitingly. Seamus said, "What do you call this?"

"You don't even know—ah, sorry. I shouldn't be surprised that Demolo taught you nothing aside from alchemy."

"Well, I mean, I know it's a… a penis," Seamus stammered. "And I've heard boys talking in the street, calling it all manner of ridiculous nonsense. Prick, poker, willy, whoreshank…."

Thio laughed uproariously. "That's a good one. In most casual parlance, the word 'cock' will do." He sobered. "You know that I'm nearly as ignorant as you. Talk among boys, nothing more."

Seamus reached out and gently stroked Thio's cock, receiving a satisfyingly excited noise in return. He said firmly, "We shall have to experiment."

They explored each other, hesitantly at first, then eagerly. Their exploration spanned weeks. They experimented with their bodies in the night just as much as they experimented with chemicals and substances in the laboratory during the day, and it was hard to say which set of experiments was more fruitful, but Seamus certainly found the nightly games more surprising.

At first it seemed most reasonable to use their hands on each other. The first night, that was what they did—stroking and rubbing each other to completion after completion, shuddering it out into each other's hands. Seamus was shocked again and again to realize how different it felt to have another man stroking him. Sweating and struggling against each other, they finally exhausted themselves and fell asleep together, loosely entangled.

The next day, Seamus's tender privates felt raw. He went to the lab with a certain determination and emerged that evening with a small vial, which he brought to the bedchamber and flourished before Thio. "Behold."

"Behold what, my genius companion?"

Seamus tipped a little of the slippery substance out into his palm. "Inert, harmless, and all but frictionless." He rubbed it around in his palm and then took hold of Thio's cock, letting his hand easily slide over and around it. "See?"

Thio's head tipped back as he moaned. "I see…. God, what a… what a sensation…."

Seamus rubbed a little on his own cock and was satisfied with the feeling. It felt almost like his hand was a… tongue?

The observation was distracting and compelling.

The following night, he decided to follow up that thought. He was nervous when he asked Thio about it, but Thio merely blushed and nodded. Seamus licked his lips nervously and felt his own cock swell at the notion of what he was about to do, or to try to do…. Then he leaned down and poised himself above Thio's cock and took a deep breath. He gently lapped at it, a small swipe of his tongue.

Thio gave a sigh that sounded almost like despair, but Seamus knew the emotion had to be something else. Seamus looked up at him. Thio's face was red, his eyes vivid. Seamus tried another lick. The skin tasted musky and somehow good, earthy and familiar. Thio groaned and took handfuls of the bedclothes, bunching them in his fists. Seamus decided he wanted to know what Thio's essence tasted like, and he applied himself wholly to that end. He took Thio fully into his mouth and sucked, gently at first, and when Thio nodded and gasped that it was good, more firmly. Thio tried to reach for Seamus's cock and stroke it as Seamus worked, but the sensation was too intense and distracting; he kept moaning, his hand going limp. Seamus found himself rather delighted that he had destroyed Thio's concentration, even if Seamus's poor neglected member was so hard it ached and throbbed for want of touch. He told it to wait and applied himself again, openmouthed and licking, to Thio's pleasure.

He noted the effects scientifically. Thio's face reddened; his jaw clenched. Soon, the veins on his neck began to stand out. He aimlessly gripped and released the bedcover with his broad hands, his arms moving frantically as though searching for some kind of relief. Seamus almost felt he was tormenting Thio with his mouth, rather than pleasuring him.... The idea sent a thrill down his spine, and he shivered. *Pleasure,* he thought firmly, and sucked long and hard. Thio groaned, nearly lifting his entire torso from the bed; Seamus rolled his tongue around the head of Thio's cock, slid along the ridge, and then gently tasted the slit from which small salty droplets were slowly issuing. He wondered if the eventual climax would taste salty like this.

But when it came—Thio gasping and helpless and undone, his cock iron hard in Seamus eager mouth, his breath heavy and his moans loud and abandoned—the soft spurting against Seamus's tongue tasted hot, and bitter, and mild. It was a very potent flavor, and Seamus realized that he was so excited, that, that... without even a touch, his own member began to pulse and flow, triggered by nothing more than the taste of Thio's ecstasy, by nothing more than the sight of his friend in so much pleasure that it was an anguish. Seamus swallowed it all, choking slightly as it coated the back of his throat. He sucked again, but Thio shook his head violently and made noises of discomfort, so Seamus left off and parted from Thio's cock with a gentle kiss on the head of it. He collapsed upon the bed.

Thio rolled over and began to fiercely kiss Seamus, his mouth like fire over Seamus's lips and throat and shoulders, and before he knew it, Seamus felt his still-hard member embraced by Thio's mouth, which was soft and hard and plunging and sliding and.... Seamus gave himself to the sensations, writhing on the bed and crying out. It took longer for him to climax, as he'd already done so once, even if without a touch, but Thio persisted until Seamus was sure no man's mouth could possibly be so determined. Seamus finally clutched his own hair in his hands as his cock wrung itself dry against Thio's seeking tongue. When it was done, he felt as though his entire sweaty, heaving body had been burned in fire and laved in syrup, lusciously floating down from the clouds.

Thio slumped to the bed beside Seamus and said hoarsely, "We must try that again, and soon."

They continued using their mouths over the following few nights, but it was Thio who suggested they position themselves so they could both suck each other at once. By the time that experience had reached its peak, Seamus felt it was possible to go mad from nothing more than pleasure. The taste of Thio and the sound of Thio's groans combined with the feel of Thio's mouth in such a way as to amplify everything tenfold. Afterward, Thio agreed with Seamus's assessment with nothing more eloquent than a series of happy, bewildered noises, and they slept heavily.

THIO watched Seamus during the days in the laboratory. He felt he would never grow tired of watching him.

The fierce, dark eyes, more alert than those of a hunting animal, matched his dark, shining hair, which was always pulled severely back lest it interfere with some vital titration or measurement. Seamus's quick, careful, slender hands and fingers were never still, always moving, but not nervously; his gestures were always precise and to the point. The utility of his motion was fascinating to Thio. Thio was powered by an often clumsy exuberance; Seamus could be still as a stone or quick as a bird. His frame was smaller than Thio's, but every part of him seemed to have been carefully crafted, as though he himself had been a part of that making.

In bed, Seamus had proven to be devilishly clever and quick to learn and try new things, wringing pleasure from Thio's body until Thio felt he was nearly dead of it. Seamus's eyes often had a wicked glint in them during those times. That glint was almost as stimulating as the work of his mouth. It was a glint that said *I know your body and the workings of it, and I will make it my own.* Thio sensed a possessiveness in Seamus.

He suspected he shared it.

They *wanted* each other in a way that seemed insatiable, a way Thio had never before experienced with another person. Standing beside

Seamus, sitting with him at meals, talking to him, and even wrapped in each other's arms and trembling with the exertions of sexual intercourse, somehow there was never an end to that sweet, aching want.

Seamus looked up from his crucible and met Thio's eyes, and Thio saw that glint again, the small quirk of Seamus's smile that said he knew things about Thio that perhaps God Himself could never have guessed. Thio had to look away, feeling his face flush. Even now, they wanted each other.

But there was work to be done.

SEAMUS was nineteen and the lover of the son of the Baron of Lessings when he made swiftsilver for the second time. This time the process was notated, and he was able to repeat it. But he knew there was a limit to how much he could make, as the materials were rare and the process time-consuming. Thio had not returned to Demolo's shop to acquire more alchemical substances, so there was a limit to what Seamus could accomplish.

The first time he succeeded, after several weeks of work, he held the precious substance in his hands and felt tears rise in his eyes. Somehow, from that one black night, his life had reformed itself into something as miraculous as the mirrored liquid that rippled in the beaker in front of him.

The question was, what was to be *done* with the soft, shimmering fluid?

Thio seemed to have the answer: it was to be dropped and spilled as much as possible. He couldn't seem to resist touching and holding it, and disaster always seemed to result. Seamus had the forethought to only make tiny amounts of it at a time, but even he lost patience with Thio and shouted and cursed at him any number of times. He was always penitent and quiet afterward, to which Thio would merely laugh. "Friend, your anger was justified, my bumbling is inexcusable, and we have work to do."

That was Thio's answer to everything: *We have work to do!* It was his mantra, his call to arms, his motto. Whenever Seamus was troubled or discouraged, Thio would bring out his pet phrase, and somehow, it worked: Seamus's spirits would be lifted, and they would throw themselves into their projects with new fervor.

It didn't stop Thio from spilling the swiftsilver every chance he got. But one day, there was an unexpected result to his clumsiness.

Thio arrived in the laboratory one morning in his Experiment Suit, a somewhat shabby tunic and trousers topped with a leather vest. The clothes looked as though they had been through some sort of a horrific war, or perhaps merely an acid bath. The latter was closer to the truth. Thio had subjected these clothes (as well as a pair of sturdy and equally shabby boots) to wear, tear, melting heat, burning cold, acids, bases, torches, nails, screws, and small animals. He had spilled swiftsilver on himself too many times to count. The fluid pearled up and slid right off fabric, as it did every other surface.

That day, Seamus was burning scraps of magnesium with a blowtorch. He was doing so for a very definite experimental purpose, and not at all because it was fun to create such a searingly bright light. Each scrap of the metal flared up, blindingly, and Thio hastily donned a pair of cobalt glasses to shield his eyes. "What are you making?"

"Pretty lights," Seamus admitted. He pointed at the vial in front of Thio. "Be careful, that's—"

Thio promptly knocked it over, spilling it all over his sleeve. He winced. "The devil...."

"I'm amazed at the fact that you only ever do that with swiftsilver. Amazed and relieved, actually; I wouldn't want to see the result of you spilling hydrogen cyanide on yourself."

Thio laughed, sounding a little weary. "Again, I am sorry, my friend. I fear that the light dazzled me."

Seamus fired up the last of the scraps and watched it burn. "I'm considering making a limelight. It would burn even brighter than this."

"Seamus."

Seamus looked at Thio, who was staring down at his sleeve, which had a thin, hard, silvery patch on it. "What is that?"

"Unless I'm mistaken or insane, neither of which ought to be ruled out, that's the swiftsilver. Did you change the formula?"

"Absolutely not. I have it memorized by now. What did you do after it spilled? Was anything else on your sleeve?"

"Nothing at all." Thio was poking at the patch of silver, puzzled. "I got it fresh off the line just now; Hazel finally managed to get it from me long enough to wash it…. I say, Seamus, this is hard as steel. I can't even bend it. Feel."

Seamus hesitantly touched the small film of silver. It felt solid and unyielding, as Thio had said, and faintly warm.

Their eyes met.

Thio smiled. "I believe we have a mystery on our hands."

"On your sleeve," Seamus pointed out.

Thio cleared his throat. "I believe mysteries are best confronted after a full night of sleep."

"Then we'll never get it worked out," Seamus said drily. "We haven't slept a full night since the first night I've been here."

Thio laughed hugely and then dragged Seamus off to bed.

SEVERAL nights later, Thio woke to the sight of Seamus's body limned in moonlight, his skin colored ice-blue by the paintbrush of night. Seamus was awake, his dark hair tousled, his dark eyes intent upon nothing at all.

Thio hesitated to break the perfection of the scene. Seamus seemed poised at the brink of doing something startling, or else frozen forever in marble.

Seamus blinked, and his gaze flickered to Thio. The severe expression on his face softened. "Did I wake you?"

"I believe I could hear you thinking in my sleep." Thio smiled. "It's the swiftsilver, isn't it?"

Seamus rubbed his face with his hands. "It's driving me to distraction, the way we can't seem to replicate the process."

"Honestly? Me too." Thio picked at the edge of the sheet. "There's nothing for it but to keep trying."

"Of course." Seamus half smiled. "Thio, I love your… unsinkableness."

Thio chuckled. "Perhaps we should refer to it as my optimism. I've tested my buoyancy various times and I assure you, I sink like a stone in water."

"You cannot swim?" Seamus frowned. "Did I know that already?"

"I think not." Thio let his hand drift over, settling it on Seamus's warm hip bone. He let it sit there gently and then began to trace the blades of shadow against the skin.

Seamus made a purring sound. His cock moved, swelling slightly. "This is almost like swimming. Breathless... alarming... energetic."

Thio moved, pressing their bodies together, and took a deep breath. "Take me for a swim, then."

They kissed, trying to breathe each other more than the air.

Seamus whispered, "There's a notion that I have...."

"Tell me."

Seamus squirmed a little, shyly. "I think you may know. I suspect you too have wondered about it."

"Ah." Thio felt his face redden. "Well. If you're saying what I believe you are, then... I only know.... Well. Jokes about it, maybe half a story or two."

Seamus grimaced. "Let's out with it, then. Buggery!"

Thio stifled a laugh against the pillow. "Ah, yes. Buggery. Were you thinking... to be... or...."

"To be buggered, yes." Seamus began giggling, and that set Thio off, until the two of them were clinging to each other and gasping with laughter. It took some time to calm themselves. Their faces flushed, they looked at each other uneasily.

Thio said, "What if it hurts you?"

Seamus shrugged. "I've been hurt before."

"Seamus, I won't be responsible for injuring you," Thio said sternly.

Seamus smiled. "You won't. I just want us to try."

Thio leaned in and kissed Seamus deeply, their bodies sliding against each other and into a configuration that felt strangely perfect, their cocks nestled against each other, legs tangled, arms linked, mouths locked. It *did* feel like swimming. Thio brushed his lips against Seamus's forehead. "What... do you want me to do? First, I mean. How do you want me to start?"

"Hmm."

They repositioned themselves, face-to-face, Seamus gently whispering suggestions as Thio fumblingly nestled his hips where he thought they ought to go. After some awkward moments, they both realized nothing was going to go anywhere without some lubrication.

They still had plenty of the fluid Seamus had created so many weeks before.

"Okay, I'm going to attempt to relax as you—ohhh. Oh, Thio." Seamus gasped as he was filled.

Thio felt himself slide completely in, and his breath stuttered. "Seamus. That's… it's… you feel like…. Blast it. Words are rubbish."

Seamus nodded, still gasping for breath.

Thio put his hand on Seamus's cheek. "Tell me that you are unharmed."

"Thio." Seamus couldn't seem to catch his breath. "I am… not hurt, exactly."

"Then what, exactly, my friend?"

Seamus pulled Thio to him, kissing him frantically, endeavoring to communicate with his lips what he could not with his words. "Thio," he gasped. "Can you feel it?"

Thio was puzzled but let himself be kissed, and soon he groaned. "I must… move…."

"Then move."

Thio's hips pushed the tiniest bit. Seamus shuddered and moaned.

"Are you hurt?"

"I'm undone."

Thio paused and felt himself shaken with a sudden need to see just how undone Seamus could possibly become. He pressed his nose into Seamus's hair and took a deep whiff of their scent—sex, skin, and something musky and dark and dangerous. Something that was always there with them, somehow. A risk of the unknown.

Seamus whispered, barely more than a breath, "Please…."

Thio groaned at the need in that single word. He let himself slide out of Seamus's body a little and then thrust himself back in, both of them grunting and sighing as the motion began and then completed. He did it again, noting the sounds Seamus couldn't seem to help making, and feeling they were not sounds of pain. Thio began a slow rhythm, something primitive in his hips taking over the act.

Seamus, for his part, shook and reacted and tried not to writhe on the bed, but soon he lost all control and clutched at Thio and moaned as though he were dying, calling for more and faster.

Thio wasn't ready for this new version of Seamus; it was a shock, like attempting to tame a wild animal. He did his best to hold Seamus down, trying not to hurt either of them, though Seamus struggled and fought against the very thing he seemed to want. Thio thrust into him steadily, groaning with the pleasure of it and the aching need that gripped him, the need for the man below him, the need to have him and keep him and plunge so deeply inside him that no other would ever know such a feeling.

Completion came all too soon, and Thio almost hated it, feeling the shuddering rise in his body, knowing it would mean the end. But he gripped Seamus firmly and finished it, fast and hard, shattering himself.

Thio fell against Seamus and panted for breath, feeling the sudden quiet in the room. He kept his eyes closed, afraid to open them, afraid to move.

"Thio." Seamus said it with such warmth and care that it was like a pair of encircling arms, like a lover's kiss.

"Seamus," Thio replied, his voice hoarse and bewildered.

"Thio, you belong to me now."

Thio gasped and realized it was true. The act, which had felt so much like a taking, so much like himself seizing the body of another and using it... that act had really been a giving of himself. And Seamus was right. Some part of Thio was no longer his own anymore. He murmured, "Only if you are mine." He knew he couldn't bargain, but still he wanted that much as a concession. Surely....

"I have been yours since the day you wrecked in the street in front of my shop." And Seamus laughed.

Thio lifted himself enough to look into Seamus's eyes, finding something there that confused him still more. He shook his head. "What has happened?"

"Don't you know?"

"How would I know?"

"How do I? But I do. Thio, this is what the songs are about, the songs and the poems and the novels. We are in love. That's what this is."

Thio paused. "I really ought to have taken those poems more seriously."

"The most dangerous force on earth, disguised as a silly little feeling in a song." Seamus stretched luxuriously. "How ironic."

Thio brushed Seamus's face with his fingertips. He could feel, pressed against his belly, that Seamus was still hard. "You didn't finish. I did, and I felt… something…."

"I didn't finish the usual way, but Thio, I am satisfied."

"I suppose we'll need to clean ourselves a bit…."

Seamus nodded. "First things first, however."

"And that is?"

"Tell me."

Thio looked into Seamus's dark, fierce eyes and felt himself quail a little. "Tell you?"

"Thio, I love you. Do you love me?"

Thio tried to catch his breath. He gave up and simply gasped out, "Seamus, I do. I love you, if this is… if I understand…. Oh, I don't even know. I just love you."

Seamus laughed. "That will do."

Thio collapsed against Seamus, feeling as though he'd just climbed a mountain.

THE next morning, Seamus opened his eyes with a feeling of excitement so profound it neared panic. "Thio! It was the light!"

"The wha—?" Thio said sleepily, raising his head. His hair made a lion's mane of tangle in the morning sun, and Seamus would have laughed at it but for the distraction of his sudden inspiration.

"The light! The swiftsilver wasn't reacting to the fabric. It reacted to the magnesium burning. It's light sensitive!"

Thio shook his head, still bewildered. "I believe I'm light sensitive at the moment. What are you on about?"

"Thio, come on!" Seamus leaped from the bed, dragging Thio with him. "We have work to do!"

"NOW, what is this thing again?"

"What this thing is, is an explosive thing, which is why I want your hands safely on the table where I can see them, Thio." Seamus steadied the lime cylinder in the clamp.

"Did you call it a lime? It doesn't look very much like a lime to me."

"It's made of quicklime."

The apparatus was as simple as Seamus had been able to make it. He had a sample of soft calico pinned to the table, with a scattering of swiftsilver droplets on it, puddling slightly in the middle. The casing of the limelight would direct the light onto the swiftsilver. It was perhaps more light than would be needed, but Seamus wanted to be sure of the effect. All he needed were steady hands and a blowlamp.

The fierce heat of the blowlamp was the bit he was nervous about, considering Thio was nearby.

"Glasses on."

They donned their cobalt glasses, Thio grinning crazily behind his, and Seamus lit the lamp, the flame shooting blue and evil into the air. He applied it to the lime, which slowly and then quickly incandesced. Soon it was shining a white-hot light bright enough to cast stark shadows off every object in the near area, and the casing directed all that fearsome light onto the surface of the fabric....

"Thio!" Seamus shut off the lamp. "Look!"

"Why look when I can touch?" Thio poked at the swiftsilver, which had formed flattened patches on the calico, hard as tempered steel. "You have once again set your genius against the powers that be, and your genius has won the day."

Seamus blushed, but he was too elated to feel embarrassed. He touched the shining patches. "And... and we can... we can...." He paused. "What do we do with it, now?"

"Well, it's light and strong at once. We can use it for parts of a flying machine, of course."

"Well, obviously, but what other applications might it have?"

Thio poked at it. "Why, we shall have to experiment."

They did. They made big patches and small patches, tried different sorts of fabric, tried paper, and even the table surface. Swiftsilver seemed, in response to intense light, to behave similarly on any porous surface: it flattened to the thinness of rice paper and hardened. Once hardened, it seemed to be unchangeable. In delicacy and strength, it rivaled spider's thread. Seamus had never known such a substance.

One day, Thio was playing with a small square of it (enameled to a piece of flannel), when he sat up. "Seamus, look at this."

"What is it?"

"Take this patch of swiftsilver and wave it back and forth in the air." Seamus did so, waving it haphazardly, and Thio shook his head. "Not like that; keep the flat side facing the push of the air. Like this." He held Seamus's hand and helped him move the patch from side to side, pushing it against the air as though waving a fan. Seamus could immediately tell what Thio had noticed: on the silver side of the patch, there was intense resistance to the air, but on the flannel side, there was very little. The effect was baffling. When one waves a fan, the air resistance is equal on both sides. To have it feel so dramatically different....

"What the devil kind of substance is this?"

Seamus said, "It's... a semipermeable membrane, Thio. Air passes through one side more easily than the other. Thio, that would be *perfect* for a wing. You would resist the air beneath on the downswing, but not the air above on the upswing."

They decided to make the patch into a small parachute and punched holes in the corners (a bit challenging, though the small sapphire drill finally managed the job) through which to tie string. They took turns fastening various objects to the strings and letting the parachute fall. The results were stunning. With the silver side down, facing the resistance of the air, objects would parachute down beautifully, until the too-flat surface gave up and turned sideways to the air, causing the object to plummet to the ground. Seamus knew it would work better if he enameled the swiftsilver onto a curve. But then, objects tied with the flannel side down simply fell to the ground. Even the natural resistance of the flannel itself should have slowed them, but it didn't. It was as though the swiftsilver had somehow changed the consistency of both materials, causing air to slip through it as easily as nothing.

Seamus formed a more reliable skin by placing some cloth in a bowl and enameling the swiftsilver into it. He now had a curved surface, cloth outside, swiftsilver inside, and his new parachute was foolproof.

But his head was buzzing with new ideas. Surely curved wings were only the beginning....

Thio seemed inexplicably aroused by the moments when Seamus was at his most creative, which was equal parts endearing and frustrating. In any case, Seamus was unable to finish his experiments that day.

That night, Thio gently took Seamus from behind, moving as slowly as possible, as they both knew Seamus was sore from the prior night. But this time, they lay on their sides, and Thio reached around to Seamus's front. Seamus knew what was coming and felt his breath catch as Thio's fingers gently cupped his balls, massaging them, pressing up into the small space behind them, and then finally moving forward.... Seamus closed his eyes and tried to be still as heat filled his body. Thio stroked Seamus within and stroked him without, and it was as though Seamus were flying, flying through the air, excited and free and amazed. He knew he would fall soon; his body could not keep up this height. But when he crested the climax of flight and then fell, he felt Thio's strong arms around him and knew it was safe, both to fly and to fall. Thio caught and held him, cresting and falling himself. They landed together, sweetly entangled.

Seamus sighed and heard Thio whispering soft, ridiculous, loving things into his ear. They were alone; nobody was there to see or hear. They could be soft with each other.

"THIO, catch!"

Thio quickly lifted his hands just in time to catch a large, rounded mass of something silver-colored. It was a hollow ball, by the feel and heft, and by the color, it was swiftsilvered. He turned it over in his hands. "How did you make this?"

Seamus smiled. "I draped cloth over an upended bowl and slowly drizzled the swiftsilver over it in the limelight. It took a few passes to get it right, and a few tries before I could make an entire sphere. What do you think?"

"It's glorious!" Thio laughed. "What am I supposed to think?"

"Now it's time to test my theory. Does it feel light?"

"Very."

"Throw it to me."

Thio threw it to Seamus and noticed something seemed to be off about the arc of its passage through the air. Seamus reached up to catch it.

"And now I throw it back to you." Seamus aimed and threw.

Thio reached up and had to leap upward to catch the sphere. When he had it, he immediately realized it was lighter than it had been before. "What the devil...?"

Seamus grinned. "It works! Throw it back. It'll get lighter with each pass."

They threw it back and forth, each time more carefully as it seemed to shoot higher and higher into the air, until finally... Seamus threw it to Thio, and it simply kept rising without falling again. They both stared at it as it rose to the ceiling and hung there.

Thio gaped. "What does it mean?"

"It's a semipermeable membrane, Thio! So when we pushed it through the air while throwing it to each other, air couldn't enter the ball from the outside, the shining side. But the inside, the cloth side, air can escape from. As we threw it back and forth, it lost a little of the interior air each time. Here, watch this; I made a smaller one." He picked up a fist-sized ball of swiftsilver and began to wave it back and forth.

"Toss it here." Thio reached to catch it as Seamus sent it over, and he copied Seamus's motion, waving it back and forth. It became slowly lighter in his hands. "Miraculous!"

"Keep waving it."

Thio kept moving the ball back and forth through the air, feeling it grow lighter and lighter, until finally he held it out and let it go. As the larger ball did, the small ball slowly floated to the ceiling and hung there.

Seamus walked over to Thio, both of them gazing up at the spheres in the air. He said, "And unless there's leakage in the coating, they'll stay up there... forever, I suspect."

Thio whistled. "Astounding. Seamus, do you suppose this could be used to build an even better flying vehicle?"

Seamus looked at Thio and gave a short, ironic laugh. "No."

"Whyever not?"

"Thio, look up there. The more these things move through the air, the lighter they become. I know that the chiefest object of a flying object is to go up… but it's really not much use to any human being unless it can also come down again."

"I see."

They spent a few more minutes gazing upward.

"Still," Thio said, "one wants to see them fly."

"You mean, *you* want to see them fly."

"Don't you?"

Seamus pursed his mouth and considered it. "I want to see what else they can do. That will take some work."

"Then we have work to do!"

THERE were days when Thio was pulled away from the laboratory by other obligations, days when Thio's father exerted his authority and forced his son to learn matters of the estate and politics. Thio hated those days but acknowledged his duty. Flighty and impulsive as he was, Thio always wanted to be a good son and a good man. So he learned the matters of the household and the dealings of trade and accounts, including charity toward the poor, for Lord Tenet was a compassionate soul. Lord Tenet had, in fact, been much like his own son at one point in time and still held to some of that expansive generosity in nature Thio had inherited.

Thio's father sat at one ebony desk, and Thio sat at another, and they discussed shipments and taxes, and Sir Tenet abruptly said something that woke Thio up in the extreme.

"Son, you will soon have to spend your profligate sums at another alchemist's shop, I fear. The alchemist in the village has fallen ill and cannot be expected to deal in his trade for much longer."

Thio blinked. "Demolo, you mean. I haven't dealt with him in—it's been some time since I have darkened his doorway."

"Best fetch your supplies while you can. Heaven knows when we shall have another alchemist, especially given that you've stolen his apprentice away from him." Sir Tenet smiled.

Thio said, "Seamus did half of everything at that shop, he would be a brilliant alchemist to the townsfolk."

"In order for him to be brilliant, you shall have to let him go and do it."

Thio stopped at the gentle rebuke in his father's voice. "But…."

"But you care for him. Perhaps more than you ever have for any friend before him."

Thio stared at his father.

Sir Tenet snorted. "I have eyes in my face, whelp. I've been known to observe things which happen to be right under my nose."

Thio felt himself turn very red. "Father, if I have been inappropriate in any way—"

"It would be because you are young and foolish, but with the foolishness necessary to the young. Without that foolishness, nothing new would ever be tried or invented, and I've always known that you would invent many new and wonderful things, my lad. But mind this: your friend has his own path, and it would seem a shame for that path to be limited to being your vassal."

Thio was too shocked for more words and merely turned and bent himself to his work, feeling deeply troubled.

"SEAMUS, you can't just charge off like this…."

"I have to go to him. I know you don't understand." Seamus was busily packing a few things into a satchel (borrowed, as everything he owned was borrowed now, it seemed—a state that had never troubled him until this moment). He mentally itemized what he might need to have with him while he was caring for Demolo.

"All right, I don't understand. Why do you have to go back?" Thio was angry, hurt in his voice.

"Thio." Seamus turned around. "I'm the apothecary. Who better to go than me?" He turned to his packing. "He might not die, after all, given the proper care."

"He doesn't deserve the proper care."

"Doubtless."

"You're going anyway."

"Irrevocably."

"Seamus, please."

Seamus looked up. Thio's eyes were darkened by some strong emotion, one Seamus felt he could share, if only circumstances permitted. Seamus said, "Thio, must I ask your leave to do this?"

Thio shook his head slowly. "You are not mine to command."

Seamus finally dropped the satchel and turned to his lover, his throat aching. "Ah, but I am yours to command, in a way. I'm just not yours to command in this way." He put his hands on Thio's shoulders. "Demolo was all I had of father or mother, and he is now all I have of kin. Do you think I want to go? No. But I must."

Thio looked as though he were laboring to understand. "I… know that if it were my own father, heaven nor hell could not stop me. But my father would at least welcome the help. Demolo may just kick you right out the door again with his bony, dying foot."

Seamus couldn't help but laugh. "Then I'll leave him. But not without first making the effort."

Thio sighed. "We won't get to finish our experiments."

"Yes, we will. That much, I swear. Now kiss me, for I am going, and I don't know for how long."

Thio held Seamus and kissed him with a kiss that said *I know it will be a long time.*

THE sign had a sash spread across it that read *CLOSED.*

When Seamus knocked upon the door of the old shop, shocked at how tiny and dingy it seemed to him now, he didn't know whether to expect a whirlwind of abuse or a tearful welcome, or any number of things in between. But even his expectations of *something* happening were betrayed: there was no answer.

He tried the door and found it unlocked and entered cautiously, looking around him as he did.

Shock gave way to horror. The usually neat and orderly shelves were now half-emptied, filled with what seemed detritus of former wares—broken bottles, spilled compounds, scraps and scrapings. The place was filthy, unswept, unwiped, unwashed. It nearly broke Seamus's heart to see it this way. And with a switch of perspective, he could see and feel the truth: Demolo might have taken Seamus in, but it was truly the shop itself that had raised him. The shop had taught him industry and responsibility, neatness and business. The shop had housed him and comforted him when Demolo had failed him. The shop was now abused and neglected, and Seamus felt it more keenly than he felt his own years of abuse and neglect.

He went up the stairs to the bedroom.

A rasping voice greeted him. "Go away."

Seamus cleared his throat and put his things down. "Good evening to you too. I don't suppose you've had anything to eat. I'll make you something."

"Away with you, boy. I have no use for you in my home. Leave a dying man alone." Demolo's hoarse voice still contained the slightly whining note it had always had when he lectured, but his face was pitifully altered, thin and drawn. "Can't a man of learning and accomplishment attain peace at his advanced age? Not when he is attempting to rest, rest sorely needed because of his very serious health condition. Why do you torment me, Seamus?" His voice dwindled weakly.

Seamus felt tears come to his eyes, and he smiled. "I suppose tormenting you is my lot in life. Come on. Let me prop your pillow up. You'll breathe easier."

Demolo muttered and complained, but he was too weak to truly argue or struggle. Seamus had come determined to help him, and help him he did.

ONE week later, there was a knock on the (clean, polished) shop door. Seamus opened it and was almost thrown off his feet by a fierce hug, delivered to him by a very distraught Thio.

Seamus laughed once he could catch his breath. "You waited long enough!"

"I thought you would come back before a single day passed with that horrible old lunatic! And here you are"—Thio looked around wildly—"cleaning?"

Seamus patted Thio on the shoulder and put down his dust rag. "Out of self-defense, I'm afraid. The shop was unbearable when I first arrived. Please come in. I've missed you, you have no idea how much....

I thought of sending for you, but there was no sense in you suffering the same things I've been tending to. Demolo isn't the easiest of patients."

"But I'm sure you're the most effective and elegant of sick nurses." Thio sighed, still touching Seamus and holding on to him as though he might float away. "I've been, oh, I can't even describe it. Without you."

Seamus laughed. "I must say, I've gone from the unwanted wastrel to every man's most essential friend in the space of a few months. Do you know that it nearly destroyed Demolo, my disappearing?" He sobered. "I ought not to have left him."

"Say that again and so help me, I'll shake the stupid out of you." Thio growled. "The way you looked at me the night we flew away from here! I've never seen the like. You were stifled in this place, and I won't see you stifled again like that, not ever."

"Hush," Seamus said softly. He closed the door and turned to place a hand on Thio's cheek. "All is well. I'm breathing quite freely here. This was also my home, you realize, and often enough a happy one. Amid my powders and metals and tubes of glass." He smiled.

Thio wilted a little. "Then Pa was right, and you're never coming back."

Seamus stared. "What?"

Thio looked away. "We had a conversation about you. He seemed to think that I was holding you back from your destiny by turning you into my servant."

"What? Thio, never."

"But I used you just as surely as Demolo—"

"And now it's I who will have to shake you. Don't be ridiculous. It was a joy to be in your house." Seamus paused. "But I can't exactly run the shop from there, and Demolo...." His face fell. "He won't last another fortnight."

"So he truly is ill, then."

"Truly. To be frank, I am not actually certain he'll leave me the shop. It's only... who else would he leave it to? He has no heirs. Perhaps in his way, he was always as alone as I was."

Thio's eyes flamed. "You are never alone if you do not want to be."

Seamus smiled. "Calm yourself, my love."

Thio blinked.

"Well, we are each other's love, are we not?"

"We are," Thio said firmly. "How strange it feels to use the words, though. My love." He pulled Seamus close. "Now kiss me, my love, for you have left me, and I require comfort."

Seamus laughed and complied. After some moments, he drew back and said, "I fear we cannot do more than this in this place. Perhaps I will come and see you soon."

"I will pine away until then."

"Oh, pffft. You will be just fine."

"Well, I brought you something, so that you shall not forget to come back to me...." Thio reached into his coat and brought out a small sphere of swiftsilver. It was wrapped in a chain of heavy gold, laced up in it and bound. When Seamus reached for it and took it, he realized the weight of the gold was intended to keep it from floating away.

He was touched. "Such a shame we cannot merely let it fly."

"Such is the way of the world. Take it."

Seamus took the sphere, feeling the way the weight warred against its weightlessness, and he kissed Thio again, and they held each other.

AT FIRST, Demolo was querulous and difficult when Seamus tried to care for him. But all too soon, he was unable to be querulous anymore and merely submitted to the care. Seamus felt a heavy sensation in his chest when this happened, knowing if anything signified a failure of Demolo's will, it was this inability to argue or lecture. He was spending all his strength on his last remaining days and had none to spare. Seamus continued to keep the shop clean and orderly. He did not open it to the public, though. His current duties were a sufficient burden on his own strength.

Thio did not trouble Seamus with visits, but long letters began to arrive, letters full of passion, pleading, and great plans for the future. It warmed Seamus to read them, and he replied to them with equal feeling, if slightly less exuberance. He hoped he didn't reveal in his words just how weary he was. He knew, now, that Thio tended to want to rescue him, and Seamus didn't want to be rescued this time—he merely wanted to survive this.

On the day Seamus turned twenty years old, Demolo breathed his last rattling breath. Seamus sat by him, holding his hand and feeling old and worn himself. When Seamus looked into the tiny mirror in the tiny room, he saw two-day-old whiskers on his face, and the depth in his own eyes said he was a man, and a boy no longer.

They buried Demolo in a small plot on Morning Hill, and Seamus was the only attendant at the funeral. It was just as he had suspected: Demolo had always been alone.

THIO, my love,

Demolo has passed on, hopefully to a less disappointing life than he always found this one to be. I am free.

I felt this almost immediately when he died: a freedom so close to weightlessness that I nearly felt my feet leave the ground below me. It was not a joyful feeling. The fact is, I have no idea what to do with myself. Always, I have worked for others. Willingly, but nonetheless, by others' will have I lived my life.

Perhaps I would still live by the will of others, if I decided to remain here and run the shop. Perhaps that is, in fact, the way of life: to pass from one set of needing hands to the next. I do what I can and then leave the rest to God.

But I have discovered a great truth in Demolo's passing, one I never suspected before. The worth of love and companionship has become real to me in a way it never was. Demolo, you see, spent his life in work and in commerce. All who knew him said he was a good man of business. He did what he felt was his duty. I was a duty to him, in fact. Perhaps an act of compassion as well, but more than that, I was a dutiful act each day he had me in his home, and never once did he forget or allow me to forget that fact.

It is a hollow, false thing to be a man of business and duty and work, without love.

In your arms, I have found joy. I have found peace there, and rest and laughter, and a respite from the loneliness that has haunted my footsteps all the days of my life. In your arms lies the life I have always needed, when I did not know it. You bear my heart. I cannot truly live without my heart, and so, I cannot truly live without you.

I do not fear the future anymore. Perhaps I will run this shop; perhaps I will leave it to work for you again. Perhaps I will own my own destiny; perhaps I will always be in thrall to others. None of that makes any matter to me now, so long as I have you. I have the firmest and most profound hope that you and I can find some way to remain in each other's arms, and hearts, and lives. If we can do that and also fulfill our duties, then that will be an excellent thing. If we cannot do both, then I would happily sacrifice a life of duty to a life well loved.

Come to me, my love, and perhaps we shall bring to life some of your grand plans.

Yours Eternally,
Seamus

Twenty Years Later

THE funeral of the Baron of Lessings was held in state with all attendant procession and honor, all the weeping and respect the good man deserved. His son was solemn and tearless, but all could see the grief on his face. The new Lord Tenet's face was lined, his hair graying more than his forty years would have implied. His father's long sickness had clearly taken some of the life from him. And yet his eyes still sparkled with that touch of mad inspiration that had always marked him and set him apart from his fellows. Thio might be mature in years, but still he was an adventurer.

Lord Tenet's constant friend and companion, Seamus the alchemist and apothecary, stood close by in support.

It had always been an odd friendship, theirs, but a fruitful one. Seamus and Lord Tenet had invented many things together—machines and devices to heal the sick, vehicles to lighten the burdens of carters and merchants, all manner of near-miraculous lamps, stoves, and tools. They had invented a material that would build the stoutest of false limbs for the lame, and firm joists for construction. That bright silvery metal was found all over town. They called it Silvus and wove long strips of it into various things. For some reason, Seamus never made a flat or closed surface with it, only long strips.

But now, perhaps grief would hamper Lord Tenet's brilliant mind; perhaps even his friend would not be able to heal him. There was some hope that Thio's ward, a young man of four-and-twenty named Allister, who, it was said, was given much of the responsibility of the estate, would bring comfort to his advancing years.

Seamus also kept a ward and assistant in the shop, a young man who it was said he had collected from the street and saved from a life of poverty. The young man was named Laurence, and his skills in alchemy and medicine were already quite advanced. In fact, the town felt it was lucky in having two gifted alchemists in their midst, in addition to the great inventor of Lessings.

"AND what is it you have to show me, my love? I haven't heard such excitement in your voice in ten years or more." Seamus smiled fondly at Thio, placing a hand on his shoulder.

Thio placed his hand over it and smiled back. Two decades on, and still their skin flamed at contact; still he looked upon Seamus and loved what he saw, and wanted him, and felt grateful to share his bed whenever they could. It had been difficult over the years to find as much time together as they wanted. It had never felt like quite enough. But they had found ways. Becoming known as collaborators in some of the most celebrated inventions in the country had lent a sense of duty and necessity to their relationship, and nobody in town would question the constant visits Seamus made to the Tenet estate. All knew this friendship had yielded wonderful things.

But none knew just how close they were, and somehow it had always felt wrong to hide it. Thio had felt stifled many times because of this, unable to be as open and flagrant in his love as he was with all his other feelings. Even Seamus, private and quiet as he was, felt a disturbance at having to suppress himself in public around Thio. It wasn't merely the fact that they were two men. It was also the difference in social and political standing between them. To the town, Thio would always be a lord and Seamus always a tradesman, and never the twain might meet except in a somewhat strange partnership; even their great friendship was suspect.

Thio said, "Seamus, I have done as you asked me, so many years ago. I have stayed upon the ground, and been who I was raised to be, and given over some of my young dreams. But I think that it is time now.... I think we are both ready. I would like to show you my masterwork."

Seamus became very solemn. He knew what it had cost Thio, so long ago, to give up flight. They had both wished for this day. He nodded. "Show me."

Thio had built the pieces in the basement laboratory and then moved the pieces to the roof of the west wing so the whole might be constructed in the open air, with nothing but a protective stretched canvas above to block it from the sky.

The airship was a thing of marvel.

No material was both light and strong as swiftsilver, and so most of the ship was constructed of woven strips of it. Interlaced were strips of wood to add weight where ballast was needed. The deck could have held twenty men, and the hold was broad and deep. Thio opened the hatch to show Seamus the quarters beneath, which were small but amply furnished and comfortable. He indicated the small bed, and Seamus, even after so many years, blushed and smiled in pleasure. No larger bed would be needed.

The forward hold was already well stocked with food and drink, blankets and candles and coal and other supplies, and a large supply of alchemists' tools and chemicals.

Above the noble prow of the ship rose a vast balloon of none other than swiftsilver, which had been cleverly designed by Thio so he could turn a crank and open rents in the sides to permit air to flow in. The rents were adjustable, from the tiniest crack (for slow descent) to a gaping hole (which would be the safest setting while on the ground). For propulsion, there was an apparatus on the back that was not unlike a slow rocket or torch, which would blow flame into the air and push the ship forward. There were also air oars like great wings protruding from the sides of the ship that would catch the wind for air sailing.

Nothing on the great airship was wanting; it was all grace and power, yet comfortable and steady. All was shipshape.

The two men looked at each other.

"Is Laurence prepared to take over the shop?"

"He has been more than ready for over three years, actually. He's a far brighter lad than I ever was." Seamus chuckled.

"Impossible, my genius friend."

"Have you prepared Allister sufficiently?"

"I have given him power over the estate and made it legally binding. My cousin's nephew has grown into a fine man, and well deserving of it. Lord knows I never wanted any of it." Thio half smiled.

Seamus gazed up at the airship. "Thio, it is a wonder. It is truly your masterwork."

"It is the work of a great love."

"Twenty years of it. It's a wonder we never tired of each other."

Thio took Seamus's hand. "Will you come aboard?"

They boarded it together, feeling a tingle with their first steps onto the ship. Thio took the helm, and Seamus manned the sails. They closed the swiftsilver balloon atop, letting the air slowly flow out of it, and the ship began, by inches over each minute, to rise. They were in no hurry to begin their journey. It had waited this long.

"Ready?"

"Forever."

The ship sailed off, over the tops of the roofs of the city, alone, and wild, and free.

BELL ELLIS made her writing debut at the age of eight with a series of truly dreadful stories about unicorns. She continued to happily produce abysmal fiction until she was distracted by several college degrees, a social life, and a steady career in software design. By the time she returned to her writing again, several of her acquaintances informed her that she'd fallen into the terrible habit of actually writing readable stories. She never recovered from this. Now she produces tolerable fiction at a furious rate in a tiny little house in the woods, to the dismay of her two cats, various family members, and legions of abandoned unicorns.

You can e-mail Bell at ellis.tales@gmail.com.

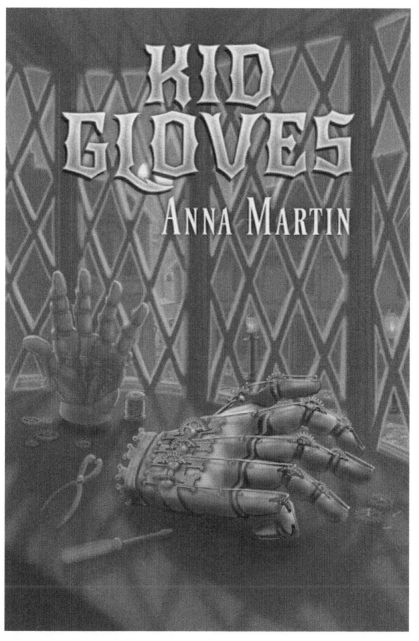

KID
GLOVES

ANNA MARTIN

http://www.dreamspinnerpress.com

Steampunk Romance from DREAMSPINNER PRESS

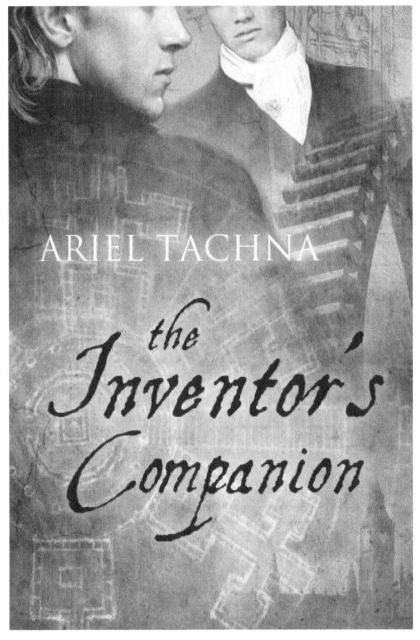

ARIEL TACHNA

the
Inventor's
Companion

http://www.dreamspinnerpress.com

Steampunk from DREAMSPINNER PRESS

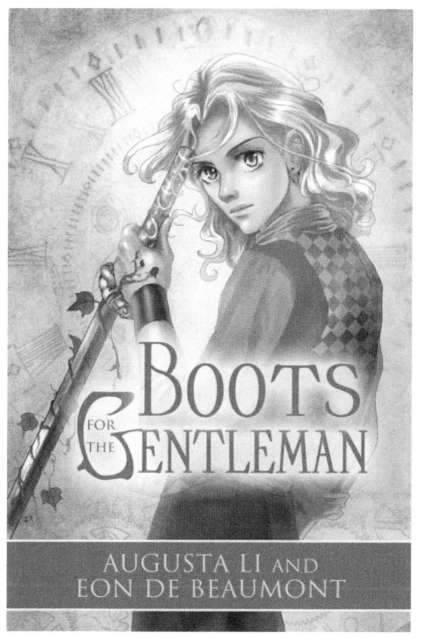

http://www.dreamspinnerpress.com

More Steampunk from DREAMSPINNER PRESS

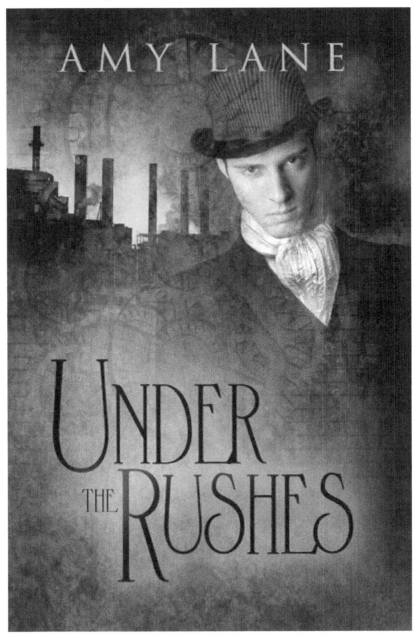

AMY LANE

UNDER THE RUSHES

http://www.dreamspinnerpress.com

Steampunk Adventure from DREAMSPINNER PRESS

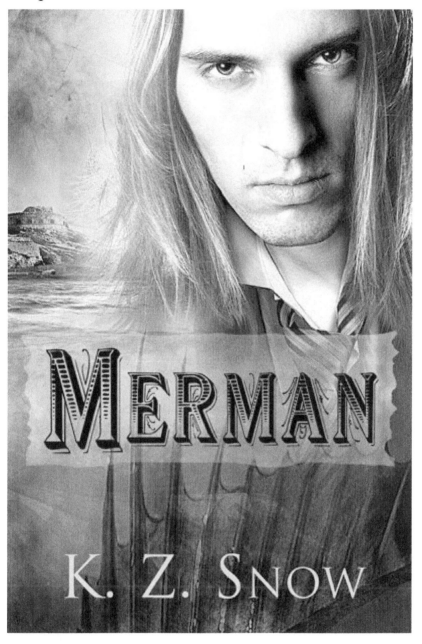

MERMAN

K. Z. SNOW

http://www.dreamspinnerpress.com

Lightning Source UK Ltd.
Milton Keynes UK
UKOW06f1808090815

256637UK00006B/257/P